Praise for

THE NIGHT SHE GOT LUCKY

"This second in Donovan's stories of dog-walking friends is a wonderful combination of love and laughter, with serious moments as well as some intrigue. The animal characters are a delightful addition to the story."

—*RT Book Reviews*

"*The Night She Got Lucky* is a sexy, sweet, and simply delicious contemporary romance."

—*Joyfully Reviewed*

"A cute, funny, and sexy tale from beginning to end."

—*Romance Reviews Today*

AIN'T TOO PROUD TO BEG

"Donovan whips up a fine frappe of romantic comedy and suspense."   —*Publishers Weekly*

"A delightful new series."   —*RT BOOKreviews*

"This is a terrific book and one that fans of Ms. Donovan, and new readers of first-class romantic comedies, don't want to miss."   —*RTR Reviews*

THE GIRL MOST LIKELY TO...

"An exceptional novel with humor and pathos and rich in detail, and the finely put-together characters make this a story worthy of our Perfect 10 award and a must-read. You'll laugh, cry, and your heart will break over this brilliant story of a man and a woman—what most wondrous stories end up being about."

—*Romance Reviews Today*

MORE...

"A wonderfully convoluted tale of love lost and found, secret pregnancies and spousal abuse, Donovan's latest shows us the healing power of forgiveness and the strength found in the love of family. It's peopled with complex characters who learn much about themselves and those they love through the course of this compelling story." —*RT BOOKreviews*

THE KEPT WOMAN
A RITA Award finalist

"Sexy and funny. Donovan takes the marriage-of-convenience plot and gives it a fun update that will leave readers grinning....these characters are filled with genuine warmth and charm." —*RT BOOKreviews*

HE LOVES LUCY
"A great book…terrific." —*Fresh Fiction*

"A fun and sexy 'feel good' story and a must title to add to your current romance reading list." —*Bookloons*

"A story of rioting emotions, wacky weight challenges, and lots of love. This is one story you will be sad to see end. Kudos to Donovan for creating such a believable and realistic story." —*Fallen Angel Reviews*

"*He Loves Lucy* has everything: humor, sweetness, warmth, romance, passion, and sexual tension; an uplifting message; a heroine every woman…can empathize with; and a hero to die for." —*Romance Reviews Today*

"An extraordinary read with intriguing characters and a wonderful plot…fantastic." —*Romance Junkies*

"Lucy is a humorous delight...fans will enjoy this fine look at one year of hard work to find love."

—*Midwest Book Review*

"A great romance...a top-rate novel...with its unforgettable characters, wonderful plot, and excellent message, *He Loves Lucy* will go on my keeper shelf to be read and re-read a thousand times... Donovan has proven that she will have serious star power in the years to come."

—*Romance Reader at Heart*

TAKE A CHANCE ON ME
2003 Reviewer's Choice Award for Best Contemporary Romance

"Comic sharpness...the humorous interactions among Thomas, Emma, and Emma's quirky family give the book a golden warmth as earthy as its rural Maryland setting. But there are also enough explicit erotic interludes to please readers who like their romances spicy."

—*Publishers Weekly*

"Donovan blends humor and compassion in this opposites-attract story. Sexy and masculine, Thomas fills the bill for the man of your dreams. Emma and Thomas deserve a chance at true love. Delightfully entertaining, *Take a Chance on Me* is a guaranteed good time."

—*Old Book Barn Gazette*

"Full of humor, sensuality, and emotion with excellent protagonists and supporting characters...a wonderful tale. Don't be afraid to take a chance on this one. You'll love it." —*Affaire de Coeur*

Not That Kind of Girl

SUSAN DONOVAN

St. Martin's Paperbacks

This is a work of fiction. All of the characters, organizations, and events portrayed in this novel are either products of the author's imagination or are used fictitiously.

NOT THAT KIND OF GIRL

For information address St. Martin's Press, 175 Fifth Avenue, New York, NY 10010.

ISBN: 978-0-312-36606-3

Printed in the United States of America

St. Martin's Paperbacks edition / December 2010

St. Martin's Paperbacks are published by St. Martin's Press, 175 Fifth Avenue, New York, NY 10010.

10 9 8 7 6 5 4 3 2 1

Acknowledgments

The author would like to thank Susan Homire, DVM, "Maryland's Dog Whisperer," for sharing her expertise about the art and science of pack leadership. This book would not have been possible without Susan's help. Thanks also to Karol Kennedy, who placed the winning bid at the 2008 auction for the Humane Society of Washington County, Maryland. A canine character in this book has been named in honor of Karol's beloved dog Gizmo. The author has fictionalized elements of the City of San Francisco's Vicious Dog laws and its hearing process for the sake of the story.

"It's a dog-eat-dog world, Woody, and I'm wearing Milk Bone underwear."

—Norm from *Cheers*

Chapter 1

The room nearly overflowed with hope, joy, and love, and Roxanne Bloom knew if she didn't get out of there within the next thirty seconds, the top of her head would blow off.

"Having a swell time?" Bea asked, squeezing her formidable figure between Roxanne and the throng of baby shower revelers.

Busted, Roxie thought to herself with a sigh.

True, her friend Bea Latimer didn't miss much, but Roxanne was sure she'd been doing a stellar job of faking it, hanging back in the corner of the big living room, smiling and nodding at all the right times. In fact, she'd just cooed with approval moments before, right when everyone else did, *and* with the appropriate level of enthusiasm. So how did Bea notice that Roxie was about as comfortable as a nun at a Chippendales show?

A new wave of *oohs* and *aahs* came and went. Roxie peeked around Bea to see her friends Josie and Ginger sniffing back tears, rubbing their equally ginormous bellies, and shaking their heads over the beauty of their matching baby jogger strollers with racing-stripe awnings and radial tires.

Roxanne checked the time on her cell phone, wondering if it would be rude to leave early. She could always say she wasn't feeling well, which wouldn't be a complete lie, because all the cooing, nodding, smiling, and teary-eyed sniffing had given her one mother of a headache.

Bea frowned. "What's up, Rox? Your face is as white as my ass in January."

Roxanne shuddered, fighting off the mental image. "I'm good," she said.

"The hell you are." Bea took a quick swig from her low-carb beer. "I'll tell you what. Why don't you take five to pull yourself together? Go outside and run around the tennis courts or something. Maybe shoot a few hoops. What's the point of partying at a wine country estate if you don't take advantage of all the amenities. Am I right?" Bea leaned closer and lowered her voice. "Whatever you do, make sure it's an attitude adjuster. You look like you're at a wake instead of a baby shower and I *know* you don't want Ginger and Josie to see you're not happy for them."

"But I'm thrilled for them!" Roxanne whispered, horrified that her friends might ever think such a thing.

Bea's expression softened. She smiled a little. "I know you're happy for them."

"I love them. I'm glad their lives are so wonderful."

"I know." Bea patted Roxanne's arm.

"I mean," Roxanne continued, "just because I don't believe in true love or marriage or happiness doesn't mean I can't enjoy a fuckin' baby shower for those who *do*!"

One of Bea's eyebrows shot up high on her forehead, but before she could respond, the front door of the old mansion opened. Everyone stopped their oohing and aahing long enough to see who the late arrival might be.

Roxanne already knew. She knew even before she got a peek at the wide brim of a black felt cowboy hat and before that hat came off and the tussle of dark blond hair was revealed. It was almost as if she *sensed* him before she could see him. So, before Eli Gallagher could stick his handsome head all the way into the room and unleash one of his modest yet stunning smiles, Roxanne was out of there and halfway through the kitchen, the back door her salvation.

Unfortunately, Bea was right behind her.

"I didn't know Rick invited *him*," Bea said, jogging to catch up.

"He works for Rick, so why not?" Roxanne reached the kitchen door latch. "Anyway, Rick can invite anyone he wants. This is Rick's home. It's Rick's party! For God's sake—it's Rick's *baby*!" Roxanne caught herself. "Well, only one of them is his baby. The other one's Lucio's. But you know what I mean."

Roxanne cringed at the sound of her own distracted rambling, hoping Bea wouldn't notice.

She noticed. "Well, well," Bea said with a snort. "I had no idea Eli Gallagher had gotten under your skin that bad."

Roxanne spun around. She pointed a finger at Bea. "That man is not under my skin. Never again is a man going to get under my skin, or anything else I'm wearing. I am not that kind of girl anymore. Got it?" She flung open the kitchen door and prepared to stomp off indignantly. She didn't get far.

A short old lady blocked Roxanne's exit down the steps. The lady's eyes were squinted and her hands were on her hips. Her sturdy legs were widespread. Her orthopedic shoes were planted firmly on the worn bricks.

Roxie gasped. "Mrs. Needleman?"

"That would be me," she said in her usual cheerful warble, her eyes now twinkling with amusement.

Roxanne shot an accusatory look Bea's way.

"I didn't know she was out here! I swear!" Bea raised her hands in surrender. "Seriously, Rox. The last time I looked she was sitting in the recliner with a cup of tea. I have no idea how she got out here so fast."

"You aren't leaving, are you, dear?" Mrs. Needleman smiled so wide that Roxanne feared the lady's dentures would lose their berth. Then Mrs. Needleman clapped her hands together and laughed. "It's such a fun party! There is miraculous power in preparing for a new life, you know. And one can't help but be touched by the pure joy of it." She gripped Roxie's wrist. "And to think— today we are lucky enough to share in the preparation for *two* new lives. That's *twice* the joy! *Twice* the miraculous power!"

Roxanne pasted a pleasant smile on her face, try- ing not to show she was now twice as likely to lose her lunch. This Gloria Needleman chick—this goofy, correspondence-course minister and self-proclaimed cosmic matchmaker (whom Josie and Ginger swore had helped them find their true loves)—was the last person on earth she wanted to chat with.

Strike that. Gloria was second-to-last. Eli Gallagher was taking up the rear.

"I was just stepping out for some air," Roxanne said, gently pushing Mrs. Needleman aside. The old lady wouldn't budge. "Excuse me, please," Roxie said, finally dislodging her enough so that she could get down the two steps to the patio. She started to jog off toward the barn.

"Roxanne."

She turned back, nearly laughing at the sight—Mrs.

Needleman looked like a garden gnome compared to Bea, who towered behind her in the kitchen doorway.

"Stop right there," Roxie said, hoping the old broad would have mercy on her. Really, how blunt did she have to be? After Ginger's wedding three months ago, right here on this very patio in fact, Roxie had informed Gloria Needleman that under no circumstances was she interested in finding a man, or, as the wrinkled old bat had put it, her *beloved*. And nothing in the last three months had changed her mind.

"Please, Mrs. Needleman," she told her now. "Don't start with the love crap again."

"I'm afraid it's already started, my dear," Mrs. Needleman whispered sweetly, shrugging. "It's out of anyone's hands now."

Roxie nodded curtly. "Great. Gotta run. See ya."

"How's your angry little doggie doing? What's her name again?"

Roxie went still. She let go with a deep sigh of surrender, aware that she'd been suckered in. "My dog's name is Lilith."

"Yes, yes, of course," Mrs. Needleman said, nodding. "The mythological demon of the night, the ancient embodiment of man's fear of everything female."

Roxie suddenly perked up, impressed by Mrs. Needleman's grasp of the subject matter. She smiled at her with renewed respect. "Right on, sister."

"A man-hating succubus."

Roxanne blinked, becoming suspicious. Was this lady mocking her? "So what's your point?"

"Oh, I was simply thinking how your dog's name reflects the whole tenor of your life, Roxanne. Even the little 'Men Make Me Sick' gift shop you operate."

Bea snorted.

"It's www.i-vomit-on-all-men.com," Roxanne corrected her. "It's hyphenated."

Mrs. Needleman shrugged, as if the details didn't matter.

"It's an online social network," Roxie pressed on. "I've created a community where women all over the world can go to tell their horror stories and find encouragement and support. And yes, I do happen to offer T-shirts and coffee mugs and a few other novelty products, but that doesn't make it a damn *gift shop*."

Mrs. Needleman dismissed the detail with a wave of her wrinkly hand. "Regardless, I'm assuming you've not dealt with Lilith's aggression issues."

"Why would you assume that? She's not here today. You don't even *know* my dog." Roxie let go with an offended laugh. "Besides, she's doing much better, for your information."

Mrs. Needleman smiled sadly. "Dear girl, there's no need to bronze the turd with me."

Roxie looked to Bea with wide eyes, hoping for some clarification. Bea was happy to provide it, even though she nearly doubled over with the giggles in the process. "She means . . ."—*snort*—"she means you don't have to put lipstick on a pig for her, you know, soften the truth."

Roxanne wasn't amused. "And the truth would be what, Gloria?"

"The truth is this—if you'd found a way to help your little doggie, you wouldn't be the angry and uncomfortable young woman I see today, still trying to run away from life."

Whoa. Roxie felt as if she'd just been punched in the gut. Her legs became wobbly and hot. She flailed her hands around behind her, seeking out one of the sturdy old portico pillars to hold her up.

Bea gently placed her hands on Mrs. Needleman's shoulders. "How about we go back inside now, Gloria?" she suggested. "I bet we're missing out on a whole *shitload* of joy in there."

Mrs. Needleman laughed, brushing Bea's hands off her shoulders. "Patience, Beatrice," she said. "You might learn a thing or two."

Roxanne leaned fully against the pillar, steeling herself as she watched the Grandma from Hell advance toward her, one rickety step at a time.

"I know you think I'm a crazy old lady."

Roxanne straightened. This would be where a polite person might say, *"Of course not!"*

"You're a fruitcake, Gloria," was her response.

The old lady giggled, her thin shoulders bouncing up and down in delight.

"Find someone else to harass," Roxie added.

Mrs. Needleman let go with a long sigh. "I'm getting quite old, you know. I'm eighty-five. Not feeling like myself lately. No time to waste." Her eyes were suddenly shadowed with sadness.

"Hey, hey! Don't talk like that!" Bea scurried up behind her and cradled her elbow.

Mrs. Needleman continued addressing Roxanne. "I know you are a thoroughly modern young woman. I can see you have no patience for fools."

Roxie shrugged.

"And I understand that you're protecting your heart."

Roxanne laughed, crossing her arms tightly under her breasts. "Damn right I am. If I don't, who will?"

"I just have one favor to ask of you."

Roxanne groaned and looked to Bea, whose eyes were large and pleading. *Just do it, for God's sake,* Bea mouthed silently from behind Gloria.

"Fine. What—*ever*," Roxanne said. "If I agree to

your favor, will you leave me alone? I'm not in the mood for one of your love interventions."

Mrs. Needleman laughed. "Thank you, dear," she said. "Once you do this one little favor for me, I'll never bother you again. I won't need to."

"Deal," Roxanne said, hoping she could trust this lady's word. "What do you want?"

"I want you to leave the door to your heart open just a crack, my dear girl—just an itty-bitty, tiny crack. That's all I ask."

Roxanne's jaw dropped. She had officially reached her limit of civility. "What the hell are you talking about? My door's already flung wide open!" She was pissed now. This lady hardly knew the first thing about her, her life, her history. "It just so happens that I love my friends and my dog and my job and I get along passably well with my neighbors, even the obsessive-compulsive ones. My mother and I are still on speaking terms, for God's sake, which is more than I can say for a lot of twenty-nine-year-old women! You make me sound like some kind of cold *bitch* or something, which couldn't be further from the truth!"

Mrs. Needleman shook her head sadly. "I never meant to imply that."

"I'm leaving."

"A man will be at your door very soon now, Roxanne." Mrs. Needleman's eyes became intensely focused as she spoke. "And this man will be different. He'll be strong enough to knock down the wall you've built around your heart, and brave enough to love everything he finds behind it."

Bea rolled her eyes at Roxanne as if to apologize. Then she pulled gently on Mrs. Needleman's arm. "Come on now, Gloria. You want to see when they open your gifts, don't you?"

As Roxanne watched Bea help Mrs. Needleman toward the kitchen door, her head got fuzzy. That lady was a whack job, plain and simple. It was like she was on some kind of mission to test the limits of Roxie's sanity. In fact, Gloria Needleman could qualify as a stalker, a senior citizen stalker! And her prophecy about some man breaking down the door to Roxie's heart? That door she'd agreed to leave open a crack?

Right.

Roxie began a casual jog toward the barn, thinking that any man foolish enough to show up on her doorstep would get a foot up the crack of his ass.

In just seconds, Roxanne found herself at the barn, her lungs burning and her breath coming hard. Apparently, her casual jog had become a full-out sprint and she hadn't even noticed.

"Sorry I'm late," Eli said. He took off his Stetson and held it to his heart as he approached the two guests of honor. The mothers-to-be were perched like fertility-goddess bookends on the oversized leather sofa.

"Come in, Eli!" said Rick's wife, Josie, her round face lit up with excitement and happiness. "We're glad you could make it."

Immediately, the dogs were sniffing his legs. Through his peripheral vision he saw four of them. Three he knew were Rick and Josie's dogs—Tara, the little terrier mix, Chen, their big hulking mutt, and Genghis, the knuckle-headed Labradoodle. With a quick glance he saw that the fourth was their friend Bea's Finnish spitz, Martina. Now *that* was a secure dog. Once the pack was sufficiently calm, Eli knelt down to give them a proper friendly greeting.

Suddenly, a fifth dog appeared, having serpentined her way through the obstacle course of folding chairs and two-legged roadblocks. It was Ginger and Lucio's little bichon frise. Today she was wearing a flirty pink bow on top of her head. Eli had to laugh. He made sure she got her share of ear rubs, head pats, and belly scratches.

"There he is, the Pied Piper of the puppies!" Lucio Montevez said in his thick Spanish accent. "Come in! Come in!" Ginger's husband waved broadly, holding up his wineglass.

Eli rose from his crouch and moved farther into the room, certain the dogs would allow him to pass. He made his way to Ginger and Josie, kissing each on the cheek as he set down one gift bag per pile of loot.

"Where might I find Rick?" Eli inquired.

"He and Teeny are carrying some of the presents out to Ginger and Lucio's car," Josie said, smiling sheepishly. "It was getting a little crowded in here."

Eli chuckled, looking around the packed room. He saw many familiar faces from the corporate headquarters of Celestial Pet, where he worked as a canine behavioral consultant, but the rest were strangers to him. He smiled politely to everyone as he took a seat. Lucio handed him a beer.

"Gracias," he told him.

Not surprisingly, Roxanne Bloom was nowhere to be seen. Eli figured she must have run out the back door.

He'd taken a single sip from his beer when he felt a heavy weight on his right foot. He didn't bother to look down, and immediately made a sharp *shh* sound. The weight moved off his foot and settled on the floor next to him. Only then did he reach down and pet the outrageous spiral curls that could only belong to Genghis, his very first San Francisco client.

Eli smiled down at the dog. "How's it hangin', my

man?" he asked, rubbing the Labradoodle behind his ears.

Eli heard the kitchen door slam and turned his head, everything inside him jumping to attention at the thought that *she* might be returning. Instead he saw Bea Latimer and the increasingly frail little old lady who'd married Josie and Rick, and later, he'd heard, officiated at the marriage of Lucio and Ginger. He watched Bea help Mrs. Needleman to a comfortable recliner and make her way to an empty folding chair next to him. Martina trotted at her side.

"Hey, Eli," Bea said, plopping down. Her voice was friendly enough but a little reserved. "How've you been?"

"Very well, thank you," he said. "You?"

"Good. Excellent, really. Since the paper went belly-up I've been working on my canine agility trainer certification. I have my exam in six weeks."

Eli smiled at the tall, older woman. "That's great, Bea. Congratulations. You have a gift, you know."

Bea glanced down at Martina lying at her feet, then gave him a self-conscious smile. "Thanks."

"Martina is a happy and stable dog," he added.

Bea's smile widened. "I really appreciate that," she said, pausing to look at him thoughtfully. "It means a lot coming from you."

Their conversation ended as a wave of delighted gasps and sighs spread through the room. Eli saw that Ginger and Josie had just unwrapped identical wood-inlay boxes, marveling at their beauty as they ran their fingers over the intricate carving. A handsome white-haired man kissed each of them, then wiped tears from his eyes as he returned to a love seat.

"That's Lucio's father. He lives in southern Spain," Bea told him, leaning in close. "The lady next to him—the one with the boobs-not-found-in-nature? See her?"

Eli coughed.

"That's Ginger's mother."

"Ah. Thanks for keeping me abreast of the situation."

Bea let go with a hearty laugh. Then she sighed, her face slowly becoming more serious. "Hey, look, Eli. I like you. A lot. You seem like a real decent guy. But . . . uh . . ."

He knew where this awkward exchange was headed, and he appreciated Bea's courage. "I'm listening," he said.

"I'm not sure I should be telling you this."

Eli nodded.

"Roxie is . . . uh . . ."

He decided to make it easier for her. "So where did she run off to?"

Bea studied him, her eyes filled with concern. "The barn."

"Because of me?"

She laughed. "Oh, yeah."

Eli stared at the beer bottle in his hand. "It's that bad, huh?"

"'Fraid so."

He nodded. It wasn't a simple matter, this thing with the stunning, raven-haired Roxanne Bloom. He'd met her only half a dozen times, usually at social situations like this one, but the energy between them was like nothing he'd ever experienced with a woman. It was dazzling in its intensity. It screamed for his attention. And it was thoroughly, maddeningly unwelcome.

Roxanne had called last fall to ask him to lunch. He'd had to say no. He'd had no choice, though she didn't even give him a chance to explain. And since then, their dynamic had been real simple: she avoided him and he couldn't stop thinking about her. It was ridiculous, he knew, and it had to be sorted out—now. Letting this kind of unfinished emotional business fester went against everything he believed in. He would not let it go on another day.

"Roxie is a little on the complicated side," Bea said under her breath.

He smiled. "So it seems."

"I love her to death, though."

Eli sipped his beer.

"She's a pussycat, really. A pussycat in a porcupine suit."

Eli chuckled.

Bea stared at him, looking slightly dazed. "Go after her," she whispered, then swiveled her head around to make sure no one was listening. "She'd *kill* me if she knew I was doing this, but I think you should go after her. Hurry. Before it's too late."

For a long moment, the two stared at each other.

"All right," Eli said. "Don't mind if I do." He grabbed his hat from under the chair and patted Bea on the knee as he stood up. "You know where to find me," he said, giving her a wink.

Eli headed for the kitchen door, knowing he had a four-legged fan club at his heels. He kept his eyes looking forward, his shoulders level, and didn't glance down at the pack. As expected, the dogs made way for him to pass through the door, alone.

"Babies, babies, babies, babies, babies . . ."

Roxanne felt free to mutter to herself out here at the paddock, because her only witness was a pretty

Appaloosa mare who loitered about ten feet away, languidly chomping on alfalfa, her big brown eyes looking sympathetic to her concerns.

Roxie propped a foot on the lowest rail of the fence and draped her elbows over the highest. "How am I supposed to be a cogodmother?" she asked the horse. "I don't know the first thing about babies. I'm not even sure I like them! Fine, they're important to the continuation of the species and all that, but there are days I'm not sure the human species deserves a pass, you know what I'm saying?"

The horse snorted and twitched its ears as if to agree.

"I mean, why keep adding extra people to the mix when the ones already here can't treat each other decently?"

The horse ambled over to the fence, where she nosed Roxie under the crook of her arm. Roxie stroked the mare's neck. "How did this happen? That's all I'm asking. A year ago we were all perfectly miserable— manless and about to lose our jobs at the paper. But at least we were a unified front in our misery, you know? We even took a vow to be alone together, just us and our dogs!"

The horse blew air from its nostrils and pawed at the dirt.

"And then, Josie goes out and finds Rick Rousseau, a hunk with a heart bigger than his bank account. And Ginger somehow conjures up Lucio Montevez, a Mediterranean sex god who basically worships her. And suddenly everybody's in a family way and happier than pigs in you-know-what and I'm still . . ." Roxie stopped herself, sighing deeply. The horse moved closer, waiting for her to finish her sentence.

"Oh, never mind," Roxie told her. She let her forehead rest on the broad and smooth plane between the horse's gentle eyes. "I think I've already missed my chance to be a mother. I guess that's what this is all about. I'm probably a little jealous of my friends."

The horse whinnied in protest. *"Fine,"* Roxanne said with annoyance. "I realize Bea isn't married and pregnant but, come on, like that's ever going to happen? My point is, she's following her dream. Becoming an agility trainer is making her as happy as Ginger and Josie, just in her own way."

Roxie lifted her head and stared off across the miles of rolling vineyard. "What I'm saying is, everyone in our little group has moved on—except me. I'm still right where I started."

"Animals are good listeners," a voice said from behind her.

Roxie froze. She knew that voice. It was an irritatingly masculine voice. Annoyingly sexy. She hated the way it flowed, like a slow and deep river sure of its destination. And she really hated the fact that the owner of that voice might have heard even a syllable of her very private musings.

She blew out air, not turning around. So *that man* had suddenly decided she was worth a little of his time? Ha! And he thought it was acceptable to follow her out here without her permission? What a complete *tool* this guy was!

"You and I need to talk," he said, his voice soft and steady. "I promise I'll be a good listener, too."

She kept her back to him. He didn't deserve her full attention.

But he moved closer and . . . *dammit*! There it was again, that weird vibration she'd felt the very first time she'd met him, right here at the ranch, the day of Josie and Rick's wedding. She would never forget the instant she noticed him. He was leaning against the stone wall between the garden and the lawn, one knee bent, the heel of one cowboy boot propped against the wall and the toe of the other tapping in the dirt. He'd pushed that stupid black hat back on his blond curls and bit down on the inside of his mouth, as if he were trying to keep from laughing. He'd focused his intense green eyes right on her.

Oh, damn, he'd been gorgeous. Big and muscular in his suit. Sun-browned skin. Sensual lips. Graceful hands.

Roxanne didn't want to think about what happened next, but she couldn't stop herself from remembering. The truth was, Eli Gallagher's intense gaze had sliced through her flesh, raced through her blood, and landed with a hot thud right between her legs.

The moment had made such an impression because, embarrassingly enough, that had been the only thing that had landed with a hot thud between her legs in a very long while. And that encounter with Eli had taken place more than *nine months ago*! And there'd certainly been no thudding since. She absolutely refused to do the bigger-picture math.

"I owe you an apology, Roxanne."

"Nope. You don't." She kept her eyes on the vineyards.

"An explanation, then."

"You don't owe me anything." She waited. She strained to hear him let go with an exasperated sigh, or a groan of frustration, or a bitter laugh—anything that would indicate she'd gotten the better of him.

"You are one tough cookie, Ms. Bloom," is what he said.

For just a second, she shut her eyes. She summoned her strength. She knew exactly what she'd see when she turned around—an extremely handsome man, some-where in his early thirties, with loose blond curls, dusky green eyes accented by smile lines, a set of full lips, an elegant chin, and a tall and fit body tucked inside a pair of worn jeans.

A man that spectacular could have any woman he wanted. And, as he'd made painfully clear a while back, he didn't want *her*.

It was for the best. Roxanne knew she was too much for him to handle. She was too much for any man to handle. That concept was introduced to her in childhood, with her own father. It was a pattern that would repeat itself through high school, college, then after college, and, most recently, with Raymond Sandberg—the one man she'd convinced herself was mature enough to appreciate everything she brought to the table.

Whoops. She'd been wrong on that one, hadn't she? But it would be the last time she'd ever be wrong about a man, because she understood now. There was no man for her. There never would be. And it didn't matter if two of her best friends had recently been sucked into the vortex of love. She would have to be okay with that. She would have to find her own peace. She was a strong woman, and if anyone could do it, Roxie could.

She shook her hair back over her shoulder, then slowly turned to face him. She crossed her arms over her chest. "Look, Ian—that is your name, right? Did I remember it correctly?"

He offered her a small smile. There wasn't even the slightest flicker of hurt in his green eyes. Her insult seemed to bounce right off him.

"Elias Jedidiah Gallagher," he said. With dramatic flair, he swept up his hand to pluck his big black cowboy hat off his head. He placed it on his heart and bent at the waist. "At your service," he added.

He was such an ass. Roxanne wanted to grab that ridiculous hat and whack him upside the head with it.

The Appaloosa whinnied loudly in Roxie's ear.

"But you know that, of course," he added, his voice teasing and pleasant. "We talked for a long while at Rick and Josie's wedding, and there was a strong attraction between us. We both felt it. And we discussed how I might help you with your rescue dog's aggression issues."

"She's cured," Roxie said, smiling. "I no longer need your help."

"And I distinctly remember giving you my card."

"I must have thrown it away," she said.

"Before or after I turned you down for that lunch date?"

Roxie enjoyed a bit of clever banter as much as the next girl. In fact, that was something she could never get enough of with Raymond. They would spar, and their words would heat up and the double entendres would fly, and they'd end up rolling around in bed together, enflamed with desire. Raymond might have been almost thirty years her senior, but the man had been sizzling *hot*. Whoever said the brain was the primary sexual organ knew what they were talking about.

But, since Roxie had no interest in banter with Eli, clever or otherwise, she decided to put an end to the barnyard ambush. One ambush per day was her limit anyway, and Mrs. Needleman had gotten to her first.

"Unfortunately for you, Ian," she said, "cowboys don't do anything for me." She stifled a yawn. "But I do know a girl with a major cowboy fetish. Want her number?"

"The name's Eli."

"Whatever."

Eli nodded broadly. "Right. I think I understand

now," he said. "The sheer force of your indifference toward me sent you racing out the kitchen door the moment I arrived. Is that it?"

"You flatter yourself," she said, her heart now at a full gallop in her chest. She didn't want any of this. Not the spark. Not the crackling attraction. Not the racing pulse. It had to end. So she delivered what she was sure would be the final blow. "Anyway, you had your chance. You blew it. I don't give second chances."

Now *that* got a flicker out of him. Understanding flashed in his eyes, but disappeared immediately. Eli had no comeback. He returned the hat to his head and tugged at the brim, as if to announce his imminent departure. *Good riddance to him,* she thought.

Suddenly, Roxanne felt something nudge her butt so hard her feet left the ground. She flew forward. She slammed right up against the front of Eli's solid body. She screamed. Eli grabbed her by the shoulders and steadied her, her toes just grazing the dirt. She leaned back awkwardly.

"Seems you got goosed," Eli said, smiling.

Roxie whipped her head around in time to see the traitorous horse lope off to the other side of the paddock. When she returned her gaze to Eli she noticed that his eyelids were heavy and his attention had shifted to her chest, throat, mouth. Then she became agonizingly aware of the touch of his strong fingers on her upper arms. Next she realized their bellies were pressed together. The front of her thighs were smashed right into his hard . . .

Oh, God.

She began to squirm. She squealed in frustration. "Let me go," she said between clenched teeth.

He didn't. His grip on her stayed gentle but seemed to deepen somehow. Roxie kicked but her feet barely skimmed across the dust. His gaze returned to hers and locked in. And that's when the strangest thing happened.

Her body began to flood with a sensation she could only call "ease." A warm, steady, calming relief that washed through her, softening her and opening her up. Everywhere.

No way was she falling for that shit.

"Settle down, sweet thing."

The words had been delivered in that deep-river voice. His muted green eyes smiled.

Settle? Down? Sweet thing?

Just four little words and it felt as if the earth had stopped turning. That comment was condescending, domineering, insulting, and, at the same time, strangely arousing. His hands maintained their grip on her as he lowered her feet to the ground. She became a little light-headed. She didn't know what was happening. The sensations swirling around inside her were confusing. Scary. Intense. Sexual. She resented all of it.

And if she hadn't despised Eli Gallagher before, she surely did now. How dare he touch her like this? How dare he talk to her with that languid voice? How dare he treat her like a wild stray animal who needed his gentle touch?

And who the hell did he think he was, knocking her off balance like this? If she'd wanted to experience ease and calm she would have gone out and gotten it the normal way—with a prescription!

"Don't ever put your hands on me again," Roxie managed.

"I won't hurt you, Roxanne."

She felt weak. Way too warm. She wanted to escape his grip but couldn't seem to muster the energy. It took every bit of strength she possessed to shake her head side to side. "No," she whispered.

"You're safe with me."

And that's when it happened. Out of nowhere, for no good reason, a sob erupted from her throat. Before she even realized what was happening, the calm had punched a hole in that giant bubble of rage and grief inside her, and it all came flooding out in one long, searing moan. There was no stopping it. She wanted to die from shame.

Eli kissed her. She knew immediately that the kiss wasn't designed to stop the outburst. Its fierceness only demanded more. The kiss—the heat, the pressure, the need—it wrenched the emotion right of her.

No. This was impossible. This was nuts! She wouldn't allow it. No man would ever again lull her into being a stupid, hopeful, defenseless, emotional, babbling idiot the way she'd been with Raymond. She would never leave herself vulnerable like that again. It had been a sacred promise she'd made to herself. No man—Eli Gallagher included—was worth the loss of her self-respect.

She shoved so hard that he lost his grip on her, with both his hands *and* his lips. Roxie gasped for breath and tried to find her bearings, quite aware of how Eli's eyes had widened with confusion. She turned and ran. Her feet pounded the hard dirt. Within minutes she was in her car heading south on Highway 121, on her way home to San Francisco, where she would undoubtedly shove everything back in its proper place, the way she always did.

Chapter 2

Eli stood on the wide front porch of Rick's Sonoma Valley estate, watching her make her getaway. Roxanne Bloom's little square hybrid car kicked up so much dust as it bounced down the lane that he could barely make out the bumper sticker advertising her livelihood:

www.i-vomit-on-all-men.com
A CYBER HAVEN FOR THE SPURNED AND BURNED

He chuckled, shoving his hands into his jeans pockets. True, there were an infinite number of things he did not know or understand about this life, but two things were beyond doubt: that woman's poor dog could not possibly be "cured," because the woman herself was a complete disaster; and he had no business messing with an emotional powder keg like that one, no matter how fucking beautiful she was, even if he planned to stay in California for the rest of his days. Which he did not.

Eli shook his head, collapsed into one of the big wooden porch rockers, and crossed an ankle over a knee. He'd kissed her. He'd grabbed her and held her tight against the front of his body and just devoured the girl. Then he'd felt empty when she pulled away. He could sit there and ask himself what had happened, but he already knew. It had been all instinct. Drive. Fever. *Shiii-it*. He made a living telling people they needed to be calm and stable. What a joke.

He clamped his eyes shut and winced as the memory of Tamara invaded his thoughts. Yes, the last time he'd lost his composure with a woman was about a year ago, when Tamara had freaked out and started packing her bags. The irony was that what happened with Tamara hadn't even been as emotionally charged as what just happened with Roxie. Or as *hot*. Eli opened his eyes with a groan and rubbed a hand across his face, realizing he'd been damn lucky with Roxie, lucky that they'd been out in the open. If they'd been behind closed doors, it could have been worse. It could have been a repeat of Tamara. He might not have been able to control himself.

And the last thing he needed was to send another woman racing off into the night, right? The last thing he needed was another reason to feel like a complete hypocrite.

He took a deep, steadying breath, comforted with the knowledge that he'd be moving back to Utah soon, putting an end to his Roxie Bloom problem. All he had to do was turn down any future social invites from Rick and Josie and he could get out of California without having to see her again. It might be the chickenshit way out, but at this point, it seemed like the wisest option.

Eli leaned back into the chair and thought about home. He'd thoroughly enjoyed working as a canine behavioral consultant for Rick Rousseau's pet store chain. It was unexpected, but it had turned out to be a productive and profitable partnership. He'd helped a lot of dogs and owners find their balance. And he'd been paid well for his services. But Eli had always known it would be a temporary gig, a fact he'd shared with the Celestial Pet CEO from the beginning.

Eli had explained that he'd come to Northern California to deal with some unfinished family business and would be leaving as soon as possible. Rick had hired him anyway.

"Are you kidding?" Rousseau had asked, laughing. "I'll take you for a week if that's all you've got."

Eli smiled to himself. It still amused him that despite his efforts to avoid the limelight, he'd become famous. Online dog training forums alone had made him a celebrity, and his reputation preceded his arrival in San Francisco.

But his stay in California was coming to an end. Eli knew that, with only two candidates left on his list, the search for his biological father had resulted in a couple new friends, but certainly not what he was looking for—the man who'd brought him into the world.

The last time he'd spoken to his mother by phone she'd had this advice: "Come home, honey. You've done your best. Some things are not meant to be."

Eli let his head fall back against the rocker, suddenly aware of the heaviness in his chest. His mom had never wanted him to find his father in the first place, so she'd be thrilled if he came home empty-handed. So yeah, he'd be headed back to Utah soon. With no idea who his father was. And no idea where things might have gone with Roxanne, had the circumstances been different.

"Hey, man, I thought your thing was whispering to dogs, not yourself."

Startled, Eli swung his head toward the teasing voice. He laughed when he saw Rick and his business partner, Teeny Worrell, crossing the wide porch and heading his way. Had he been mumbling to himself? Jesus! He was worse off than he thought.

Eli managed a grin. "Turns out that some days I *am* the dog, Teeny."

Rick and Teeny laughed as they lowered themselves into nearby rockers.

"Are you seeking refuge from the toxic estrogen levels in there?" Rick tilted his head toward the front door, behind which the baby shower was still in full swing.

Eli chuckled. "Not really—just taking a moment to regroup." He didn't miss the quick *I told you so* look Teeny shot Rick.

"So you had an encounter with the Man-Eater?"

Eli laughed at Teeny's keen observation. "How did you guess?"

"'Cause you got that 'I barely escaped with my balls intact' kind of stare," Teeny said. "We've all been there, my brother."

"What could she possibly have against you?" Eli asked, perplexed. "You're not even the enemy."

Teeny shrugged. "She had no way of knowing I was a gay man when we first met. To her, I was just another one of *them,* just another opportunity for target practice."

Eli sighed. "Sorry to hear that."

"Gotta love her, though," Rick said. "Roxie's been through hell and has come out on top—even made a career out of it."

"She'll net six figures this year," Teeny added, clearly impressed. "She's got advertisers beating down her door at this point—you know, feminine hygiene, Midol, self-help books, shit like that."

Eli nodded. "Good for her."

"I was walking down Market Street the other day and saw a woman wearing one of the Web site T-shirts," Rick said. "I tried to approach her, just to tell her that Roxie was a friend of mine, but she pulled out a container of Mace before I could open my mouth."

Teeny chortled. "You lie like a dog, Rousseau."

"Hey, it's probably happening to some poor guy, somewhere," Rick said, grinning.

The three men sat in silence for a moment. Because it was impossible not to, their gazes wandered out to the stunning view of the early-season vineyards and the scraggly mountain backdrop. Eli realized that Rick's Sonoma Valley retreat was a refined version of his own Utah paradise, but with a whole lot more luxury and fewer dogs.

A pang of loneliness shot through him. Eli missed his motley bunch. He knew they were in good hands with Sondra—after all, his sister was his first protégée—but that didn't mean he didn't miss them like hell. Especially old Gizmo, his huskie-shepherd mix, the four-legged leader of the pack and the dog he'd known the longest. Eli spent every day surrounded by dogs, of course, but they weren't *his* dogs. There was no replacement for the eight friends who shared his life and, since Tamara had bolted, his bed.

A vision flashed through his brain—Roxanne in that same bed, flushed, breathless, naked, all that gorgeous dark hair thrown across his pillow, reaching for him. Again.

"You do know her story, right?" Teeny asked, his voice more serious.

Eli tore his mind away from the fantasy and looked to Teeny. He shook his head, knowing the reality wouldn't be nearly as pretty.

"She had a real hard time as a kid," Rick said. "Her dad was a scum bucket who walked out on her and her mom when she was six. They never saw him again."

"And when she was older, Roxie started hooking up with a string of bad boys," Teeny said, shaking his head wistfully. "God knows I have no right to judge that particular weakness, but she's made some questionable calls in the relationship department."

"Hmmm," Eli said, frowning. "So that's where all the anger comes from—father issues and bad relationships?"

Rick jumped in to answer Eli's question. "No," he said. "It was the last one that did her in. Josie tells me that before the last guy, Roxie was pretty much your average woman—a little skeptical but holding out hope. But this last one really fucked with her head."

"How so?" Eli asked, turning toward Rick in fascination. He couldn't help but be interested in the how and the why of Roxie Bloom.

"He was an older dude," Rick said, "a lawyer she met while covering the court system for the *Herald*. She really loved him. She thought for sure they were headed for the altar."

That surprised Eli—the age difference *and* the fact that Roxie had ever dreamed of being somebody's bride. "How much older are we talking?" Eli asked.

"Dirty old man territory," Teeny said, chuckling.

"Josie told me about the night it all went to hell for Roxie," Rick said.

Eli nodded uncomfortably, aware that learning more about the destabilizing force that was Roxie Bloom sure wouldn't make it any easier to walk away. "I'm not sure I want to hear this," he said.

Rick continued anyway. "One night, Josie and Roxanne decided it would be fun to surprise the old guy while he was kickin' back with his boys at a cigar bar."

Eli's eyes got big.

"I know, can you believe it?" Teeny asked, shaking his head at the severity of Roxie's blunder. "Rule number one: always call ahead."

"So they caught him with another woman?" Eli asked.

"Another woman would have been a blessing." Teeny leaned forward and whispered conspiratorially. "They found him in the middle of a nasty little story."

Eli groaned. "He was talking about Roxie."

"Oh, yeah," Rick said. "Josie told me the guy was bragging to his friends about how he liked his women young and stupid, and that Roxanne would have been the ideal girlfriend if she only knew how to give a blow job."

Eli was speechless.

"But this is where it gets good," Teeny said. "Roxanne reaches down and grabs the man's lit cigar and then grinds it into his hair."

"No, no, no," Rick corrected his friend. "The guy's going bald. She put out the cigar on his bare head, man. Josie said you could smell burning skin and everything."

Eli got the rocker moving back and forth, stalling for time while he tried to figure out how to respond. One quick glance at Teeny and Rick confirmed that they expected some kind of reaction from him. The truth was, his heart ached for Roxie Bloom. The old dude sounded like a real pig. But to carry around all that hurt and not deal with it, to wrap yourself up in it, define yourself by it—and even rely on it to pay your bills? That was a recipe for disaster. Roxanne needed to make some changes. And soon.

"And now the bald mutha is threatening to sue her for talking about him on her Web site," Teeny said.

Eli shook his head real slow. No wonder Roxanne exploded into sobs when he'd told her she was safe with him. First her father, then the bad boys, then the father-figure lover who'd led her to believe she'd be getting a proposal, not a knife in the back.

Telling Roxanne Bloom she'd be safe with him probably sounded like something right out of the Rat Bastard Playbook. She had no way of knowing that Eli always meant what he said and said what he meant.

Rick cleared his throat. "So, Eli, we're basically recommending that if you're interested in Roxie, you should wear riot gear."

"Hazmat shit if you got it," Teeny said.

Eli stopped rocking, and looked to both men, his mind racing with the information he'd just received. He felt a smile spread across his face.

"Contents under pressure," Eli whispered.

Teeny and Rick cocked their heads in unison, confused.

That was it, Eli knew. Roxanne Bloom had shoved and pushed and crammed the hurt way down inside herself, then secured it with a big old lid of anger. Somehow, Eli had pried open that lid out there at the paddock, and look what happened! Within seconds she was sobbing, kissing him, wiggling up against him like she was trying to get inside his clothes with him. She was a volcano, ready to blow.

"We're not following you," Teeny said.

Eli nodded, giving himself a moment to settle. "I was just thinking that Roxanne Bloom should come with a warning label. You know, 'Contents Under Pressure; Do Not Use Near Heat, Sparks, or Open Flame.'"

Even as the three men enjoyed a good belly laugh, Eli realized that there was nothing funny about his observation. He'd just articulated his problem, and his problem was that he was on fire for Roxie Bloom.

And if he didn't keep his distance, there was sure to be an explosion.

Chapter 3

Pulling into the entrance of the Komfy K-9 Day Spa, Roxanne dreaded what was to come. She'd been through this enough times, at enough establishments, that she had a standard timeline mapped out in her head. Here's how it usually went: Lilith gets dropped off; Lilith growls and barks at male kennel workers and male dogs; the kennel calls Roxie to complain; Lilith gets so worked up she froths out of the sides of her muzzle; other customers demand to see the dog's vaccination record on file and threaten to never use the establishment again if *that animal* is there; Roxanne apologizes over the phone; Roxanne arrives to pick up Lilith; Roxanne begs the kennel management to give her another chance; Roxanne has to pay extra.

All this could be avoided, of course, if someone were willing to check on Lilith while Roxanne was out of the house for long periods. Unfortunately, she'd been blacklisted among Bay Area pet sitters. And her neighbors were distinctly uncomfortable around Lilith, even the neighbors with dogs of their own. Of course, Bea was willing and able to look after Lilith, but she was often attending the very events Roxanne had to leave home for in the first place.

Sometimes, Roxanne felt as if she and Lilith were the lepers of the pet world.

She opened the glass door to a cheerfully tinkling bell and the smiling face of a young woman at the reception desk. The smile quickly disappeared. The woman snatched the desk phone.

"She's here," she whispered, obviously speaking to one of the kennel workers. "Well, excuse me, but *somebody* has to bring that dog up here!" She slammed down the phone.

Roxanne took a deep breath. She walked to the desk, credit card already in hand, barely able to look the girl in the eye. "How much extra?" She decided to just cut to the chase.

The girl let go with a sarcastic laugh. "Well, our six-to-eight-hour doggie day care package is usually $49.95, but considering the fact that we had to call in extra staff, it's going to be twice that amount."

Roxanne's jaw hung limp. "That's embezzlement," she said.

Suddenly, the door to the kennel slammed open, and Lilith came bounding through with the force of a sled dog solely responsible for pulling a three-hundred-pound fur trapper through twenty-five feet of snow. Unfortunately, the employee in question, slipping and sliding on the vinyl flooring, weighed one twenty, tops.

"Ring me up," Roxanne said, handing over her card.

"You should really try some obedience training," the counter girl said, swiping the card.

Roxanne rolled her eyes. Because she refused to repeat Lilith's Litany of Failure (thrown out of three obedience classes and two behaviorally challenged dog programs) she simply signed the receipt and slid it across the reception counter.

"In your case, you might want to go right to one of those dog whisperers. I hear they're supposed to be, you know, the last-chance Texaco for psycho dogs like yours." The girl looked askance at the now foaming Lilith. "One of our regulars told me about some guy who's temporarily in the area. Very exclusive. Jennifer Aniston was his client a while back. Supposed to be fabulous. He works out of Celestial Pet. Wait—I think I entered his name in our database."

Roxanne grabbed Lilith's leash and stroked her dog's short, smooth fur in an attempt to calm her down. She nuzzled her nose into Lilith's neck and whispered softly to her, all while backing up toward the exit. Her plan was to be out in the parking lot by the time the girl found what she was looking for.

"Hey, wait! I got it! Oh! And our customer said this dude is smokin' hot, which is always a nice bonus. Hey, maybe I should call him myself!" She giggled.

Roxanne was at the door.

"The guy's name is Eli Gallagher. Don't you want his number?"

"I already have his number," Roxie said, escaping into the parking lot.

She cried during the entire twenty-minute drive between the kennel and her house, hating that she'd fallen into one of her black holes of self-pity but knowing there was nothing she could do about it now. It always took several hours to dig herself out of one of her emotional recessions.

As if on cue, the pity-party remix began spinning in her head, DJ Miz Fortune at the mike.

It all started when Millie died. *My collie had been*

with me since middle school. She was my best friend, my one constant.

Then, Raymond showed his true colors. *I loved him and he lied to me, played me, and never respected me.*

The next two weeks were pure hell. *I find out I'm pregnant. Before I can even catch my breath, I wake up in the middle of the night with cramps, blood dripping down my legs, and the baby is gone.*

Enter Lilith. *I adopt a behaviorally challenged dog no one likes.*

Hello, joblessness! *The paper cans me because I won't shut down the Web site, which is just an excuse. Firing me means one less reporter who'd need a severance package when the place goes under, which it soon does.*

Then Eli Gallagher shoots me down. *The only man since Raymond to catch my eye turns me down for lunch, among the least threatening of date options.*

Happiness finds Josie, Ginger, and Bea. *But skips me entirely.*

And Raymond comes back in my life. *But only to threaten me with a lawsuit and a promise to shut down my Web site.*

And so, here I am.

Lilith snuggled her head into Roxanne's lap, occasionally looking up at her owner with the biggest, most beautiful brown puppy eyes that ever were. Roxie stroked her petal-soft ear. Despite everything, Roxie never regretted adopting Lilith. Not for a second.

No one seemed to consider her a particularly attractive dog, with her muddy brown mix-up of boxer, pit bull, and some kind of hound, possibly beagle. But what did they know? Lilith was a survivor, beautiful and brave, Roxanne's Warrior Priestess sidekick.

According to the dog rescue people, she'd had a hard

and lonely life before Roxanne saved her, spending most of her days tied to a clothesline on a nasty old man's back stoop, left without proper food, water, or attention. A neighbor had reported suspected physical abuse of the dog and the SPCA swooped in, taking her to a shelter. Because of her poor health and exotic looks, she'd been on the fast track to euthanasia when the rescue group found her.

Roxanne would never forget the day she arrived for her first interview with the Best Friends Canine Rescue Agency of Northern California. Lilith had only been in a foster home for a week. Her fur was falling out in patches. She had a festering cut across the top of her head. Roxanne could see every rib in her body and every vertebra in her spine. The dog's eyes were hollow.

"I'll take her," Roxanne had said. The three-person approval committee laughed at her enthusiasm.

"It takes a special person to accept this type of responsibility," one of the committee members had said in a kind voice. "This is a dog that needs to start from square one. She needs lots of time and lots of patience. And there's something else you should know." The woman glanced nervously at her fellow female committee members. "It seems she doesn't like men very much."

"I'm your girl!" Roxanne assured them, knowing a sign from heaven when it fell on her.

Of course, Lilith didn't come home with her that day. It took four additional weeks, two more interviews, four personal references, a written application process, a criminal background check, and a home inspection before Roxanne was approved to be Lilith's new owner.

As Bea had said, "You can squirt out eight artificially inseminated babies in this state without so much as a howdy-do, but you can't adopt a beat-up mutt without getting Top Secret security clearance? *What the fuck?*"

The memory made Roxanne smile, even through her sniffles. As fate would have it, the day she'd brought Lilith home marked the three-month anniversary of the death of her beloved Millie, and the two-month anniversary of the Night of the Cigar, as she and Josie had since referred to it. And it marked the beginning of a new phase in Roxie's life.

When the paper was preparing to fire Roxie, Lilith became her primary sounding board and shoulder to cry on. When she sank most of her savings and all of her energy into the Web site, Lilith became her one-woman cheering section. Of course, she also had Bea, Ginger, and Josie, but they weren't exactly shy about dispensing advice along with their encouragement. Lilith, however, had no agenda. She would sit on the couch with Roxie, lay her in head in her lap, and look up at her with soft brown eyes filled with adoration.

And really, sometimes that's all a girl wanted. No advice. No "I told you sos." Just some freakin' adoration.

Roxanne rubbed her dog's head and tried to keep her focus on the road, the tears flowing harder now. Wouldn't it be nice if that were the whole story?

Well, it wasn't.

The truth was, something wasn't right with Lilith. Love, patience, and time hadn't been enough. Lilith had a feral and volatile part of her that Roxanne hadn't been able to reach. Lilith might be strong and healthy now, with a shiny coat and bright eyes, but Roxanne hadn't been able to give her the one thing she needed most—a deep belief that everything would be all right, that she could let down her guard.

For whatever reason, Roxanne hadn't been able to make Lilith feel safe, no matter what she did, how hard she tried, or how relentlessly she wished for things to get better. But nothing had changed. The reason she got Lilith in the first place was to enjoy her company, but that only happened when they were alone at home. Doors locked. No sounds coming from outside. No other people or dogs in sight.

The bottom line? Owning Lilith was exhausting.

They pulled up Roxanne's drive and into the little garage of her Noe Valley house. They went for a quick walk around the block. Of course, Roxie had an encounter with the Sweeping Lady. She always had an encounter with the Sweeping Lady on days when being nice to an anal-retentive nut job required more energy than she possessed.

"Good afternoon, Mrs. Delano. How are you?"

The Sweeping Lady's broom stopped in mid-jerk. Mrs. Delano looked up from her perpetual task, one eye squinted beneath her sunhat. After a barely noticeable nod to Roxie, her eyes darted to Lilith. "Pit bulls should be illegal," she said.

Roxie made a polite "hmmm" sound, as if she were giving the woman's comment some serious thought— for the thousandth time. This had been their topic of conversation since the day she brought Lilith home. Not that the pre-Lilith Mrs. Delano had been any friendlier. Roxie had bought her little two-bedroom bungalow on Sanchez Street four years before, and Mrs. Delano lived two doors down. From what Roxie could tell, the widow's motto was, "I sweep, therefore I am."

She swept morning, noon, and night. She swept leaves, twigs, dirt, pebbles, and stray blades of grass. She swept in the rain, wind, and occasional cold. She swept the driveway. The sidewalk. The porch. The porch steps. And, on her most anxious days, the street itself. Once, Roxie even caught her sweeping the small patch of grass in front of her house. That time, Mrs. Delano had scurried inside, broom clutched tight to her body, ashamed that she'd been caught.

"Lilith is a mixed breed, Mrs. Delano," Roxie said, sounding as sweet as she could. "She may have some pit bull in her but she's also part boxer and beagle or something."

With a shrug, the woman went back to her sweeping. *Swssh, swssh. Swssh, swssh.* "I liked your other one better. It was a normal dog."

Lilith chose that moment to growl. Roxie's head swiveled around to see a man walking a well-behaved standard poodle on the opposite side of the street. Lilith began to tug and bark.

"Have a nice evening, Mrs. Delano," Roxanne managed to say as she was dragged down the sidewalk by a now frothing Lilith.

"This one's not normal!" Mrs. Delano called out, just before she recommenced her sweeping.

Ten minutes later, Roxanne had managed to take off Lilith's muzzle and put away her leash, order a pizza with mushrooms and black olives, and change into a pair of comfortable sweats and a tank top. Popping open a Diet Coke, she began updating her blog while Lilith rested peacefully at her feet. Today's topic: men who turn you down for lunch one day and try to kiss you the next. She titled it "The Vacillator." It would make a nice follow-up to yesterday's essay about how relationships can go from champagne and kisses to civil litigation in the blink of an eye. That one she'd called "Tort, Anyone?"

She went on to read some e-mails, then three entries for the Jerk-of-the-Week contest. She came across one entry from a grad student who ran into her ex at a dance club and, against her better judgment, took him back to her place, just like old times.

At first, the guy was all over her, telling her he'd made a huge mistake letting her go. Suddenly, he stopped all the sweet talk and asked if he could use her bathroom. While he was occupied, she put on some nice music and changed her clothes. When the ex came out fifteen minutes later, he announced he had to leave. No explanation. No small talk. And suddenly he was gone, leaving behind a foul-smelling bathroom and a really confused girl.

Roxie felt chills race through her. *I've found this week's winner!*

She was just about to review the day's merchandise orders when she heard the doorbell. Roxie was shocked at what had to be a record for pizza delivery. After grabbing a twenty out of her purse, she opened the door just a bit, leaving the chain lock in place. This was her tried-and-true routine: stick the money through the crevice, tell the delivery guy to leave the pizza on the doorstep, and wait for him to get safely to his car before she opened the door. It was a foolproof method that insured the delivery guy's safety and minimized Lilith's agitation.

But this time, something went terribly wrong. The instant she eased the door open, it slammed against her palms, throwing her back onto her butt as a loud *crack!* echoed through the house and the chain ripped away from the wood door frame.

"You bitch!"

Roxanne barely had time to prop herself up on an elbow and catch her breath before he was standing over her, rage on his face, sweat beading on his balding head. She realized she had a headache. Had the door hit her? She lifted her hand to find a lump forming under her hair.

" 'Tort Anyone?' How dare you? Who the hell do you think you are, you stupid, hardheaded sluuu—?"

Uh-oh.

From her vantage point down on the hardwood floor, Roxanne saw only a brindle-brown, white-bellied blur sail overhead, sharp white fangs bared. She heard a horrible low-level growl rumble through the air.

There was nothing she could do to prevent it. Lilith ended her flight with a thump, hitting a terrified-looking Raymond Sandberg on his upper chest. His head flew back. Lilith promptly sank her teeth into the side of his neck. Raymond crumpled to the floor, but Lilith hung on.

"Stop, Lilith! No! Oh, God!" Roxanne was up. She threw her body on top of Lilith and gripped the dog's collar. She tried in vain to pull Lilith off Raymond. Her ex-boyfriend, in the meantime, began screaming. He begged for his life. He threatened to kill Roxanne and/or sue her for everything she was worth. Even in the panic of the moment, Roxanne noted that Lilith had done a half-assed job—the man still had use of his vocal chords.

Thrashing. Tearing. Screaming. Growling. It seemed to go on forever. But it ended abruptly, when there was a faint sound of someone clearing his throat.

It was the pizza guy. The kid's eyes darted to the bloody scene before him as he simultaneously opened the Velcro closure of a thermal carrying case and removed a cardboard box that guaranteed a hot and fresh pizza or your money back. "Medium thin crust with black olive and mushroom?" he asked nonchalantly.

This interruption distracted Lilith from her murderous intent—if only for an instant—and when the dog turned her attention to the new arrival, Roxanne was able to grip her snout and collar. While Raymond continued to scream and curse, Roxie dragged Lilith's muscular body down the hallway to the kitchen, where she crammed her inside and slammed the door. Roxie raced back to the living room, grabbing her cell phone as she went, already dialing 911 with trembling, bloody fingers.

She fell to her knees in front of Raymond. He lay on his back, limbs spread, eyes huge with shock, a blood-covered hand clutching the side of his throat. He was alive.

And boy, was he *pissed*!

"That fucking dog tried to kill me! You trained it to attack me, didn't you? You did this on purpose!"

"I need an ambulance," Roxie said to the 911 operator. "My dog just bit a home intruder."

"What?" Raymond struggled to a sitting position, his face scarlet with rage. The veins in his neck—the ones not shredded by Lilith—pulsed wildly. "You bitch!"

Only then did Roxanne notice that Mrs. Delano stood on the stoop, broom in hand, head pivoting back and forth as she passed judgment.

Next, Roxanne noticed that the pizza box had been carefully placed in the doorway, along with the receipt. The delivery guy was gone, and so was the twenty-dollar bill that had slipped from Roxanne's hand in the melee.

Chapter 4

"I'm so sorry," Roxanne whispered, dropping her head into her hands, pressing the ice pack into her lump. "I know this isn't the traditional way to wrap up a baby shower."

Josie patted Roxie on the shoulder. Ginger stroked her knee. Bea paced wildly between the rows of waiting room chairs in the emergency room of the California Pacific Medical Center, mumbling obscenities to herself.

A sudden outburst from Lucio surprised everyone. "That sohn uva towzand *beet-chez*!" Ginger's husband waved his hands around wildly the way he did when he got worked up. "*¡Gilipollas!*"

Bea stopped her pacing and looked to Lucio with approval. "Amen to whatever it is you just said," she told him.

From her slump of defeat, Roxanne laughed sarcastically. "You know what I just realized? Mrs. Needleman was almost right." She peeked up at Bea. "I left my door open just a crack like she suggested, and voilà! A man waltzes right in. Only he wasn't the man of my dreams. He was my worst nightmare!"

Bea pursed her lips. "That was supposed to be a metaphor."

"Oh, really?" Roxanne asked, laughing harder. "I've never seen a metaphor bleed like that!"

Just then, Rick and Teeny came marching through the waiting room, provoking openmouthed stares from most of the women within visual range. Teeny was very big, black, and bald, and he wore a substantial diamond in one of his ears. Plus he dressed like a movie star. Rick was his usual hunky self, part casual and scruffy surfer dude and part *GQ* CEO.

Roxie stood up to greet them.

"Door's fixed," Teeny announced. "We built a whole new frame, put in a sturdier chain, and added a dead bolt. We recommend you use it."

She nodded.

"Don't forget to prime the frame before you paint," he added.

"Of course," she said, overwhelmed by the kindness of her friends. She gave both of them a quick hug. "I can't tell you how much I appreciate everything you've done."

"It's nothing," Rick said. "How's the head?"

Roxie absently touched the sore bump a few inches above her left temple, where the door had hit her. "The doctors said it's just a minor contusion."

Rick nodded, looking worried. "Listen, Roxie, I left a message for my lawyer to see who he'd recommend for this kind of situation. Hope you don't mind."

Roxanne shook her head. "You didn't need to do that. I'll find someone." She returned to her seat between Josie and Ginger and resumed her slump.

Teeny frowned. "You'd better listen to what he's telling you," he admonished Roxanne.

"Yeah. Listen to the man, Rox," Bea said.

Rick stepped closer to Roxanne and squatted, putting a hand on her knee. "If you don't have the best defense money can buy, Raymond Sandberg's going to chew you up and spit you out."

Roxanne moaned, returning her face to her hands. "Raymond *is* the best defense lawyer money can buy," she mumbled.

"What you really need is a damn time machine," Teeny said, his voice soft. "Then you could go back in time and take out any mention of him on your Web site."

Roxanne raised her eyes and huffed, offended. "I've never once used his name! I only provided a general description of him!"

"Come on now, Rox," Bea said, pacing again. "It's common knowledge that Raymond Sandberg is your ex-lover. The breakup was dramatic and acted out in front of the patrons of a crowded cigar bar. Plus, how many other men in this town can be described as 'San Francisco's most successful criminal defense attorney and all-around champion pig-faced, misogynistic asshole?'"

Rick nodded, his brow crumpled in seriousness as he looked into her face. "You hung this guy in virtual effigy, Rox. You turned him into the Internet poster boy for pig-faced men everywhere. He was already planning to sue you for that—and now *this*?"

Bea snorted her agreement. "The man shows up and your dog promptly tries to rip his throat out. This doesn't look so good, babes."

"The man didn't just *show up*!" Roxanne wailed. "He busted down my whole freakin' door! Lilith was protecting me! She might have saved my life!"

The group of six remained quiet for a moment. Rick's phone rang and he wandered off to speak with his lawyer. Josie continued to rub Roxie's back. Ginger stroked her hair. Their attention felt very sweet and maternal, but Roxie was too upset to appreciate their attempt to comfort her.

Suddenly, the doors leading from the ER slammed open. Raymond Sandberg appeared, looking like an extra in a Quentin Tarantino flick. Blood droplets were spattered all over his white slacks and tangerine-hued Ralph Lauren polo shirt. A large, square gauze bandage was taped to the side of his neck. The same two San Francisco Police detectives who'd interviewed Roxie strolled out behind him.

Raymond's dark blue eyes burned with hatred as he headed directly toward Roxanne. She stood up, swallowing hard. All her friends stood up with her, and gathered close. Rick hurried back to the waiting room chairs, the phone still to his ear.

Raymond came to a stop, breathing hard. "I so look forward to our various courtroom rendezvous," he said, his voice laced with mock politeness. "It seems you'll be kissing both your business *and* your fugly mutt good-bye."

"You wait just a damn second, mister." Josie stepped forward before Roxanne could even open her mouth to speak. The mother-to-be's cheeks were flushed as she peered up into Raymond's face. She poked a finger in his chest. "You are a brute and a bully and you're dressed like you belong in a *Miami Vice* rerun."

Ginger stepped forward next. "You got exactly what you had coming to you, you pompous douche bag."

Then Bea sauntered up. "Ain't karma a bitch?"

Raymond said nothing for a long second, studying the little group, taking note of Josie and Ginger's very pregnant silhouettes and angry faces. Then he produced a deep laugh and displayed one of his jury-worthy grins. His gaze flew to Roxanne.

The force of that stare pinned her down. She felt trapped. She hated him. She'd once loved and trusted him with everything in her, and he'd blown a hole in her soul with his betrayal. It was interesting how hate had filled up that hole, spilling over into everything in her life.

Oh, and how she despised those eyes of his. How she cringed at the sight of that stellar smile.

The image of Eli Gallagher flashed in her mind. In her head she watched him tug on the brim of that stupid hat. She remembered the sound of that velvet-calm voice as it assured her she was safe. But she especially recalled the sadness she saw in his eyes when she pulled away from his kiss.

She remembered it so well because she'd felt the very same way.

Roxanne squeezed her eyes shut to block the vision. Why was that man haunting her? And why now? Didn't she have enough shit to deal with? She didn't want Eli in her head. She didn't want Raymond in her life. She just wanted these men—*all* men—to go away and leave her in peace.

Raymond leaned in close. She kept her eyes closed so she didn't have to see him. But she smelled him— the crisp, light scent of his expensive cologne mixed with blood and sweat. It almost made her heave.

"My complaint has already been processed," he whispered. "Your dog will be impounded. She's going to be put down." Raymond chuckled in her ear. "May I just say, in advance, how sorry I am for your loss?"

With that, the smell and sound of Raymond Sandberg dissipated. He was gone. She opened her eyes.

"Miss Bloom?" One of the detectives moved toward her. His partner followed.

"How could he already have an order for my dog to

be impounded?" she asked then, not bothering to hide her panic. "He hasn't set foot out of the hospital! What's going on here?"

The two officers glanced at each other. "He made some calls from his bed," one said.

"Mr. Sandberg knows a lot of people in this town," the other officer added.

"No," Roxie whispered, feeling her throat close up with panic. "He can't do this to Lilith. I won't let him."

Because home for Eli was a four-thousand-acre ranch in southern Utah, there was no such thing as a quick trip there and back. The drive was twelve hours each way. Flying wasn't much better, with a jet from San Francisco to Salt Lake, a long layover, and then a puddle-jumper flight to St. George. From there it was another two-hour drive to the outskirts of Panguitch, then down three miles of bumpy access road that ended at the gate to Dog-Eared Ranch. Despite all this, a few days at home was always Eli's preferred method of relaxation. It was the only foolproof way to return his mind, body, and spirit to a state of equilibrium.

What did it say about his current state, Eli wondered, that he'd canceled all appointments for the week and set out for home on a Monday afternoon? Did it mean he was so out of whack he couldn't wait for the weekend? Did he need to put about eight hundred miles between himself and Roxie Bloom, the long-legged, dark-haired sensual volcano who'd nearly rocked him off course?

Eli hoped to have it all figured out in a few days. In the meantime, he'd remind himself to breathe and enjoy the trip.

It wasn't that he didn't like San Francisco. He did. The city hummed with energy from the diversity of human beings who lived there. It had food, music, art, and architecture for every palette. Then there were the magical blue stretches of ocean and bay. The parks. The wind that whipped around the Golden Gate Bridge. The beauty of the city at night was a vision that sent shivers through him.

But it all got to him after a while. The people and concrete and traffic and noise could make him feel jumpy. His core—that unshakable sense of who he was as a human being and a man—would start to feel just the slightest bit fuzzy. And when that happened, he knew it was time for a dose of never-ending mountain and sky, and the rolling waves of sagebrush topped by high-altitude cedar forest. He needed to be in a place that had more coyotes than cabs. He needed to go home.

That's how he found himself at the Salt Lake City International Airport that Monday evening, waiting for the SkyWest connecting flight to St. George. He looked at his cell phone and sighed with relief. In a few hours he'd be sitting on his porch, his dogs around him, a cold beer in his hand, and his familiar mountains rising in the darkness beyond.

Of course, this idyllic homecoming would include the usual interrogation from his sister, Sondra, who'd never understood his San Francisco sabbatical in the first place.

"Are you crazy?" she'd ask first, followed up with *"Can't you just let this go?"* and, Eli's favorite, *"What are you—a glutton for punishment or something?"*

He smiled softly to himself and cradled the back of his head in his hands, watching, through the glass wall, the maintenance crew at work on the small sixteen-seat commuter plane. Of course she didn't understand—how could she? Sondra knew who her mother and father were. When Bob Gallagher died last year, her world stayed in order. She grieved, of course, but the universe still made sense. It hadn't been that way for Eli. He'd found out by accident, while getting his father's papers in order for the attorney. In his hand he was suddenly holding a slightly yellowed legal document he never knew existed. In it, Robert W. Gallagher of Denver, Colorado, became the legal guardian of the illegitimate son of his new wife, the former Carole Broward Tisdale, also of Denver. The identity of the biological father was unknown. At the time of the adoption proceedings, the child in question was eighteen months old.

Eli had sat there in his father's study, numb with shock. It took a good half hour for him to thaw out, but when he did, he was on fire with anger, hurt, and the knowledge that he'd been betrayed. He'd been thirty-one years old, for God's sake! When had they planned on telling him? How could they have justified keeping this from him for his entire life?

In the depth of her mourning for her husband, Eli's mother begged Eli to understand—it was about her shame, she said. She sat with him at the kitchen table, crying, telling a story about how she'd been a freshman at Berkeley when she found herself pregnant. It was 1977, a time closer to the dawn of Young Republicanism than the Summer of Love, but his mother apparently missed the memo. She'd spent her freshman year living the life of a UC Berkeley wild child—sex, drugs, and rock 'n' roll, as the saying went. She told him, with her head bowed, that Eli had been a product of one of those random moments of abandon, during one of those pot-fogged nights, with one of those faceless (and occasionally nameless) men.

His mother assured him that his father had loved him like his own, and was so very proud of his son.

She told him that Bob Gallagher always saw Eli as a gift from God.

Eli remembered how he had sat there at the table in silence as she told him the truth, listening to the sound of his own breathing and the howl of coyotes in the desert night. He had tried to take it all in, put the new information in some kind of order in his heart, but Eli's understanding of the world had shifted that night.

Unknown? His father was *unknown?*

From that moment on, Eli was determined to fill in the blank.

His cell phone vibrated inside the front pocket of his jacket. It was Sondra, making sure his flight was on time and informing him she'd already left the ranch for St. George to pick him up. Should they plan on stopping somewhere for supper? she wondered. Did he want to pick up supplies in town before they headed back? Should she go back for a couple of the dogs? Or maybe all of them? Or, since a storm was forecast, should she just keep driving and forget the dogs?

An overhead announcement told him to board the plane, so he ended the conversation with Sondra. Eli stood, grabbed his carry-on, and set his hat back on his head. He was just one passenger away from handing over his boarding pass when the phone buzzed again. Not even looking at the number, he stepped out of line and answered with a laugh. "Let me guess—you called to remind me to use the bathroom before I get on the plane?"

When he heard silence in place of one of Sondra's chuckles, he removed the phone from his ear and checked the screen. The call hadn't come from home—it was a San Francisco number he didn't recognize. Eli put the phone back to his ear. "Pardon me. Hello?"

The woman's voice was so soft he could hardly hear

it with the airport background noise. "Have I reached Eli Gallagher?" she asked.

"Yes. Who's calling? Can you speak a little louder?"

There was a tap on his shoulder. "Sir, you really need to board now," the SkyWest employee said, smiling politely.

"Sure. Be right there." But with the momentary distraction, Eli had missed whatever reply he'd gotten from the caller. "I'm sorry, could you repeat that?"

The mystery woman laughed. "Of course you'd want me to repeat it. You get off on hearing women beg for help, is that it?"

Eli blinked. The voice was clearer and louder now. He felt his belly drop to his boots.

"What did I expect?" she continued with renewed vigor. "That you'd be something other than an arrogant bastard about this? My God, I must have been crazy to think you'd help me."

"Roxanne?"

More silence.

"This is Roxanne Bloom, correct?"

"How in the world would you know it was me?" she asked sharply.

Eli laughed and was about to answer her but lost his train of thought when the airline employee tapped his shoulder again, this time without the friendly smile. He held up his index finger to indicate he'd just be another minute.

"Because I know you, Roxanne," was Eli's answer. Immediately, he realized how odd his statement sounded. What he'd meant to say was, *Because I know your voice.* Talk about losing his equilibrium!

"I hardly think so," she said, her words flat.

"Ms. Bloom, is there something I can do for you? I don't mean to be rude but they're holding a plane for me."

"A plane? But you can't!" Roxie's voice softened again. She sounded truly frightened. "Oh, God! What am I going to do?"

If Eli heard right, Roxie then began to cry.

"Tell me exactly what's happened," he said, already guessing the general nature of this call. With everything that had transpired between them, there could be only one reason Roxanne Bloom would ever contact him— her dog had attacked someone and she needed his help.

"Yesterday, Animal Control took her . . . they're going to destroy . . . Oh, God . . . I have to prove she can be re-habilitated or they'll put her down!" Roxie stopped a moment, unable to speak. Eli heard her struggle to contain her emotions. "There's a hearing . . ."

That's when Eli heard Bea Latimer's voice in the background, insisting Roxanne spit it out.

"Please! I can't let them kill her! You've got to help me. *Please come back!*"

Eli sighed deeply, then made his way to the chair he'd vacated only moments before. He let his overnight bag fall to the floor and took a seat. "Did she bite someone, Roxie?" he asked calmly, his voice free of blame.

She cried hard.

"Roxanne, please listen to me."

She cried some more.

"Was the injury serious?"

"No!" She sniffed, pulling herself together. "It was totally minor stuff. He had some lacerations to his throat, but no major arteries were severed or anything."

Eli's eyes went wide. "I see."

"All it took was ten stitches and some intravenous antibiotics and he was outta there!"

Eli coughed. "But he'll be all right?"

"Oh, sure. He's going to need some plastic surgery down the road, but, you know, nothing major."

"Ah," Eli said, realizing he'd hate to hear what Roxie considered a serious injury. "And who, exactly, did Lilith bite?"

"My pig-faced dickhead of an ex-boyfriend."

Eli sucked on the inside of his cheek a moment before he continued. "And where is the dog right now?"

"They've got her. They said I can't take her home until after . . ." Roxie stopped. In fact, it sounded like she'd stopped breathing altogether.

"Roxie?"

She let out a long, low howl of grief. The emotional pain he heard in her cry would've brought him to his knees if he weren't already sitting. It reminded him a great deal of the way she'd cried at the horse paddock just the day before.

Eli took a slow and steady breath. He pulled air into his chest and let it out through his nose. He saw where this was headed, and he would need to be steady. In fact, he would need to be steady enough for the three of them—himself, Roxanne, and her dog. And that was saying something.

He smiled softly, realizing that the whole situation had the feel of inevitability to it. Here he was, in an airport, trying his best to run away from Roxie Bloom, and now it seemed he'd be running *to* her, instead.

Eli grabbed his bag once more and made his way to the gate. As Roxie continued to cry into the phone, he informed the airline that he had an emergency and would be returning to the main terminal to book a flight back to San Francisco.

He started walking, the phone to his ear.

"Everything is going to be all right, Roxie," he told her. "I'll be back by morning. We'll figure this out together."

"But . . . you mean you're not leaving town?" She sounded incredulous. "You're going to help me?"

"Yes. I'll help you."

What came next was clearly a stretch for Roxie. She'd become a little rusty at it, no doubt. But she managed to fix her mouth around those two little words and then say them out loud—*to a man,* no less. To Eli.

"Thank you," she whispered.

"You're welcome," he said.

Chapter 5

Roxanne sat at an outdoor table at the Starbucks on Diamond Heights, waiting for Eli Gallagher to show. Not that he was late. She was early. Roxie's plan was to appear relaxed and businesslike from the get-go, so she'd given herself a little extra time to accomplish that. She wanted Eli Gallagher to come down the sidewalk and see her sitting with perfect posture, legs crossed casually, sipping on her café au lait with an air of dignified nonchalance.

To aid in this, she'd taken extra care with her appearance that morning, following a grooming routine much like the one she relied on back when she covered criminal courts for the *Herald,* back when she was forced to leave the house every day to do her job, back when her livelihood required regular, actual, face-to-face human contact. So that morning she'd applied a tasteful amount of makeup and straightened her long hair into a sleek but casual style. She'd chosen a pair of peep-toe heels, charcoal gray dress slacks with a scarf belt, and a tailored blouse in a pale lilac color. She wore modest silver hoops in her ears and an heirloom marcasite ring on her left hand.

The goal was get an immediate positive reaction from Eli. She wanted him to see her and say something to himself along the lines of, *That woman sure has it together!* She'd even settle for, *She certainly looks sophisticated and lovely today.*

Roxanne reached for her cardboard-wrapped coffee cup and took a large slurp. Ha! Who was she kidding? She'd be lucky if the guy didn't stop dead in his tracks and then run away in horror. She knew better than to think that a little lip gloss and under-eye concealer would hide the fact that she hadn't slept for two nights in a row. Instead of sleeping, she'd been crying and blowing her nose, eating caramel corn and cheese puffs while dividing her zombielike attention between a cable shopping network's "Cavalcade of Beauty" clearance special and the 2,351 Google results that appeared when she typed the words "Eli Gallagher, dog whisperer" into her laptop.

How was she supposed to sleep? Lilith wasn't with her. For the first time in nearly a year, Roxanne had been spending the night completely, utterly, and pathetically *alone,* all while her sweet girl was locked up in dog prison, unjustly accused. Sleep hadn't even been an option.

Roxanne sighed deeply. She put down her cup. She could do this. She could deal with Gallagher. As much as it pained her, she would do whatever it took to save her dog. Whatever he said to do, she'd do it. She owed Lilith that.

Besides, Roxie Bloom had never been short on balls. She'd interviewed mass murderers on death row. She'd coaxed scoops out of the most uptight assistant DAs. She'd waited in parking garages at night to corner hesitant sources. She'd been on the scene for child pornography arrests, foiled bomb plots, and murder-suicide investigations. Surely, she could ask one measly cowboy for a hand with dog training!

All it would take was a little self-discipline. She would put aside her own anger and hurt and graciously accept Gallagher for who he was—an animal handler known for miraculously turning around even the most aggressive dogs. She'd just forget all the rest—the way her body caught fire the first time she saw him, the pain of his rejection, how she couldn't stop thinking about him, how that single kiss at the paddock two days ago had contained enough electricity to light up the city of San Francisco for a month . . .

"Excuse me."

Roxie nearly rocketed from her chair, the deep voice scared her so much. "Uh. Sure. No problem." She scooted in a bit for the college kid trying to pass between tables. She realized her heart was pounding and her palms were sweaty.

No more caffeine today, she decided.

She checked her phone. Fifteen minutes to go. She let her eyes roam, scanning the morning neighborhood crowd. She noticed an elderly couple holding hands as they took a slow walk. She saw a happy, laughing man and woman pushing a stroller with a happy, laughing toddler occupant. She saw a middle-aged married couple a few tables away, chatting cheerfully.

She knew it was an exaggeration, but right at that moment she felt as if she were the only single person in San Francisco. It had been so long since she'd been part of a couple that she'd forgotten what it felt like.

Had she really held hands with Raymond on the street like that? Had she looked up into his eyes and laughed? Had they had cheerful conversations? Had there really been good times before it all went to shit?

Of course. It had been good with Raymond—right up until the Night of the Cigar.

She'd been such a stupid, stupid girl.

Roxie smiled tightly, recalling a conversation she'd had at that very same Starbucks table eight months before. Bea, Josie, and herself had sat here, eyes wide and faces flushed, as Ginger described her hot-and-heavy hookup with Lucio Montevez, the famous nature photographer. With a perfectly straight face, Ginger assured everyone she was starting menopause and was no longer fertile. What a crock! What a layer cake of delusional thinking! Because not only was Ginger not going through menopause, she was already pregnant as she spoke those words, but just didn't know it.

Then, Josie had served up her own delusion du jour, insisting that a woman could, indeed, find great sex and a great relationship all with the same man. She'd assured Ginger, "If it could happen for me, it could happen for you or Roxie or any woman!"

Roxie recalled how, in her mind, she'd battled with her options: should she cut Josie some slack, seeing that she'd only just returned from her honeymoon and was drunk on love, or should she do everyone a favor and tell them the truth, for God's sake?

Since Bea was still reeling from Ginger's kissing-and-telling, Roxie knew it was up to her to spread the gospel of reality. "In my experience, the hotter the sex, the harder the fall," she'd told them. "You can't have great sex and a great relationship with the same man. You're going to have to settle for one or the other. It's a universal law."

Ooh, had Josie been mad! In fact, it was the only real argument she'd ever had with her best friend. They'd gotten over it, in time. Roxie supposed that friends sometimes had to agree to disagree.

Still, to this day, Josie was sure she'd caught the brass ring with Rick. Ginger still felt the same about Lucio. So Roxanne prayed her friends were right but waited in the wings to offer them solace, just in case.

"Is this seat taken?"

Roxie allowed a self-satisfied smile to spread across her face. She felt smug, and so very grateful she hadn't jumped out of her seat at the sound of that voice. She turned and looked up. "Hello, Eli. Thanks for coming."

He pulled out the chair across from her. He tipped his hat back a bit and leveled his gaze, studying her. "Rough couple nights, huh?" he asked.

Roxanne laughed, somehow relieved to get that out of the way. She stared down into her cup. "Well, truthfully, yes. When I wasn't busy reading about you online, I was ordering crap I don't need from the cable shopping channel."

She heard his chuckle and decided to meet his eye once more. *Holy shit, that man is gorgeous,* was all that went through her mind.

"Buy anything for me?"

She laughed again, thinking, *How the hell am I supposed to pretend that I haven't spent the last nine months picturing this guy naked?* "Do you have any need for a vibrating eyelash curler?" she asked.

"Not in the foreseeable future."

"How about a holiday nail care collection featuring twenty-five festive polish colors and a year's supply of emery boards?"

"Can't say that I do," he said, pursing his lips while the lines around his eyes crinkled in amusement. "What else you got?"

Roxanne leaned back into her chair and crossed her arms over her chest, sighing deeply. "What I got, Eli, is one incredibly fucked-up dog."

He nodded kindly, and in that deep-velvet-mellow voice of his he said, "It kind of looks that way, Roxie Bloom." She watched him take a slow, deep breath. "Did you bring a copy of her records?"

"Yup." Roxie reached in the bag at her feet and pulled out a manila envelope. "Everything's in there— the report from the rescue group, her adoption papers, all her shot records and vet visits. I even enclosed the letters I got from the dog trainers who kicked her out of class."

"Wonderful. Thank you." Eli pulled the papers out and glanced at them quickly before he shoved them back inside the envelope sleeve and slid it back across the table.

"You don't want to keep them? You're not going to read them?" Roxanne asked, puzzled.

"Nope. Just wanted to make sure she was up to date on her shots."

"Hmmph," Roxie said, thinking that all he had to do was ask her for that information, for God's sake. Maybe he didn't trust her to tell the truth. *Men.*

Why does this particular man have to be so drop-dead hot?

"Now, before we get started, there's one thing I need to ask you."

Roxie felt her eyes go wide. "Of course," she said, her head spinning with the possibilities. What did he want to know? she wondered. *Are you seeing anyone? Do you know how wrong I was to turn you down for lunch? Do you think you could orgasm at just the sound of my voice?* (*Why, yes, Eli! I believe I could!*)

"How do you picture your ideal relationship with Lilith?" was his question.

"Huh?"

"Lilith," he repeated. "Your dog. Picture the perfect relationship with Lilith. What do you see?"

"Oh." Roxanne flipped her hair over her shoulder, slightly embarrassed that her imagination had roamed so far off topic. That had been a good question, and it just so happened that she'd asked herself that very thing many times over.

"I want us to enjoy each other's company," she said, her voice confident. "I want Lilith to stay calm and feel safe, no matter where we go, what we do, or who we're with. I don't want to worry that she might growl, lunge, froth at the mouth, or bite again. *I just want to have fun with my dog.*"

Eli blinked a few times, then unleashed one of those supernova smiles that seemed to appear for no reason, without any effort. Roxanne had never seen anyone—man or woman—produce such a white-toothed, full-faced smile of joy without it looking fake. Where did that smile of his come from? she wondered. Why did she find it so engaging? And why did it feel so fascinatingly familiar?

"Good answer. Now tell me why," he said.

"Why what?" Roxie sat up straighter.

"The ideal relationship you just described with your dog—why do you want that?"

She smiled a little, enjoying the way this conversation challenged her. She might have known the answer to Eli's first question, but that was where her introspection had ended. "You know, I'm not sure why, exactly. Give me a minute to think about that, okay?"

"Of course."

Roxie closed her eyes. She was prepared to reach deep down into her heart for some kind of sensible reply, but, as it turned out, a deep reach wasn't necessary. The answer was lurking right below the surface. But as the words formed in her mind, she was hit with a wall of emotion. Loss. Longing. Sadness. She tried to stop it, but tears began to well behind her eyelids. It took a moment before she could speak.

"Because we both need some peace," she whispered. Even though her eyes were tightly closed, the tears threatened to drop onto her cheeks. "I don't want to fight anymore. I'm exhausted. All I want is to love my dog and have her be happy." She opened her eyes and smiled at him. "I want to get rid of the garbage so there's room for happiness."

When her words got no response from Eli, Roxie figured she'd made a fool of herself with her blubbering. With a nervous laugh, she swiped at her cheeks. "I must sound like Wayne Dyer on crack or something."

That's when the strangest thing happened. Roxie was treated to a slide show of emotions playing on Eli's face. First, he looked stunned. Next, he seemed slightly amused. Then, he looked downright proud of her.

The rest happened quite fast—his smile softened and his green eyes darkened. His breathing slowed and his jaw twitched. And Roxanne swore she could feel him ripping her clothes off with his eyes. Her whole body began to tremble.

Okay, perhaps the part about undressing her with his eyes was wishful thinking, but still, something extremely *powerful* had just passed between them, and not a single word had been spoken. It made their barnyard kiss seem like a snippet of static electricity.

She tilted her head and stared at him, befuddled. He was the most unusual man she'd ever met, and the effect he had on her was stranger still. He had a calm charisma. He was dominant and masculine but gentle. And the combination of those traits seemed to soothe Roxie and stimulate her at the same time. She couldn't put a name to it, but whatever was going on between them seemed like a chemical reaction of sorts, a collision of Eli's assured maleness and Roxie's mishmash of longing and anger and need.

They studied each other for a moment, then Eli sprang up from his seat.

"Let's walk," he said, nearly tossing aside his wrought-iron chair as he moved from the table.

Roxanne smiled, relieved that the unnaturally serene Eli Gallagher could be made uncomfortable. She took her time disposing of her coffee cup, then caught up with him at the curb. His back remained to her.

"So, where are we headed?" she asked, trying to sound casual.

Eli looked down at her. Because his eyes were shaded by the brim of his silly hat, she didn't have a clue what was going on with him. Suddenly, he burst out laughing.

"What?" she asked, surprised by his reaction.

"I believe we're headed into unknown territory," he said.

"Seriously?" Roxie frowned up at him, a little disappointed. "So Lilith and I are an extreme case? You don't have experience with this sort of thing? I thought you were some kind of guru or something."

He brought his hand to the small of her back and escorted her across the street, chuckling the whole way. When they reached the opposite curb, he smiled down at her. "I'm just a man, Roxie. But I'll give it everything I've got."

Sometimes, he marveled at the depth and breadth of his abilities. If there ever was a man who could make things happen simply by the force of his will, by the power of his mind, it was he, Raymond Julius Sandberg, Esquire. On occasion, it felt as if the world itself unfurled at his feet, a ruby-red carpet of possibility spread out to the horizon. All for him. Just him. Damn, but he loved this life he'd created for himself. It felt awfully good to be him.

"Christ," he muttered, a lightning sting of pain shooting down the side of his neck. The doctors had told him how lucky he was—the vicious she-devil of an attack dog had ripped some skin and a little muscle but had miraculously avoided tendons and arteries. Truly, he couldn't have asked for a more jury-ready injury, a savage and hideous-looking bite wound that caused no permanent damage. Wasn't that interesting? Even this nasty slice out of the right side of his neck was to his benefit. It might be slightly uncomfortable, but it would allow him to pull the plug on that fucking Roxie Bloom bitch forever.

Raymond sighed with satisfaction. He led a charmed life. No doubt about it. A life where even his physical pain led to personal gain.

"Is the light sufficient?" he asked his assistant. "Natural light is always best—is there enough? Should I turn a bit to the left?" Raymond adjusted his position to catch the maximum sunshine from his office suite window, suddenly doubting his new employee's ability to execute this particular assignment. "Are you sure you know how to use a digital camera? These images will prove vital to my complaint. They must show how bruised and swollen I am, even two days after the stitches. Are you getting the caked blood?"

Her response was borderline disrespectful. "Bruising and swelling, check. Caked blood, check."

Raymond rolled his eyes at the subpar attitude of his latest assistant. She was young. Extremely hot. Smart.

But surly. Why did the hot ones always have attitude problems? Awkwardly enough, he suddenly couldn't remember her name. It was Ricky or Randy or something inanely boyish, that he knew, because he'd almost condemned her résumé to the shredder pile when his eye caught reference to her four years in Stanford's women's tennis program.

Looking at her now, in a tight little skirt and blouse, he could say with confidence that there was nothing boyish about that ass. She was all girl. All over.

He smiled at her. "Maybe you should scoot over here and get a closer shot, Ricky," he said, hoping his tone was at once suggestive and authoritative.

"Dusty," she said flatly. "And the zoom worked fine. Here." She handed him the digital camera.

Raymond felt a sudden hot rush of uncertainty. What was he supposed to do with the camera? He didn't see any pictures on the screen! How was he supposed to find the pictures? How did he turn the fucking thing on? It enraged him that she'd seen his obvious lack of mastery over his own digital camera.

"Ahh," Ricky said, ripping the camera from his hand. She hit a few buttons. "There you go." She shoved it back at him. "Click this arrow and you'll see every picture I've taken, in the order taken. Can I go now?"

Raymond's lip began to twitch. Who did this little bitch think she was? He'd hired her from a pool of thousands of applicants. She was nothing. She wouldn't even graduate for another two weeks. She wouldn't start law school for another three months. Didn't she know who he was? Didn't she realize he could crush her? Ruin her before she even got started?

True, she looked nothing like Roxie. This Ricky girl had curly reddish-blond hair and the palest gold eyes he'd ever seen. She was all peachy and perky and freckly, with a set of big tits and legs honed to perfection by Division 1 varsity tennis. Roxie, on the other hand, had been leaner and taller, and her looks were at the opposite end of the spectrum—strikingly dark hair and eyes and porcelain skin. Roxie's boobs had been a nice handful, but they were at least a cup size smaller than this girl's. Yet there was a similarity between them. Maybe it was the ridiculous, flippy sound of their names. Maybe it was the disrespectful attitudes.

Roxie hadn't always been that way, he knew. She'd started off in awe of him. She'd done whatever he said. She'd looked up to him. She'd admired him and catered to him and talked about having his children.

Then she'd made it her life's work to fuck him over.

"You're fired," he told the disobedient Ricky.

"Whaa—" she choked. "But . . . what did you just say, Mr. Sandberg?"

"I said you're fired." Raymond tossed the camera to the leather inlay surface of his desk and rather jauntily circumvented his office suite, as if deep in thought. He headed for the door and put his hand on the knob. "Get out."

Ricky or Randy or whatever her name was, bless her little feminine soul, started to cry. She was sputtering and spewing and whimpering and her emotional implosion was just the kind he preferred—all helpless limbs and big, scared eyes.

Raymond let his shoulders droop dramatically and nodded, as if he'd reached a difficult decision. He crossed over to where she stood on her three-inch heels, looking a bit shaky. He slid a hand around that firm waist and let it slide along the curve of her perfect hip. With his other hand he gestured for her to sit on the sofa.

Once he got her snuggled up in the cushions, he joined her. Then he reached into his pants pocket for a clean, starched, monogrammed handkerchief, and noticed his dick was harder than Chinese calculus.

"You are a very intelligent and capable young woman, Randy," he murmured, insisting she take his hanky. "I chose you to be my assistant because I saw great potential in you. But the way you just spoke to me is unacceptable. Do you understand that?"

She nodded, dabbing at the mascara pooling under her eyes. She looked like a twelve-year-old kid who'd just been yanked into the principal's office.

How perfect. He wanted to rip her clothes off.

"I'm sorry, Mr. Sandberg," she said, sniffling. "Please give me another chance. I . . . I just get a little woozy at the sight of blood, that's all. I thought I was going to help with litigation when you hired me to be your assistant. You know, do legal research and draft briefs and stuff. I guess I got mad that you called me in here just to take pictures of your dog bite."

Raymond chuckled softly. He reached up and stroked her curls. She flinched, but just barely. He smiled at her, noticing how she'd started to breathe fast. He watched those luscious tits move under her blouse.

"Randy, I *am* this firm. This is *my* creation. Sandberg and Associates would not exist if it weren't for my reputation and skill. I am king here."

She nodded.

"Your entire future is in my hands. If I like the work you do, you're set for life. I may even hire you right out of Stanford Law as an associate. Someday you could even be a partner! But if I'm not pleased . . ." Raymond trailed his fingers down to her collarbone. He watched her eyes flash, but she didn't move away. This was all very promising. "If I'm not pleased, I'll fire you. For real next time.

And I'll make your life a living hell if you try to practice law in this town."

She gasped. But it was a small gasp. She'd obviously tried to suppress it.

"If you are to be my assistant, you will remember all that I've just explained to you, and you will afford me the respect I deserve. Do you understand?" Raymond let his hand fall to the top button of her blouse, and he insinuated a finger down into her cleavage. Her mouth dropped open.

"Well, do you?" he repeated.

"Yes," she said meekly.

"And, should there ever be any kind of unpleasant misunderstanding between us, no one would ever take your word over mine. The idea is laughable."

She stared at him, but he knew she got the message.

"Good." Raymond removed his hand from between her perfect tits and then gave her knee a friendly pat. He stood up and smiled at her. She looked baffled. Once more, her mouth hung open.

Raymond liked the view from where he stood, looking down on her young, pretty, confused face—and open mouth. It wouldn't be long before she spent most of her time on her knees exactly like this, with his dick between her lips. Just like all his other assistants.

"How would you like to help me prepare for vicious dog court?" he asked her brightly. "It will be our job to convince the hearing officer that the horrible animal who did this to me should be destroyed."

Ricky's brow crumpled. "Destroyed?"

"Euthanized. To protect the public from further attacks."

She bit her lip. "Uh, well, okay, I guess," she said.

"It was a pit bull, you know," he added.

"Oh," Randy said, nodding, as if that explained every-

thing. "What exactly do you want me to do, Mr. Sand-berg?"

God, he loved his life.

Eli hadn't planned for this.

It seemed that beneath all of Roxanne's anger lurked a smart and sensitive woman. The way she'd described her perfect relationship with her dog had been the most insightful answer he'd ever received from a prospective client.

And he wasn't comparing it to the real doozies he'd gotten over the years, either, like the guy who thought having control over his Doberman pinscher in public would make chicks dig him. No, Roxanne's answer was the best—period.

She didn't mention control. She didn't say she was embarrassed or ashamed of her dog. She didn't need to prove anything to herself or others. She simply wanted peace to replace the struggle, so that there would be room for happiness.

He hadn't expected an answer like that from Roxanne. Eli was aware that there was more to Roxanne than her Web site or her anger, of course. Everyone had multiple aspects to their personality. It was what made us human. And Bea had given him a heads-up the other day by assuring him that Roxie was a pussycat in a porcupine suit. He smiled at the memory.

But from what he could tell, Roxanne was far more complex than he realized. In addition to the father issues and bad dating karma, she happened to be funny. She possessed a deep compassion for her dog. She truly cared for her friends. She was willing to try something new. And when Roxie smiled . . .

Eli glanced at her sitting next to him on a bench overlooking Dolores Park, the dog park where Roxanne and her friends met up three mornings a week. The afternoon sun was on her face. She looked composed and beautiful. He was almost relieved she didn't look overly happy at the moment, because when that girl smiled, he could barely breathe. When she laughed, it was if his whole being strained to get closer to the sound.

"What?" she asked, now frowning severely. "Are you getting ready to tell me how much this is going to cost? Is that it?"

He laughed. "Uh, no. That's not what I was thinking, but I suppose we should get that out of the way."

As she probably already knew from her Internet browsing, Eli's customary fee was between seven-fifty and three thousand, not including travel, and it could go much higher depending on the number of dogs in the family, the aggression level of the dogs involved, and whether he would be called to testify at a civil or criminal court hearing. Under normal circumstances, Roxie and Lilith's case would land at the high end of the spectrum, because it involved a rescue dog with longstanding aggression issues, a dog bite case, an already scheduled appearance in vicious dog court, and probable civil action. But as Eli looked into those dark, doubtful eyes, he knew nothing about this case was normal. There was only one price he could charge for this assignment, and that was nothing at all.

They were acquaintances. She was a friend of Rick Rousseau's, and Rick was his boss. Plus, there was something real interesting going on between Roxanne and himself, something that had to be resolved. So money would only muddy the waters. Money didn't have a place here.

Besides, he'd never gone into a case with the dual hopes of saving the dog and bedding the owner, and if he were to be honest with himself, that's exactly what was going through his head. No, it wasn't a smart move, but he'd already admitted to himself that smarts had nothing to do with his instinctive response to Roxanne.

"I know you're expensive," she said, her voice sharp. "I don't want any favors. Just tell me how much."

Eli draped an arm over the back of the park bench, fully aware of how Roxie flinched at his friendly maneuver. He'd been studying her during their walk. She was about five eight, lean, with an elegant neck and liquid black eyes flecked with tiny sparks of gold. She had the sweetest little chin, and stunning cheekbones. Her waist was toned and she had the nicest kind of female bottom there was—not flat but not too big, not too wide but with a good amount of flair to the hips. And her hair—now that was really something extraordinary. It was long and shiny and black and he licked his lips at the thought of how it would feel cascading across his bare chest as she rolled with him, naked.

Yep, Roxanne Bloom was an exceptionally pretty woman—but she was wound up tighter than a two-dollar watch. He could see the spring-loaded tension in her shoulders and back. He noticed that even her most relaxed sitting posture featured balled fists and tightly crossed legs. Her jaw was clenched most of the time. She had a variety of nervous gestures, including sighing, flipping her hair over her shoulder, fiddling with the antique ring she wore on her left hand, swiveling her neck around until it cracked, and, on those occasions when she did relax her fists, she ended up drumming her nails on whatever surface was available—the tabletop, her thigh, the bench slats. Eli thanked God Roxie didn't chew gum, because he was sure she'd be a smacker and a popper.

"My customary fee for this type of case would be at least three thousand," he said, settling back into the bench and moving just an inch closer to her. He'd timed his maneuver so that in her shock she'd forget to move away.

"Say *what*?"

Eli smiled. "But I'm not charging you anything."

He watched her blink a few times, squint her lovely eyes at him in suspicion, and flip her hair over her shoulder. Then she let out a laugh. "Oh, I don't think so. Nuh-uh. I'll definitely be paying you." She scooted away to reclaim her buffer zone. "I don't want any gray area with you, Eli. No favors. No way. This is a business proposition. I need your professional help, and I will pay for it like everyone else does."

He nodded, aware that he'd encountered yet another of Roxie's emotional land mines. The woman's psyche was littered with them. He'd take care to tread lightly. "But you aren't everyone else, and that's my point. You and I know each other."

"Hardly," she said, cutting him off.

"I would feel uncomfortable if money were exchanged."

"And I would feel uncomfortable if it weren't."

Eli sighed, feeling a small smile creep onto his face. "Look, Roxie, can we clear the air between us first, before we go any further?"

Her frown intensified. She moved another inch away. "There's nothing to clear."

God, but this woman was hardheaded! Eli took a moment to breathe. Focus. "Do you want my help?"

Roxie shifted uncomfortably. "Yes."

"Do you want to work together to ensure that Lilith can be calm and happy?"

She sighed. "Of course I do."

"Then there can't be resentment or distrust between the two of us. If there is, Lilith will sense it."

Roxie laughed a little. "Yeah, I read all about that

online. You think that dogs pick up on the anger or nervousness of their owners."

"I know so."

"Fine," she said.

"In fact . . ." Eli paused before he stepped over the line between acquaintance and teacher, but the time had definitely come. "If you want Lilith to stay calm and feel safe, then you have to show her how to do it. She takes her cues from you, Roxie."

She blinked. She looked offended, as if he'd insulted her. That meant she was following along just fine.

"The truth is, Lilith is unsettled and insecure because you are, Roxanne. She doesn't know there's another way to be in the world."

"Excuse me?" She flipped her hair again and drummed her fingers on her tightly crossed leg.

"She doesn't want to be filled with anxiety. No dog does. Lilith longs for a better way, and, as her pack leader, it's up to you to show her that path."

Roxanne's dark eyebrows arched high on her forehead. She leaned forward as if she couldn't believe what she'd just heard come out of his mouth. "Eli," she said, her tone obviously held in check with a great deal of effort. "Lilith was a mess when I got her, right? Beaten. Starved. Scared. Lost. She's always hated men because she was abused by one. I'm the one who saved her. I didn't *do* any of this shit to her. She came this way. You do understand that, right? God! I thought you'd worked with rescue dogs before!"

Eli nodded slowly. At this point in their conversation, every bit of knowledge and experience he desperately wanted to share with her came to a screeching halt in his head, like rush hour traffic in San Francisco. And it would be a long while before things started moving again.

This was not the time to explain to Roxie that dogs don't carry around emotional scars from the past the way humans do, that they live in the moment. True, dogs may develop conditioned responses, but nearly all their behavior is based on the current pack dynamic and not some past trauma. He knew she wasn't ready to hear that her dog's anxiety and fear was just a reflection of her own, that the problem wasn't that Lilith hated men—the problem was that Roxanne hated men and Lilith was simply picking up on the fear, anger, and mistrust her owner had whenever a man was around.

If he told her this right now, she'd argue with him. She might even back away from the process. And the dog would lose out in the end.

So Eli would go slow enough to avoid overwhelming her but fast enough to get Lilith cleared of vicious dog status at the hearing in less than two weeks. That's what this was all about in the first place—keeping the dog from being destroyed.

"Roxanne, I need you to do something for me."

She cocked her head and clenched her jaw.

"You've got to trust me. There's no way around it."

Roxanne was silent and still.

"I am here because I want to help you and your dog, but you must trust me and do what I say. If you don't, I might as well get right back on that plane because there's no point in even starting."

Slowly, Roxanne's spine began to soften. She leaned back into the bench, so careful with her movements it looked like she was in pain. She sighed deeply. When she spoke, her voice was so soft Eli could barely hear it. *"I want to, but don't know if I can."*

"Now we're getting somewhere," Eli said, smiling. He fought the need to reach for one of her small, soft hands. God, he wanted to touch her again, but he knew he couldn't.

"I realize you didn't go looking for this," he said, his voice as gentle as he could make it. "I know the last thing in the world you want is some man insisting that you let him into your head and your heart, but I'll be real straight with you. That's what you have to do to save Lilith. So you can do it with me or you can do it with somebody else—and maybe finding a woman to help you would be the smartest move—but that's what it's going to take."

Roxie nodded but quickly looked away. "Do you know any woman dog whisperers in town?"

"I know there are a few, but I don't know them personally and I'm not in a position to recommend their approaches." Eli paused a moment. "But I'll make some calls if you'd prefer that route."

"I just want Lilith out of that horrible place," Roxanne said, fighting back tears, her face still turned away. "I just want her home with me."

"Ah. Well, that just happens to be the easy part." Eli reached into his front jeans pocket and pulled out a folded piece of paper. "This is Lilith's release form. All you have to do is go pick her up at Animal Control anytime before five P.M."

"What?" Roxie spun around on the bench and ripped the form from Eli's fingers. "But they told me I had to get approval before I could pick her up, some kind of release signed by the magistrate!"

"That's what you're holding," Eli said, nodding at the yellow computer printout. "I pulled a few strings. I told them I'd be responsible for Lilith's behavior so she can stay home until the hearing, which should be enough time for us to turn things around."

"You mean . . ." Roxanne choked on her words,

stunned. "I can go get her? Today? *Now?* You bailed her out for me?"

Eli laughed a little. "You are free to pick her up at Animal Control at Fifteenth and Harrison, but you have to sign for her and agree to enroll her in—"

Roxanne threw herself into Eli's arms and grabbed him tight. He could feel every curve and muscle in her body. He had to struggle to keep his hands off her. Good God, she felt so fucking good against him he nearly groaned with the pleasure of it. While she hugged him, he reminded himself again why this was not a wise idea: his priority was finding his father; he'd be moving back to Utah as soon as he did; and he wasn't interested in getting involved with another woman who'd expect him to be calm and serene twenty-four/seven, a dog whisperer in the world and a lapdog at home.

"Thank you, Eli. Thank you, thank you, thank you." Her warm breath tickled him as she muttered into his right ear. "I don't want to find someone else. Let's do this. Thank you so much." Suddenly, Roxanne pulled away, looked into his eyes, grabbed his face hard, and planted a kiss right on his lips.

The kiss went from zero to sexual in an instant, just the way it had out by Rick's paddock two days before. Eli knew what Roxie had intended the kiss to be—a friendly peck, a spontaneous burst of joy and gratitude. No more. But the hunger flared between them immediately, hot and intense and wild. And now her lips had parted and his tongue began to explore the silky heat inside her mouth and his Stetson got knocked off his head and hit the dirt. When exactly did her thigh get wrapped around his waist like that? How was it that all that gorgeous hair of hers got twisted up in his hands?

Dear God, who *was* this woman? What was she *doing* to him? What were they doing to each other?

Breathless, dizzy, shocked, it ended. Roxie leaned back and stared at him, her eyes filled with tears and a thousand questions of her own. She wiped her mouth with a trembling hand. Eli did the same.

"I didn't mean for that to get so, you know, wild," she said.

Eli laughed in surprise. "Holy shit," he muttered.

"I'll go get Lilith now. At the animal place. Fifteenth and Harrison, right? Right." Roxie jumped up from the bench and stood in front of him, the paper clutched in her hand. She started to leave but pivoted back around, and with an awkward lurch forward she kissed his cheek, then bent down to retrieve his hat. She brushed off some of the dirt and stuck it back on his head. "Sorry about that. Anyway . . . so we'll start tomorrow?"

He nodded. She ran off down the hill.

"See you tomorrow," Eli said, but she was too far gone to hear him.

Chapter 6

"Where's Lilith?" Bea stood at the top of the hill at Dolores Park with Ginger at her side, waiting for Roxanne to reach them. "I thought our girl got parole!"

"She's at home," Roxanne said, approaching her friends, watching Martina and HeatherLynn romp on the dog park's grassy hillside. "I won't be bringing her out until this whole thing blows over."

"How are you doing, sweetie?" Ginger reached out and hooked arms with Roxanne. "Are you holding up okay?"

Roxanne nodded.

"Have you heard anything more from Raymond *Sleaze*berg?" Bea asked.

"Not yet." Roxanne let out a sigh she knew sounded too pessimistic, even for her. "But I will. He won't be satisfied with the vicious dog case and the misdemeanor criminal charges. He'll come after me for damages, no question."

So far, Lilith's outburst had resulted in charges of harboring a vicious animal, which brought an automatic $500 fine plus court costs for the hearing in two weeks.

Roxanne knew it would be a mistake to think Raymond wouldn't sue her for every penny she had.

Ginger pulled Roxie tighter to her bulbous body. "One step at a time," she said reassuringly.

"Fuck the old buzzard," Bea said, draping an arm over Roxanne's shoulder as they began to walk.

Roxie knew why she'd come to the dog park that morning, even without Lilith. She needed her friends. So much was changing in their lives. Once the babies came, it would all change some more. But right then—on that morning—Roxanne needed the comfort and reassurance of her best friends and a routine that felt familiar and safe.

Roxie's head suddenly snapped up. She'd only then realized Josie wasn't with them. "Hey, where's—"

"Everything is just fine," Bea said, smiling sweetly and patting Roxie's back as she preempted the question. "Josie is just *great*."

Roxie jolted to attention. The tender optimism in Bea's voice sounded downright unnatural. Something was wrong. "Tell me what's going on," Roxanne demanded.

"Josie's fine, really," Ginger said. "She's just not feeling too great this morning. She told me she thought she better stick close to home for a few days until she knows what's going on."

Roxanne's pulse spiked. Her breath came sharply. She stopped walking. "Is it the baby? Is something wrong with the baby? Is something wrong with Josie?"

"God, no," Bea said, waving off her concern. "She's just getting some of those Taylor Hicks contractions."

Ginger shook her head. "My God, Bea. Taylor Hicks is the guy from *American Idol,* not a medical condition." Once she'd finished laughing, she turned back to

Roxanne. "They're called *Braxton* Hicks contractions. They're a kind of false labor, or prelabor pain, and it's perfectly natural to have them in your last trimester. I had them all the time in the weeks before the boys were born."

Hearing all that made Roxanne feel a little better, since Ginger, also the mother of twin teenagers from her first marriage, surely knew what she was talking about. But Roxie had been so preoccupied with her own crisis that she hadn't heard Josie's voice since their ER vigil two days before. She had no way to verify that all was well. "But if these contractions are so normal, then why isn't she here?"

"Because she's a little jumpy," Ginger answered her with a soft smile.

"It's her first, you know," was Bea's observation. "She's not an old pro like Ginger."

"Please don't call me old," Ginger said wearily, rubbing her distended tummy. "In about two weeks I have to fake the strength and flexibility of someone half my age."

Bea snorted. "You'll do just fine, Mrs. Montevez," she said, grinning, getting them all walking at a steady clip again. "But there is something going on up at the ranch that concerns me."

"My God, what?" Roxanne asked.

"Oh, Bea's just referring to Rick and Teeny," Ginger said. "They're not exactly helping Josie relax, you know?"

"How do you mean?" Roxanne asked. "The last I heard they were spoiling her absolutely rotten."

"Well, it may be too much of a good thing," Ginger said cautiously. "Rick's been working at home so he'll be there when she goes into labor. He doesn't go in to the office anymore. In fact, he won't leave her side. He's got her all packed for the hospital already."

"That doesn't sound bad," Roxanne said. "It sounds like he's just being responsible. And really sweet."

Bea laughed. "Yeah, but Teeny has the back of the SUV outfitted into a mobile maternity ward."

Roxanne laughed. "What?"

"The guy's an absolute wreck," Bea continued, shaking her head. "He's gone to every one of their Lamaze classes and now's he's freaking out that Josie will deliver before he can get everybody into the city. So he's bought a ton of books on home childbirth and ordered something called an 'emergency birth kit' off the Internet."

Roxanne felt her eyes get huge just before she burst out laughing. "You're kidding?"

"You saw him at the baby shower, right?" Ginger asked. "The man's put on at least twenty pounds from all the weird crap he's been eating—peanut butter and mayonnaise sandwiches, Cherry Garcia ice cream with Chex Mix crumbled on top. It's scary."

Roxanne laughed more. "God, I absolutely love that guy. Why aren't there any straight men as sensitive and loving as Timothy Worrell? Why did he have to be gay?"

When she felt Bea's body flinch next to her, Roxanne could have kicked herself. In all the years their little group had been hanging out together, Bea had never once revealed anything about her own sexual preference. Josie, Ginger, and Roxie gabbed away about their sex lives at any and every opportunity, but Bea had always hung back. Nobody had ever pushed her, or ever even asked her directly what was going on. Once, early on in their friendship on a day when Bea wasn't with them, Ginger, Josie, and Roxanne took the opportunity to wonder aloud about their friend's big secret. They agreed right then not to make an issue of it, and they never talked about it again.

Of course, for many years now Roxie had half expected Bea to show up one day with a girl pal on her arm. But it never happened. And, after all this time and after all they'd been through together as friends, Roxie figured if Bea hadn't let them in on her secret by now, she probably never would. In fact, Roxie often wondered how Bea could have lived for more than fifty years in the world's most gay-friendly city yet never felt comfortable coming out.

Bea cleared her throat. "People can't choose to be gay or straight," she said quietly.

"You're absolutely right," Roxie said, trying to sound nonchalant, but knowing that, for Bea, that simple statement was a damn-near breakthrough.

"Besides," Ginger said, grinning. "There really are straight men just as sweet, thoughtful, and devoted as Teeny."

"Oh, yeah?" Roxanne asked. "Where?"

Ginger jabbed a thumb over her shoulder. "Second car from the corner."

Bea and Roxanne whirled around on the Dolores Park walking path and peered past a grove of palm trees. "What the hell is he doing?" Bea asked.

"Probably the crossword puzzle. He says it helps expand his English vocabulary," Ginger said, laughing.

"But he could have come on our walk with us," Roxanne said. "He doesn't have to wait in the car like your driver or something."

"Oh, no, no, no," Ginger said, shaking her head. "He told me he'd rather not know what happens on these walks. He said an ignorant man is a happy man."

Everyone laughed.

"Lucio is all right by me," Bea said, nodding with approval. "So how's it going with Gallagher?" she asked Roxanne, changing the subject with no grace whatsoever as they resumed walking.

"I'm surprised it took you so long to ask," Roxie said. "I've been here ten minutes already."

Bea shrugged. "I must be losing my touch."

"Did you meet with him yesterday?" Ginger asked, squeezing Roxie's arm tighter. "Did he tell you why he turned you down for lunch that time?"

Roxanne sighed again, which bothered her. She was beginning to sound like her mother. If sighing had been an Olympic sport, her mother would have so many gold medals around her neck, she'd be unable to remain upright.

"Yep. We got together," she answered.

"Well? What happened?" Bea asked.

Roxie didn't want to talk about Eli Gallagher. It hurt her brain just to think about him. She was so confused. She hated every single thing that had happened between them—the connection they felt, the way he'd grabbed her and kissed her at the barn, and the way she'd done the same to him only yesterday. In this very same park.

What—was she completely insane?

The confusing part was that for every thing she hated about him, there was something she loved about him. He had canceled his plans and come back to the city for her. Without even being asked, he had gotten Lilith out! Eli Gallagher had actually gone in person to that horrible place, vouched for her and her dog, and gotten Lilith's release approved. Then he'd said he'd help her free of charge! Of course, she appreciated the offer but had no intention of honoring it. She'd be writing him a check when they were done.

But the whole situation was making her crazy, and she had no idea how she was supposed to sort it all out.

She supposed it didn't matter. The only reason Eli was giving her the time of day was because of Lilith. If she didn't need his help so badly, she never would have seen the man again.

Roxie checked her cell phone for the time. Bottom line: Eli Gallagher would be coming to her house in less than six hours.

"All that stuff is water under the bridge," Roxanne assured her friends. "Eli and I are working on a plan to get Lilith rehabilitated in time for her vicious dog hearing in twelve days. We have a lot of work to do. We don't discuss anything personal."

Bea snorted.

"What?" Roxanne demanded.

"Nothing," Bea said.

"So what's his plan?" Ginger asked.

Roxanne sighed again. *Oh, God,* she needed to stop that. "Well, he's coming over this afternoon. He's got some forms for me to fill out and he wants to meet Lilith."

"That sounds nice," Ginger said.

"Yeah. He said the idea was to gently introduce Lilith to the concept of a nonthreatening pack leader, you know, show her what the rules are and reinforce them until she calms down and seems stable. Once she's comfortable with the concept, I will take over as pack leader. Eli's going to teach me how to do that."

Both women suddenly stopped walking, which brought Roxie to a halt, as well. They stared at her. They both looked extremely puzzled.

"Did I say something weird? You're looking at me like I just sprouted a third boob or something."

"No, no," Bea stammered. "It's not that."

"It's just . . ." Ginger's eyes flashed toward Bea. "Well . . ."

"What?" Roxie asked.

"Uh," Bea said, her eyes big. "Did you just say that Eli planned to stay until Lilith is calm and stable?"

Roxanne flexed her neck until it cracked. "Well, yeah. Eli said that's the whole point of this. It's his standard approach."

"So how long will that take, do you think?" Ginger asked, her voice a little high. "Is he going to move in with you?"

"Excuse me?" Roxanne blinked at her friends. "Are you nuts?"

"Well, it's just that . . ." Ginger shrugged. "You know. Something like that could take a while."

"Funny," she said.

Bea snorted. "We're not joking, Rox. The man's gonna pull up to your house in a flippin' U-Haul. Just you watch."

"Here's how it's going to work," Raymond said, explaining to his new assistant the ins and outs of the vicious dog hearing in less than two weeks. Sure, his plate was full of motions and plea agreements, pre-trial conferences, sentencing hearings, appeals, and general client hand-holding—in other words, billable hours—but *nothing* on his calendar promised to be as personally satisfying as this piddly little hearing.

Bitch Bloom was going down.

As Raymond talked, he admired the skintight blue suit his assistant had chosen to wear to the office that day. Not that there was anything inappropriate about her choice. That's what he loved about the current women's fashions—you could have half your tits on display, your skirt as tight as a tourniquet, and be prancing around in heels so high that your ass was sticking out screaming *"Come and get it!"* and you'd look just like the women who graced the pages of *Vogue* or even, thank the gods, women who practiced in a court of law. They were all dressed like hookers.

God*damn,* this was a good time to be alive.

"City code discourages the use of legal representation for either the complainant or the defendant," he said, staring at her legs as she sat on the couch and took notes.

The girl cocked her head in confusion. "But in this case, the complainant *is* a lawyer, while the dog owner is not. That seems a little unfair."

"Exactly," he said, wagging his eyebrows. "Now, the hearing is not considered a legal proceeding, per se, so there's no judge. There will be a hearing officer or magistrate instead, and that person is often an investigating officer from the dog bite unit."

His assistant crinkled her pretty brow, pen poised in midair. "Yeah. I wondered about that," she said. "It seems the SFPD's dog bite division investigates the case and then gets to rule on the merits of their own evidence."

Raymond tipped his head back and roared. "You're sharp, Randy. I like sharp girls."

"Dusty," she said.

"I see you've been doing your research."

"Yes, sir. I have."

Raymond enjoyed this girl. He bet her boob would feel great cupped in his hand. And he looked forward to finding out how she tasted. He bet she tasted like saltwater taffy. And his plan was to get the little taffy-tasting smarty-pants all worked up. He'd drive her absolutely crazy with his tongue. Then he'd pile-drive her.

"Once the magistrate rules in my favor, I can proceed with the tort complaint," Raymond said, admiring her cleavage.

She nodded, her eyes cast downward.

Raymond sat down next to Ricky on the leather sofa of his office suite. He stared across the room, pretending to be lost in thought, while he pressed his leg up against her knee. She moved away.

This was no problem. He loved a good chase. It made going in for the kill that much sweeter.

Raymond nodded pensively. "I don't know if I mentioned this, but, in a way, this case is personal." He kept his eyes focused off in the distance and sighed, as if he were deeply troubled by the situation. "Unfortunately, the vicious dog in question belongs to a woman I was once romantically involved with. She was unstable. She even stalked me and attacked me in a public setting. It's a very sad story, really, but the last straw was when she sicced her pit bull on me. I do hope she finds the help she needs."

"I know all about her," she said.

Raymond's head swiveled around. "You do?"

"Sure," she said, smiling. "When you asked me to prepare for the hearing, I researched the vicious and dangerous dog laws as described in Section 42-A of the San Francisco Health Code. Plus I obtained the police report, the vicious dog complaint you filed from your laptop in the emergency room, the order for impounding the dog, your request for—and the approval of—an expedited hearing, and a copy of Animal Control's signed release form. Then I researched Roxanne Bloom's background."

Raymond must not have heard her right. A release? What fucking release? He took a second to calm himself before he turned toward her. "Excellent work," he said, smiling in approval while the blood pounded in his brain.

How the hell had Bloom gotten her little bitch dog out of there so fast? The creature was supposed to be impounded until the hearing date! It was a matter of public safety!

He watched Ricky nod her pretty head. "So, I gather this is the very same woman you've been preparing to sue for defamation of character?"

"The same," he said.

They were quiet for a moment. Then she cleared her throat. "You did know that the dog had been released, right?"

"Oh, sure. Of course."

"I spoke to the desk supervisor at Animal Control, and it seems there were special circumstances."

Raymond's lip began to twitch. It took every fiber of his being and every shred of his concentration to stop it from becoming a full-out seizure. "Yes. I found that development quite interesting, myself. I seem to have forgotten—what exactly were those circumstances, again?"

The slow smile that spread over Ricky's face made Raymond want to choke the living shit out of her. He watched her calmly riffle through the papers on her lap.

"The special circumstances were not even circumstances," she said. "They were a person. A man named Eli Gallagher."

"Who the fu—" Raymond caught himself. He pulled at the tie knotted loosely at his injured throat. "Of course. Now I recall. He's an attorney, right?"

"No," Ricky said. Or was it Randy. *Oh, fuck! What was this chick's name?* "He's a dog whisperer from Utah."

Raymond just gave up. There was no way he'd ever be able to fake his way through the remainder of this inane conversation. So he roared with laughter. He slapped his knee. Roxie was a complete *lunatic*! What next? Dog psychics? Eventually, he calmed down.

"Now, I admit that's something I didn't know, Randy."

"Dusty."

"Did the desk clerk say why in the name of God she let some New Age dufus take the dog from the pound?"

"Oh, he didn't remove the dog from the premises, sir. Ms. Bloom did. Mr. Gallagher only visited Animal Control in advance and negotiated the dog's release, putting in writing that he will be responsible for the dog's actions while it is enrolled in rehabilitative training."

Raymond blinked. "But . . ." This simply could not be. If Roxanne showed up at the hearing with a well-behaved dog, the whole complaint could get thrown out. That development could diminish the merits of his personal injury case. His defamation case might even be weakened. The dog would live.

And Roxie would be vindicated.

"Also, Ms. Bloom's statement to police indicates she has a legitimate defense for her dog's actions," his assistant said.

Raymond studied the girl carefully. Was it his imagination, or did the little slut have a twinge of glee in her eye?

"She claims you broke down her door, physically and verbally assaulted her, and threatened to kill her. She claims her dog was merely protecting her property and trying to keep her from additional bodily harm. Oh! I almost forgot!" She reached down to the bottom of the pile.

"She's pressed charges against you. Assault and battery, breaking and entering, and destruction of private property."

Raymond's upper lip began to spasm like a herring on dry land. There would be no stopping it.

Gloria knew her daughter was overreacting. Whenever Rachel came to the house it was such a production—reviewing her prescriptions, going over her scheduled doctor's appointments, examining the contents of her refrigerator. You would think Gloria was a helpless toddler, the way her eldest daughter carried on about her.

"Mother. Why do you have a box of Velveeta in here?" Rachel pulled open the meat and cheese tray and popped up from her crouch in front of the refrigerator.

"Because that's where it goes," Gloria said, raising her hands to the heavens. "It says it right there on the clear plastic drawer—*meats and cheeses*!"

Rachel held the cardboard carton aloft and turned it to and fro, studying it. "This is not cheese, Mother. It's not even food. It's nothing but a log of Day-Glo chemical goo."

Not this again, Gloria thought. Her vegan daughter was a zealot. She came over here and preached and chided until Gloria agreed to remove from the premises whatever food item Rachel found most offensive. It was hard to believe the girl used to love nothing more than her mother's homemade brisket or a good veal chop. She used to be the first to belly-up to the table, as a matter of fact.

"It is so cheese," Gloria said, collapsing into one of the kitchen chairs, suddenly a little out of breath. "Read . . . the label. It's says 'cheese' . . . right . . . on there."

Rachel didn't seem to care about the box of cheese

anymore. She tossed it onto the counter. She was suddenly kneeling in front of Gloria, her face creased with worry.

"Are you feeling all right, Mama?" Rachel grabbed Gloria's wrist and started checking her pulse against the second hand of her watch.

Gloria didn't know what had gotten into Rachel. She was acting so strange. Why did she keep changing the subject to ask if she was feeling well? What had they been talking about, anyway?

"I'm taking you to the hospital."

"No," Gloria said. "Why do you do this to me every week, Rachel? You sashay in here and tell me how to live and what to eat and then you look at me like I'm dying. I'm nearly eight-five years old! Of course I'm dying! And if I want to eat Velveeta in my last few days on earth then I'll eat Velveeta! If I tell you I feel fine, then I feel fine!"

Her daughter ignored her. She'd already grabbed her car keys. "Hold on to my arm, *bubeleh*."

Oh, why did she have to be like this? Out of Gloria's four grown children, Rachel was the only one who didn't trust her to live her own life. Why did she have to be so bossy?

You raise your children, praying to God at least one of them will grow up to be a doctor or a lawyer, and then what happens? Your daughter the lawyer thinks she can manage all your affairs, including your health and what you put in the meat and cheese tray of your refrigerator!

"Mother?"

Gloria reached out in front of her, wondering why someone had dimmed the lights. Her legs gave out from under her.

Chapter 7

Roxanne was nervous, which was the one exact thing she wasn't supposed to be. Eli had made that very clear. He'd called a couple of hours before to go over the ground rules for his arrival and tell her that he'd e-mailed her the questionnaire he gave all clients. She'd since printed out a hard copy and started filling it out.

Apparently, the only information the man didn't want was her cholesterol level!

What in God's name would her childhood have to do with Lilith's aggression? Why did he want to know about her hobbies? Whether there were seasonal changes in her energy level? Or how many people she'd dated since she brought Lilith to live with her? Why had he included a bunch of questions that were obviously right out of some psychology textbook? (*How do you see yourself? A. Equally worthwhile and deserving as others. B. Less worthwhile and deserving. C. More worthwhile and deserving.*) Did he think she was a sociopath or something?

She'd followed all his instructions, however. She'd taken a thoroughly muzzled Lilith for a long walk to relax her, which didn't really work because they encountered other humans and dogs. Roxie even had to endure a few choice comments from the Sweeping Lady, including this tidbit: "The police came around the other day, asking about your pit bull. I told them she wasn't normal."

Swwsssh. Swwwssh.

Once they were home, Roxie removed Lilith's muzzle and let her relax for about a half hour, as instructed. Then she fed the dog some cooked chicken and brown rice, just the way Eli told her to. Next Roxie sat quietly with her on the living room floor and stroked her fur and rubbed her ears, which was her all-time favorite thing.

"You both need to be comfortable and relaxed when I get there," Eli had told her. "Roxanne, I can't emphasize enough how important it is for you to come to the door without any anxiety. Please breathe deeply before you open the door. Greet me in a soft and friendly voice. Don't shout or move quickly."

"It sounds simple enough," she'd said.

"Simple isn't always easy."

"So they say."

"But here's the single most important thing to remember—whatever happens, do not interfere. I can handle whatever Lilith might do. Do not reach for her or yell at her. In fact, do not look at her or talk to her at all. Remain still and calm and let me handle anything that comes up."

"Of course."

"I will not hurt Lilith. I might have to restrain her as a way to communicate with her, but nothing I do will hurt her. Please do not interfere. Do you hear what I'm saying?"

Oh, she thought, *so he thinks I'm the slow-learning type of sociopath.* "I understand," she'd assured him.

"Even if she gets aggressive."

"She won't do that."

"Be sure to keep her muzzle off."

"What? Are you completely whacked? She'll eat your face!"

Eli had paused for a moment, somehow keeping himself from pointing out her contradictory logic. "You cannot be afraid she'll hurt me, Roxie. This is very important. You cannot come to the door worried that the worst will happen. If you do, she will pick up on your apprehension, and she'll make your worst fears a reality."

His deep-river voice made all the psychobabble sound like it made sense. Someday, Roxie would tell Eli that if the dog whisperer gig didn't work out for him he could talk people off ledges for a living. Or negotiate for the release of hostages. Or be the host of *Cowboy Masterpiece Theater*.

"But above all else," Eli had said, "you've got to let go of your own anger for just a moment. Do whatever you need to do so that when I arrive at your house, you're not thinking about your old boyfriend, or the vicious dog hearing, or anything anxiety-provoking."

"No problem," she'd said, once again wondering why the hell he'd turned her down for lunch six months before. *God, that had pissed her off.*

But that entire exchange with Eli had been a couple of hours earlier, and she'd already let it all go, just as Eli had suggested. And now, as she sat cross-legged on the living room rug with her doggie all sweet and sleepy in her lap, she really believed she could do this.

She would be calm. She would be relaxed. She would radiate stability.

Roxie glanced at Lilith. She loved those little prickly hairs that formed her eyebrows. She loved the white stripe that ended at her little dark brown nose. She loved her white back paws and soft white belly. She loved the muffled noises she made in her dreams, where she ran free through open fields with her dog friends. Maybe someday that would be more than a dream for her. Maybe, with Eli's help, Lilith would one day be a happy dog.

She suddenly sat up straighter, tears in her eyes. How could anyone have been so cruel to this little animal? How could some man have tied her up the way he had, and hit her with his fists, and just left her to starve the way he had? That asshole was the one who should have gone to jail, not Lilith! What was wrong with people, anyway?

Breathe. Breathe. Let it go.

She checked her watch. Eli would be there in a couple of minutes. "Okay, Lily Girl," she whispered, still stroking her ears. "Let's wake up, all right? You're going to get to meet a new friend. You'll like him, I promise."

Roxie stood, taking a deep breath. Lilith got up, too, stretching and yawning as she looked up at her owner, excited about whatever wonderful thing they were going to do next. Lilith wagged her tail.

That's when the phone rang. Roxie picked it up. Then there was a knock at the door. Lilith barked.

"Hello?"

"You fucking stupid bitch! Do you really think you can put anything past me? This is Raymond fucking Sandberg you're fucking with! Don't you get it?"

Roxie froze.

"You were a lousy lay, did I ever tell you that? I'd have gotten off better with a blow-up doll."

She felt the rage begin as a tight ball in her chest, spreading to her head, her arms, her feet . . .

Lilith was at the door snarling like a guard dog at a prison break. She was already frothing.

Roxie exploded. "Go to hell, you prick! I *hate* you!" Then she threw the phone across the room.

There was another knock.

Lilith went insane. On reflex, Roxie reached for her collar. Her hand shook with rage. She tried her best to drag her dog away from the door.

Oh, shit. I wasn't supposed to do that, was I?

Roxanne screamed over the barking. "Lilith, no!"

Oh, shit. I wasn't supposed to do that, either.

Roxanne tried to salvage the moment. She took another breath, then opened the door just a crack. *Fuck Raymond! Just fuck him,* she thought, as she slipped off the door chain.

"Hello," Eli said.

"Hi," Roxanne said, wiping the hair from her face, hoping she sounded stable, hoping to God that in a few seconds there wouldn't be another massacre. Her mind flashed with the image of Raymond lying on his back clutching his throat, spewing obscenities and blood in equal measure.

Roxie let go of Lilith's collar. Oh, God, she hoped Eli hadn't noticed how she was shaking, or how unraveled she was, or the mistake she'd made by holding on to Lilith's collar in the first place. Or shouting at her. "Come on in," she yelled over the barking.

Eli stepped inside.

Roxanne had a very bad feeling about this.

Bea rapped her knuckles lightly on the door to Room E-451 of the Neurology floor. She waited a moment, then heard an unfamiliar voice say, "Come on in."

Bea pushed at the door, peeking around cautiously.

She didn't know what she expected to see when she entered that hospital room. But it wasn't this.

A tall, lovely woman stood up from her seat next to Gloria's hospital bed. The woman's eyes were a strange brownish-green color, but instead of looking muddy or bland, they were luminous. She had a nice, wide smile. Her hair was streaked blond and gray and it looked soft as it settled down in choppy layers at her jawline. She was dressed comfortably, but there was a sense of fun to what she wore. It was probably the funky earrings and the silk scarf wrapped around her neck.

"Thank God you're here," Gloria said from under the blankets. "Would you please take Rachel down to the cafeteria for coffee? I need my rest."

Then it hit Bea—Rachel was Gloria's daughter, the lawyer. Gloria had spoken of her often. A lot more often than her other three kids, now that Bea thought about it.

"Rachel, this is Beatrice Latimer, my apprentice. Bea, this is my eldest, Rachel Needleman, attorney-at-law."

Whatever was in that IV drip at Gloria's bedside had to be making her delusional. An apprentice? An apprentice to *what*? The only thing Bea knew about being an apprentice was what she'd seen on Donald Trump's reality show, and that shit wasn't for her.

But Bea managed to put a smile on her face as she stepped forward, holding out her hand to Rachel. The hand that found hers was soft but firm, and it was infused with a deep and warm strength that nearly knocked the wind out of Bea. She tasted a mix of vanilla, lemon, and cinnamon-sugar on her tongue.

What the fuck was that?

Bea tried to speak. Nothing came out. She cleared her throat. "Uh, hey. Hi," was what she came up with.

Bea was mortified. The only other time she'd been at a loss for words was when she'd interviewed Michael Phelps in Beijing's Olympic Village. And she'd always considered that the peak experience of her life.

Until right this second.

"Oh, sure! Hello, Bea. Mother told me you might stop by. That's very kind of you."

Bea nodded, swallowing hard.

"Excuse me, but did you think I was joking?" Gloria asked, staring at Bea. "I need my rest. Take her out of here before she makes me so crazy that they transfer me to the psych ward."

Bea snorted. "I'm glad to see you're in good spirits, Gloria," she said, arriving at the side of the bed across from Rachel. Bea stole a quick glance and saw Gloria's daughter smiling at her.

Wow.

Gloria reached out and patted Bea's hand. "I am glad you came, Beatrice."

"Well, of course I came! I came as soon as I got your message." Bea looked at Rachel again. "What exactly happened? Have the doctors found anything yet?"

"Yes," Rachel said, her voice straining to be strong. "It seems Mother had a ministroke, a 'TIA,' they called it."

Bea thought the floor had been pulled out from under her. She blinked. The image of Rachel's face became blurry in Bea's tears. "Is she going to be okay?"

"Well, she should be all right," Rachel said, trying to maintain a pleasant smile. "They're a little concerned because of her age and the weakness she experienced in her legs, so they're going to do some more tests."

Bea nodded, trying to take it all in without morphing into a snot-soaked mess. She felt weakness spread in her own legs. This could not happen to Gloria. In the short time Bea had known her, she'd become incredibly important to her. She was a dear woman. Bea sometimes saw her as the mother she'd always wished she'd had.

"How long will she be here?" Bea asked Rachel.

"We're not sure."

"What is the next step?"

"Hello?" Gloria called from the bed below. "Would you mind going down to the cafeteria before you start discussing my burial arrangements? I would like to take a nap."

Bea saw Rachel laugh and shake her head, then watched as she bent down and kissed her mother on the cheek. "We'll be back to check on you in just a bit, *bubeleh*."

Bea squeezed Gloria's hand. She squeezed back. Hard. Her eyes looked into Bea's with an intensity that didn't seem right coming from a woman who'd just had a stroke.

"Yes?" Bea asked, leaning in close to hear the crucial information she was sure Gloria was about to convey.

"Have a nice time," was all she said. Then she smiled a little, closed her eyes, and folded her hands over her chest.

Bea walked out with Rachel at her side. Gloria's daughter was as tall as she was. She guessed that she was about her own age, as well. She looked like she could have been an athlete, too. She wondered what sport— lacrosse? Tennis? Diving? Suddenly, Bea felt there wouldn't be enough time in the world to find out everything she wanted to know about Rachel Needleman.

The first bit of information came quickly. Bea

glanced down and discovered there was no wedding ring.

It was a start. A start of what, she couldn't say.

He let it unfold.

The dog rushed him, but Eli set down his duffel bag and kept walking. With his eyes on Roxie he took a few steps into the foyer. Lilith barked and nipped the air near his hip and arm, but there was no physical contact. Eli didn't acknowledge the animal or her level of aggression.

He gently touched Roxie's arm. He saw the fear in her eyes, and he couldn't say he was surprised. Being calm was a lot to ask of her. He knew this was one assignment that couldn't be rushed—it would take however long it took.

"How are you today?" he asked Roxie, paying no mind to the mixed-breed Tasmanian devil now delivering a clear warning. He heard a chest-deep growl and then the sound of his shirtsleeve being shredded as she bit the fabric.

"Shh!" Eli hissed matter-of-factly, giving Lilith the human equivalent of a growl. At the same time, he pressed two fingers into the side of her neck, his version of a bite. With that, Eli had leveled the balance of power: her one growl and bite to his one growl and bite. They were even.

Lilith didn't much like that arrangement. She immediately jumped up and clamped her teeth onto Eli's forearm, ripping the fabric further and puncturing his flesh.

Roxie screamed. Not exactly the calm reaction Eli had asked for. He squatted, flipped Lilith on her side, and pressed her body into the floor, all while Roxie repeatedly gasped in shock.

"Please remain calm," he told Roxie, his gaze soft and focused toward the kitchen at the end of the hallway. "I am not hurting her, Roxanne. I am not angry with her. I am putting her in a down position because it's the best way to communicate the fact that biting me will not be tolerated, that I am the leader here."

"But—" Roxie groaned. "God, she looks so upset! And you're bleeding all over the place!"

Eli briefly noted that she was right about that last bit. It would have to wait. "Just breathe, Roxanne," Eli said. "I'm breathing steady and deep, see? Watch me. Try to keep in rhythm with my breathing, okay?"

"Huh? What the hell good is *that* gonna do?"

From his squat, Eli slowly tipped his head and raised an eyebrow at her. Words were not needed. She got the message just fine.

"Sure. Right. Here I go. I'm breathing now." Roxanne raised her nose toward the ceiling and inhaled loudly.

"Excellent," Eli said, hiding a smile. "Just keep breathing. Observe what is happening. Stay detached."

"Yeah, sure, but it looks like you're strangling her."

"I'm not," he said. "This is standard. I held her collar, twisted it slightly, and pressed her head toward me and down to the floor. Then I pressed my fingers into her hip, flipped her, and pulled her so that her back is up against my legs. Now I'm keeping my fingers pressed into her neck, which is the closest thing I can do to mimic a bite to her throat."

"How long are you going to do that?"

"Until she relaxes."

Roxie laughed. "Seriously? But she's stiff as a board!"

"Yes, and she'll stay that way until she accepts my dominance. The instant she does, she'll be allowed up."

Just then, Lilith began to squirm and growl. Her compact and muscular body was strong, and she was nowhere ready to give up her position as top dog. "Shh!" Eli said again, pressing his two fingers deeper into her neck while adding the pressure of his other fingers to her hip.

"Maybe you should have a seat," Eli suggested. He watched as Roxie slid down the wall and sat cross-legged about six feet from Eli and her dog. "Remember not to look at her," he said.

Roxie nodded, closed her eyes, and let her head fall against the wall. It gave Eli a chance to study her. Such a lovely contrast between her pale skin and dark hair. A perfectly straight nose. Such a beautifully formed mouth, pouty, pink. He watched a single tear travel down the swell of her right cheekbone, and wondered why she was crying. He had a feeling it was more than Lilith's display of one-upmanship.

About ten minutes into the hold, Eli felt Lilith's body go from a rigid board of resistance to a soft pile of surrender. And thank God—ten minutes in a squat had Eli's knees throbbing.

"Such a good girl," he said, stroking Lilith's body as he released the pressure from his fingers. As he did so he noticed that blood had coursed down his forearm and pooled between the fingers of his right hand.

Lilith jumped to all fours. She blinked. She yawned. She looked at Roxie.

"You can pet her now, too. Tell her how good she is," Eli said.

Roxie called her dog and Lilith went right to her, burrowing her head into her owner's side. Roxie stroked Lilith's head, rubbed her ears, and praised her dog for her bravery, all while raising doubtful eyes toward Eli.

"She'll be fine," he said, offering Roxie his non-bloody

hand and pulling her up to a stand. "Now I need you to tell me you're pleased to see me, and welcome me into your space. Then lead me toward the kitchen."

"But . . ." Roxie quickly glanced down at Lilith and her dog looked back at her, the sudden anxiety in the animal's eyes a mirror reflection of her owner's. Roxie caught her mistake and let go with a whine of regret.

"Go on as if nothing happened," Eli coaxed her.

"All right, well, come in, then." Roxie announced this and swept her arm up a little too wide and a little too fast. "Welcome to my space!" she shouted enthusiastically.

This startled Lilith. She growled again, but Eli kept walking. He headed into Roxanne's kitchen, and immediately saw two steel dog bowls by the back door. He would get to them in a moment.

He started with the cabinets over the stove, and slowly, mechanically, he began to open and close every single cupboard door in the place. Lilith circled, slowly at first, then gaining momentum as her growling intensified. She wasn't ready to give in, apparently. Of course not. Lilith was Roxie Bloom's dog.

"Is there anything I should be doing?" Roxanne asked meekly from the kitchen doorway.

"Yes." Eli kept his tone friendly as he crossed to the opposite bank of cupboards. "You can relax, please. Speak with a confident but calm voice." He took out a single drinking glass.

"Okay," she said, obviously trying hard to sound calm. "But you're still bleeding and I don't know what the hell you are doing going through all my cabinets. If you wanted something to drink I could have gotten it for you."

Eli chuckled a bit, moving to the refrigerator and

taking out what looked like a pitcher of iced tea. "But then Lilith wouldn't learn anything, Roxie. This way, she'll get to see me help myself to your food supply."

"Hey, whatever rocks your socks," Roxie said.

Lilith continued to growl. She paced around at Eli's feet. Her snarling was punctuated with nasty-sounding barks. She jumped again, and her teeth sliced through his jeans and boxers and hit the flesh of his left butt cheek.

Here we go again, Eli thought.

"Ssh!" he hissed, returning to a squat. He gently twisted Lilith's collar, brought her head forward and down toward the ground, and flipped her.

"God," Roxie said, shaking her head. "I can't believe she bit you again. She's so incredibly stubborn."

Eli nodded.

"So is this why you needed her shot records?" Roxanne asked, her voice quite small.

"It certainly is," he said.

After five minutes, Eli asked Roxie to fetch his duffel from the foyer and lay out his first aid supplies—he'd need to bandage up soon.

After ten minutes, Eli had to adjust his position from squatting to kneeling, relieved when the circulation returned to his lower legs.

After fifteen minutes, Lilith let go with a great sigh and unclenched her muscles in surrender. Her head fell against the kitchen tile with a thud. Once more, Eli praised her, stroked her, and allowed her up.

While Roxie was busy loving her up, Eli returned to the refrigerator and pulled out the plastic food container of brown rice and chicken. Just as he turned to pick up the dog bowls, Lilith barked, tore across the floor, then jammed her body between Eli and her bowls.

He paid no mind. With calm, smooth movements, he reached down and gathered the empty stainless-steel food bowl and took it to the counter. He dumped about half a cup of the rice-and-chicken mixture into the bowl, then put his hands in it, mushing it all around.

Lilith was growling. The hair on her back was standing up.

"What the—" Roxanne's mouth fell open. She scrambled to her feet. "I have spoons, you know."

"No, thanks," Eli said, ignoring Lilith's frantic growling and barking as he ran his fingers through the mixture. "I am putting my scent all over her food," he told Roxie.

"Right," Roxie said. "But why would you want to do that?"

Eli chuckled. "This is not what I want—it's what she *needs*. It demonstrates to the dog that she only eats after the pack leader has had his fill. I would suggest you do this at every feeding, until she understands the concept."

"Gross, but okay," she said.

Eli put the bowl down and walked away, heading to the kitchen sink. Lilith sniffed at the food but seemed more focused on the intruder than her snack. Eli turned on the water and waited a moment, not acknowledging the dog. But when she failed to eat any of her food, Eli promptly removed the bowl from the floor and placed it on top of the refrigerator. He returned to the sink. "How about you give me a tour of your house once I've patched myself up?" he asked Roxie, rinsing his hands in the water.

She laughed, walking toward him. "I don't get it. Why would you tease a dog like you just did?"

"I never tease," he said. "That was part of her lesson—she eats immediately after the pack leader, not at her leisure. She didn't touch the food I gave her, so the food disappeared. It will be like that at every feeding from now on."

Roxanne crossed her arms over her chest. "But I don't feed her that way."

Eli smiled as he glanced over his shoulder. "You do now." He pointed to a ceramic dispenser on the counter. "Is this the soap?"

Roxie sighed, and joined him at the sink. He could see her try her best to smile.

"Here, let me help you."

That's when she touched him. She gently rolled up the sleeve of his denim shirt, sucking in her breath at the sight of the lacerations on his arm. He'd had worse. This wasn't nearly as bad as the Saint Bernard from Spokane last year.

Roxanne squeezed out a couple drops of the soap, and worked it into bubbles in her hands. She had very pretty hands, he noticed. Slim fingers. Clean white nails kept short. He ran his arms under the warm water and looked down at her. He grinned. She frowned.

"She tore you up," Roxie said.

"I'll be fine."

All the while, Lilith paced and patrolled at their feet, snarling and barking.

Roxanne placed her soft hands on his arms, spreading the soap. Her touch was quite gentle. She managed to get soap into all the places where the skin had been broken, but didn't rough them up. The sting of the soap was already plenty bad.

"She hates men," Roxie said suddenly. She looked sheepish. "Did I tell you that?"

He laughed. "I believe you did."

Roxanne sighed. He almost sighed, too—the feel of her hands caressing his forearm was overtly sexual. He wondered how he could convince her to dole out the same first aid treatment to his ass. Suddenly, a vision flashed in his brain—Roxie's hands moving on his hard cock like that, up and down, up and down.

"The girls told me a long time ago that I was the cause of Lilith's aggression toward men," she whispered, her hands still moving. "I didn't want to believe them."

She stopped her ministrations and reached for the spray attachment of the faucet. She directed a stream of water onto his flesh, dialing down the force of the spray so it wouldn't hurt him. Then she unfolded a soft cotton towel from a drawer and patted him dry.

"You're going to need stitches," she said.

"Won't be the first time. Would you mind handing me one of those bandages?" Eli nodded toward the supplies she'd placed on the counter.

Roxanne nodded, her face full of concern. She unwrapped a roll of gauze. "I see you're prepared for everything," she said.

"Always."

Roxanne helped him cover the deepest cuts with square bandages, wrap gauze around his whole arm, and tape everything in place. When they were done, she raised those gorgeous dark eyes to his face. "I'm trying not to look at her, you know? But I'm really worried she's going to bite you again."

"No worries, right?" Eli smiled at her. "I'll survive. Shall we?" Eli asked, gesturing for Roxie to show him around.

"She's doing better, isn't she?" Roxanne asked, the hope evident in her voice.

"Much," he said, feeling the dog begin to sniff at his ankles. In fact, if she'd gone from biting to sniffing, they were definitely headed in the right direction. Sniffing was normal behavior for dogs. Biting wasn't.

"This is the dining room," Roxie said. "My mom gave me all her old furniture when she moved to Mexico a few years ago."

"Mexico? Is she running from the law or something?"

Roxanne laughed, and it was the first real laugh he'd heard from her that day. Yes, things were going much better.

"Not exactly," she said. "Mom just wanted to retire in splendor, so she's living in a beach house in some town full of aging hippies and artists. She didn't want to keep anything from her old life."

"Ah," Eli said. "She sounds like an interesting woman."

Roxie grinned. "Yeah. She is." She led him into the living room, and as he glanced around, he decided he really liked the way she'd fixed up her house. They were smack in the middle of the city, but the place felt comfortable. Solid. It was quiet, too. Her choice in furniture was simple but it seemed just right. All the while, Lilith continued to sniff at Eli's legs.

He stopped in his tracks. Above a small fireplace mantel was a poster-sized photo of Roxie and Lilith, dressed as some kind of all-girl jungle warrior gang. A laugh exploded from Eli before he could pull himself together.

"Yeah. There's a story behind that," Roxie said.

"I bet."

Roxanne sighed. "Lucio has his own fantasy pet photography business, right? Well, he let all of us do a photo sitting of our choice with the idea that he'd use them in a promotion. I chose the Amazon Woman motif, you know, the whole warrior priestess vibe. I thought it was perfect for me and Lilith."

"Excellent choice," Eli said, giving himself a few

moments to take in the details of Roxie's photographic splendor, from the feathered headdress, to the thigh-high animal-hide boots and matching ragged-edged mini-skirt, to the figure-hugging breastplate and coordinating spear. Eli had to admit that despite all the ways he'd imagined Roxie in his mind's eye, never once had he pictured her in a breastplate. Apparently, he'd done himself a disservice.

"You make a fine warrior woman," he whispered.

Roxanne sighed. "You're teasing me. Go ahead. Everyone else has."

Eli smiled and shook his head, looking down into her eyes. "I mean it," he said. "Look at you." Eli placed his hands on Roxanne's shoulders and turned her to face the photo, her back to him. He leaned into her ear. "That woman is strong and beautiful. She's nobody's fool."

He felt her relax beneath his touch. It seemed every time their bodies made contact there was a hot electric rush that moved through him. Just like now. Roxie must have felt it, too, because she leaned into him briefly before she caught herself and straightened again.

Eli smiled, unable to take his eyes from the framed photo above the mantel. He saw much more in that image than he was letting on. Obviously, it had been difficult enough for Roxanne to ask for his help, to let him into her home, and trust her dog to his care. Eli knew he'd be pushing it if he told her what he really saw in that photograph.

That girl up there was a tigress, a sexual goddess standing on firm, parted thighs, creamy breasts shoved forward by the ridiculously tight costume, a sensual smirk on her mouth. And in those dark eyes was rock-solid determination. *Holy hell, it would take a strong man to handle all of that.*

Eli's mind flooded with a vision: he was slashing his way through the thick and tangled jungle to get to her, braving alligator-infested waters and slobbering pumas, the sweat soaking through his clothing and running into his eyes as he pressed on . . .

"So you think I have what it takes to be a good pack leader for Lilith?"

Roxanne's voice shocked Eli from his imaginary quest.

"Ah, yeah," he said, clearing his head.

"You don't sound very sure."

Eli grinned to himself and gave her shoulders a friendly squeeze. "If you ever doubt you have what it takes—in pack leadership or life in general—just take a deep breath and be the woman we see right here, in this photo."

Roxie giggled.

"Look at yourself up there, Rox. Your head is held high. Your shoulders are back. Your eyes are scanning the horizon. You are at peace with your own power. At peace with the world. This is no joke—just look at your dog in this photograph." Eli pointed to the image of Lilith, who, despite the ludicrous costume, seemed perfectly composed.

"She seems really calm, doesn't she?" Roxie asked, amazement in her voice.

"She does."

"Was it because I was pretending to be a powerful and competent warrior priestess and she picked up on the change in my energy?"

"Stranger things have happened."

Roxanne turned and looked over her shoulder at Eli. "Thanks for pointing that out," she said, giving him a crooked little smile.

She showed him the rest of the living room. Eli took

note of the corner she'd made into her office. A modern, U-shaped desk of pale wood held her laptop, phone charger, and a lamp. A credenza behind the desk held her files and books. A table beneath the desk housed her all-in-one printer.

Displayed on the edge of her desk was a selection of man-hating novelties including coffee mugs, bumper stickers, and baseball caps.

"So this is where all the magic happens?" he asked her.

She let go with a genuine, happy laugh. Truly, that jubilant sound sent shock waves through him. He'd never heard anything as delightful. And at that moment, with her head tilted back and her eyes shining, he'd never seen a woman more beautiful.

Roxanne Bloom and her laugh gave him the shivers. How sad that she hadn't had many opportunities to laugh like this lately.

It was then that Eli noticed a portable phone on the floor in the corner of the room, its back panel lying in several pieces a couple feet away. "Hey, your—"

"Got it," she said. Roxie snatched the phone and threw it in a desk drawer. She slammed the drawer shut. Then she returned to him and smiled. "So, what's next?"

Eli decided not to ask. Clearly, she'd thrown the phone across the room at some point in the recent past, but she'd tell him about it when she was ready. Eli smiled.

"Take me upstairs," he said.

"Say *what*?"

Eli watched the panic hit her wide eyes. As if on cue, Lilith snarled and barked at him.

"Did you catch that?" Eli asked, gesturing for Roxie to proceed ahead of him up the stairs. "You got scared, and your dog got scared."

"I . . . I am not scared," she said, heading up the steps in front of him, wagging her hips. He wasn't sure it was intentional, but he appreciated it, regardless.

Eli chuckled to himself. If he went by the standard routine here, he'd be the one leading the group upstairs. The leader always went first. But he didn't want to miss the chance to admire Roxie's ass. Besides, Lilith stayed behind both of them on their walk up, which was the main objective.

"Why would I be scared?" Roxie asked, catching him ogling her when she whipped her head around.

"That's for you to ponder," Eli answered, giving her a reassuring smile.

Of course she was scared. Roxie Bloom, Chief Emasculating Officer of i-vomit-on-all-men.com, was taking a man upstairs. And the man had been staring at her booty. It probably freaked her the hell out. He'd love to know what she was thinking at this very moment.

If things were different, Eli would have reached out and stroked those perfect globes of female flesh that wagged and wiggled right in his face. The girl looked downright delicious in jeans. He had a suspicion that she'd look even better out of them.

But this wasn't the time or place. The ferocious Lilith was right behind him, her nose suddenly sniffing at his crotch. He needed to stay focused.

"Why are we up here, anyway?" she asked when they'd reached the top of the steps. She was frowning.

"Haven't you figured out what I'm doing yet?" Eli walked past her, helping himself to the second floor of her home.

"Maybe not. What exactly *are* you doing?" she asked.

"I'm taking over, babe," he said. "And I need to mark my territory." He headed into the bathroom without an invitation, glancing her way. "I'll be leaving the door open, so, if you must, step into the other room until I'm out of your line of sight."

He watched her mouth fall open. When he started to unzip his Wranglers, Roxie skittered into what looked like the spare room. He kept talking to her through the open door.

"This is for Lilith's benefit," he said.

"I'm sure she appreciates it as much as I do," Roxie answered.

Eli chuckled as he raised the toilet seat and unzipped his jeans the rest of the way. Showmanship aside, he really did have to go.

He sensed Lilith inching closer. He hadn't yet looked at her. From the moment he'd entered the front door, and through all the jumping and the biting and the growling, he'd never made eye contact with the dog or looked at her directly. In the language of dogs, that would have indicated one of two things: aggression or that the pack leader had lost his focus as protector and provider. If he'd looked at her, or if he'd ever once displayed the tiniest hint of anger or fear, it would have been the signal for Lilith to step into the role of emergency pack leader. It's what had happened with Lilith and Roxie. It's why Lilith didn't trust her owner to keep her safe. It's why Lilith couldn't relax and enjoy being a dog in the loving care of a human.

As of today, Lilith was no longer in charge around here. The pecking order had changed.

Eli began to relieve himself, and Lilith was fascinated. She sniffed the air. She ventured closer. But all it took was one soft *shh* from Eli and she backed away.

Oh, yes. Things were getting a lot better.

Eli finished up, flushed the toilet and washed his hands. He stepped out of the bathroom and into the upstairs hallway, Lilith at his side, more curious than concerned.

Roxie emerged from the spare room. She flipped her hair over her shoulder and raised her chin in defiance. Eli had to concentrate on his breathing, because his own animal instincts were rattling the cage. He wondered just how satisfying it would be to sink his teeth into that flawless female flesh of hers.

"What next?" she asked, balling her fists at her sides. "Is this where you change into your jammies and get in my bed?"

Eli smiled. "Never wear 'em, sweet thing," he said.

Chapter 8

Roxanne went numb with disbelief. Eli Gallagher just strolled right into her bedroom like he had every right to. Her brain ricocheted back and forth between fury, terror, and trying to remember which books were on her nightstand and which panties might be lying on the rug.

Then it hit her. Oh, God, no . . . before she fell asleep last night she'd been reading a DIY guide to female orgasm. She'd even used a yellow highlighter on critical passages.

Why? *Why?* What had she ever done to deserve this?

"Nice," she heard him say. "Real nice."

Was this guy for real? Who the hell did Eli Gallagher think he was? And what in the world was going on in her bedroom?

Then she heard Lilith growl. She heard Eli make that hissing sound that was really starting to get on her nerves, and then it got quiet.

Roxie ran across the hall and into her room, stopping with a gasp. Eli Gallagher had opened her closet and was sorting through her clothes. "I like your taste," he said, sensing that she'd come to stand in the doorway behind him.

Lilith revved up her growling again. Roxie didn't blame her. If Roxie were a dog, she'd have responded to Eli's alpha male exhibition in the very same way—bites to the ass included. She wondered if God's Gift to Dogs and Girls would expect her to wash those wounds, as well. Ha! Like that would ever happen!

She watched Lilith pace at Eli's feet, clearly upset about how he was helping himself to her owner's sanctuary. The dog's lips peeled back over her teeth. The hair along her spine bristled. A deep rumble emanated from her chest.

Poor Lily Girl. This was too hard on her. This was cruel.

"I liked what you were wearing yesterday—that pale purple shirt was very pretty against your skin."

Roxanne watched as Eli sorted through her hangers, then closed the closet door. He headed straight to her chest of drawers.

She could not freaking believe this guy! "All right. That's enough," Roxanne spat out. "This is getting ridiculous. I've never *once* seen Cesar Milan go through some chick's closet on his TV show."

"Calm tone of voice, please," he said, smiling at her over his shoulder. "Most people who call themselves 'dog whisperers' share some basic approaches to the job, but I'm not Cesar Milan, in case you haven't noticed."

She nearly laughed out loud. "I've noticed."

Eli opened her underwear drawer. "We're making a lot of progress. Please don't give up now."

She was at his side in a flash. She gripped his wrist, intending to rip it away from the dresser pull. But she noticed how blood had spotted the white gauze. She stared at the golden skin and light hairs of his upper forearm, mesmerized by the hard bone and muscle. And then it was too late. She'd already touched him. That unbelievable rush went through her again, the way it had several times already today.

She'd first felt it when Eli stepped into her house, the chaos doing nothing to lessen its effect on her. She'd felt it again downstairs at the sink, as she gingerly tended to his bite wounds, and then as they stood in front of the photo over the fireplace. And if she were to be perfectly truthful about it, there was a part of her that got insanely hot at the sound of Eli's zipper going down, followed by the sight of him marching into her bathroom like a barbarian.

Roxanne closed her eyes a moment, fending off dizziness. What was wrong with her? Why was she having these absurd thoughts? It was stupid, that's what it was. Laughable. Hadn't she had enough of the big-shot macho caveman routine with Raymond Sandberg? Hadn't that taught her anything *at all* about herself, about men, about reality? Hadn't she decided that she was never going back there again?

"You need to get out of my house," Roxie said, making her voice as sickeningly sweet as possible, for Lilith's sake. She withdrew her hand from his arm as if she'd touched a hot stove. Her eyes flew open. "You need to gather up your bag of tricks and your dominant-male bullshit and get out of here. Now. Got it?"

Roxie stared up at him and smiled pleasantly, just the way he wanted it. She was so pissed that the effort it took to smile actually hurt the muscles around her mouth.

Eli's face showed nothing. It was smooth and serene and handsome. "I know this is hard for you," he said. She felt his fingers brush along the side of her face.

"Don't do that."

Eli frowned slightly, then he looked away. It was the first time today she'd seen him less than completely in charge. Eli shook his head quickly, as if to clear his thoughts, then returned his gaze to hers. His soft green eyes were filled with emotion.

"We're dealing with three separate challenges here today," Eli whispered.

"I don't want to hear about any of them."

"And only one is about your dog."

"You need to go."

"It's important that we keep them separate, Roxanne. I am a dog whisperer here to help you and Lilith, but I'm also a man who's being thrown off his game because he's so damn attracted to you." Eli paused, searching her face.

Roxie couldn't move. She could barely breathe.

"All I'm saying is it's going to be a trick to keep everything separate."

Roxie took a step back.

Eli took a step closer. Their faces were inches apart.

"I came here to introduce Lilith to the concept that she's not in charge in this house. She's struggling, but she's starting to get it. With every line I cross I erode some of her control, and this is the first lesson she has to learn—that she is not the pack leader anymore."

Roxanne looked away from his gorgeous male face and shut her eyes. She longed to stick her fingers in her ears like a petulant little kid, just to block out the liquid heat of his voice. She couldn't stand that voice anymore.

"I know it's hard to watch, but it is not hurting Lilith. She is very stubborn, but she'll be immensely relieved once she settles into her new place. She will be a much happier dog."

She shook her head.

"Roxie, please listen to me. The reason Lilith has resorted to aggression is because she's convinced you aren't qualified to be the boss. Your energy is so unstable and full of anger that she doesn't trust you to take care of the pack. She thinks she has to do it."

"That's enough." Roxie's knees were beginning to feel wobbly.

"You say you want her to feel safe, right? Well, the only way she's ever going to feel safe is if you give her a reason to."

"I want you to leave." Her legs began to shake.

"The second thing happening here is *your* reaction to me being in your home, your safe haven, telling you all kinds of shit you don't want to hear. I am well aware that you hate having a man here as a matter of principle. I know it feels like an invasion." He ran a feather-light finger down her hair.

"If you don't get out of here, I'm calling the police."

Eli's voice never wavered. "The third thing that's going on is something completely unrelated—the force that is drawing us together. I know you feel it. I've never felt anything like it in my life, and I'm a man who makes his living picking up on energy from humans and animals. It's . . . well, honestly, it's a little intimidating. It's almost as if it's coming from somewhere outside of the two of us."

Roxanne had been trying not to hear a single word out of this man's mouth. Yet, again, because of that deep-river lullaby of a voice, she couldn't help but listen.

And everything he'd said was spot on. It made her want to scream.

"Please, Roxie," Eli said, his hand traveling down to cup her chin. He lifted it so she had no choice but to look at him.

"There's got to be another way," she said. "This is too much."

"There is no other way," he said.

"But I saw a cable TV ad for an electric shock collar that works wonders. It comes with a money-back guarantee."

Eli nodded, as if giving it some serious thought. "It's going to sting your neck pretty bad, but we could give it a try, I suppose." He smiled.

"Funny," Roxie said, rolling her eyes. She was losing this fight. She could feel it. Something was breaking apart inside her, and it was so incredibly scary. She'd felt this very same sensation before—at the paddock the day of the baby shower, when Eli had grabbed her and kissed the hell out of her. She'd busted out sobbing then, and she absolutely refused to give a repeat performance.

Why did Eli Gallagher affect her this way? It seemed if she let her guard down for an instant, she was toast. He just pushed the rest of the way through, right into the core of her.

Roxie swallowed hard, suddenly recalling the deal she'd made with Gloria Needleman. *". . . leave the door to your heart open just a crack, my dear girl . . ."*

"Roxie, can we acknowledge the attraction we feel for each other?"

". . . this man will be different. He'll be strong enough to pry open the door of your heart and brave enough to love everything he finds inside."

Eli put his hands on her shoulders. "Can we accept it as a fact, and see where it takes us? There has to be a reason it's so strong."

Roxanne focused her eyes right on Eli's. She tried to make sense of all the emotion roaring through her, and this was the one thing she knew: if it weren't for Raymond Sandberg, she'd find Eli's offer irresistible. If

Raymond hadn't scooped out the last bit of trust she had left inside her, she'd have gone for it.

"You said you were tired of the fight, Roxie," Eli whispered, his eyes clear and true. "You said you wanted to get rid of all the bad stuff so there's room for peace. For happiness."

"I was talking about Lilith."

"I don't think so."

Roxie sighed, long and deep. She felt so overwhelmed, she needed to sit down. The floor would be fine. But just then, Eli opened his arms to her, and she fell against him. He didn't do anything—no ass-grabbing or boob-tweaking or sticking his tongue down her throat. There was nothing but the heat and comfort of his strong body against hers. Once again, it felt as if she were being filled, as if she'd pulled up to the pump and had selected the ultra-premium grade of calm. It was as if Eli could transfer some of his own rock-solid peace through physical contact. It was an awesome feeling.

"I don't understand any of this," she said, her voice muffled by the cotton of his shirt. "This is way over my head, Eli."

He laughed. She clutched at him, then closed her eyes and reveled in the rocking motion of his chest. For that instant, Roxanne felt completely safe. She felt completely loved.

Perhaps for the first time in her life.

Then she heard a loud thud as Lilith collapsed right next to her foot. The dog let out a very dramatic and deep sigh of submission. Roxie smiled to herself because the outburst sounded awfully familiar.

"She just reached another level of surrender," Eli said, his hand gently stroking along the length of Roxie's hair. "Let's love her up some."

Roxie pulled away from Eli and smiled at him.

"Remember," Eli added. "With some practice, you'll take over and she'll make the same transition with you. It's just this first part that's the real bitch."

Roxie raised her lips to his. Eli met her mouth and offered her the sanctuary she so desperately wanted, delivered with a sweet gentleness. Somehow, he knew exactly what kind of kiss she needed.

And why wouldn't he? He knew everything else about her, it seemed.

The two separated from their embrace and knelt down to the dog's level. Roxie let Eli touch Lilith first, watching as he rubbed her ears. Next, Eli murmured a stream of reassuring words in his laid-back baritone.

"Such a good girl. What a good dog you are, Lilith. We knew you could do it."

Apparently, his voice affected Lilith the same way it did Roxie. She watched her dog roll over on her back and bare her white belly, her ears flopping back on the rug over her head. Eli stroked her short, coarse fur and continued to speak to her. "You're a fine dog. You're the best dog ever."

Her tail began to wag.

Roxie put her hand on Lilith's belly and stroked in rhythm with Eli. "That's my Lily Girl," she said, her voice calm and soft. "What a good dog."

Eli placed his hand over hers. The rubbing stopped. Lilith rolled back over, paws in front, panting happily, tail wagging.

Eli took Roxie by the hand and pulled her to a stand. His face looked relaxed and kind. He placed a delicate kiss on her forehead, then nuzzled her neck.

"Okay, Ms. Bloom. *Now* it's time for bed," he said.

Gloria waited until the girls were gone and the door had fully closed. Then she waited a few more minutes, just to be sure they'd made it all the way down the hall. When she was certain the coast was clear, she allowed herself to cry.

Life was such a glorious mystery. Lately, when her thoughts would wander—and that was happening a lot—she'd picture the passing of time as a kind of poem, a poem that looped around and repeated itself in places, yet always charged ahead toward the inevitable end. And when it was over, love was the only thing that remained.

She reached for the tissue box on the rolling cart at her bedside, startled by the sight of the plastic tubing jabbed into a big blue vein on the top of her knobby hand. That same hand had once been soft and graceful. It seemed like yesterday. Where had the time gone?

She would never forget the moment she first laid eyes on him. Ira Needleman was nothing to write home about in the physique department, that was for sure, but that face! Those eyes! That head of dark and thick curls! *Oy!* Right there on the train platform, in a sea of people, he'd stood out like the Northern Star to Gloria, the clearest, brightest burst of energy she'd ever experienced. It was like he'd plugged into her. She hummed with his essence.

Then she lost him in the crowd. The girlfriend she'd come to meet tapped her on the shoulder and he was gone.

Two weeks later, she saw him again, this time at a second cousin's bar mitzvah. As it turned out, Ira Needleman was the nephew of a friend of her grandmother's. A loose association to be sure, and it was many years later that Gloria was told the sole reason Ira had been invited was to meet *her*. Her grandmother was always doing things like that. That's where Gloria got the gift.

She blew her nose. She took a sip of the metallic-tasting water from a paper cup at her bedside. She hated it here. She'd had a very good life. A blessed life. She missed Ira. And that was why she had no intention of hanging around this joint any longer than she absolutely had to. Frankly, she couldn't decide which would be worse—a hospital room, a nursing home, or living with Rachel! Oh, her eldest was a mensch, a real sweetheart. But she didn't want to live by Rachel's rules. She didn't want to be a burden. What kind of life was that?

Gloria cried. Then she cried some more. Then she stopped crying and wadded up her tissues and hid them under the blankets. Rachel and Bea would make such a fuss if they knew.

She stared at the ceiling panels, thinking that up until quite recently, she'd been baffled by how her children had turned out. They were wonderful children, good people. Two doctors, a lawyer, and a college professor—what more could a mother ask for? But none of them had the gift, and as far as she could tell, none of their children had it, either. Oh, how Gloria had prayed that Rachel would show a knack for it one day, but Rachel was in her fifties now. If there were going to be a knack it surely would have surfaced by now.

Then Gloria met the girls—Josie, Ginger, Roxanne, and Bea—and the four young ladies had brought such adventure to the last year of her life. Now two babies were on the way! If that wasn't proof of the power of love, she didn't know what was. With a nod, Gloria promised herself that no matter how challenging hanging on might get, she'd stick around to see those babies born. No question about it.

She remembered how Josie had been the first to need Gloria's help, with her funny spirit and her cute freckled nose. And Josie had led her to Ginger, always so glamorous, even in her maternity smock. Nothing had eased the pain of losing Ira like joining their circle of female friends. The day Josie walked in her front door with her reporter's notebook to write about Ira's passing—that was no coincidence.

Neither was meeting Bea. Dear, kindhearted, no-nonsense, solitary Beatrice Latimer. She might think her only gift was for teaching dogs to run through sewer pipes or whatever nonsense she did these days, but Gloria knew better. Bea hadn't even acknowledged her real gift yet. And that was another piece of unfinished business Gloria needed to stick around for. She had to explain to Bea that in addition to reveling in the light of her eldest daughter's love—with Gloria's full blessing—Bea would be taking over the family business. Knowing that gave Gloria a sense of peace.

And then there was Roxanne Bloom.

Gloria rolled her eyes. She'd never seen such a difficult case. What a *meshugeneh*! Through the years she'd worked with plenty of angry women. Of course she had. And a few of them had harbored bitterness toward men in particular. That was the way of the world. But never—*ever*—had she known a woman as twisted up with hostility as Roxanne.

Rage had become the girl's all-purpose approach to life. It was the excuse she used for shutting herself off from the world. It was her livelihood. It was her religion.

Gloria had known it would take someone very special to break through all that. Then Eli Gallagher had shown up as a guest at Josie and Rick's wedding. He was so good-looking Gloria had to blink a few times. And the man radiated a pure and forceful energy that nearly knocked her over.

Never had Gloria been so sure about putting two

people together. When Eli and Roxanne had looked each other at that wedding, Gloria had wanted to stop the proceedings and ask if anyone else felt the earth shift. But just because it was meant to be didn't mean it *would* be.

Roxanne might very well blow it. If something spooked her—if anything spooked her—she could close up and never let Eli in again. And Eli was the kind of man who needed an invitation. Though his spirit was powerful, he was no brute. He would never simply kick in the girl's door, the way that perverted old lawyer had. Roxanne would have to welcome Eli in.

Gloria closed her eyes tight. She summoned all the strength she had left inside her worn-out body and directed it to Eli, Roxanne, and that poor abused mutt of hers. Mazel tov to them all!

Her shoulders drooped from the effort. Gloria would have to enlist Bea's help on this one. There was no other way. She wasn't strong enough, and time was running out.

The hospital room door opened. She kept her eyes closed and pretended to be asleep. She felt both the girls lean down close to check that she was still breathing. Bea fiddled with her IV. Rachel pressed the blankets close to her side. Then Gloria felt them move away.

She strained her ears. Damn that her hearing was going right along with all the rest of her. She could only catch a few snippets of their whispered conversation, but she could hear enough to know that there was excitement in their voices, and wonder. Bea sounded like she was in shock. Rachel sounded happier than she'd heard her in years.

Gloria opened one eye just enough to see that the two of them had scooted their armchairs close together and sat beneath the window, their gray heads nearly touching. Bea tenderly held Rachel's hand in her own.

Gloria smiled to herself. And what about this match, the one blossoming right here under the window of her hospital room?

She took a deep, satisfying breath.

This one was a piece of cake. A real no-brainer, as Bea would say.

Eli kissed her silky-soft forehead, kicked off his shoes, and made his way to Roxie's queen-sized platform bed. He stretched out on the cream-colored comforter, laced his fingers behind his head, and crossed his ankles. Eli wiggled his toes and sighed in relaxation.

Lilith went nuts.

"I thought she was doing better," Roxie said, coming near the bed, frowning in disappointment.

"Oh, she is." Eli grinned and patted the top of the comforter, urging her to join him. "But in a dog's mind, this is the Holy Grail of dominance. The food bowl is bad enough, but the bed is where dominant dogs draw the line."

Roxie cracked her neck. "Great."

Eli laughed. "So, do you sleep alone?"

Roxie's eyes went huge. He watched the anger flare on her face. Clearly, her first instinct had been to lash out at his presumptuous question. She was just like Lilith—falling back on what was familiar though she knew it would only bring more misery. Eli wondered if Roxie had figured out what he was up to yet—that he was chipping away at her old patterns right along with her dog's?

"What exactly—"

"I'm asking whether Lilith sleeps with you at night."

"Oh." Roxie let out the breath she'd been holding. "Sometimes," she said. Then she cautiously lowered her perfect little bottom onto the edge of the bed, keeping her feet on the floor.

The instant Roxanne's butt hit the mattress, Lilith doubled the decibel level of her incessant barking. The dog was up on all fours, teeth bared once more. Eli did not look at Lilith and did not raise his voice when he spoke to Roxie.

"Who decides when she sleeps with you? Is that your decision, or hers?"

Roxie looked down at her dog, then snapped her head back to Eli. "Sorry. I forgot," she said.

"No problem."

"I guess Lilith decides," she answered, fighting to keep her voice calm in the mayhem. He had to hand it to her—she was really trying. "Some nights she wants up and some nights she sleeps on the floor next to the bed."

"So once she's up here, would she get down if you told her to?"

Roxie laughed a little. Once more, Eli was mesmerized by how pretty she was when she laughed.

"I tried that once. It didn't work out so great."

He nodded. It was what he had expected to hear.

"She wouldn't budge. She even growled at me."

Roxie had never mentioned that before. "What did you do?"

She flipped her hair over her shoulder and sighed. "I let it go. I didn't press the issue. But that was right after I got her, so I figured she was, you know, still getting settled in."

"Hmm," Eli said, knowing it was time to read her questionnaire. "Can you go get the forms I asked you to fill out, and then come up here on the bed with me? We'll read them together."

Roxie's mouth pulled tight, but she nodded, leaving the bedroom. He heard her feet run down the steps, then come right back up. Lilith didn't move or change the cadence of her barking. Eli didn't acknowledge her.

Roxie was soon back, and Eli observed her as she walked to the other side of the bed and climbed up next to him. She lay down quite close. His instinct was to wrap his arms around her, but he knew he was going to need them for other things. Immediately.

Lilith jumped up on the bed and put her paws on Eli's chest, assuming the top-dog stance as she barked and growled in his face. Slowly, without a trace of emotion or fear, Eli rose up and pressed his fingertips into the side of her neck. *"Shh!"* he said, gently grabbing her collar and guiding her to the floor.

As if nothing had happened, he returned to his spot on the bed with Roxanne. They started to review the questionnaire but Lilith continued to bark and growl. After about five minutes of that, Lilith jumped on the bed again. Eli repeated the routine. Then again. Then once more.

Eli thought Lilith would try for a fifth time—which would have been a record in his many years of this exercise—but she stopped in mid-jump. Lilith dropped her paws from the side of the bed and decided it wasn't worth it. After spinning in place a few times to find that perfect spot, she collapsed on the floor with a loud thump and a sigh.

Eli and Roxie lay in silence, waiting until they could be sure the dog wasn't launching another attack. "My God, what a nightmare," Roxie whispered into Eli's ear. "I think you actually broke a sweat." She touched her fingers to his damp temple and then ran her fingers through his hair. "Now what do we do?"

He turned to her. Her face was so close to his that he could smell her sweet breath and a light floral scent floating from her skin and hair. Eli breathed deeply, pulling the warm flowers inside himself.

He wanted to do the same with all of her—body and soul—just grab Roxanne Bloom and pull her to him. But he knew that slow and steady would be the only way with Roxie.

"How about we chill for a while and review the questionnaire?" Eli answered her.

"What about Lilith?"

"What about her?" Eli said, smiling. "Take a peek."

Roxie rose up and leaned over Eli's body so she could see down to the floor. When she did that, those gorgeous breasts of hers pressed into his belly. Her right hip pushed up against his left one.

"Her eyes are closed," Roxie whispered, her voice full of wonder. "That's absolutely amazing."

Eli's eyes were closed, too, as he focused all his senses on each point of contact between their bodies. Breast to belly. Hip to hip. The way Roxanne's hair fell loose and brushed across his lips.

Absolutely amazing was right.

Chapter 9

They made it through the client survey, but, because Roxie had a question for every question, the process had taken nearly an hour.

Why did Eli need to know such intimate details about her personal life? she'd asked him. Why did she have to tell him how she spent her typical workday? Or why she occasionally had trouble sleeping? Or whether she fretted over her finances? Or what she did for relaxation?

Eli laughed out loud at what Roxie had written down for that one. *"The only thing I do for relaxation is take Lilith on her walks, which is anything but relaxing, so I guess it would be accurate to say I never relax."*

"Ah, Roxie," Eli had said, pulling her tighter to his side. "We're going to have to work on that."

"I do run," she added, raising her head from his shoulder, looking and sounding pleased with herself.

"Really? That's great." Eli scribbled that information along the questionnaire's margin.

"But I only do it to stay in shape," she admitted. "I don't really like it much. I hate it, actually. But I love keeping a running journal so I can see how I've pushed myself to go harder and farther. It's kind of a competition with myself."

"Right," Eli said, crossing out his margin notes as he shook his head. "Out of curiosity, who usually wins that competition?"

Roxie squinted her eyes at him. "Is this a trick question? Another way to judge me, show me how uptight I am?"

"This is not about judging you, Roxie." Eli reached down and tweaked her delicate chin. "I'm just trying to figure out what makes you tick, and how your personality and lifestyle might be linked to Lilith's difficulties."

"Why do you keep touching my face?" she asked.

He chuckled. "Because it's a beautiful face. Very soft and sweet, and I'm blown away when you smile."

"Really?"

"You have a great laugh, too."

"I do?"

"I hope I get to experience a lot more of both."

She nodded. "Are we almost done?" she asked, dropping her gaze to the papers in Eli's lap.

He laughed, knowing the answer to that question would be a resounding *no*. They were just getting started. But Eli knew she'd meant the client questionnaire, not the dual journeys they'd begun together. "The only section that's left has to do with your love life, but you left it blank. Did you run out of time?"

Roxie popped up to a sitting position on the bed. Lilith raised her sleepy head to check that everything was all right, then tucked her snout between her paws and went right back to sleep.

"No," she said, pulling up her knees and hugging them close to her chest. "And I'm not avoiding the subject, either. I just didn't think there was enough room on your little form to say what needed to be said."

Eli nodded neutrally. "Care to elaborate?"

Roxie laughed, pulling her knees right up under her chin and lowering her head. She reminded him of those strange little pill bugs he often saw on the ranch, creatures that could roll themselves up into a perfect armor-encased ball when threatened.

He sure didn't want to threaten her. "It's okay, Roxie. We have plenty of time. We can get to it whenever you feel comfortable."

She raised her face then, and he was struck by how young she looked. Her eyes were big and black and her pretty mouth was pulled tight.

"It's my fault things were so rough when you first got here today," she said. "My ex-boyfriend called right as you knocked on the door. He starting talking shit to me, threatening me, telling me I was nothing. I screamed at him. Then I threw the phone into the corner. Then I answered the door, already in full flipping-out mode."

Eli nodded, saying nothing.

"I did everything wrong," she said.

"It was bad timing. I appreciate how hard you tried." He wanted to touch her again, but the way she was curled up was a clear warning to stay away. "Want to tell me about him?"

"Uh," Roxie looked around her bedroom. She sighed. "Maybe a little, okay?"

"As much or as little as you want."

She nodded at him, then gave him a fully unexpected smile. "You're very good at this," she said.

He wasn't sure what she meant by that.

"You know, with dogs and with people. You're real gentle about it, but you don't mess around—you get right to the heart of things."

"Thanks—I think," he said with a laugh. Eli felt

that old familiar stab of guilt in his gut—if his fierce attraction to Roxie was any indication, he'd have a hell of a time with the gentle part of the equation. And then what would she do? Would it be a repeat of Tamara? Of college?

She studied Eli for just a moment, her face becoming serious. "You look worried, but he never hurt me physically, if that's what you're thinking. Well, not until he knocked the door into my head." She gave a quick rub to her scalp and sighed before she continued. "He was almost thirty years older than me, a very handsome and powerful lawyer I met while covering a big murder trial."

Eli nodded, glad she'd misinterpreted his worry.

"He's a high-profile defense attorney. A legend in this city, really. He hardly ever loses a case."

"I see," Eli said, not indicating he'd already heard part of this from Teeny and Rick.

"I got totally sucked in. I was hypnotized by how brilliant he was and how sophisticated he seemed and all the important people he knew. He took me to A-list parties and the best restaurants and got front-row seats to everything. I know now it was all an illusion, but he made me feel safe. I thought he adored me." At that point, Roxie's eyes met his, and they were swimming with tears. "The girls—Bea, Ginger, and Josie—they warned me. They told me he was too old for me and he couldn't be trusted and that I'd let my father-figure complex get in the way, but I told them they were wrong, that this was the real deal."

Eli smiled sadly. "We can all get carried away sometimes. The combination of physical attraction and wishful thinking can be particularly deadly."

Roxie bit her lip. "You're damn right about that. The physical thing was very, uh, you know . . ."

"I can guess," Eli assured her.

"Look, I knew at the time that he could be an asshole. I saw how he was with people he didn't like or who he couldn't use to his advantage. But there was something about him that hooked me and reeled me in."

She looked away uncomfortably. "I was downright *high* on wishful thinking, you know? I just wanted it so badly. I wanted him so badly. I wanted to be loved and be a part of something special." She swiped at a single tear that had managed to drop to her cheek.

"So what happened?" Eli wanted to hear it from her.

She shrugged. "Josie and I had this great idea to pop in on him while he was out with his cronies. We walked into the cigar club where he hangs out, and strolled up to his table while he was talking—about me." She closed her eyes. "He was telling his friends about how he prefers his women young and stupid. He called me a 'pack mule,' saying he loved the way he could just keep piling the bullshit on me and I'd keep coming back for more. Then he said . . . he said—"

"You don't have to tell me if you don't want, Roxanne." Eli reached out then, and placed his hand on her knee. "You can stop whenever you want to."

She shrugged, then plowed ahead. "He said, 'that girl I'm with now, that reporter chick, if she could give a decent blow job she'd be perfect.'"

Roxanne's eyes shot toward Eli, as if challenging him to come up with a gentle yet pithy response to *that*. No way was he even going to try. He stayed silent.

She continued. "So I reached over his shoulder and grabbed his cigar—which was lit, by the way—and started grinding it into the big-ass bald spot on his head."

Eli shivered, remembering Rick's claim that the whole place smelled like burning flesh.

"That's when I started the Web site," she said, perking up dramatically. "I started it because I needed to vent. I needed to tell the world about my experience. At first, I was sure I was the only woman who'd ever been through something so horrible—but guess what? I'm not! Women like me are everywhere!" Roxie's arms flew up over her head. Lilith popped up from her sleep and rested her snout on the edge of the bed, keeping a wary eye on her mistress.

Roxie noticed, and stopped herself in mid-rant. She took a deep, ragged breath and reached out to pat her dog calmly. "It's okay, Lily Girl," she reassured her. The dog sat on her haunches, tail wagging.

"Anyway," Roxie continued. "Women started writing in from all over. Their stories blew me away. I posted them. And the thing just grew and grew." Roxanne swiveled her head back and forth, cracking her neck.

Eli leaned back against the pillows of Roxie's bed, thinking that this girl needed a masseuse as much as she needed a dog whisperer. He smiled to himself. Lucky for her, he was skilled at both.

"Can I ask you something?" he asked her.

"Of course."

"All this venting on the Web site. Your Jerk-of-the-Week award. All the blogging you do about your horrible ex-boyfriend. Has any of it helped?"

Roxie looked puzzled. "You know about my Jerk-of-the-Week contest?"

Eli grinned. "I have a computer, too, Ms. Bloom."

She laughed.

"So?" he asked again. "Has it helped?"

"Helped what?"

"You," Eli said, sitting up straighter. "Has it helped you to heal? Has it helped you feel happier? Brought you any peace?"

She choked in surprise. Her lips parted and she stared at him. "Hell yes, it has," she said, as if he'd missed the point entirely. "I've got steady income. I have a reason to get up in the morning. I have something to be passionate about."

Eli smiled.

"What?" she asked. "Why are you looking at me like that?"

He reached out for one of her hands and waited until she slipped it into his palm. He held it softly. "I wondered if it might be the opposite."

She frowned.

"Have you ever considered that being the ambassador of angry women might make things worse for you on a personal level?"

"It makes things better," she said with a crisp nod of her head. "I should know."

Eli let that settle for a moment, and he had an idea. "Out of curiosity, have you taken a break since you started your Web site, just stepped back for a few days?"

"I couldn't possibly."

"You could leave a message saying the site is down for a week while you're on vacation."

"No."

"Everyone takes vacations."

"I don't."

Eli realized that a grin had begun to spread across his face. His gaze wandered to Lilith and then back to Roxie. "Would you consider it?"

Both her eyebrows were raised now.

"Would you consider taking a road trip? You, me, and Lilith?"

Roxanne blinked. "Are you serious?"

"Yes."

"But . . ." Roxie laughed. It was a real laugh, deep and loose. "You only just *met* me! We don't even know each other. That would be totally nuts!"

He chuckled. Yes, it would be. Eli held up the questionnaire. "I know a whole lot about you, Roxie Bloom," he reminded her. "And by the time we got back, you'd know everything there was to know about me. We'd be even."

She lowered her chin, leveling her gaze on him. "Where did you have in mind?"

"Ever been to Panguitch, Utah?"

"What the hell is that and why would I want to go there?"

Eli laughed. "It's my home. My ranch."

Her lips parted.

"I've got one thing I need to take care of in town tomorrow—plus I'll need to swing by the doctor's and get stitched up, but then I'm free. How does early Friday morning sound? We'll be at the ranch by supper time."

She stared at him blankly.

"C'mon!" he said. "When's the last time you went on a road trip? A wind-in-your-hair, music-blaring kind of road trip?"

"It's been a while," she said.

"So how about it?"

She tapped her fingertips on her lips, weighing the offer.

"Just think—no harassing phone calls from your ex. A few days away from the city and the Web site. Nothing to do but work with Lilith and relax and build your pack leader skills. And when we come back, we'll go to the hearing and kick some ass."

That last bit must have hit a nerve, because Roxie

looked at him and nodded. "I guess it wouldn't kill me," she said.

He stretched up and placed a kiss on her cheek, smiling to himself. From what he'd seen of Roxanne Bloom, that response had been downright enthusiastic.

Eli closed his eyes for a moment, keeping his face hidden in her hair as he wrestled with the weight of what he'd just done.

That instant—as the sip of forty-year-old Glenfiddich merged with the CAO Gold's creamy smoke at the back of his throat—that was Raymond's version of a religious experience. The walls of the Havana Club formed his church. Blended Scotch was his altar wine and cigar smoke his incense. Raymond's disciples were gathered at his table, enjoying the tale of how his ex-girlfriend's attack dog had gone for his throat, and how he planned to eviscerate her in a court of law.

"A bitch with a bitch," said one of his buddies, to much hearty laughter.

Ah, yes. A bitch with a bitch. *Dos biatches.* It amused him, really. Poor little pathetic Roxanne. She had to go out and get herself an ugly, vicious bitch-dog to keep her company after he dropped her ass. She must have needed something to keep her warm at night that could also double as the mascot for her castrating Web site. Raymond took another puff of his CAO Gold, then twirled it in his fingers, mesmerized by the series of perfectly round smoke rings he'd just produced.

She'd been such a fresh-faced go-getter when he first met her, wide-eyed and in awe of him. Raymond couldn't help but smile as he remembered. Those were truly satisfying days. She would come when he called. She would drop everything when he had a few hours to spare. He had the girl on a schedule, for Christ's sake! If she wasn't in his bed, Roxanne would call him when she woke in the morning and when she went to sleep at night. She relied on him to advise her, comfort her, guide her, and fuck the hell out of her.

Raymond knew that for good or ill, relationships were like litigation—you found the hole in your opponent's case, and you went in for the kill. And like a whole lot of fucked-up young women these days, Roxie Bloom was looking for a daddy, whether she realized it or not. So that's what Raymond gave her—a mean ole daddy she could worship.

It wasn't his fault that he was more than she could handle.

"I saw your new assistant," said one of his disciples. "She's got a hell of a booty on her."

"I'd do her," said someone else.

Raymond chuckled.

"How long is it going to take you to start tapping that ass?" someone else asked.

Raymond took another sip of golden nectar, swirling it around in his mouth. "Already tapped and flowing, gentlemen," he told them, to a burst of appreciative laughter.

He smiled to himself, thinking he might hurry things along with Ricky. Maybe it was time for a late night at the office with some Chinese takeout. He'd let her think she'd made a real contribution, then he'd let her suck him off.

"Damn, I wish I were you, Sandberg," said one of his disciples.

Raymond raised his glass to that.

Chapter 10

Eli entered the revolving door of the downtown skyscraper, glad there weren't many more of these meetings ahead of him. He'd survived ten of them in the last ten months. That meant that he'd reminisced with ten middle-aged men about their years at Berkeley. He'd cautiously asked ten men whether they remembered a pretty yellow-haired anthropology major named Carole Tisdale. Then he'd talked ten men into giving a sample of their DNA to a diagnostics lab and waited, sometimes for weeks, for the results.

Each time there was no match. And Eli was downtown that day to find out about number eleven, a guy who ran a real estate leasing company. Milt Horvath was fifty-three, on his second wife, with three grown children. His hobbies included cruises to Hawaii and golf at least twice a week. That's how Eli had originally cornered him—in the parking lot of the Union League Golf and Country Club. It had been one of his more blatant stakeouts.

"Mr. Horvath," he'd said, as the man unlocked the trunk of his BMW and stored his clubs.

"Yes?" He sat down on the fender of his car to remove his golf shoes. "Can I help you?"

Eli broached the subject gently. The guy looked at him with shock and wonder as Eli explained why he'd tracked him down. Then the man shook his head as if to clear his mind. "Sure I remember her," he said. "I always wondered what happened to her—she just disappeared."

Eli filled in the blanks for him. Carole Tisdale had moved back home to Denver to have the baby; she'd gone back to school, where she'd met a great guy named Robert Gallagher. Eli had assumed Bob was his biological father until his death last year, when he'd discovered otherwise.

Milt Horvath looked up at Eli for a moment, quite serious, then slammed the trunk door before he turned to him. "That sounds tough," the man had asked. "You're, what, thirty-two? Why didn't they ever tell you?"

Eli gave Milt Horvath the same antiseptic story he'd told the others: his parents didn't want to upset him when he was younger, then believed it was pointless to bring the subject up once he was an adult. He'd told Milt that with his mother's help, he'd narrowed it down to a dozen possibilities. Two of the men had moved to other areas of the country—New York and Atlanta—and Eli went there first. Then he moved to Northern California to find, contact, and get lab results for all the rest. If Milt wasn't a match, he told him, there was just one more possibility.

Of course Eli left out the more personal details. Like how he'd been so furious at his mother that he hadn't spoken to her for six months, not even during the funeral. How he'd become obsessed with filling in the blank of his origins. Who was he? He needed to know. What kind of man was his real father? What parts of him had Eli inherited?

Milt Horvath listened patiently, studying Eli's face with intensity. He gave Eli his card and Eli handed him the packet containing everything he'd need to complete the DNA test. When they agreed to meet again to review the lab results, Milt looked melancholy.

"You seem like an exceptional young man," he'd told Eli, placing a hand on his shoulder. "There's one thing I want to ask you to do for me."

"Sure," Eli said.

"Don't think too harshly of your mother. We were kids. I'm not saying that Berkeley was any more wild back then than it is today, but those were the days before a one-night stand could kill you outright. We didn't see things the same."

Eli nodded. He'd heard the same excuse from a few other men, though they were usually asking Eli not to judge *them,* not his mother.

"It was nice to meet you, Eli," Milt had said, getting in his car and driving away from the country club lot.

That had been three weeks ago, and now Eli was taking the elevator up to the twenty-first floor to meet with Mr. Horvath, who'd received the results several days before.

Eli went to a reception desk and waited for only a few minutes before Milt came out to greet him. He ushered him into his large, tasteful office and had him take a seat near him at a grouping of comfortable chairs.

"Shall we?" he asked, holding up the FedEx envelope. "Would you like to do the honors?"

"Sure," Eli said, pulling at the envelope's tear strip. He reached in and slipped out the results. The findings weren't exactly a shock. Eli handed the paper over to Milt, saying, "Looks like you're off the hook."

He watched Milt read and reread the test results, then sigh deeply. "I'm sorry, Eli," he said.

"No problem. I appreciate your willingness to do this," he said, standing.

Milt put out his hand. "If there's anything else I can do for you, you just let me know." He shook his head and laughed. "You know, while we were waiting for these results I started thinking back to when I knew your mom. It was, uh, you know, pretty crazy. Things got a little out of hand sometimes." Milt looked down at his shoes, embarrassed. "I hadn't thought of all that in a long, long time."

Eli cocked his head. "How do you mean?" None of his mother's accounts painted her as a saint, obviously, but nothing she'd described sounded "crazy" or "out of hand," words Milt had just used.

"Oh." Milt shifted his weight and shrugged. "I only meant that I'd been with your mother a couple times. She and a bunch of her girlfriends came around the off-campus hole in the wall where I worked as a part-time disc jockey." Milt laughed. "And I'm talking right at the peak of disco. Polyester wide-collar shirts and gold chains and the whole bit. Jesus, it's funny to look back on that now."

"So what happened with my mother?" Eli asked, suddenly uncomfortable.

Milt cleared his throat. "Nothing terrible. It's just that I'm not very proud of myself for my behavior back then, that's all I'm saying." He pasted a smile on his face and extended his hand again. "It was a pleasure. I wish you the best of luck in sorting all this out."

Eli nodded, knowing two things: Milt Horvath wasn't telling him the whole story and Eli had just been told to get the hell out.

"Thank you," Eli said, ending the handshake. He headed for the office door. "I'll be out of town for a week or so. If you should think of anything else I might need to know, please call."

Eli decided to glance behind him. Milt's expression had frozen. His mouth was still smiling, but his eyes sure weren't.

"Unless you want to tell me now," Eli offered.

"No, no, it's nothing," Milt said, laughing it off. "Just tell your mother that Milt-in-Your-Mouth sends his regards."

Eli lowered his jaw and blinked. "Right," he said.

On the elevator ride down to the parking garage, Eli calmed himself by noting he had just one more of these god-awful errands to run. One more possibility. One more guerrilla meet-and-greet. One more sales pitch. One last lab test.

As Eli reached his truck he made himself a promise. Even if suspect number twelve wasn't a match, he was done looking. That would be it. He'd given this his best shot, but it would have to be over. He'd survived three decades without knowing the identity of his biological father, and he could survive a few more.

Milt-in-Your-Mouth?

There was only so much of this shit a man could take.

Five hours into the drive, Roxie looked over at Eli's golden-boy profile and it hit her—this thing between them wasn't fading. It was only getting stronger. It felt right to be with Eli Gallagher. She felt calmer in his presence. And the peacefulness had nearly lulled her usually pragmatic mind to sleep.

She'd almost forgotten that she hated men. That she didn't trust them. She'd nearly forgotten the sacred promise she'd made to herself—she would never again be the kind of girl who got lied to, used, and disrespected. No more stupid moves. No way. No how. Not her.

Roxie took another quick peek at Eli and frowned. He did have quite a few redeeming qualities, no question, but that didn't change the fact that she was taking a whopping risk, putting herself in this position. She was in a strange man's truck, on a deserted highway, headed to the strange man's remote Utah compound, where God only knew what she'd encounter. Some kind of dog whispering religious cult? A survivalist fringe group? A polygamist's paradise? She was headed to *Utah,* for crying out loud. Willingly. And with a man she hardly knew!

Roxie stroked Lilith's fur, thinking this through. She'd never been to Utah. She'd never had any desire to go to Utah. There had to be a reason for that. Maybe she should insist Eli turn right around and take her back to the city, where she belonged.

God, what am I doing?

Roxie concentrated really hard, willing her heartbeat to steady, her breath to slow. It didn't work. In her mind she pictured events as they might unfold a few years on. A lone hiker on a nearly inaccessible Utah trail would stumble upon a partially decomposed body in a shallow grave . . . dental records would finally solve the mystery of whatever happened to missing San Francisco blogger Roxanne Bloom . . . and people would shake their heads and say, what a pity . . . the girl had been an idiot to put herself in such peril . . . she should have known better . . . the girl had been too stupid to live . . .

"What are you thinking over there?" Eli asked, shooting a clean and sweet smile in her direction.

"Huh? Uh, nothing. Just thinking how relaxing all this is."

"Yeah?" Eli asked, laughing. "I thought maybe you

were sittin' over there trying to convince yourself I'm not a psycho killer."

Roxie laughed, a little too frantically, she knew, but by then it was too late to do anything about it. She continued to stroke Lilith's fur and stare out the window.

Speaking of being pragmatic, Roxie had to acknowledge that this wasn't exactly her idea of a fun time. She was windblown and sweaty. And she didn't much care for the country music coming out of Eli's sound system, even if it was the cultural icon variety. Truth was, she'd never been attracted to men who wore cowboy hats and Wrangler jeans and listened to Johnny Cash while driving their trucks down deserted highways. She'd always preferred the cool, sexy, intellectual types who wore gray flannel and drove their sports cars along city streets while listening to vintage Pearl Jam or Public Image Limited. In addition to all that, Roxie's jeans were now covered in dog hair and silvery streaks of Lilith drool. As a bonus, she had to pee like Secretariat.

"Would you be up for stopping for lunch in Baker? It's another half hour or so. It's my usual watering hole."

"That sounds perfect," she said.

"If Lilith is crowding you, you can scoot over here a little and let her have the spot next to the window. I think she wants to let her head hang all the way out."

"Oh. Sure."

As she rearranged Lilith and edged closer to Eli, Roxie felt a shiver go through her. This whole situation was embarrassing. Confusing. Miraculous. And boy, was it ever *different*.

The macho-man pack leader routine aside, Eli had been nothing but a gentleman. When he left her house the other night, he left behind a dog with a wagging tail and a woman with her honor intact. Eli had patted Lilith affectionately and kissed Roxie softly. He'd promised to call her the next day. And he actually had. During the call he suggested what she should pack and promised to pick her up at six A.M. He'd been right on time. It was truly unusual.

And now, five hours into the trip, Roxanne was stunned to realize that they'd talked and laughed most of the way from San Francisco to close to the Nevada border, covering everything from favorite movies and food to the collapse of American journalism, politics, music, and travel. And despite her occasional worries about cults and shallow graves, Roxie had felt herself unwinding with each passing mile, inching closer to reaching an understanding with herself. Maybe this hadn't been a stupid call, after all.

Roxie grinned at Lilith, happy that her girl was discovering the joy of hanging her head out the window of a moving vehicle, just like a normal dog, her ears flying back and her eyes half closed in ecstasy.

Maybe her decision to come with Eli to Utah would turn out to be the smartest thing she'd ever done.

Bea had certainly thought so. "That's awesome!" she'd cried, nearly jumping with glee as she'd hugged Roxie. "You're going to have a wonderful time—I just know it."

Ginger had been supportive, as well. "Good for you," she'd said. "Relax and enjoy. You deserve to have some fun."

On the phone, Josie squealed with delight at the news.

But Bea also mentioned that Mrs. Needleman had had a minor stroke and was in the hospital. And Josie confessed that her doctor had ordered bed rest for the last couple weeks of pregnancy. Then Ginger had informed Roxanne that her baby's head had dropped, a development Roxanne didn't quite understand, nor did she want to. All she knew was it couldn't be good.

After hearing all that, Roxanne decided the time wasn't right for her to leave town.

"We'll all survive a few days without your supervision, I guarantee it," Bea had said. "Besides, I'll strangle you with my bare hands if you don't go."

"We're here," Eli said, slowing the truck and pulling into the Baker Town Diner parking lot. "I'll take Lilith for a stroll if you want to freshen up before we eat."

Roxanne nearly ran to the ladies' room. When she came out, Lilith was content under the shade of the front porch, lapping at a bowl of water. Remarkably, the dog barely seemed to notice the three men who strolled out of the diner just a few feet from her bowl, which shocked Roxanne, seeing that her dog's usual reaction would have been snarling, barking, and a display of fangs.

"It's a miracle," Roxie said, striding up to Eli. She noticed he wasn't even holding her leash.

"No, just simple communication," he said, glancing from the dog to Roxie's face. "I show her how it is. She knows it's in her best interest to follow the program."

"Because she feels safe? Because it makes her happy?" Roxie looked up into Eli's smoky green eyes when she asked her questions.

"You've been paying attention, Roxie Bloom."

Over a lunch of barbecue sandwiches and homemade potato chips, Eli dropped the bomb. "I've got eight dogs at the ranch," he told Roxanne, wiping his mouth with a napkin. "We'll introduce Lilith to a couple at a time. There's only one who might give her a hard time."

"Excuse me?" Roxanne stared at him in disbelief. "You're going to force her to deal with eight strange dogs in a strange environment? She'll go ballistic!"

Eli smiled. "Let's give her a chance to show us what she's made of, okay?"

Roxanne had barely recovered from that news when,

as an afterthought, Eli mentioned that his mother and sister would be stopping by.

Roxie fell back against the vinyl booth and let her chin fall toward her chest. "You're taking me to meet your *family*?"

Eli laughed. He tilted his head back and Roxie watched in wonder as his whole handsome face relaxed into happiness. Hot desire swept through her. She wanted him. She wanted to get her lips and hands all over that man, all over his flesh and his happiness. She wanted to wrap herself up in him, pull up to the pump of everything good and wonderful that was Eli Gallagher.

"*Damn,*" she breathed.

Roxanne hadn't wanted any man since Raymond. She hadn't dared. Only Eli. She'd wanted him since the second she laid eyes on him all those months ago and she still wanted him, right here at this diner in the middle of nowhere.

She wanted Eli Gallagher with a fierce and bright longing that wiped out her memory of every other man she'd ever given herself to. Even Raymond was reduced to a shadow in Eli's light. Eli made Raymond seem like a cheap imitation. Her head was spinning with the heat of her thoughts. The way she sat in the booth suddenly felt unbearable. Her underwear felt too tight. Then it felt too loose. She began to fidget.

"My sister Sondra only lives about a half hour away and she's been taking care of my place while I'm in California," Eli was saying. Roxanne had to force herself to pay attention. "My mom lives in Cedar City, but she wants to come up and make dinner for us tonight."

Roxanne took a sip of her iced tea and tried to pull herself together. She worried she wouldn't be able to hide her interest in Eli from his mother and sister. How could she play it cool when this man made her so *hot*?

"Are you okay over there?" Eli asked, a grin on his face.

"Fine. So . . ." She paused, smiling. "Do they know you've got a woman and her psycho dog in tow?"

"They do."

"What have you told them about me?"

Eli reached over the table and held out his hand palm up. She slipped her hand into his, the soothing warmth of his touch moving into her center. Like always.

"I've told them the truth—that you are a client and a woman I want to get to know much, much better."

Roxanne managed to take a deep breath. "So I'm a client and a potential . . . uh . . . well . . . ?"

"Whatever you want to call it is fine with me," Eli said. "A woman I'd like to start dating. A potential girl-friend. A friend who happens to be a girl." Eli unleashed a grin so sly and sexy that Roxie feared she'd slide off her booth.

"Girlfriend?"

"That's how I see it." Eli raised one of his eyebrows. "How about you? How do you see it?"

Roxanne went very still. She removed her hand from his. Technically, there was nothing wrong with his description of what they were doing, but she didn't know that she wanted to be anyone's girlfriend. Ever again. Plus, she needed clarification on a few things. Immediately.

"Have you ever felt that way about a client before?" she asked.

"Never," he said.

"Do you kiss all your clients?"

He shook his head. "No. Just you."

"Not even Jennifer Aniston?"

"Nope."

"Do you stretch out on the bed of all your clients?"

"Pretty much," he answered, the corners of his mouth turning up in delight.

"Aha!" Roxie felt smug. "So everybody gets in the bed and snuggles with you?"

"No and no. You were the first one invited to join me for a snuggle."

"Have you ever brought a client to your ranch?"

"Hell, no," he said, chuckling. "In fact, I do my best to keep my address out of the public domain. That's one of the benefits of using a P.O. box in town."

She felt herself smile. This was just the kind of clarification she needed.

"I can't get enough of that smile, Roxie," he said.

She felt her cheeks redden. This thing was going really fast. In a few hours she'd be in Eli's home, with his family and his eight freakin' dogs! But something didn't feel right, and she remembered what her city editor used to tell her—if she felt uncomfortable turning in a story, it meant she had more reporting to do, more information to get.

"I have to know everything about you," she whispered.

"I'll tell you anything you want to know," he said.

She sat up straight, suddenly inspired. "Would you fill out one of your own questionnaires for me?"

Eli roared with laughter. "You drive a hard bargain, Roxie Bloom."

"So you'll do it?"

"Absolutely."

Roxie nodded, relieved. "All right, then," she said, relaxing back into the booth, hands clasped in her lap. "But there's one thing I need to know right away."

"Have at it."

"Why did you turn me down for lunch?" Roxie said. "I think I'm ready for that explanation now."

Eli nodded. He reached for his wallet and placed a twenty on top of the check. He stood, offering his hand to Roxanne and helped her from her seat. "We've got a seven-hour drive ahead of us. That'll be just enough time for an explanation."

She laughed at what was obviously a joke.

"But only if I talk real fast."

Carole hopped out of the front seat of her ancient Ford F-150 to unlatch the gate and smiled. She did that every time she drove up this dirt road and looked out at the endless sparse beauty framed by desert mountains. Eli had managed to carve out a little piece of hallelujah for himself here, and she was proud of her son.

She hopped back in the truck and continued on, marveling at the sight of her boy's log home as it appeared above the rise in the lane, behind the stand of towering cedars. The simple elegance of the structure still surprised her, even after five years. That Eli had paid for this place by using his God-given talent to help the world—that was plenty. But knowing her son had designed and then helped build the house with his own hands always made her shake her head in wonder. Eli was something special. Her son was one of a kind. He always had been.

God, how she wished she'd done things differently with him. She had let her own fear—her own vanity— outweigh the truth. Eli had a right to know Bob wasn't his biological father, and he'd had a right to be told as much early in his life, so he could ponder it and settle it in his own mind. Sure, Eli would have been angry if they'd told him when he was twelve, the way Bob wanted. But it wouldn't have been anything compared to the rage of a thirty-one-year-old man who was convinced his parents had betrayed him.

As Carole arrived at the end of the lane and parked near the wide front porch, she closed her eyes for an instant to say her usual prayer: *Please, God, help Eli take another step toward forgiveness today, and have mercy on me for all my mistakes. Amen.*

She took the keys from the ignition and let her thoughts return to the one question she'd been mulling over during the whole drive from Cedar City. Why in the world had Eli decided to bring a client home to the ranch? Who was she? And why now? Carole didn't pry into the details of her son's life, but she knew he'd not been in a relationship since his breakup with Tamara eighteen months before.

When Eli first told Carole he'd be spending a year in California to find his dad, she nearly lost her mind with worry. What good could possibly come of this? What if his father didn't want anything to do with Eli? What if his father was a scoundrel? A weak man? An evil man?

But if there was anything positive to come of his foolishness, Carole knew it was the boost it could give to Eli's love life. After all, there were more eligible females in one block of San Francisco than in the entire five thousand square miles of Garfield County, Utah. True, Eli had often reminded her that his plan was to find his biological father, not a girlfriend, but still, she could hope.

Simply put, Carole was baffled. Who could have caught his eye, she wondered, and what kind of woman could make him cross that line between his business and his personal life? He'd never done it before, and his clients had included beautiful movie stars, recording artists, and even a model or two. The woman he was bringing home today had to be someone extraordinary.

Carole smiled as Sondra clomped down the porch steps to greet her. Her daughter's short brown curls looked as wild as usual, and her sun-pink face just as cheerful. Sondra was the spitting image of her Bob—solid and freckled, and with the palest of blue eyes.

She looked nothing like her brother, of course. Even as young children, when Sondra and Eli sat side by side, it was obvious to everyone that Bob Gallagher was father to one but not the other. *Was I more concerned about myself than my child? How could I have been so selfish?*

"Mom!" her daughter called out, arms outstretched. They pulled each other tight, and Carole was happy to feel Sondra's warm welcome, even though it was cut short by the arrival of "the horde," what she called Eli's collection of eight stray dogs plus Sondra's chocolate Lab. Carole pulled away from her daughter's hug to look down at the group and laugh.

There were a couple of real cuties in the bunch. Gizmo, the regal shepherd mix, and the silly little terrier mutt were Carole's favorites. The rest were ugly as the day was long, creatures only a dog whisperer could love. But every single one of them was perfectly behaved. Calm. Respectful. Friendly. Every time she visited she was greeted with the same vision—a pack of assorted dogs with their butts planted on the ground, their tails fanning the dirt, and their eyes filled with enthusiasm. Carole took a moment to pat each on the head in greeting.

"Do you know anything about this chick Eli is bringing home?" Sondra asked, suddenly frowning. "Did he tell you anything?"

"No. I was hoping you'd have details."

"Me?" Sondra waved her away and opened the passenger side of the truck, pulling out the large insulated casserole carrier. "Are you kidding? Eli never tells me anything juicy. He avoids all talk of romance with me.

I think he doesn't want to stir anything up—he hates to hear me cry." Sondra unzipped the carrier so she could sniff at dinner.

"Careful, that's probably still warm." Carole's heart sank for her girl. It was a shame that a whole year had passed since Sondra's divorce and she still couldn't move on. As her mother, Carole would have given anything to see Sondra get back out there, going to a movie or grabbing an occasional dinner with a handsome young man. It didn't have to be true love. It didn't even have to be serious. She only wished Sondra could relax and have some fun.

But who was Carole to judge? Her own Bob had been loyal and true, and she'd been spared the kind of heartache Sondra had endured. How was a woman supposed to recover from that kind of thing, anyway? One day you think you have a sweet and loving husband and the next day you discover he's a serial cheater with women lined up in several states. Carole knew it would take Sondra a long time to heal from that hurt, if she ever did.

Sondra lowered her nose close to the glass lid on the carne asada with green chiles. "God, that smells good, Mommy. I've been fantasizing about this all day."

Carole smiled and placed a hand on Sondra's back as they walked up the steps, across the pine-plank porch, and through the twelve-foot-high front doorway. The dogs followed them as far as the door, but didn't cross the threshold without being invited.

"Eli and Madame X won't be here for hours, so I'll stick this in the fridge." Sondra spoke over her shoulder as she headed into the large, open kitchen. "I can't figure out why they decided to drive—twelve hours is quite a chunk of time to spend trapped in a truck with someone you hardly know."

Carole had considered that, too. "Exactly how long has he known this girl?" she asked.

Sondra shrugged. "From what I understand, she's a brand-new client. It's the girl who begged him to go back to San Francisco on Monday, when he was already halfway home."

"What in the world . . . ?" Carole stopped and leaned her elbows on the large center island of Eli's kitchen, trying to let that information sink in. "He's known her for a matter of days and he's bringing her *here*? That doesn't sound like Eli."

Sondra snickered, pouring both of them a glass of white wine. "Yeah. He's not exactly the most spontaneous dude in the world, is he?"

"No," Carole said without hesitation.

"I hope to hell Tamara never hears about this," Sondra said, shaking her head.

Carole sighed. After waiting more than three years for Eli to commit, Tamara apparently gave up on him, leaving Eli and Utah for Seattle. The last she heard, Tamara was engaged, which is what she'd wanted all along. She'd been a fine girl, and Carole never really understood why their relationship had ended so suddenly. She and Sondra assumed that Tamara was simply sick of waiting.

"What in heaven's name is that boy up to?" Carole wondered aloud.

Sondra laughed. "I asked him about that. I said, 'Eli, you spend half your time hiding from fan-girls. Are you sure you want to bring a stranger to your home?' "

Carole popped upright. "And what did he say?"

"He said he's got it under control."

Carole nodded, admitting he probably did. Eli always seemed to have it under control. In fact, the only time she'd ever seen him lose his cool was when Bob died and he discovered those damn adoption papers. True, Eli's whole career was showing other people how to remain calm, but she'd love to see him let his hair down once in a while.

"And . . ." Sondra sipped her wine and wiggled an eyebrow. "I asked Eli if I should make up the guest room."

"You did not!"

"I sure did."

"That's pretty darn nosy of you."

Sondra shrugged off her mother's comment. "So did you have a nice drive?" she asked, walking into the living room and plopping onto one of the soft leather armchairs. "Is there still construction on I-15?"

Carole knew when she was being tortured. She played along, bringing her wine into the room to join her daughter. After a refreshing sip, she stretched out her legs and admired the high vaulted ceiling, then gazed out the west-facing wall of windows to the mountains. There would be a dramatic light show at sunset, like most evenings.

Carole stayed silent for as long as humanly possible, hoping she could contain her curiosity longer than Sondra could stand the silence. Eventually, she surrendered. "Well? *Are* you?" Carole asked.

"Am I what?" Sondra inquired, looking perfectly innocent.

Carole laughed. "Lord, but you are hard on your old mother. Are you making up the guest room or not?"

"Oh, that." Sondra set her wine glass down and folded her hands in her lap. "Eli told me not to bother."

Carole sat back into the deep chair, stunned. She stared at Sondra a moment.

"Oh, my God," she said.

Chapter 11

Roxie had been so riveted by Eli's tale that she hadn't moved, and the legs she'd tucked beneath her body hours before had fallen asleep. She shifted her weight in the front seat of the truck and stretched out, willing the blood to start circulating. Only then did she notice that the quality of the light had changed, leaving shadows on the endless dry and flat landscape around them.

"I've bored you to death," Eli said, reaching for his bottle of water. "They should rename this area Bored to Death Valley."

Roxanne chuckled, grabbing the bottle before Eli could, twisting off the cap for him. "Here you go."

Eli looked sideways at her, the corners of his eyes wrinkling with a smile behind his dark aviator sunglasses. He nodded his thanks and held the bottle up, as if drinking in her honor.

Roxanne studied him for a slow, suspended moment as the afternoon light gilded his hair and skin. He was a beautiful man. There was no doubt about it. She considered how his strong jaw moved as he gulped, the up-and-down bobbing of his Adam's apple, how starkly white the gauze bandages were against his tanned skin. She winced.

"Everything okay?" Eli asked.

Roxie shook her head. "No, Eli. I'm sick that Lilith did that to you. Does your arm hurt? Are the stitches itchy?"

Eli shrugged. "Not so bad. They're the self-dissolving kind. I should be as good as new in a week or two."

Roxie continued staring at the bandages, her heart sinking. "I sincerely apologize for my dog trying to eat you alive," she said.

Eli laughed, then reached over to brush a section of wind-whipped hair from Roxie's face. She felt herself lean into his touch. "And what about you, Roxie? You did pretty much the same thing, you know," he said, letting his fingers trail down the side of her neck.

She nodded, figuring what he said was true. She remembered how pissed she'd been the day of the baby shower, when Eli followed her out to the paddock. She'd bitten the man's head off. Obviously, she'd lashed out at him because she was embarrassed to be caught in a moment of self-pity. Plus it angered her that she continued to feel such an attraction to Eli when she'd been trying desperately to forget all about him. And clearly she'd still been stinging from his rejection all those months before. It seemed so simple now, so easy to put together. But a week ago, Roxanne couldn't have admitted those things to herself if her life depended on it. A lot had changed since then, she realized.

"At least I didn't sink my fangs into your forearm," she said.

"True," Eli said. "You went right for the jugular."

Roxie scrunched up her face. "It wasn't all that bad."

Eli took another swig of water and returned the

bottle to the cup holder. "Well, you told me you didn't much care for cowboys. Then you told me I'd blown my one chance with you."

"But that was before I knew about . . . everything," she said.

Roxanne let her head fall against the seat back, staring straight ahead through the windshield at the flat ribbon of road. Eli had just spent the last few hours telling her about how he'd learned his father wasn't really his father, how it had made him question everything he'd assumed about himself, his family. He'd told her how he'd come to California to find his real dad, and the string of disappointments he'd faced. He'd explained that he'd turned Roxie down because he didn't want to start something he had no intention of finishing. But when he got her phone call asking for help with Lilith, he knew there would be no more denying his attraction for her.

"And now?" Eli asked, shooting her another smile. "How do you feel now? You gonna give this cowboy another chance, Miss Bloom?"

She sighed, mostly at her own foolishness. "That's what this is," she said, surprising herself with the candor of her answer. "When I asked for your help, I told myself it was about Lilith. But it was about you, too. You and me. There were probably a few other people who could have helped with my dog, but there was only one person I couldn't get out of my head, and that was you." She looked sideways at Eli, giving him a sheepish smile. "And here we are."

Eli nodded gently. "I hope you never regret this decision."

Roxanne laughed. "You and me both," she said.

They drove for several moments without talking, but Roxanne knew, based on Eli's story, that they had something in common—absentee fathers—and she wanted to see how forthcoming Eli would be on his end.

"Are you angry at your real dad, whoever he is?"

Eli shrugged, keeping his eye on the road. "All the anger was directed toward my mother and father. I couldn't stop thinking how selfish they'd been, and how careless and stupid my mother had been when she was young. I came down really hard on her—you know, her lack of moral fiber and all that."

Roxie laughed. "Oh, yeah. I knew all about moral fiber when I was in college."

"Exactly." Eli turned toward her briefly and shot her one of his dazzling smiles, then moved his attention back to the road ahead. "But I eventually talked it out with my mom, and I made a decision not to be angry at this man who's my real father, whoever he is, because he doesn't even know I exist. My mother left Berkeley without a word to anyone about her predicament."

Roxie nodded. "But you were lucky to have Bob Gallagher as your dad."

"Definitely." Roxie watched a smile tug at the corner of Eli's mouth. "He may not have donated any of his genes to me but he gave me everything else of himself. His time, his love, his support." Eli quickly looked over the rim of his sunglasses to make eye contact with Roxie. "He taught me carpentry and ranching, and a respect for the natural world. But more than that, he taught me what being an honorable man looked like, every day of his life. Yeah, I was lucky."

Roxanne was humbled by that answer. She looked down at her hands, thinking she had no idea what it felt like to know, love, and respect your father.

"My dad left me when I was six," she said, turning away from Eli to look out the other window.

Eli nodded silently, waiting for her to go on with her story. But Roxie knew that wouldn't happen. She didn't talk about her dad. She never had.

"But I'm sure he didn't leave *you*," Eli said, his sentence ending with the lilt of uncertainty. "Right? I mean, his relationship with your mother fell apart and he left *her*. You got caught in the cross fire, the way children too often do."

"Sure. I guess you're right," she said, letting her head fall back against the seat. There was no point in correcting him. The truth was still too tender and raw to expose, even twenty-two years after the fact.

With a sigh, Roxie decided to change the direction of her thoughts and the course of the conversation. Something had been nagging at her brain the whole trip. Eli still had no intention of staying in California. One of the reasons he'd turned her down in the first place was still valid. Nothing had changed. So why were they even bothering to do the whole "get to know you" thing?

"I don't hate San Francisco, you know," Eli said, as if he knew where she wanted to take the conversation. "It's a beautiful city. I'd be happy to spend part of my time there."

Roxie swiveled her head to look at him, still leaning against the seat. "How big a part?"

"I don't know," he said, eyes on the road. "My home is in Utah. That's how I'll always feel. My home is a big part of who I am." He reached for her hand and squeezed it tight. "I hope once you see it, you'll understand."

"Is that why you're taking me there? So I'll fall in love with Utah?"

She watched him bite down on the inside of his cheek to subdue his grin. "Something like that," he said, squeezing her hand even tighter.

Her face opened in a wide smile. Right there on that seat, smack in the middle of nowhere, between a grinning Eli and a joyously windblown Lilith, Roxanne felt happiness sneak up on her. She laughed out loud at the strange sensation. It was as if a warm wave of relief had just washed over her, leaving a giddy tingle in its wake.

She was only nine hours and five hundred miles away from her world, and she suddenly felt free. She felt open to whatever might come her way. Her dog had obviously experienced a similar change of perspective. Lilith took playful gulps of wind as her ears flapped around and her tail wagged nonstop. What a remarkable transformation—for both of them. It was the weirdest thing.

Eli was the reason. The man holding her hand was responsible for bringing them this far. Roxie figured she might as well trust him to lead the rest of the way.

When she closed her eyes, the image of Mrs. Needleman flashed before Roxanne's eyes, standing there with her fists on her hips and her feet splayed wide, a white-denture smile on her face.

She took the opportunity to make a silent plea to God or Mrs. Needleman—whoever was in charge of things these days.

This time, let it be more than wishful thinking.

"You've got to hold on a little longer," Bea said, rubbing the T-shirt stretched tightly over Josie's belly. "Squeeze your thighs together or something. Just don't shoot that puppy out until next week, okay?"

"For God's sake, Bea! You can't control when you go into labor!" Ginger made that observation from her half-reclining position on the bedroom love seat, looking just as round as Josie.

"You can't?" Bea asked, baffled.

"Please! Stop talking about me like I'm not here! I'm pregnant, not deaf!" Josie hoisted herself up on her stack of pillows, then threw one of them at Bea's head.

"No need to lash out, my pet." Bea calmly retrieved the pillow from its landing place on the Oriental rug in Josie's bedroom. She then dutifully rearranged the pile to Josie's satisfaction before she returned to her chair.

"You don't have any idea what this feels like," Ginger said, fanning herself dramatically. She flashed a hateful look toward Bea. "I can't sleep at night. I can't tie my own shoes. In fact, my feet are so swollen I can't even wear actual shoes. Look!" She straightened a leg and held it parallel to the floor. "Slippers! Ugly, flat-footed, fat-lady slippers!"

"You think you've got it bad?" Josie pushed herself up on her elbows. "At least you're allowed to get up and walk around! My biggest thrill of the day is a quick shower. I'm getting so big that I have my own gravitational pull. I wake up sometimes and see my toiletries orbiting around the bed."

Bea rolled her eyes. All she'd wanted was to have a friendly visit—and convince both of them to avoid going into labor while Roxie was out of town. Why did they have to go all hormonal on her like this?

"Here's my only concern," Bea said, venturing forward with caution. "We can't do anything that would cut this trip short for Roxie. This is her shot at happiness, I'm sure of it. Eli is the man she needs. He's the right guy for her. I've got a wonderful feeling about this."

Ginger pushed herself to a mostly upright position, her mouth ajar. Josie went perfectly still upon her bed throne.

"What's wrong?" Bea asked, surprised by the silence. "Did I say something off the wall?"

Her friends had no reply.

"It's just that I know Roxie will come racing back here if either one of you goes into labor. And that can't happen."

No response. Just wide-eyed stares.

"Don't get me wrong—I want these babies to be born! I can't wait to be a co-godmother! I'm only asking that you wait until Roxie's home. A few days with Eli is going to change everything for her, just you watch."

Ginger scooted her robust form to the edge of the love seat and began rocking back and forth to gain momentum, then pushed herself to a stand. She shuffled over to where Bea sat, and stared down at her. "Who *are* you and what have you done with Beatrice Latimer?" she asked, her eyes wide with mock terror.

Josie chortled. "No kidding, Bea. What's up with you? You been watching *The Bachelor* again?"

"Funny," Bea said. "I'm serious."

"So am I," Ginger said, relocating her roundness to an antique boudoir chair next to Bea. "I've never heard you get all gushy about love like this. You are usually the one telling us to maintain our grip on reality. So what's gotten into you?"

Bea snorted. "Nothing. Don't be ridiculous."

It went quiet again. Other than the sounds of Genghis snoring in the corner of the room—where he was flopped over a sleeping Martina, who was in turn curled around HeatherLynn—it was uncomfortably silent. Bea did not miss the raised eyebrows on her friends' faces.

Josie patted the comforter on her big four-poster bed. "Come up and sit with me a minute, Bea," she said. When Bea didn't budge, Josie said, "Please. Just humor the irritable pregnant lady, would you?"

Bea sighed, making her way to one of the bedside stepstools, then climbing up. She swung her legs off the side of the mattress and kicked off her sneakers, eventually collapsing back against Josie's decadent collection of bed pillows. She crossed her arms over her chest.

Bea knew what was coming. It was inevitable. For years now, every time a sea change was detected in the emotions of one of them, the woman in question would be expected to spill it to the group. It was therapeutic, they'd always told each other. Sharing the ups and downs of life and love was how they helped each other stay strong and smart. It was how Ginger had made it through her divorce from Larry-the-driveway-fornicator, how Roxie had survived Raymond Scumberg, and how Josie had managed to hold on to her self-respect through the likes of Lloyd, Spike, and the guy who stole her turkey baster when he moved out. It was what they'd always done for each other.

And now, Bea's turn had come. She was fifty-four years old, always the one who somehow managed to stay above the muck and mire, but today she was the one with the story to tell. She only hoped that Josie and Ginger could handle the plot line. God, how she wished Roxanne were there with them. She'd be cool with the situation.

Bea took a deep breath and prepared herself, but nothing came out. This was harder than she ever would have imagined.

"Here, pull me in. " Ginger stood on the stool on the opposite side of the bed and Josie grabbed her hand to steady her. It was like watching a couple of life-sized Weebles, Bea decided.

Once everyone was settled, Bea felt Josie's soft hand

tug at her tightly crossed arm until she loosened it. Then Josie patted Bea's hand and Ginger put her hand on top of Josie's. Her friends smiled at her.

Bea opened her mouth.

She couldn't do it.

"Oh, Lord, Latimer!" Ginger shook her head. "Do you think we're stupid? Do you think we're small-minded? Do you think we would ever judge you?"

Bea was stunned.

"We love you, you big ninny." With that, Ginger unleashed a beautiful smile. "We love you like crazy, Bea. We always have and always will."

Bea felt tears stinging her eyes.

"And no one deserves happiness more than you," Josie said, tilting her head sweetly.

Bea didn't know what to say.

"All right. Fine." Josie rolled her eyes toward Ginger. The two of them nodded in agreement, then focused on Bea.

"What's her name?" they asked in stereo.

Bea swallowed. She blinked. She felt the inside of her skull heat up so much she worried her hair gel would combust. "Her name is Rachel," she said.

Josie and Ginger nodded. They waited for more information.

"Rachel Needleman," Bea whispered.

The explosion of shrieking and laughing was so loud that Bea tried to cover her ears. Ginger and Josie fell on her, nearly suffocating her in their fleshy embraces. Within seconds, three dogs had joined them on the bed, adding their barks, yips, and howls to the celebration.

"I knew it!" Ginger yelled. "This is fabulous!"

"How long have you known her?" Josie screamed, shaking Bea by the shoulders. "How long has this been going on? This is Gloria's daughter, right? Why didn't you *tell* us, Bea? How could you have kept something like this from us!"

She was about to address those questions—and come clean about how Gloria had been hospitalized—when the bedroom door flew open. Three panting and wide-eyed men filled the threshold. Two more dogs ran into the room.

"I'll start the car!" Teeny yelled, running in and taking a sharp cut to his left, as if he were about to intercept a mid-field pass.

"Which one is in the labor?" Lucio called out, hands above his head.

"Nobody panic!" Rick shouted, sweat beading on his forehead. "Holy shit, where did I put the hospital bag?"

The women on the bed stared at the men. The men stopped in their tracks to stare at the women on the bed. For a moment, nobody said anything.

Then Bea, Josie, and Ginger began howling with laughter. All five dogs joined in. The men—who'd entered the room visibly primed for battle—began to deflate. Teeny staggered to a nearby chair and collapsed.

"No babies?" Lucio asked, waving his arms around. "But we heard the screaming! The birth screaming!"

"No babies. Sorry," Josie said, giggling. "Nobody's in labor. We were just goofing around."

"Oh," Rick said. He wiped his face. "So everybody's okay, then? Nothing's going on?"

"Well, that's not entirely accurate," Ginger said, her voice soft.

Teeny raised his hand as if to stop the proceedings. "Just tell me—whatever this is about, is it going to involve me driving? Because I suddenly don't feel so good."

"No driving," Josie said.

"Thank you, sweet baby Jesus," Teeny said, sighing.

"Then what is it?" Rick asked. He and Lucio wandered to the edge of the bed and stood guard.

Lucio cleared his throat. "Before we continue, may I say that before today, I have never had the pleasure of seeing so many women and dogs in the same bed?"

Soft laughter spread through the room.

"And here I thought you'd seen it all, pal." Rick patted his friend's back.

"Such a thing is not possible," Lucio said, grinning at his wife. "Every day, life brings us another surprise, is it not true, *guapa*?"

Ginger's cheeks flushed and her eyes sparkled. "That's an understatement," she said.

Suddenly, Bea felt the heat of Josie and Ginger's stare. She sighed.

Teeny perked up. He sat up straight in the chair. "Bea? Is this about you? Is everything all right?"

She sighed again.

"Come on now, girl. Don't scare us like this." Teeny leaned forward, resting his elbows on his knees. "What's going on?"

Lucio cleared his throat. "You aren't . . . you know . . . ?" He gestured to Ginger and Josie.

"Pregnant?" Bea shouted, nearly jumping off the mattress. "What the *fuck*?"

"Yes. Sorry," Lucio whispered.

Teeny collapsed again. Rick wiped his mouth in anxiety. Ginger and Josie laughed.

"Oh, just go ahead," Josie said, landing a soft punch on Bea's upper arm. "Nothing you could come up with now would be a shock after that!"

Bea rose from the bed. She walked to the center of the room, giving herself a moment to pull her thoughts together. Martina scurried over to sit at her left side, tail wagging, eyes filled with devotion. Bea reached down and patted her loyal companion's head.

She raised her gaze to her friends, who waited in rapt attention. She had to chuckle to herself. Never had she pictured it would be like this, that her moment of truth would take place in a Victorian-era whorehouse in front of a bunch of dogs, a crazy Spaniard, a pet store tycoon, and a two-hundred-and-fifty-pound former Syracuse cornerback.

But Josie and Ginger? Two of the best friends she'd ever had in her life? Two of the best people she'd ever had the honor to know? Bea had always hoped they'd be here for this. She only wished Roxanne were with them. She was the only missing piece.

Bea took a deep breath. "I've met someone," she said, keeping her eyes shut for courage. "I'm pretty sure I'm in love."

A loud crash made her eyes fly open in alarm.

"Sorry," Teeny said, shards of an antique bowl and pitcher at his feet.

Rick shook his head, not caring in the least. He turned to Bea. His face was frozen in shock. "And?"

She nodded, steeling herself. "It's Gloria Needleman's oldest daughter, Rachel. She's . . . she's incredible. She's a child advocate lawyer. She was a record holder in women's giant slalom. She loves dogs. She's devoted to Gloria. She thinks I'm . . . you know . . . pretty special, too."

For thirty years, Bea had fantasized about how magical it would have been to stand on that center podium at the 1980 Olympics to receive her gold medal in the five-hundred-meter breaststroke. Of course, because of Jimmy Carter and the boycott, that moment would always remain a fantasy. But she figured this particular real-life situation had to come pretty damn close.

Teeny jumped from his chair, ran to Bea, and lifted her into his arms. He spun her around as he laughed and hooted. The room filled with cheers. And barking.

"This calls for a celebration!" Lucio screamed.

"Champagne for everyone!" Rick said.

"But I can't get out of bed!" Josie yelled.

So, once everyone calmed down and Lucio and Rick had fetched a couple bottles of the good stuff—along with a bottle of mineral water for those who didn't imbibe—they gathered around the bed for a toast in Bea's honor.

"To happiness," Ginger proposed.

"To love," Josie said.

"To freedom," Teeny added.

They drank to all those things, then Rick insisted that Bea bring Rachel to the ranch as soon possible. "We'll have a party," he said. "This group of friends has a whole laundry list of things to celebrate."

Bea knew Rick was right. She put one hand behind her back and crossed her fingers, silently adding Eli and Roxanne to that list. Oh, how she hoped fate was unfolding as it should, somewhere in Utah.

He'd never had to force himself on a woman in his life. It wasn't his style. Nor was there ever a need for that kind of thing. Women found him, then they found him irresistible. Women offered themselves to him by one of two paths: they came already mad with desire, or as a willing participant in the game of seduction. But no woman ever refused him.

Raymond's latest conquest was a feisty little specimen. The way she'd been panting and growling against his neck was turning him on something fierce. He loved the way she feigned a struggle, pushing the flat of her palms against his chest, as if she didn't like what was happening, as if she didn't like the damp friction of his fingers inside her panties.

"Stop. Please. God, no."

He chuckled, nipping the skin over her collarbone. "So you like a fight, do you?" he asked, increasing the pace of his pumping hand. "You like to play rough, baby?"

She pushed harder.

He lowered his mouth, searching for the excited nipple he knew he'd find poking up through the silk of her blouse. He rooted around, perplexed when his lips failed to find it.

"Get the fuck off me!"

Raymond felt a slam to his gut, then tumbled off the office couch. He thudded to the floor, landing flat on his back, his head slamming against the carpet. A strange tingling pain began to shoot through his left shoulder and arm.

Stunned, he observed the scuffed bottom of a woman's high heel headed right for his face. It stopped millimeters from his nose, then moved away, hovering over the bandage on his throat. Under normal circumstances, he would enjoy the view this position afforded him—a direct shot right up the tight skirt to the parted inner thighs and beyond. But these weren't normal circumstances.

The shoe's pointed toe began to tease his windpipe.

"You gross, sick-fuck, asshole *grandpa*. You perverted old bastard dickface."

Raymond took a moment to assess the tone of voice of his assistant. This went beyond the realm of sex play. She sounded positively furious.

"I should crush your fucking throat," the voice said. "I should finish off what that dog started, you twisted fuck! I'm reporting you to every single place I can think of! The bar association, the Humane Society, the AARP, the SPCA!"

"Now just a—"

The assistant's pointy-toed shoe hadn't even touched him, yet he was barely able to lift his head off the carpet without searing pain. There appeared to be something wrong with him.

The girl's shoe pulled away, but her face bent down close to his. He was struck by how young and beautiful she looked this close up, how tight the skin remained to the bone as she hung over him. No sagging whatsoever.

"This is quite unnecessary," he said, using his famous suave baritone, a tone of voice known for sucking the fight right out of the most stubborn of jurors. "There seems to be a misunderstanding, Ricky."

"My name is Dusty, you dirty old narcissistic senior-citizen fuckhead!"

"Remember, your future is in my hands "

She leaned even closer. Her shiny hair swept over his cheek. "Guess what? I don't even *want* to go to law school anymore! You've cured me of that particular affliction! All I want now is the satisfaction of seeing you hung by your shriveled old gonads!"

Raymond winced.

"Roxanne Bloom is my new hero!" the girl added, a gleam in her eye. "Ha! That's right. You heard me. The way I see it, that chick is a prophet—a fucking *saint*!" She leaned in so close that her nose bumped his. "I wish that dog had ripped your guts out, you disgusting old loser."

Suddenly, she stood up. From her position high above him she looked down, smirked, and said, "By the way. I told my brother about you. He's gonna kick your sorry ass."

Then she was gone. The door to his office suite

slammed with a sense of purpose. He tried to sit up, but he quickly reached that same limit to his range of movement. The sizzling pain in his shoulder and arm had now moved to his fingers. He gauged his position on the floor—he was in front of the couch but several feet from his desk, certainly not within reach of his intercom.

Raymond fished around in his trouser pocket for his BlackBerry. He must have left it on his desk. *Fuck.*

"Oh, Yvonne?" he called out casually, hoping his voice was loud enough for his secretary to hear but not loud enough for any of his associates to notice. He couldn't allow anyone important to see him like this.

"Yvonne?" he called out a little louder. "YVONNE!"

Raymond rolled his head around to get a look at the ancient cherry grandfather clock across the room. *Wait—did that little bitch just call me a "grandpa"?* The clock read ten minutes past noon—Yvonne was probably at lunch. That meant that unless he could get his ass up off that floor, he'd be lying there like roadkill for another fifty minutes.

Fuck.

He pressed his palms flat to the floor. He used every bit of strength he had to push, push, push . . . but it hurt so bad he gave up.

Raymond didn't know which was worse—the discovery that he was now paralyzed for life or that Roxie Bloom and his new assistant had obviously been in cahoots. Had the Bloom bitch somehow set him up? Why else would Ricky refer to Roxie as a saint? A prophet? Damn! He'd been framed!

"Somebody?" he squeaked, hoping that nasty young woman was bluffing about her brother. "Help me!"

Chapter 12

Eli was glad he knew every curve and dip in this part of Highway 89, because it had become increasingly difficult to keep his eye on the road. As soul-stirring as the scenery was—and as glad as he was to be on his home turf—he couldn't stop looking at the sleeping Roxie Bloom. His travel companion had taken on the beauty of a dark-haired angel in her repose, and a softness had settled over her. There wasn't a single frown line to be seen on her pretty face. He wanted desperately to stroke that rosy cheek and tweak that cute little chin.

But not as much as he wanted to kiss her.

As startling as it seemed, it had only been five days since he'd approached Roxie at the baby shower, hoping to grab a few minutes of her time, just to clear the air. Instead, he'd ended up grabbing her and kissing the hell out of her—which didn't clear up a damn thing. He'd gotten his very first taste of Roxie's penned-up fervor that day, and it had only made him want more. It had made him want everything she had to give him.

Looking down at Roxie now, Eli had a better handle on why things had unfolded the way they had with her.

It was no fluke that he hadn't been able to stop thinking of Roxie for all those months. It wasn't an accident that once he got his hands and his lips on her, he couldn't let go. And it was no coincidence that when he'd tried to run away from Roxie Bloom, the universe had pulled him back to finish what he started.

He smiled to himself, remembering how surprised he'd been when his cell phone rang at the Salt Lake airport and Roxie was on the other end. Sometimes, Eli knew, you couldn't avoid destiny, no matter how hard you might try.

"Rrrr . . . umph," Lilith said, watching him carefully, the white whiskers over her eyebrows twitching in concern.

Eli laughed. It seemed Lilith had been keeping an eye on him, and the sound she'd just made wasn't a growl, really, but more of an inquiry. In the language of dogs, Eli figured Lilith had asked where they were going and what his intentions were with her owner.

"Everything's going to be fine," he told her. After a quick check of the road, Eli reached over Roxie's sleeping form to rub the dog's ear. "You're a good girl," he assured Lilith. "Such a very good dog."

Roxie stirred. She mumbled something in her sleep. Carefully, Eli put his right arm around her and pulled her tight against his side as he drove. She let her head fall onto his chest. As much as he was enjoying the warm pressure of her body against his, he knew he'd have to wake her up in a few minutes. He wanted to give her enough time to be prepared when they arrived at the ranch. Eli knew his mother and sister would spy the truck coming from a mile off, and they'd likely be waiting in front of the house like sentinels.

That wasn't the kind of thing you should spring on someone still half asleep.

He stroked Roxie's long, silky hair and consciously focused on his breathing. Eli would face a lot of questions from his mom and Sondra. That was a given. And they'd ask who Roxie was, why he'd brought her to the ranch, and what made him change his mind about finding a girlfriend in San Francisco.

He had no idea how he'd answer.

The truth was, this was a first for him. He was kicking logic to the curb and trusting his instincts in a way he never had before. Of course it wasn't smart to get involved with a woman who lived nine hundred miles away, let alone a woman who excited him so intensely. But something about Roxanne was making him take a leap of faith. Maybe, just maybe, this woman who hated men for a living was the one who could truly love him. *All of him.*

It was funny, really. Eli was about to take the ultimate risk. He was about to start something with a woman while simply being himself. For the first time in his life. And who did he pick to bare his soul to? Roxanne Bloom, the man-eater.

He'd learned early on that his gift was more of a curse when it came to matters of the human heart. The precisely tuned antenna at the core of him—his basic nature—made him highly sensitive to the energy of other living things. It was what had led him to become a dog whisperer. And it was what turned his relationships with women into complicated messes, or worse.

He'd never been able to fall in love. Not all the way. If what he sensed about a woman didn't feel exactly right, he couldn't move forward. That was the problem with Tamara, like every woman he'd ever been involved with, though he tried for three years to turn it into something it wasn't.

Tamara was sure and steady, deeply spiritual. They

had a lot in common professionally—she was an equine vet who specialized in traumatized horses. But Eli had never felt they created anything unique when they were together. He had never felt their union had a life of its own, its own force. He had never felt like they fit together.

He glanced down at Roxie again, shaking his head in wonder. Roxie was another story. She seemed all wrong for him on the outside—pissed off and suspicious and full of anxiety. But they clicked somewhere deep down, where it mattered. When he was with her, he felt a profound sense of joy. He knew she felt it, too. Their attraction was so powerful that every time they'd met in the last year they'd ended up doing the same dance. They'd circle around one another cautiously, sniffing, ears pricked to catch the faintest sound, eyes trained on each other's slightest movement. But that was as far as it ever went—until now.

He let a handful of her hair slide through his fingers, watching it reflect the evening sun like a mirror, thinking that the only real explanation he could give his mom and Sondra—or himself—was that he'd brought Roxanne here because he had to. He had to see what would happen once they spent time alone. With no distractions. He had to allow this fascination to unfold. Thank God the ranch had plenty of open space for the explosion to occur. His as well as hers.

"Roxie, you better wake up." Eli pulled her tighter to him, then rubbed his hand up and down her upper arm. She grumbled again in her sleep but didn't move. Eli bent down and kissed the top of her head, inhaling the soft scent of her hair and skin. "Roxie?"

"What!" She popped up so fast that the top of her head cracked into the underside of Eli's jaw.

He let her go and began feeling his face for anything broken or dislodged.

"Oh my God, I am so sorry!" Roxie placed her hand on top of his. "Are you okay? Did I hurt you?"

"No problem," he muttered, moving his jaw back and forth until a loud pop filled the cab of the truck.

Roxie collapsed, leaning her head back against the front seat. "You're going to look like you've gone six rounds with Mike Tyson by the time we get there."

Eli laughed. "And to think, it was just a couple of days with the Bloom girls."

Lilith began licking Roxie's face, happy to see her owner awake. Roxie stroked her until she sat quietly at her side. "So where are we?" she asked, looking out the windows.

"We're here."

"Where?"

"We're home," he said, pulling off onto the county access road that would lead to Dog-Eared Ranch. Roxie sat up again, her eyes big with trepidation. He stopped the truck.

"Come here, Ms. Bloom," Eli said, gathering her against him once more. "How are you feeling?" he whispered, leaning close to her. "You doing okay?"

"Sure. I'm just a little . . ."

"Terrified?"

Roxie laughed, her lovely dark eyes looking right into his. Interestingly enough, his raven-haired angel was awake, but the usual lines of tension hadn't returned. She smiled at him cautiously. "I think I might need a kiss for encouragement," she said. "Can you still kiss with a broken face?"

Eli chuckled. "Never tried before." Gently—so gently—he cupped Roxie's face and brought it to him, then lowered his mouth to hers. Eli closed his eyes as the wave of bliss moved through his being.

This was what he'd searched in vain for with Tamara. *This* was the unidentifiable thing he had wanted to experience in her company, but never could. With Roxie, it was always there, even in the sweetest, simplest of kisses.

"Let me get the gate," Eli whispered against her lips.

Sure, Roxie thought. *You go ahead and do that. I'll be in here picking my bottom lip up off the floor.*

This was Eli's ranch? It looked more like a national park, or something from a PBS special on frontier living. The sun was beginning to set over the desert mountains to her left, layering red-gold stripes of color on top of blue sky. The rolling hills seemed to be covered with some kind of short grass, with stubby little bushes and scraggly trees dotting the ground. Tall, thick stands of evergreens popped up here and there.

Eli returned to the truck and drove forward a few feet, then went out again to lock the gate behind them.

"It's beautiful," Roxie said when he hopped behind the wheel again.

"Thank you."

"How much of it is yours?"

"Pretty much everything you see to the mountains over there and the ridge over there," Eli said, pointing to either side of them. "Beyond that is mostly BLM land."

Roxie shook her head, not understanding.

"Bureau of Land Management—federal property."

"Ah."

"So, are you ready?"

She nodded, then swallowed hard, trying not to allow the sea of doubts take her under. It didn't matter that coming all the way out here with Eli was a giant gamble. It didn't matter that it went against everything she'd been telling herself about men and the world for the last year and a half. They were bumping along the road toward his ranch. It was happening. She'd put herself—and her dog—in Eli's hands, and there was no turning back.

When the truck began to climb a rise in the dirt lane and took a gentle curve, a house appeared from behind the trees. It was half-glass and half-wood construction, not quite two full stories high, with huge solar panels on the roof, a big front porch, and pretty spring wildflowers popping up along the walk. The backdrop for the house was a dramatic red mountain ridge and an endless stretch of sky.

"Holy shit," Roxie muttered.

Eli stopped the truck. Two women came out onto the porch, huge smiles on their faces. They waved. Roxie waved back. Her heart pounded in her chest. Lilith began barking furiously when a long line of dogs ran toward the truck.

"Give me just a second to get the dogs settled, and then we'll let Lilith out. Can you hold onto her okay?"

Roxie nodded.

Eli smiled at her. "Everything's going to be fine," he said in that deep-river voice.

He snatched his cowboy hat from behind the seat, opened his door, and stepped onto the dirt. He moved toward his mother and sister with open arms, hugging the women together. The group of dogs was barking in excitement, but keeping their distance. What happened next was obviously the standard routine around here. Sondra and Carole backed away from Eli and he walked off a few feet to a thin patch of grass, where he plopped down. Eli let loose with a brief and shrill whistle, and it

was like the starting gates were opened. The dogs—
Roxie counted nine altogether—were all over him.

She watched as Eli rolled around with his pack, allowing them to lick him, sniff him, and snuggle up to
him. She was amazed at the sight. Eli looked like he
was in heaven. So did his dogs.

Lilith, in the meantime, had reverted to her old psycho self. She was frothing at the mouth, growling, snarling, and barking machine-gun style.

After a few moments, Eli stood, then began walking
toward an outbuilding a couple hundred feet to the side
of the house. Roxie figured it was a kennel compound
because of the chain-link fenced–in areas around it. She
watched how Eli managed to separate the pack with a
few spare hand gestures. He put four dogs in one kennel,
two in another, and three were told to sit and wait outside on the grass.

In a few moments, Eli sauntered back to the truck,
three dogs at his side. He nodded at Roxie, giving her
the go-ahead to open the truck door.

"Are you sure?" she called out over Lilith's frantic
barking.

He nodded.

So she did it. Lilith went flying out of the truck,
heading right toward the three calm dogs at Eli's feet.
She kicked up the dirt as she raced headlong into the
group. She skidded to a stop before she reached Eli and
his companions, then arched her back, lowered her hind
end and head, and hid her tail between her legs. Lilith
growled and exposed her teeth, all while displaying her
hackles. Roxie thought she looked as mean as a hyena.

She sighed. Eli must have heard her, because he
glanced her way. With a barely discernible nod of his
head, he relayed to her that she had nothing to worry
about. Roxie smiled slightly, hoping he was right.

The largest dog of the group decided he wasn't much impressed with Lilith, and wandered off to the friendly-looking woman Roxie assumed was Sondra, Eli's sister. The big brown Lab sat at Sondra's side, tongue hanging out and tail wagging.

Another of the dogs, a shepherd mix at least twenty pounds heavier than Lilith, took a couple steps forward. The dog's tail wagged high and slow; its ears were cocked forward and its head was held high. It seemed to Roxie as if the dog were giving Lilith a friendly warning: *You're welcome to hang with us, but you'd best be gettin' your shit together.*

The other dog, a homely-looking thing with a pointy, wolflike snout, decided to roll over on her back, exposing her belly. The move seemed to take Lilith by surprise, and she backed off. Her barking stopped and the arch in her back relaxed. Slowly, she approached the animal on the ground, the bigger dog keenly aware of every move she made but not at all threatened. Lilith moved in to sniff the dog still on her back.

Through it all, Eli had done nothing. He simply stood there, his posture relaxed and his face pleasant, but his presence clearly felt by all. Roxie was fascinated by that aspect of Eli's personality—he did nothing obvious, but his authority was always evident. She smiled to herself, remembering how she'd felt him even before she saw him that day at the baby shower. It was as if Eli carried around his own personal power source, made all the more intense because he did nothing to promote it. It was just part of who he was.

Suddenly she wondered—what would that kind of man be like in bed? What kind of sex would a woman get with a man that sure of himself, that in charge? Roxie's body flooded with heat, the question landing with a thud right between her legs. Again.

Something must have set Lilith off, because she suddenly barked and growled, then lunged at the relaxing dog. The other dog stepped between them, using his body as a buffer but maintaining his easygoing posture. Lilith relaxed again.

With a wave of his hand, Eli sent his two dogs off to play. After just a second of hesitation, Lilith ran after them—no barking, no hackles, no froth. Roxie blinked. As impossible as it seemed, her dog was living her dream. She was running free with other dogs, having fun, simply happy to be alive.

It had taken Eli minutes to give that gift to Lilith. Roxie had been fighting for it for over a year.

This was the absolute wrong time for this, but Roxie's chest swelled with tender emotion and she began to cry. Eli was immediately at the passenger side door.

"I'm sorry," she said, shaking her head and looking anxiously to Sondra and Carole, who were staring at her in concern. "Your mom and sister are going to think I'm a spaz."

Eli laughed, pushing the brim of his hat back on his head. "Well, you *are* a spaz, Ms. Bloom," he said.

Roxie sniffed, smiling. She loved it when Eli pushed his hat back like that. It made him look sexy as hell, in a mischievous kind of way.

"C'mon, Roxie," he said. "Time to stretch your legs."

Eli made quick introductions. Almost immediately, Roxie received warm hugs from Carole and Sondra and was guided up to the porch, their friendly chatter pinging in her ears. They ushered her through a strikingly pretty hand-carved door and into a room with a soaring cathedral ceiling, criss-crossed by huge wooden beams. One entire wall was glass, making it hardly seem like she was indoors. Roxie blinked in wonder.

"My God, Eli," she whispered. "This place is incredible."

"Eli's bringing in your bags," Sondra said, her eyes twinkling with delight.

"Oh," Roxie said, embarrassed.

"It's lovely, isn't it?" Eli's mother arched her brows high on her forehead. She was a tall and trim woman with thick gray hair, managing to look pulled together in jeans and a denim jacket. "He designed it himself and worked right alongside the contractor to build it."

Roxanne felt her mouth fall open.

Eli came in the door and shut it with the heel of his boot. "I'll get the guest room set up for you, Roxie," he said, smiling as he moved through the main room, bags in his hand. Roxie didn't miss how his mother and sister widened their eyes.

"I checked on Lilith, and she's doing great, so I let everyone out of the kennel."

Roxie swallowed hard, watching Eli disappear with her bag. She sure hoped he knew what he was doing.

The meal was delicious and the conversation was easy. Not once did Roxie feel as though she were being scrutinized by the women in Eli's family, but it was obvious that Carole adored her son and that Sondra looked up to her brother.

Over a lovely fresh fruit dessert tart—and Roxie's third glass of chardonnay—she got the question she'd been waiting for. Sondra was the one to ask it. Frankly, Roxie was amazed it had taken this long to get to. In the city, asking what someone did for a living was among the first things you wanted to know about a new acquaintance. It must be different out here in Utah, since they'd already covered topics like Roxie's family, the drive, dogs, nearby natural wonders, ranching business matters, and a general overview of Eli's childhood years. That's how Roxie learned that he'd worn braces, played the oboe, and had a tendency to wander off into the woods and lose track of time. Carole said the police were called more than once.

But it was Sondra who'd innocently asked what Roxie did for a living. On the long drive, Roxie had thought about how she'd never been even slightly embarrassed by her career, even when Mrs. Needleman chided her for bringing negativity and venom into the world, or some such drivel. But this was different. Roxie had been invited to meet the family of the most remarkable man she'd ever known, and she cared what they thought of her.

Roxie just told them the truth. She told them about her six years at the *Herald,* how the paper fired her just before it declared bankruptcy and closed, and that she was now blogging for a living.

Carole frowned. "You can support yourself doing that?"

"Some bloggers can," Roxie explained. "I've been quite lucky to attract a wide audience and get the interest of major advertisers."

Sondra put down her glass of wine. She began to stare at Roxie, her brows knitting together in intense scrutiny. A few seconds of that was enough to make Roxie squirm. She quickly looked to Eli, who smiled and raised an eyebrow.

Uh-oh.

"Oh my fucking *God!*" Sondra suddenly shouted, her mouth falling open in disbelief.

"Sondra!" Carole looked horrified at her daughter's expletive.

"You're *that* Roxie Bloom?" Sondra slapped her palms

down on the surface of the dining room table. "No fucking way!"

"*Sondra!*"

Eli cleared his throat, which got Sondra's attention. His sister stared at him, blinking. She pointed in Roxie's direction. "Do you know who she is?"

"I certainly do," Eli said. "She's an intelligent, beautiful, sweet, and funny woman who just happens to hate men for a living."

Carole's eyes went huge.

"I knew it!" Sondra stood up from the table. "<u>I-vomit-on-all-men</u>!"

"Oh, Sondra. Please," Carole said with a weary voice. "This is bad enough without you starting on that." She let her forehead drop to her hand.

"No, Mom." Sondra nodded toward Roxanne. "*She* vomits on all men, not me. I mean, that's the name of Roxie's Web site. It's what's advertised on the T-shirt I won when she published my true story about Alex and his roadside bimbo collection! Remember the T-shirt you won't let me wear out in public? Mom? Do you?"

Carole slowly raised her head. She looked around the table, stunned.

Roxanne slouched into her chair, suddenly putting it all together. "You're Sonny from Utah," she said, her words barely audible.

Sondra smiled. "Yes! My husband was the regional sales manager for a mattress company. He was named Jerk-of-the-Week for February twenty-first through twenty-eighth!" She shrugged. "I missed the Cupid Sucks Award by just a week, but, hey, it was an honor anyway."

Eli laughed.

Roxie lowered her gaze to the hands she was now

wringing in her lap, trying to figure out how she could possibly rescue the evening—the entire trip—from the disaster pile.

"And you knew about this?" Carole asked. Roxie peeked up to determine where that question was directed, and found it had been directed to Eli.

"Of course I knew what Roxie does. I just discovered that Sondra knows her, too, however." Eli glanced at Roxie and offered a crooked smile. "You're famous."

Roxie let out a mewl of distress.

"Well." Carole grabbed her plate, utensils, and wine glass and went into the kitchen. Eli followed her.

Sondra collapsed into her chair, sighing with great satisfaction. "It is a real honor to meet you, Roxie." She raised her wine glass.

Roxanne tried to smile.

"But you know we've got a situation here, right?" Sondra leaned forward on her elbows. "I mean, truly, my brother isn't one of those guys. He's honest and decent and trustworthy."

Roxie nodded. "I'm learning that about him."

"Plus he's really cute."

"I know," Roxanne said.

Sondra smiled. "Good. As long as we're clear on that, then I'm cool with everything."

It took a few moments before Eli and his mother returned to the table. Carole tried her best to offer Roxanne a brave smile. "It was nice meeting you," she said, slipping her purse strap from the chair. "I think we should head home, Sondra. We should probably give them some time alone. I'm sure they have a lot to sort out."

Sondra shrugged and got up from the table, taking her dishes into the kitchen. A few moments later, Eli and Roxanne walked them out to their trucks. Sondra's chocolate Lab jumped into the front seat with her.

Roxanne had to give Carole credit—she'd remained pleasant enough, even though she probably hated Roxie's guts. And understandably so. If Roxanne ever had kids, she sure wouldn't want her boy hanging out with someone like herself.

Carole drove away first. "We'll swing by later this week, but we'll call ahead!" Sondra waved as she drove off. "You two crazy kids have fun!"

Roxanne stood in the dirt, surrounded by the darkest kind of dark she'd ever experienced, and shuddered. Eli slipped a strong, warm arm around her shoulders, pulling her tight against him.

"That sure was exciting," Eli said.

Roxanne didn't say anything. She suddenly felt quite sad. The idea that Eli's mom hated her didn't sit right, and she'd never once given a damn what anyone thought of her or the way she lived her life. *Ever.*

Roxanne took a deep breath of the cold air and looked around at the strange shadows and shapes surrounding her, figuring that people in Utah must not put a premium on outdoor lighting. A shiver went through her that had nothing to do with the chill. "Where's Lilith?" she asked.

"Let's find out." Eli let go with one of his quick, high-pitched whistles, and Roxie immediately heard the canine stampede coming their way. She anxiously scanned the group, looking for Lilith. She found her in between a little terrier and the dog with the wolf snout. Her tail wagged and her eyes sparkled in the dark.

"I want her to sleep inside tonight," Roxanne said.

"Oh, everybody sleeps inside around here," Eli said. "The pack needs to share a den with the leader, right?"

He walked Roxanne back up the steps and through the front door. Only after he'd made a gesture with his hand did all the dogs follow them inside.

"I know you're tired," Eli whispered into her ear, leading her down the hallway to her guest room.

"Exhausted."

They stood in the bedroom doorway, where he turned her to face him. A small smile played on Eli's lips but his eyes were intense. Roxie's whole body began to hum as her brain went wild with competing thoughts. *I shouldn't have come here. I love the way Eli's touch feels. So what if his mother hates me? God, I just want to go home. It's so pretty here. Thank God he didn't assume I'd sleep with him. Why didn't he want to sleep with me? Is there something wrong with me?*

But all that stuff was nothing compared to the horrible thought that had been lodged in Roxie's mind since Eli began describing his search for his biological father. She hadn't had the guts to ask him then, but she knew she wouldn't be able to sleep until she did.

"There's something I absolutely have to know right now," she said. Roxie was aware that her voice sounded shaky.

"Sure. Anything."

"Does the name Raymond Sandberg mean anything to you?"

Eli frowned. "Should it?"

Roxie groaned with relief. Then she laughed at herself, embarrassed. "That's excellent news."

"What's all this about?" Eli gave her a smile but his eyes were concerned.

"Oh, I had the most horrible thought on the drive here, but if I tell you, you're going to know how much of a spaz I really am."

Eli laughed. "I already know. Who's Raymond Sandberg?"

"He's my pig-faced ex."

"Ah. So why did you think I'd recognize the name?"

She shook her head and looked at her socks. "You know how you told me I shouldn't expect the worst possible outcome with stuff?"

"I remember."

Roxie raised her eyes to him. "Well, when you were telling me about all the men you'd gone to in an effort to find your biological father, and how you had just one man left on your list, I had this horrible thought . . ."

"Oh, Jesus, Roxanne." Eli closed his eyes. "That *is* horrible."

"Yeah. Crazy. But it's not completely out of left field, you know. I think Raymond was at Berkeley Law about the same time your mom was on campus. It's not outside the realm of possibility."

Eli slipped his arms around Roxie and pulled her tight. "Roxanne. The last guy left on my list is a Palo Alto accountant named Arnie Weatherholder. And I'm happy to report that my mother didn't have sex with *every* male on UC Berkeley campus. But then, she was only there one year."

Roxanne hugged him tight, resting her cheek against the warmth of his chest. She was suddenly, completely relaxed. And so tired she could hardly stand.

"With that good news, I should let you get some rest," Eli said. He held Roxie in front of him then lowered his mouth to hers, giving her the gentlest kiss—so tender and respectful—while he tilted her chin with his fingertip.

Roxie melted. An embarrassing groan came from deep in her throat. She wanted more. Why hadn't Eli ever kissed her again in the way he had at the paddock, or at the park? Why had all his kisses since been so cautious?

Once he ended the kiss, his smoky green eyes smiled down at her. "We'll start in the morning."

"Start what?" she asked, licking her lips.

Eli laughed softly. "Working with Lilith."

"Oh." Roxie swiveled her head to find Lilith already curled up in a ball on the guest room floor. "We're doing really good, aren't we?"

"We are," he said, grinning. "But I have a feeling that good is just the beginning."

Chapter 13

When it was still dark outside, Eli padded down the hallway in thick woolen socks, his entourage clattering along with him. Eli heard Lilith whine and scratch at the guest room door, wanting to join her new friends, so he let her out. He couldn't resist a quick peek in at Roxie, but all he could see was a fall of dark hair and one slender hand hanging over the edge of the bed—the rest of her was buried under a mound of quilts. He smiled as he closed the door, figuring she must have raided the hall closet in the middle of the night searching for warmth.

Maybe soon, she wouldn't need extra blankets to keep her warm—because she'd have him.

Eli let the dogs out and made a pot of coffee. Within minutes he was out on the front porch sipping from his favorite pottery mug, hoping Roxanne packed the way he'd advised her to. It was colder than usual for a May morning in southern Utah.

Eli's eyes moved from one wonder to the next. To the east was the first glow of orange sun coming over the Cedar Breaks. To the west were the dark purple remnants of night, just about ready to fade away. He observed the steam of his breath and beverage rising into the morning chill.

This was what he loved about his home—the stillness, the peace, the magnificence he found in the simplest things. He couldn't wait to share it all with Roxie.

But he wouldn't delude himself. He had no idea if the woman buried under three quilts in his guest room would take to this world—his world. She might. But she very well might not. Like everything else about Roxie Bloom, it was something that couldn't be forced.

He'd tried to explain that to his mother last night. He told her that Roxie had issues but that her career didn't diminish all the wonderful things he saw in her. "Man-hating is just a stop on the road, not her destination," he'd assured his mother. She hadn't seemed convinced.

That was when he tried to change the subject by telling her that Milt-in-Your-Mouth was the latest to be eliminated. Bad move. She'd glared at him as if he'd slapped her. "How many more do you have on that list, Eli?"

"Just one. The nerdy math major who lived in your dorm."

She'd nodded curtly. "I can't *wait* for this to be over, Eli. Not for my sake, but for yours." She'd put her hand on his cheek. "You've been through so much. This crazy business in San Francisco has brought you nothing but more disappointment."

"And Roxanne," he pointed out.

His mother gave him a tight smile. "Then there's that."

Eli sighed, watching his breath rise and disappear. He didn't want Roxanne to change for him or his mother or anyone else in the world. In fact, she didn't have to change at all. But she'd come to him tired of the fight. She'd said she wanted her dog to be happy and her life to be peaceful. That would require change, and it was Eli's job to help her get to where she wanted to go.

He brought the mug to his lips for another sip, feeling the liquid warm his insides all the way down to his toes. He had to admit that Roxanne's struggle was a fascinating process to observe. She seemed incapable of hiding her internal battle—each twist and turn of thought was written on her face, especially when it came to Eli himself. *She was interested. No, she wasn't. She was willing. She was afraid. She thought she'd be safe with him. No, wait—you never can tell with men.*

It was like watching an emotional wrestling match televised right there in her pretty dark eyes.

Eli observed the dogs break out into small groups for their morning rounds, Lilith finding a place for herself without even the slightest hint of drama. The dog was already coming into her own. Her owner would have to catch up.

Eli tapped the toe of his boot onto the porch floor, thinking. The biggest challenge he'd face from here on out would be with himself, he knew. He wanted Roxanne. Bad. And the strength it took for Eli to keep his kisses nonthreatening—and his raging hard-on in check—was nearly superhuman. And as he'd told her up front, he was only a man.

But if what he said last night was true—if good was only the beginning for them—then he'd have to be patient. He could have her rolling around in his bed with him before lunchtime, if that's what he wanted. But even if things went smoothly, that first time together would also be their last. Roxie would decide she'd been manipulated—yet again—and Eli would only provide further proof that men were scum and not to be trusted. She'd end up adding Eli to her most reviled list. He might even be named Jerk-of-the-Week!

He turned just in time to catch it—the instant the night gave way to morning with a flash of light. He looked out at a suddenly altered landscape, aware that this was the way of all things. In an instant, everything could change. It was a thin line that separated one reality from the next.

It would be that way with Roxanne and him. And then there'd be no turning back.

As Eli headed down the steps to watch the light spread out over the land, his thoughts floated back to the dream he'd had last night. It was a typical man dream—big on sensation and short on plot. He and Roxie had hiked down from the southern ridge and ended up at Snow Creek hot spring. They got naked and immersed themselves in the water. Eli found a ledge to sit on. Roxie straddled him. He felt as if he'd shatter into a billion shards of pleasure as he pushed up inside her, his hands gripping her water-slick body, his lips and tongue conquering her mouth. He'd woken up then, so frustrated he'd nearly jumped out of his skin.

Eli took such an enthusiastic gulp of coffee that some of it spilled down the front of his denim jacket. He laughed at his clumsiness, deciding he better take a few minutes to center himself. No woman had ever knocked him off balance from the get-go the way Roxie had. No woman had ever made him feel so alive. It was as wonderful as it was terrifying.

He'd need to wake her up soon so he could introduce her to the rhythm of life on the ranch. Each day started with an early-morning hike. That was followed by breakfast, for both man and beast, then quiet time for reflection, meditation, or reading—all before he even thought about work. Sondra called it "living on monk time," but she followed something quite similar at her own place. Eli always believed that if your morning was peaceful—pornographic dreams aside—the rest of the day would flow.

"It's beautiful here."

Eli swung his head around to see Roxie on the porch, still buried in a quilt. He laughed. "Beautiful in a cold way, right?"

She nodded. "No kidding. I nearly froze my butt off last night."

Eli headed back up the porch toward his houseguest, thinking that particular loss would be a national tragedy. "We have a typical desert climate here—warm during the day and cooler at night." He stood next to her. "I'll turn the heat on for you if you'd like."

Her dark eyes darted toward him, and he could see that the day's wrestling tournament was already in full swing in her head. The closer he came, the more she fought with herself. Eli had left a few inches of space between them—for her comfort, not his. He'd rather get inside that quilt with her. Then get horizontal. And naked. He cleared his throat. "Feel free to grab some coffee if you'd like, but you should get dressed. We're going on a hike."

She narrowed her eyes at him. "Now?" She looked around. "But it's, like, six in the morning."

"Yup." Eli flipped open the flap of his jacket pocket and pulled out one of his short and thin nylon training leashes. "We've got a lot of work to do."

Roxie's eyes went huge.

"You look surprised."

"Uh . . ." Roxie's eyes darted from the lead to Eli's face. "For a minute there, I thought the leash was for me."

Eli nodded, biting the inside of his mouth to stop from laughing. "Do you need one, Ms. Bloom?"

She pulled the quilt tighter to her body. "You know what? No. I'm feeling uncharacteristically agreeable

today, so I think you can trust me not to wander off."
She gave him a wry smile. "Besides, the last man who
tried to keep me on a leash lived to regret it."

"So it seems. Now scoot!" Eli located the quilt-
covered lump that was probably her lovely bottom and
gave it a smack. "We're on a schedule."

Roxanne emerged from the guestroom a few minutes
later in a sweatshirt and jeans, feeling guilty because
she hadn't paid much attention to Eli's packing recom-
mendations. Thermal underwear in May? In the desert?
She'd thought his suggestions were overkill.

She heard clanking in the kitchen and wandered
toward the noise, but at first she didn't see Eli. When
she rounded the island, she was greeted by a man ass
so spectacular that even a pair of ugly Wranglers didn't
diminish the effect. He stood up from his crouch in
front of a cabinet and spun around.

"Hi," she said.

His eyes immediately scanned her body from head
to toe. He raised his chin and an eyebrow. "What you
got on under there?"

Roxie's jaw dropped. She immediately felt the heat
of anger spread through her, and she crossed her arms
over her chest. "Wow. Let me guess—you want me to
feed your male fantasies and tell you I'm wearing a
black demibra and a matching pair of crotchless panties? Is that it? Well, sorry to disappoint."

She watched Eli swallow, then nod slowly. He came
toward her, his hand outstretched. "Come on, Ms.
Bloom," he said, guiding her at the curve of her lower
back and escorting her from the kitchen.

"Where are you taking me?"

"My bedroom."

She twisted away from him, amazed at this sudden personality change. She *knew* it. The gentleman thing was an act. Roxie panicked, knowing her cell phone didn't have any reception out here. In a rush of fear, she calculated that no one would ever hear her scream.

Eli stopped in his tracks. He shoved his hands in his jeans pockets, and Roxie nearly lost her breath at the way they stretched tight over his body. He looked so good she could even forgive the cowboy belt buckle.

"I asked you what you were wearing because I'd hoped you remembered to bring thermal underwear." Eli looked down at her with vexation, and it occurred to Roxanne that it was the first time she'd ever seen anything like that in his eyes. He grabbed a bit of sweatshirt at her waist and pulled at it with his finger and thumb. "Obviously not. So let's get you something warmer to wear."

She followed him into the bedroom, ashamed of herself. She didn't like the fact that she'd automatically thought the worst of him, but how could anyone blame her? She had battle scars. She couldn't just pretend she didn't.

Out of the corner of her eye she noted his huge four-poster bed. It was a bit on the rustic side, but the red flannel sheets looked real cozy. There was a big stone fireplace on the other wall, too. She'd never need extra quilts in here.

Eli opened the double doors to a walk-in closet and pulled out a set of silk long johns, then grabbed a wool sweater, shoving the bundle in her arms. "The sweater's going to be way too big, even though it shrank in the wash. But it's better than nothing." Before he shut the doors he grabbed a knit hat and some gloves and slapped them on top of the clothing pile. After a quick examination of her footwear, he said, "I'll meet you out front."

Eli had put all but two of his dogs in the kennel, so it was just five of them, now well into their hike in the hills. Lilith was on the little flimsy leash, the strap of which was draped loosely in Eli's open hand. He'd been showing her how she was expected to walk—at his side with her nose even with his leg, never edging out in front. Amazingly, Lilith had tried only twice to defy him, and after two gentle tugs on the leash and two of his hissing corrections—along with his usual steady demeanor—the dog was done rebelling.

Roxie was in awe at the spectacle. She began rubbing her arm reflexively, thinking of all the times Lilith had nearly ripped her shoulder from its socket despite the use of a much thicker leather leash, a heavy-duty choke chain, and a muzzle.

Eli eventually came to a stop. All three dogs did the same. He unhooked Lilith's leash, and with a gesture, permitted the dogs to explore. Roxie watched Lilith race down a hill, the look of delight on her face.

In a way, Roxie was jealous.

He directed her to follow him farther up the ridge. "We'll be able to keep an eye on them from up here. Don't worry."

And for the next half hour, as the sun finally started to warm her bones, she listened to Eli chatter away about sagebrush, cedar and aspen, and the two-hundred-million-year-old geological formations of southern Utah. Roxanne had never known a man could get so excited about sandstone and shale.

"So you majored in geology in college?" She was hoping she could coax out his usually friendly nature. She got nothing but matter-of-fact answers.

"Zoological anthropology." He glanced over his shoulder at her and noted her blank stare. "It's the study of the human being's place in the animal kingdom, especially in relation to other primates."

"So why did you choose to work with dogs?"

Roxanne was trying to catch up to Eli when he answered. "It was the other way around. Dogs chose me." He looked over his shoulder again as he said this, and a faint smile widened his lips. *Finally,* she thought. *A mile.* She'd gone over an hour without seeing one of Eli's grins, and she'd felt deprived, and extremely lonely. She exhaled in relief and kept climbing.

"I've had dogs all my life," he went on, "and I always had a way with them. I had planned to get my doctorate and maybe teach one day, but friends kept asking me to help them with their dogs." He shrugged. "I began studying canine behavior on my own and it just happened."

"So you didn't mean to be a dog whisperer?"

"Hell, no," he said with a laugh, whisking his hat off to run a hand through his hair. He squinted into the wind and replaced his hat.

Thank God he's laughing again.

"Friends and acquaintances started giving me that title. At first it was a kind of joke. Then it snowballed into a career. And here I am."

At that moment, Eli reached the top of the ridge, propped a hiking boot on a boulder and a forearm on his knee. He reached for her hand to help her up, and Roxie gasped, not from the exertion as much as the shocking beauty of the view that had just opened up before her. Giant red cathedrals shot up from the earth. Sheer cliffs were topped off with thick evergreen forest. Vast stretches of hills rolled away toward the horizon, dotted with deep canyons as far as the eye could see.

"Oh, my God," Roxie whispered, suddenly under standing Eli's passion for rock. "So this is what you were talking about."

When she turned back to Eli, he was studying her like she'd been studying the landscape. Roxie noted how the morning sun formed a halo around his hat, how the wind ruffled the dark blond hair curling below his ear. His dusky green eyes bored into hers. She gasped again—this time because the intensity in his gaze had knocked the wind from her.

As they studied each other's faces, a humming energy swirled around them, like a living thing, like the wind, demanding their attention. Roxie blinked, trying to understand what she was seeing. But there was nothing to see. Whatever was happening was happening inside the two of them. It was pure sensation.

Roxanne tried to hold on to the awareness for as long as possible. It felt so wonderful that she wanted to lock it away so she could remember it for the rest of her life.

But the moment passed and the intense energy dissipated into the breeze. Eli looked away. When he spoke her name, his normally smooth voice caught in his throat. "Roxanne—"

"I'm sorry, Eli," she said, cutting him off. Maybe her timing was rotten. She had no idea. She'd never been all that good with timing—or apologizing from the bottom of her heart, for that matter. "I'm sorry I behaved like that back at the house. Please forgive me."

His brows crinkled together under his hat.

"I don't want to be that kind of girl anymore," she said, suddenly needing to sit on the closest boulder. "I don't want to go through the rest of my life expecting the worst from every man I encounter. I don't want to be lying in wait for the moment I can say, 'Aha! See? He's

an asshole, just like I thought!' God, it's the most exhausting thing you can imagine."

Roxie sighed, closing her eyes and lifting her face to
the sun. She realized she was crying only when her
tears began to sting from the wind. "But it's not easy to
change who you are."

When Roxie opened her eyes, she saw Eli looking
down at her with gentle affection. She started to cry in
earnest then, which mortified her. How could he be so
kind and patient with her when she was such a hardheaded case? How could he look at her like that when
she was making a mess of this apology, of their whole
first morning in this beautiful place? The same way
she'd made a mess of every relationship she'd ever had
with a man? Roxie wiped her cheeks with the cuff of
Eli's sweater, figuring she'd take it to the cleaners once
they were back in the city.

He sat down next to her on the rock, his hip touching
hers. Eli picked up a pebble from the dust and turned it
over in his hand for a long moment, lost in thought.
"The anger and distrust is not who you are, Roxie. It's
your defense. It's your porcupine suit."

"Excuse me?"

Eli laughed loudly, tossing the pebble over the ridge
and into the sky. "At the baby shower, Bea told me you
were a pussycat in a porcupine suit."

Roxie's mouth fell open, then she snapped it shut.
"How thoughtful of her," she said sarcastically.

Eli chuckled. "She adores you, Roxie. She sent me
out to the barn to go after you, did you know that?"

Roxie felt her left eyebrow shoot up. "Oh, *really*?"

"Yep." Eli's eyes were smiling now. "She warned me
that you were a little on the complicated side but worth
the effort. She told me not to let you get away."

Roxie snickered and shook her head. She'd be sure

to discuss this with Bea when she got back to town. "That girl sure is funny."

"She was right, you know. You are a creampuff inside here." He touched the sweater just above her left breast. "You are a very good person."

"I keep telling myself that, but it's hard to believe sometimes."

"Maybe it's time you hear it from someone else."

When Eli glanced sideways at her, smiled, and pushed up the brim of his hat, Roxie knew she was in trouble. And it wasn't the shallow-grave kind of trouble anymore. It was heart trouble. She'd just figured out what had happened between them a few moments before, when she'd gasped at the intensity of the moment. She'd been opening the door to her heart—just a crack—and Eli had simply let himself in.

". . . This man will be different. He'll be strong enough to pry open the door of your heart and brave enough to love everything he finds inside."

Eli reached for her hand. "It takes courage to change," he said.

She nodded.

"I have a theory about it. Would you mind if I shared it with you?"

Roxie smiled at him, thinking that the man's reservoir of graciousness had to be bottomless. "Please," she said. "I'd love to hear it."

"Okay, then," he said, his voice soft. "There are basically two ways a person can change. One way is through some kind of awakening, where they slowly begin to see that their life doesn't work for them anymore, that they're unhappy, unhealthy, lonely, or a combination of all those things, and they decide to try something new."

Roxie nodded.

"Or, change can come with crisis." Eli smiled sadly

at her. "Something so devastating can happen that it's impossible to put the pieces of a life back together the way they were." He gestured toward the dramatic scenery before them. "That's what happened here over the millennia. Asteroids hit, seas flooded then dried up, volcanoes exploded, giant slabs of ice ripped open the earth—and this was the result."

Roxie chuckled. "Sounds like the last year of my life."

Eli laughed, then wrapped his strong arm around her shoulder. "Do you know what I think?"

She shook her head.

"I think you were already in the process of changing, but the asteroids and explosions and vicious dog charges just helped move things along."

Roxie smiled at him. "Yeah, but you forgot the giant slab of an ice-cold ex-boyfriend who ripped my heart open."

"I didn't forget him." He leveled his gaze at her. "But *you* need to."

"No problem," she said sarcastically.

"All right. If you can't forget, then forgive." Eli slowly reached up to remove the knit hat from her head, then smoothed her hair. He stored the hat in his jacket pocket. "Try looking back at the relationship with compassion— for him *and* yourself—and let it go."

She leaned back so quickly that his arm fell from her shoulder. "You're kidding, right?"

"Nope."

"I'm not freakin' Mother Teresa, you know."

Eli laughed. "No, you're Roxie Bloom—brilliant, funny, loving, and sexy Roxie Bloom, and the second you forgive this guy, he loses all power over you. Poof! It's gone."

Roxie blinked at him in surprise.

"Once you do that, he can't make you angry. He can't make you miserable. He can't make you see each and every man who comes your way as a potential enemy." Eli's grin expanded. "And suddenly, your life is your own again."

Roxie looked away from Eli's face and stared out at the vast display of beauty. None of this was exactly news to her, but she'd never heard it put in such a doable way. "They say forgiveness is for the forgiver," she said.

"Every single time."

After a quiet moment, she suddenly turned to Eli. "So do you practice what you preach?"

Eli blinked. He opened his mouth to answer her when the sound of barking echoed up from the canyon below, and a bolt of worry shot through Roxie. She stood. "Where are they?"

"Not far," Eli said, standing without a hint of concern. "Are you hungry? Do you think you'll be ready to eat by the time we get back?"

Roxie's eyes scanned below for Lilith or any of the dogs. "I don't see her. What if something's happened to her?"

Eli put his fingers to his lips and let loose with a short, shrill whistle. Instantly, she heard the sound of dogs scampering up the ridge. The moment Roxie saw Lilith's little brown and white face and dark, sparkly eyes, she was filled with love and relief.

She looked up at Eli. "Thank you," she said. "For everything. I . . ." Roxie burst out laughing. She'd almost blurted out that she loved him. *Loved him.*

"You what?" he asked, cocking his head at an angle.

"I think you're very good at what you do. You're also a pretty incredible man."

He gave her a gentle kiss on the lips, then motioned

for her to go ahead of him down the ridge. "And just think—you haven't even tasted my cornbread yet."

Raymond turned away from the rebuilt door at the little house on Sanchez Street, enraged. He'd peeked into the garage windows and seen her car, so he knew she was home. But she was refusing to come to the door. All the blinds were down. And the bitch hadn't answered her phone or returned any of his e-mails. Her Web site claimed she was on vacation, which was a lie, clearly.

As Raymond returned to where his car was parked on the street, he heard a strange *swssh*ing sound to his left. He turned to see a dowdy-looking middle-aged woman with a broom, her eyes on him even while she mechanically moved the broom back and forth along the sidewalk in a zombielike fashion. He remembered her.

Raymond nodded his greeting. But he'd forgotten about the damn neck brace, so a shot of pain sliced down his left arm again. His fingers went numb. He hated this fucking brace. But the doctor said if the ruptured cervical disc didn't heal on its own, he'd have to have surgery, and keeping immobile would accelerate the healing.

Unfortunately, Raymond didn't want to be immobile. He didn't want to look like a gimp. Raymond Sandberg wasn't either of those things—he was smooth, sexy, and in complete command. Unfortunately, he'd quickly discovered that the world didn't see him as such with a brace on his neck. Women who bothered to glance his way did so with a twinge of disgust or pity. It just wasn't right.

"You the victim?" the woman asked.

He walked up the sidewalk in her direction, casually

scanning the path for a sign of the dirt or grass she was so diligently chasing away with her broom. He didn't see a speck of anything. Raymond smiled at the loony old hag. "As a matter of fact, I am the victim."

She kept sweeping but rolled her eyes to Roxie's house. "She's not here."

"All right. Well, thank you."

"She and the attack dog went somewhere with a man in a truck."

Raymond felt his eye twitch. "Interesting," he said.

"She left with a suitcase."

"Ah." Raymond felt awkward obtaining such useful information from someone he'd never officially met. "I don't believe we've been formally introduced. I'm Raymond Sandberg, and you?"

"I know who you are—you used to come over here for a little nookie. You'd leave early in the morning, around five. You're pretty old for her. You've got to be close to my age, and I'm fifty-six."

Raymond choked. He was only a year younger than this batty old street-sweeper? It wasn't possible . . .

"That pit bull tried to rip your throat out. I know. I saw you flat on your back. I watched the ambulance come and take you away. That dog's not right in the head."

Raymond attempted to smile politely, thinking that madness must be contagious in this particular neighborhood.

"Is that why you're wearing a brace?" she asked.

Raymond had already grown tired of the rather one-sided exchange. He was a busy man. "Yes. I was severely injured, I'm afraid. Well, it was nice to meet you." He headed back to his car.

"The truck had Utah plates."

Raymond spun around, a little too quickly, apparently, because the shooting pain and numbness were back. "I see. Yes, well, since I'm here—may I ask if you've ever seen a young blond woman visiting Roxie? About twenty-two? Extremely attractive? A college student named Ricky?"

The crazy lady glared at him. "You mean the pregnant redhead with the little white fluffy doggie?"

"No."

"The pregnant freckle-faced brunette with the hairy brown—"

"No."

"The big, tall lesbian with a—"

"No!" Raymond snapped. He took a moment to collect himself. "I am talking about a very pretty, very unpregnant, very heterosexual college student. She's probably here quite often."

"Never seen her."

As Raymond drove away, anger built in his chest. These stupid conniving girls wouldn't get away with their plan. Who did they think they were? He might be temporarily off his mark, but he was still *Raymond-Fucking-Sandberg.*

Chapter 14

Chapter 14

Roxie woke up disoriented, the pitched pine ceiling above her head not what she expected to see upon opening her eyes. The savory scent of slow-cooked meat shocked her senses. She patted the strange bed, relieved to encounter Lilith's snout. She was glad her girl was at her side.

She flipped on the bedside light and searched the guest room for a clock. After finding none, she supposed no one bothered with clocks up here. Why would they? If the sun was up, it was day. If not, it was night. It wasn't like they'd miss the seven P.M. screening at the Cineplex if they didn't get a move on.

Roxie jumped from the bed and threw open the heavy drapes, encountering fiery streaks of sunset. She paused a moment to stare in awe. It was breathtakingly beautiful here. But how long had she been napping? The last thing she remembered was deciding to lie down for a few minutes after breakfast. She must have slept the day away.

She walked right past the jeans she'd tossed over the back of a chair and wandered toward the big mirror above the dresser, laughing in surprise at what she saw.

There she was, all bare legs and bed hair and nearly drowning inside a man's sweater, the crotch of her white lace underwear peeking beneath the shrunken knit hem. Roxie watched the smile as it spread, taking over her entire face. She was smiling because it was Eli's sweater. She was smiling because of the things he'd said to her that morning on their hike—things that soothed her and challenged her and made her feel she still had a chance at love. Roxanne crooked her arm so she could bury her nose in the wool, and inhaled. It smelled like him, like the cedar forest and the clean wind of his home.

Damn. She lowered the sweater from her nose. Eli had gotten to her. He'd gotten inside her heart and under her skin and there was no point pretending otherwise.

What had Bea once told her? That if she admitted she liked Eli Gallagher she'd have to change the name of her Web site to i-vomit-on-almost-all-men.com? Roxie laughed out loud.

She peered closer at her reflection, suddenly intrigued by what she saw. Despite the dishevelment, she had to admit that she hadn't looked this good in years. Her eyes were bright, her skin radiant, and her face relaxed. She looked . . . well, she looked *pretty*. She looked *happy,* of all things!

The mirror showed Lilith hopping down from the bed and sniffing at the guest room door, her tail wagging.

There was a soft knock. "Are you alive in there?"

"Sort of," Roxie said, still giggling as she turned and went to the door. The instant she pulled it open, Lilith ran through her legs to greet her new friends. "I must have passed out. Sorry if I put you off schedule."

Eli produced a crooked smile and let his eyes scan her from socks to bed hair, spending an inordinate amount of time on her bare upper thighs, which made

Roxie remember how she was dressed. Or not dressed. She tugged on the bottom of his sweater, hoping to cover her panties if nothing else.

"That means you're winding down," Eli said, swallowing hard, trying to keep his eyes on her face. "You'll probably end up spending most of the week in my bed."

His eyes popped wide when he realized what he'd said. "I meant my guest room bed," he added, laughing uncomfortably.

Roxie laughed, too, thinking that there were about a dozen smart-ass comebacks sitting right on the edge of her tongue, but she wasn't interested in any of them. She was only interested in Eli Gallagher's handsome, golden-skinned face, those outrageously sexy eyes, and that lightning-bright smile. She was only interested in finding out what this unusually kind and sweet man would be like in bed—his bed, just like he'd said—that big four-poster, red-flanneled bed in front of the big stone fireplace.

Was Eli a serene lover? she wondered. Was he as calm and composed between the sheets as he was hiking his beloved ranch? Was Eli capable of kicking the serene shit to the curb and going for it?

Roxie watched him lick his lips. The sight made her belly burn with hot lust. "Uh, let me grab my jeans and—"

He cut her off. "That's okay. I didn't even notice you weren't wearing any pants. I won't ever again notice anything about what you're wearing because you'll just bite my head off if I do."

She laughed, surprised by his reaction. The master of mellow suddenly seemed downright rattled.

"You know I wasn't coming on to you this morning, right?" he asked her, falling against the doorjamb as if he could no longer support himself. "You know I wasn't dragging you to my bedroom to have my way with you, correct?"

Roxie felt her face flush. "I apologized for—"

"Then why, Roxie?" His eyes looked tortured. "Why did you lash out at me like that? I've been completely up-front with you. I'm crazy about you and I want to find out if we could have something special—hell, we already do! Don't you feel it?"

She nodded again, embarrassed that seeing a peek of her underwear had derailed the poor guy like this. What would he do when she was naked in front of him? It occurred to her that she might not have to worry about him being sedate in the sack.

"Look, Roxie." Eli rubbed a hand all over his face, then shook his head as if he were trying to reclaim his composure. It didn't seem to work. "I want you so fuckin' bad I can't see straight."

"Okay—"

"I'm trying to give you your space. I know you're still trying to figure out if you're ready, but, unfortunately, I'm ready now! Shit! I've *been* ready since the moment I saw you at Josie and Rick's wedding!"

She couldn't help it. Roxie let her eyes wander down the front of his body to the bulging front of his Wranglers and the zipper that was strained to its limit. And to think, just days ago she'd disapproved of his choice of denim. How silly of her.

"Do you remember that first time we saw each other?" Eli asked, straightening up from the doorjamb.

Roxie trailed her eyes back up his torso, over the flat stomach, to the open neck of the smoky blue Henley shirt he wore. She could see light curly hairs in the hollow of his throat. She could see his pulse banging against his skin. The guy was on fire.

"Yeah, I remember," she croaked out. Her mouth had suddenly gone dry. "You were leaning against the stone wall in your suit and cowboy hat. I couldn't believe what I was seeing."

"And you were in that fucking green dress with your hair up and you had this perfect face and the cutest chin and Jesus, Roxie. You were the most beautiful thing I'd ever seen in my life."

She sucked in air, now left speechless by his confession.

"I'm goin' down, Roxie." Eli raked his fingers through his dark blond curls, desperation in his voice. It suddenly occurred to her that he wasn't wearing his hat. He didn't wear it indoors, apparently. She actually missed it. She loved his head of silky, tousled, touchable curls, but she liked the way he looked in his hat, too. The black Stetson suited him. He looked like himself in it. Hadn't she ridiculed his hat at first, as well? She must have been blind.

Eli reached out and ran a fingertip down her disheveled hair. "I'm just afraid that if we fall into bed too fast you'll bolt. You'll put my face on your Most Wanted poster and I'll never see you again."

She felt her eyes go wide. Surely, there were better places to put his face.

"I'd do anything to avoid that. Even if it means walking around the ranch with a piñon branch in my pants!" When he said that he waved his hands around, and Roxie noticed he had papers rolled up in his fist.

"What's that?" she asked.

"What?" Eli seemed surprised to see something in his own hand. "Oh. That's my questionnaire. I've filled everything out for you."

"Really?" Roxie's mouth gaped open. She let go of the hem of Eli's sweater, feeling it rise on her thighs.

"Of course," he said, unable to keep his eyes from the vee of her legs. "I keep my promises, Roxie. All of them." He stopped himself. "Except maybe promising not to notice when you're not wearing pants."

She went perfectly still. She stared at him, thinking this through one last time. She wanted him. He obviously wanted her. And the guy had been nothing but truthful, respectful, and patient. He'd filled out a questionnaire, as promised.

Plus, he was wise, but not egotistical. He was in command but not bossy. And those first two kisses they'd shared—the one at the paddock and then on the bench at Dolores Park? They were so hot she still felt them. Maybe she always would.

Roxie took a step toward Eli and looked up into his eyes. As usual, she suspected her timing was off. She didn't want to make a mess of this, but she had to have him. *Now.*

Besides, the whole reason they were here was to rehabilitate Lilith, right? And hadn't Eli himself said that would happen only after Roxie found a way to relax? Her eyes strayed once more to the big lump in the front of Eli's jeans.

Well, she'd found it.

Roxanne reached out for the papers in Eli's hand, his fingers relaxing as she tugged. Without a word, she turned toward the bed, climbed up, and stretched out. She patted the still-warm sheets next to her and smiled at him teasingly. "Why don't you hop on up here and we'll go over your questionnaire?"

In an instant, everything changed. Roxanne felt it, like an electric charge sizzling in the air. Suddenly, Eli looked different. His eyes had darkened. Every trace of awkwardness was gone, replaced by calmness. She saw the knowing gaze, the small tug at the corner of his mouth, the confident way he held his body.

Roxanne blinked in surprise, recalling the last time she saw him like this. Eli had strolled through her front door, dealt with the blood and the chaos, and proceeded to strut through her kitchen, living room, bathroom, bedroom—as if he owned everything in sight! She struggled to remember how he'd described his method . . . *"I'm taking over, babe. And I need to mark my territory."*

She gulped. Eli was walking toward the bed. She dropped the questionnaire. She pushed herself up on the pillows. She felt her eyes go huge.

In a flash, he hovered over her, big and blond and smiling. He planted his palms on either side of her bare legs, the inside of his wrists pressed against her outer thighs. Then he moved in even closer.

Roxanne felt herself start to pant. In seconds she was shaking.

"Settle down, sweet thing." The deep velvet baritone was back with a vengeance. *"Ssshhh,* now," he said. "You're safe with me."

Then he put his mouth on her.

Roxie stiffened at his kiss, and stiffened again when she felt his big, hard cock press against her shin. She leaned back into the headboard, suddenly unsure.

Eli ended the kiss. He studied her, nothing but absolute certainty in his expression. "When we met at the Starbucks to talk about Lilith, do you remember what I told you had to happen before we went any further?"

She nodded, her eyes going wider. "You told me I had to trust you."

Eli brought his mouth so close to hers that when she

breathed it was his air she brought into her body. She felt heat transfer from his skin to hers. His erection poked even harder into her leg. "Do you want this, Roxie Bloom? Be honest with yourself and with me."

She tried to steady her heart. She felt her hands tremble at her sides.

"I will be here and I will feel the same, no matter what you decide."

Oh, God, that did it—even at the peak of arousal this guy put her welfare first. It was the biggest turn-on she could imagine. Roxie's entire body began humming with need and she felt the wetness between her legs.

"I want this," she said.

"Do you trust me?"

She closed her eyes. If she didn't trust Eli, she might as well give up, for real, not just like the silly pledge of manlessness she'd taken with Bea, Josie, and Ginger last year. She'd already trusted this honorable man with the most important thing in her life—Lilith. And look how far she'd come already. If she couldn't trust Eli to take equal care with her own body and heart, then she'd never trust any man.

Suddenly, she pictured Raymond and Eli together in her mind's eye. She nearly laughed at the contrast. Eli Gallagher was as far away from Raymond Sandberg as a man could possibly get. It was as if they weren't even the same *species*.

She was twenty-nine. How much more of her life was she willing to throw away on anger, on ridiculous Raymond?

Not another second, that's how much.

Roxanne opened her eyes. She slid her hands up around Eli's neck and pushed her fingers into his thick hair. "I want you, and I trust you." Her lips brushed his as she spoke. "I'm ready to be rehabilitated."

* * *

Each of Gloria's old bones seemed as heavy as lead and as dainty as a single strand of hair. The exhaustion was so deep that it left her unable to think straight, to move, even to feel. It was a blessing to have all her children with her—and her many grandchildren—but truly, she was so tired that the kindest thing they could do for her was to leave her be.

She was hooked up to tubes and wires now. Soon, she'd be in Ira's arms again. She wondered what love felt like on the other side, where you didn't have your hands to caress and your lips to kiss. Oh! She prayed that she'd done enough with her time on earth to make a difference.

What had been her favorite things of this life? Her most treasured memories? It was difficult to choose from the abundance of pleasures she'd been privileged to experience.

Of course, her passion for Ira was where she discovered the power of love. He was her first and only romance. There was never another. And it was this union with her beloved that gave her the strength and courage for all that would be required of her.

Then there were those sacred times with her children, especially when they were babies. She recalled one night in particular. It was 1949. Her firstborn was about six months old and had awoken in the middle of the night hungry. The house was dark. The world was silent but for the crickets beneath the nursery window, singing their love songs. Gloria had rocked back and forth, feeding her little one with the riches of her own living body. The moment had struck her as so sacred that the tears had flowed as hard as her milk.

Ira had found her a few minutes later. Her sobs must have woken him from his sleep. He had kneeled at her feet and asked her what was the matter.

"Ira?" she had whispered, barely able to discern his face in the dark. "Have you ever experienced a moment when life was so beautiful you didn't know if you were strong enough to bear it? Have you ever been humbled by the beauty of being alive?"

He'd nodded his dark head, pulled up the hem of her nightgown and kissed her knee. "I have, my darling," he'd said to her. "Right now is one of those moments."

And that, in a nutshell, was why she'd loved Ira Needleman until the day he died.

Then there were the weddings. She remembered every one of them. Every kind of human face imaginable had stood before her. She wouldn't lie to herself—some of those weddings were shams. Some didn't last. But for many brides and grooms, the moment they offered their heart to their beloved was a moment of consecration. They were telling the world that they believed in the importance of love.

Among those faces were three of her four children and their spouses. Sadly, Gloria knew the combination of politics and illness would keep her from sharing that moment with Rachel and Bea. But she knew the two of them would figure something out. They were resourceful women. *Oy!* How difficult could it be to catch a plane to Vermont?

"Mother?"

Gloria felt one of her children wrap their warm hand around her own. It was nice, but she needed to sleep.

More faces began to float in and out of her vision, like clouds, like smoke, like a sheer bridal veil billowing in the wind.

Josephine and Rick.

Genevieve and Lucio.

She'd already placed Roxanne and Eli in Bea's capable hands. Even if—by some miracle—she were to live, Gloria knew the pair was too hot for an old lady like her to handle.

Rehabilitated?

Even as Eli slid his hands up under the hem of his old sweater, even as his palms spread out over the tight silk of Roxie's abdomen and as his lips sizzled as they landed on her sweet belly button, he couldn't stop laughing.

Roxie Bloom might need some help learning to let go of her anger, but she needed no remedial guidance in bed. Eli felt her fingers clawing at the shirt on his back, trying to yank it from where it was tucked into his belt. She was wiggling under his kisses, digging her heels into the mattress in an effort to feed herself to him. His head reeled with the hot musk of her arousal.

Eli wondered if he might be the one in need of rehab when this was all said and done.

"Oh, God, Eli. Oh, God."

She'd managed to pull his shirt over the back of his head, but it caught under his arms, putting him in an awkward half-Nelson. But he kept his mouth busy on her skin, licking the edge of her ribs, kissing down her center, tugging on the edge of her little lace panties.

Roxanne's hands began racing up and down the bare skin of his back. Her hands felt hot and soft. Like all of her. But he knew he would suffocate if he didn't take a second to get situated.

He stopped kissing her belly. He pressed his hands on her thighs to stop her wiggling and pushing.

"Roxie. Hold up."

She started wiggling again. She was making little squealing sounds.

"I can't breathe, baby."

"Oh." She relaxed under him. "My bad."

Eli pushed himself up with his nearly immobile arms, then reached over his head to rip the shirt off him. He pushed his knees between her spread legs, and smiled down at her.

"Holy shit," Roxie whispered, her wide eyes moving all over his torso. "You're incredible."

His thoughts exactly. What he saw there beneath him was similar to the fantasy vision he'd once had of Roxie. Dark hair spilling out across a pillow. Arms reaching for him. Face flushed with desire. Legs open beneath him. But in the fantasy, she hadn't been wearing a big ole baggy sweater.

"Eli," she said, her voice nearly frantic, her hands tugging at the sleeves. "Please get this off me. I need to get naked. I want to feel your skin on mine. Hurry!"

"Ssshh," he said. "Roxie, baby, there's no rush. We have all the time in the world."

She nodded, all the while attempting to wriggle her shoulders out of the wool neckline.

"Oh, fuck it," he said, reaching down and ripping it from her body in one tug. He dove on top of her, reached underneath her body, and unclasped her little white bra. In a matter of seconds she was bare from the panties up, and he didn't know what kind of feast he wanted first—the visual kind or the tactile kind. God, she was so beautiful. Eli had not exaggerated when he told her how he felt the first time he saw her. She'd been the most beautiful thing he'd ever laid eyes on.

Such pale, delicate flesh crowned with all that dark hair. Her eyes were like black diamonds fringed by long and thick lashes. That mouth. That pretty pink mouth. Oh, God, how that mouth could kiss.

He let his eyes drag down her throat, across her slender shoulders, to those two bouncy, creamy breasts with small brown nipples. She was perfect. She was utterly perfect.

"Eli," she said, her voice heavy with need.

He looked into her eyes and saw that they had filled with tears. As mind-blowing as this moment was for him, he knew it was even more so for Roxie. She'd gone from despising him to offering herself up to him in the span of a week. She'd put it all on the line for him. She'd decided to trust him. It had to be scary as hell.

"Baby," he said, slowly leaning down to place tender kisses on her forehead, her cheeks, her nose. He tasted the salt of her tears. "You'll be safe with me. I promise," he said.

"Because you keep your promises."

"Each and every one of them." Which reminded him . . . Eli gave her a gentle smile and slid off the edge of the bed. "Don't move. I'll be right back. Promise."

Roxie shot up to a sitting position, those exquisite breasts swaying with her movement. He nearly choked at the sight. He thought he'd explode in his pants.

"But why?" she wailed. "Where are you going?"

He wiggled an eyebrow. "Take a guess."

"You're getting a condom?"

Eli shook his head. "No, Ms. Bloom. I'm getting the whole fuckin' box."

Chapter 15

Roxie fell against the pillows and tried to steady her breathing. That guy was unbelievable. She was going to die if she didn't feel all his perfect man parts rubbing all over her in the next thirty seconds. She hadn't had sex for more than a year. She was so wet she was afraid she'd leave a puddle on the mattress.

She heard the front door open and close. He must have let the dogs out. Then she waited. She counted to ten. Her fingers wandered down to the elastic band of her underwear. Where *was* he? She trusted him to keep all his promises and all that, but she was done waiting.

Roxie jumped from the bed, cornered the doorway in a sock-footed skid, and tiptoed down the hallway. She saw him standing at his nightstand, his back to his open bedroom door. As she eased toward him she appreciated how his waist tapered in and the muscles of his upper back flared and rippled. She loved that he had such a small, tight bundle of muscle for a butt. He was gorgeous. And very soon now, he'd be naked.

Roxie was glad Eli was young and strong, because what she was about to do wasn't something she'd try with just any man.

She jumped him, wrapping her legs around his middle and her arms around his neck. Instantly, his hands reached behind to grab her ass and pull her in tight. He immediately began kneading the globes of her panty-covered bottom.

Roxie laughed in surprise. "You knew I was coming!" she said, giggling.

"You'll be doing a lot of that today." Eli crooked his neck around so he could see her. Roxie leaned in and kissed him. Their mouths slammed together, hot and slick and demanding. Eli's tongue pushed between her lips, behind her teeth, then licked at the inside of her mouth. This was wilder than the kiss at the paddock, or in the park. Not that she was complaining. She'd happily take whatever he had for her, the wilder the better.

Without warning, Eli backed up and wrenched her legs from his body. Then he pushed her arms up and away so that she lost her grip. Roxie fell back on his big bed, yelping in surprise. The man seemed to be filled with surprises.

Eli spun around. "Roxanne," he said, the deep-river sound of his voice making her even wetter. She loved how her name sounded coming from his mouth. She opened her legs.

"Yes?" She could see her breasts rising and falling with her breath. They felt swollen and tender.

"You're mine," he said.

That was it. No elaboration. While staring down at her with those ethereal green eyes, Eli began to undo the cowboy belt buckle.

She let out a little moan of helplessness, feeling paralyzed. Interestingly enough, Roxie had always imagined that the first time she saw Eli naked would be at her hands. She'd always pictured that she'd undo his belt and unzip his jeans and then pull everything down his legs. Then she would sit back on her haunches and savor the view.

But the moment was here and she couldn't move. Eli's alpha male eyes had pinned her to the bed, flat on her back, with her legs open.

"Oh, my God," she breathed.

The jeans were unzipped. She got a peek at a pair of gray boxer briefs about ready to split at the seams. She watched as Eli hooked his fingers into the waistband of both items of clothing and ripped everything off his hips without a bit of fanfare.

Fuck fanfare. The man didn't need it.

"Oh, God. Oh. My. *God*." Roxie had noticed that the more aroused she got with Eli the less she cared about her vocabulary. The less she cared about anything, really, except getting that beautiful, sexy man on top of her and up inside her.

Eli gave her a wicked smile. He knew exactly what he was doing to her. And he just stood there, hands relaxed at his sides, allowing her to get her fill of what he had to offer. She stared at everything. The smooth swell of his biceps. The veins that protruded down the inside of his arms and along the top of his hands. His defined chest. The small pink nipples. The rippled abs. The dark blond hair that dusted his pecs and ran down the center of his body to his . . .

For a second there, she forgot the word for it. Cock. Dick. Shaft. Penis. What*ever*. The exquisite beauty of Eli Gallagher had reduced her to a panting, vocabulary-challenged mess. She was wet. Everywhere. She feared there was spittle trickling from the corner of her open mouth.

Eli's cock was so rigid that it nearly grazed the surface of his hard belly. She could see the underside of it, all engorged and covered in veins and as thick around as . . . She lost her train of thought, because, while she'd been staring, Eli had executed a series of quick, efficient moves and had rolled on a condom.

He leaned forward, placing his hands on the edge of the mattress between her spread feet. "I'm going to show you how it is with us," he said. "Are you listening, Roxie?"

She nodded. Without realizing it, she began to play with her own nipples, pinching and twisting until shivers went through her. Eli's grin widened. "Go ahead, baby," he said. "Those are mine now but you certainly have my permission to play with them."

Roxie gasped. *His?* Her breasts were *his?* When his eyes slid up and down her nearly naked body she shivered with delight.

Just then it occurred to her that there was something decidedly different about Eli Gallagher.

"You know it will be in your best interest to follow the program, right?"

"God."

"And do you know why?"

Did he want her to say something? Had he asked her a question. "Huh?"

"I asked if you know why it's in your best interest to follow the program?"

She nodded. She swallowed hard, finding barely enough concentration to form words. "Uh-huh," she said. "Because I'll feel safe. I'll feel relieved that there's someone looking out for me. I'll be happier than I've ever been in my life."

Eli nodded, a sly smile spreading his lips. "You've been paying attention. You're a very good girl." He brought a fingertip to her sternum, then dragged it between her breasts and down the middle of her body, not stopping when he reached the band of her panties.

"Let's see what we have here," Eli said, his melted-butter voice driving her completely insane. She tensed up, expecting him to push his finger down into the lace. He didn't. Instead he let his finger tease her through the fabric of the crotch. He touched her so lightly she thought she'd scream with frustration.

"You seem a little damp," he said.

Roxie laughed. This was nuts. She felt as if she'd pass out. Or die. Or come. Just from the way he teased her, barely touched her. *The sound of that fucking voice.* "Please," she hissed. She raised her hips off the bed in desperation.

"Settle down, sweet thing," he said. He pushed her hips back to the bed. He put his mouth so close to her that she felt his hot breath brush against the inside of her thighs.

Those four words. *Settle. Down. Sweet. Thing.* He kept saying them. He had to know how they messed with her head, aroused her.

"I better check that you're ready for me."

Finally!

Eli slipped his finger under the lace crotch and pulled it slightly to the side. Lightly, so lightly, he used his tongue to explore the seam of her sex. She was so wet that she could hear the sound of his tongue as it flicked at her. She breathed a sigh of relief when she felt him pull the entire crotch away. His tongue touched her clit.

She came. Her whole body shook and seized and a shockingly loud scream of pleasure filled the room. Somewhere in the back of her mind it registered that her panties had just been torn away from her body. She felt something incredibly thick push against her opening. She wanted it more than anything, but she was still coming, still squeezing tight with an orgasm. She didn't know if it was possible for him to get in there.

It was. Eli put his forearms up under her legs and pulled them wider apart and farther back, then brought his mouth to hers. He covered her lips with his. He pushed his slick tongue into her mouth as he pushed his cock into her body.

Roxie could do nothing but ride the wave of ecstasy, feel the heat and power of Eli as he took her. *You're mine. You're mine.* The words repeated in her head over and over. Then she realized it was Eli's voice she was hearing.

He developed a rhythm. He took his lips from hers, said the words, then put them right back, spreading her mouth open with his hungry tongue as he spread her body open with his cock. He pulled away again, but only for the time it took him to say it again. *"You're mine."*

He shoved every inch of his big cock into her. His mouth went back to hers, stifling a series of cries suddenly exploding from her. He bit down on her upper lip, not hard, but it certainly got her attention. Then he reached under her body and gripped her ass hard as he pounded into her.

"You're mine," he said, pushing, pulling out, taking her, taking all of her with every stroke. She began coming so hard that black spots swam in her vision.

That was when Eli moved one hand from her bottom. He placed it gently but firmly around her throat. And he said it again. *"You're mine. You're mine. You're mine."*

Roxie didn't know what was happening to her. Never in her life had she had this kind of sex with a man, a man who had her pinned down in two places: at her pussy and at her throat, a man who clearly saw her as his to command, his to take. Somewhere in the back of her mind she found it hilarious—that a woman who professed to hate all men would be allowing herself to be dominated like this, controlled by a man because he knew the perfect combination of words and deeds.

Her fears had been unfounded. Eli wasn't reserved when it came to sex. He was all alpha male. He was authority. He was in control. Yet at the same time, Eli was giving himself to her with unrestrained delight.

It made her head spin.

"Let go, Roxie, baby." His hand slipped from her throat as he whispered in her ear. "Let yourself go with me. Don't hold anything back. I'm not holding anything back from you, and I never will. Let go. I've got you. I promise."

She could feel it. This man loved her. This man was strong enough to break down all her defenses and brave enough to love everything she was. She wasn't making a mistake this time. Eli Gallagher was the one for her. He was the one man who could handle her, the good and the bad. He was the one who could take her places she'd never even dreamed of.

Roxanne wrapped her legs around his waist and her arms around his neck and held him with all the strength she had in her, arching up against his body as he drove down into hers. And just when she'd decided this was the most searingly hot sexual experience she'd ever had in her life, Eli rooted his mouth into the side of her neck and pressed his teeth into her flesh. He bit down. He released.

"You're mine," he told her. "Do you feel it? How perfectly we fit together? I found you. I finally found you."

She went rigid from head to toe as she came. She leaned her head back and let the hot pleasure burn her all the way to her fingers and toes.

"That's it. Come all over me. Come on me while I come in you. Oh, sweet Roxie—*you're all mine.*"

It had taken some persuasion, but Raymond was glad he'd agreed to meet his boys at the club for a CAO Gold and a bit of Glenfiddich. It had done him good to get out and have a few laughs, even if he hated appearing in public in his neck brace.

Raymond walked the half block from the club to the parking garage, his keys dangling in his hand. The last few days had been hard on him. He'd had to do some serious damage control at the courthouse, quelling nasty rumors that he'd ruptured his disc chasing after young pussy. He'd set everyone straight, however, explaining with a bit of self-deprecating humor how he'd tripped over a putter propped against his desk.

But he did worry about Ricky. Or Randy. Had she gone around blabbing her mouth? Was she serious about not wanting to go to law school? If that were the case, then Raymond had lost his leverage. But what baffled him the most was *why this particular girl*? He'd been messing with his assistants for at least twenty years now. Only the females, of course—he wasn't one of those twisted motherfuckers who got their jollies in the airport men's room! And in all those years, not a single one of those girls had made a fuss. They'd simply opened their legs or lips and understood they were paying the admission fee to their future success.

And clearly, he'd been a fine mentor. His former assistants held a variety of important positions. Several were assistant prosecutors. Two were now sitting judges. There were even a couple of CEOs and law school professors in the mix. And why? Because at one time, they'd been willing to assume the position for Raymond Sandberg.

Which led him right back to what bothered him about his latest assistant, Randy. Why did a little smart-mouthed cunt think she could take him on like this? Had Roxie whipped her into some kind of revengeful frenzy? Was Roxie out on the streets trying to recruit members for a man-hating cabal? An all-girl hit squad? He wouldn't put it past her. Raymond knew that in the end, he'd discover that bitch Bloom was behind all the nonsense with Ricky.

By God, if it weren't for his neck brace, he'd be out in Utah right now, hunting Roxie down like a dog.

After he said good night to his crew, Raymond took the parking garage elevator down two levels. He pressed his key fob and heard the comforting *beep-beep!* of his Lexus sedan reverberate through the nearly empty structure. Ow! Even that tiny movement of his fingers had resulted in discomfort. The shooting pain in his arm seemed to be getting worse, not better. Damn if he hadn't started feeling his age this past week. It all began with the dog attack. Then the accident with the putter. He had to reassure himself that fifty-five wasn't *old*. He wasn't really an old man. Maybe once he'd gotten Roxie's little bitch dog hooked up to the gas pipe he'd get the spring back in his step.

"Raymond Sandberg?"

He spun around. Way too fast. He brought a hand to his neck and howled with agony. "Who are—"

Holy fuck. Raymond had to tilt his head back to get a good look, which hurt even more. The guy standing in front of him had to be at least six foot four. And a third his age. With more muscle in one of his arms than Raymond had in his entire body.

"You don't need to know my name," the kid said. "It doesn't matter. I'm here on someone else's behalf."

His attacker seemed quite self-assured for a young

criminal. Raymond moved his thumb across the car key and prepared to activate the panic button.

The guy snatched the keys from his hand. He threw them midway down the ramp of the parking garage, where they clattered and slid. The assailant slowly backed Raymond against the concrete wall between parked cars, his eyes serious but his hands to his sides. "I need you to pull out your wallet," he said.

Raymond scrambled, digging into the front pocket of his suit coat. "Here." He shoved it at him. "Take it all. Just don't hurt me."

"Thank you, but I'll only be needing your driver's license."

Now, *that* was bizarre. Raymond fumbled trying to pull his license from its plastic case. He handed it over to him.

"Excellent," the man said, examining it. "I'll return this in just a moment."

Identity thieves were now prowling city parking structures? Raymond wondered. What was this world coming to? Was there a soul left in this town with a modicum of decency?

The man returned his attention to Raymond. "Well, shall we get on to the business at hand, Mr. Sandberg? I believe you're acquainted with my sister."

Shit! Fuck! It was Ricky's brother.

"You're making a huge mistake," Raymond said, knowing he was so scared he was about to soil his custom-tailored suit trousers. The kid would never suspect that, however, because Raymond had used his rich, steady baritone voice, the one that could hide a full-out panic from the most attentive juries. At least that gift hadn't failed him.

The kid grinned. "You're the one who's made the mistake, you Viagra-popping piece of crap."

"I'm sure we can sit down and discuss this—"

The young man reached into the pocket of his cheap, baggy nylon jacket and Raymond thought for sure he was going for a gun. Instead he produced a document of some kind.

"Sign your name to this and I won't break both your legs."

Raymond choked on his surprise. "Whaaa—"

The young man unfolded the document and held it out for him, along with a ballpoint pen. "It's real simple," he told Raymond. "You sign and date this and I don't beat the fuck out of your pathetic needle-dicked self." The kid suddenly laughed. "Look, I try not to pummel old dudes in neck braces if I can help it, okay? It's a point of honor with me. So let's just get this over with."

Raymond's legs became weak with fear. He reached out for the pen with a shaky hand, wondering what in the name of God he was being forced to sign. This was an outrage! A travesty!

In a matter of seconds, it was all perfectly clear to him.

Raymond skimmed the one-page affidavit, smiling to himself. It was kind of cute, really—his assistant had done a decent job with it. His only criticism was that her description of Raymond's alleged sexual harassment was so clinical that it made him sound like a vile pervert. Also, she'd conveniently skipped the part about how she'd loved every fucking second of it. But, all in all, bravo for her.

Too bad she'd never be a real attorney.

"Did you read it carefully?" the young man asked.

"Yep," Raymond said, smiling bigger now, signing his name with his usual lavish swoops and swirls and adding the date where indicated.

"Do you pledge that the information is true and that you understand the importance of this oath?"

Raymond snickered, looking up at his misguided attacker. "Sure, why not? Can I get my keys and go now?"

The kid stared at him as though he knew something Raymond didn't, which was idiotic, since the exact opposite was true. As well written and clever as the affidavit was, it was a worthless scrap of paper in the state of California without a notary public's seal, which was clearly something that big-titted and small-brained former assistant of his hadn't bothered to find out.

The young man cleared his throat and began reading off from the numbered list of adverments, one for each individual act of sexual harassment to which Raymond had just admitted. If doing so somehow made the guy feel better about the behavior of his slutty sister, then, hey, Raymond was willing to donate a few more minutes of his time.

"'At this aforementioned date, I, the affiant, Raymond Julius Sandberg, Esq., do hereby swear that I shoved my hand into my employee's underwear and fondled her sex organs without her permission, expressed or implied.'" He looked at Raymond curiously.

"Can we wrap this up?" Raymond asked.

The young man slipped the pen into his shirt pocket. Again, he studied Raymond, holding the document in his hand. He reached across his body into the pocket of his baggy jacket again, and this time, Raymond *knew* he was going for a gun. The instant he saw the peek of gleaming steel he fell to his knees and began to beg for his life. He shut his eyes, leaned forward, and crossed his arms over his head, waiting for the sound of the trigger to be cocked.

Raymond's last earthly thought was: *Fuck everyone*

If I had to do it all over again, I wouldn't change a fucking thing!

Then came the sound. It was a gentle *ka-thud*, definitely not the expected click of a gun ready to fire. The sound was vaguely familiar to Raymond, nonetheless.

He lifted his head just in time to see the kid slip a notary public device back into his pocket. The sound he'd just heard was the embossing of the seal! Raymond's mouth went dry.

"I know," the kid said with fake pity, folding the affidavit and sliding it into his shirt pocket. "This must be a huge shock for you, Mr. Sandberg. Here, let me help you up." He reached down with his hand extended.

Raymond reached up. He was so numb and weak that he could barely keep his balance as the kid pulled him to stand. It was then that Raymond noticed the girl walking up behind her brother. She had a blank look on her face and was dangling Raymond's keys out in front of her as if she were delivering a dead mouse by the tail.

She dropped the keys into Raymond's open hand.

"I see you've met my brother. He's a vice president for commercial loans at Pacific Trust, and, of course, a licensed notary public."

Raymond gulped.

"And this is just the beginning, boss," she added brightly.

Raymond's mouth hung open. "What in the fuck does that mean?"

"That means that I've already found six other women willing to join in a class action lawsuit against you."

"You're bluffing."

She took a step closer. "But I'll drop the whole matter

if you can answer one simple little question correctly. Are you game?"

Raymond nodded, the knowledge that his life was over slowly seeping into his brain. He was totally, utterly fucked—unless he could answer her question. This went beyond vile. This was just plain cruel. "I'll try my best," he said.

She smiled. "What's my name?"

"It's Ri—" Raymond stopped. He shook his head, feeling as if he were about to cry. "I don't actually know your name, darlin'."

"It's Dusty," the girl's brother said, opening the car door for him. The young man was kind enough to support Raymond by the elbow and help lower him into his seat. Then he twisted Raymond's arm until it snapped.

"I sure hope you like desiccated venison stew."

Roxie scrunched up her nose. "Sounds delish, but I think I'll pass." She sat down on one of the stools at the cooking island to watch Eli putter around the kitchen, but couldn't seem to find a comfortable position. Up until a few hours ago, she'd had zero sexual encounters over the span of nearly thirteen months. But boy oh boy, had she just made up for lost time. Roxie smiled to herself, deciding a little temporary discomfort was a price she was happy to pay.

She watched Eli use potholders to remove a heavy-looking cast-iron Dutch oven from the big Aga range, then kick the oven door closed with his sock-covered foot.

"Just out of curiosity, how long was that supposed to cook, Eli?"

"Four hours."

"How long was it in there?"

He smiled and shook his head. "About nine."

She blew out air. "We're lucky it didn't catch fire."

Eli tossed the potholders to the kitchen counter. He leaned his palms against its edge and doubled over in laughter. For a long moment, he simply let his head hang between his arms and laughed.

"What?" she finally asked.

He raised his head, a look of amazement on his face. "Roxie, baby, this whole place could have gone up in flames and I wouldn't have noticed. Or much cared. I'm serious."

She grinned at him. It really was embarrassing what had been going on in that bedroom for the last several hours. They'd completely lost themselves in each other. They seemed to have unleashed one another's wild sides. And they couldn't get enough. And it all left Roxie feeling joyful.

She also felt raw, and not just in her previously dormant body parts. She felt raw in her spirit, like all that lovemaking had laid her bare, made her new. Maybe she'd been bare even before they began to make love. After all, she'd revealed her worst fears to a man and given herself to him anyway, willingly and completely. Or maybe the raw feeling was normal after you'd had head-banging sex with someone you love—*who actually loves you back*.

Roxie tried her best to hide the fact that she suddenly had trouble breathing. Her hands began to shake. Had she already decided that they loved each other?

"You're a little hellcat," Eli said, groaning as he stood straight.

"And you're a maniac," Roxie said. "I can't believe I was worried you'd be boring in bed."

"No kidding?"

"Absolutely." She propped her elbows on the countertop and rested her chin in her hand. "I thought there was a chance you'd be . . . you know . . . *restrained,* the way you are when you're dealing with unruly dogs and bitter women."

She watched Eli bite the inside of his mouth, which meant he was trying not to burst out laughing. It was interesting, all the little things she knew about him already, along with the important stuff. Like how good it felt to be held in his arms, or how nothing was off-limits when they talked, and how being with Eli made her simply . . . happy.

"Restrained, huh? Interesting." Eli turned his back to Roxie and opened the refrigerator, as if changing the subject. He put his weight on his left leg and tapped his foot, the way he did when he was mulling something over.

"You know, living out here is a little different than living in San Francisco. You can't just decide at midnight that you'd like a big plate of chicken pad thai or a warm-from-the-oven French baguette and then run down the street to get it."

Roxie chuckled. "What *can* you run down the street for around here?"

Eli looked over his shoulder. The light from the fridge glowed on his golden skin and danced in his green eyes. He was so strikingly handsome that she nearly gasped. He was her angel. Her teacher. Her lover. He was the best thing that had ever happened to her.

"Elk," he said, unleashing one of his big, charming, effortless grins. "Plus coyote, deer, and sage hen, but you're going to have to work hard for your supper if any of those items are on your menu."

"So there's no drive-through at the Kentucky Fried Sage Hen?"

"Unfortunately, no," he said, laughing. Roxanne loved the way his eyes wrinkled up when he laughed.

"Is this your way of telling me I have to learn to hunt if I live here?"

Whoops.

Roxanne's eyes widened in surprise at what she'd just said. Apparently, she was already so comfortable with Eli that she would just let any old thing fall out of her mouth. Still, she wasn't looking forward to hearing how he'd react to something *so completely, stupefyingly premature*!

"Oh, jeesh," she mumbled.

Eli shut the refrigerator door. He crossed the space between them and stood in front of her, his eyes soft and kind. He cupped her face in his hands. "Hunting is optional around here, but speaking your mind is required."

She nodded quickly and tried to lower her eyes.

"So would you?" Eli leaned toward her. "Would you consider living here with me? At least part of the time?"

He tapped under her chin to get her to look up. He must have seen her anxiety level begin to rise because he kissed her softly, which made her forget what she'd been anxious about.

"If it helps put things in perspective, I don't think the rules are ever going to apply to us, Rox." His voice was warm and kind. "I have a feeling we'll always do things our own way, however and whenever it feels right to us. It won't matter what the world thinks. The only thing that will matter is how it feels to us."

Roxie smiled softly. Relief flooded her. If what Eli said was correct, then throwing out all her promises to herself and falling for a man in a matter of days wouldn't necessarily mean she was certifiable. "I like the idea of that."

Eli reached for her and pressed her cheek against his warm, bare chest. She felt him kiss the top of her head and stroke her back. "Nobody has to make any decisions about anything right now. Except what to eat. I'm so hungry I could eat one of those elks from down the street, antlers and all."

Chapter 16

Monday went by in a blur.

Roxie and Eli did their morning hike, this time heading west toward the part of the ranch Eli called "the feed bowl"—a dip in the earth where his cattle preferred to graze. Roxie got a quickie education in all things Angus, including how the weekly livestock auction worked, price per pound, and the butchering process, which effectively eliminated her craving for a double cheeseburger.

After a breakfast of baked apples and some of his rich, crumbly cornbread, Eli gave Roxie a reading assignment. He got her settled in the big leather couch in the main room and handed her a thick stack of printer paper he'd had bound and covered at a discount print shop. It was entitled "Stable Owner, Happy Dog—A Manual for Aspiring Pack Leaders."

Roxanne smiled and flipped through the booklet. "You wrote this?" she asked, looking up at him as he hovered nearby.

"I had to. After my first few professional clients, I realized there was far too much information to pass on verbally."

"So will I start working with Lilith today?" she asked.

"Not quite yet."

"You want me to read this first?"

"Yep," Eli said. "Please keep in mind that I'm no writer."

"But I am," Roxie said, wagging her eyebrows. "Maybe I could whip this into shape for you. I could make you more famous than you already are."

Eli plopped down on the arm of the couch, intentionally sending Roxie toppling over on the cushions. They both laughed.

"This isn't an editing assignment, Ms. Bloom," he said, falling on top of her. "It's for you to read, study, and make notes for any questions you have."

She giggled. "You're squishing me," she managed to say, though hardly enough wind remained in her lungs to speak.

"My bad," Eli said, wrapping his arms around her and rolling to the floor, his body cushioning her landing. Roxie tossed the book across the room.

"Hey, careful with that. It's an original."

"So are you," she said, kissing him quickly before she straddled him and began unbuttoning his pale denim shirt to his waist. When her fingers began tugging at his cowboy belt buckle, Eli laughed. "What are you doing?"

"Getting you naked."

"But it's time for reading and reflection," he said, the amusement in his eyes deepening his crow's feet.

"Reflect on this." Roxanne unzipped his jeans and pulled everything down his legs, scooting back as she went. Once she'd tossed everything to the side she crawled back up the length of his body and began kissing him again. She started at his luscious lips. She let her kisses trail along his smooth cheek, down to his chin and throat. She dragged her lips and tongue down across his chest, teasing his small, hard nipples, then continued down the center of his body. Long before she reached his belly button, she felt his erection prod her breasts.

With a series of teasing stops and starts, Roxanne let her mouth play with him. She licked the underside of his cock and let her tongue swirl around the thick, hard root. Then she slipped her lips around the head of his penis, softly suckling at him until he began to moan.

"Are you reflecting?" she asked.

Eli laughed so hard that Roxanne was treated to the sight of his cock dancing and the muscles of his hard belly rippling. He covered his face with his hands and groaned.

"You need to write your own book," he said, his voice muffled by his palms.

"Oh, yeah?" she asked, putting her mouth back on him. In between licks and sucks and twirls she asked, "What would it be called? I wonder."

Eli lifted his head off the floor and looked at her for a moment, then let his head fall back. *"The Dick Whisperer,"* he said.

Roxanne let go with a raucous laugh, shaking her hair back, feeling free with the knowledge that her outburst wouldn't bother anyone but the cattle.

She stood up. Slowly, teasingly, she began to undress while looking down at Eli. She watched his smoky green eyes get heavy lidded as she removed her shirt and bra. She watched his chest rise and fall with ragged breaths as she ripped away her jeans, and his cock twitch as she whisked away her panties. When she was completely naked, Roxie stepped over Eli's body and straddled him, her hair falling into her face as she smiled down.

"Goddamn, Roxanne," Eli said, pushing up to his elbows, shaking his head.

"What's wrong?"

He sighed, closing his eyes, but said nothing.

Roxanne was a little disappointed. She thought for sure this pose would elicit more than a shake of the head and a sigh.

That thought had barely formed when Eli sprang up from the floor, picked her up like a big bag of dog food, and ran with her into his bedroom.

"What are you doing, Eli?" she called out, laughing as she got bounced around on his shoulder.

"What kind of question is that?" he asked, breathing hard. "I'm going to fuck you senseless, you naughty minx!"

Of course, Roxie didn't get back to the manual until evening. While Eli prepared dinner, she studied. She took detailed notes on what were the characteristics of a stable leader, plus the benefits of walking your dog, providing nutrition free of food additives and ingredients that might cause allergies, and setting clear rules for behavior at home and out in public. At dinner she asked a slew of questions, and Eli answered every one of them.

"So," Roxanne asked. "Can I start with Lilith tomorrow?"

"Not sure," Eli said.

"But I'm ready," she told him. "I know I am."

Eli grinned at her. "That's for me to decide."

"You're an awfully mean teacher," she said, taking her dishes into the kitchen.

Eli sneaked up behind her, propped her on the island, and ripped off her pajama pants so that he could lick her and nibble at her and torture her with his fingers and tongue until she came all over him.

Roxanne retracted her mean teacher comment.

Tuesday began with a hike to the farthest southern border of Eli's ranch, marked by the rocky Snow Creek. Eli took Roxie's hand and led her behind a huge outcropping of rock and down a path to what looked like a strange paradise. Steam boiled up from a natural hot spring.

"Are we allowed to go in?" she asked, her eyes big.

"It's ours," Eli said with a grin. "It's part of the ranch. Do you feel like—"

"Yes!" Roxie began stripping off her clothes.

They lingered at the hot spring for more than two hours, taking dips, talking and laughing, making love in the water and on a sun-heated boulder.

At one point, Roxie rested her head against a smooth rock, letting her body float in nature's hot tub, and stared up into a blue sky dusted with streaks of clouds. Before she realized what was happening, she began to cry. Within moments, great sobs were wrenching out of her. Eli's naked body slipped in behind her in the water. He put his arms around her and cradled her.

"I was pregnant with Raymond's child," she heard herself say. The words sounded shocking spoken aloud—she'd never uttered those words to anyone, not her mother, not Josie or Ginger or Bea. She'd always thought that if she didn't mention it, then maybe she could forget it ever happened. Of course, that didn't work. If it had worked, she wouldn't have spontaneously broken down here in this most beautiful and serene of places, in the company of the most loving man she'd ever known.

"Tell me, sweetheart," Eli whispered, his breath at the nape of her neck.

"I didn't even know until a couple of weeks after we broke up. Then I miscarried one night. I woke up covered in blood."

Eli kissed her shoulders and held her tighter as she cried. "I am so sorry, Roxie."

She sniffled, nodding, deciding to herself that she might as well get to the rest of it. "I think I should tell you about my dad, too," she said, turning so she could see his face. "My parents weren't exactly the Cliff and Clair Huxtable types."

Eli smiled sadly. "Are anybody's parents?"

She offered him a small smile of her own. "Yeah, well, mine were more like Cheech and Chong."

"Ah," he said, stroking her upper arms.

Roxie turned and resumed her position in the water, her back to Eli's chest, the hot bubbles skimming her chin. "My dad got tired of having a wife and kid, basically. I know that sounds awful but it's the truth." Roxanne felt her heart beat wildly in her chest at the memory, but knew it was a secret she needed to share with someone, just like the pregnancy.

"I was six years old the day he left us. I heard them arguing. My mom was screaming at him and he kept saying, 'Hey, I'm just telling you like it is.' And he packed up his crap in his little beat-up Datsun and started to drive off without saying good-bye to me."

Eli's hands stilled on her arms. "Jesus," he whispered into her hair.

"But I ran out in front of the car. I blocked him in. Then I stood on my tiptoes at the driver's side window and I asked him why—why was he leaving me?"

"That was very brave of you," Eli said.

"Yeah, well, I would've been better off just letting him go. Because what he said . . ." She choked, her throat closing up at the memory.

"Go on, Roxie. Get it out."

"He . . ." Roxanne didn't think she could do it. The words felt like shards of broken glass lodged in her throat, so sharp and jagged that they'd slice her to pieces if she tried to speak them. But then she felt Eli's arms pull her close to his solid body. That familiar stillness seeped into her bones. Her heart steadied. Roxanne opened her eyes to see a huge, blue heaven sheltering her from above, the way Eli's embrace sheltered her down here on the ground. "He told me he'd never wanted to be a dad. That my mom forced it on him. He said a wife and child weren't what he pictured for himself." Roxanne swallowed hard. "He said 'Sorry, kid,' and he was gone."

She had no idea how long she cried. Sometime later, she got dressed and they began hiking back. She felt so wobbly and scraped out inside that she nearly fell asleep about halfway through the hike. Eli carried her piggyback for a while, but she couldn't bear the thought of hurting him so she made him put her down.

After food and a two-hour nap in Eli's arms, Roxanne slipped out of the bed, got dressed, and made herself a cup of tea. She wandered out onto the porch and sat on the top step, enjoying the day's last bit of sunshine. Within minutes, Lilith found her, plopped down right next to her, and leaned against Roxanne's body in a show of camaraderie.

"Lily Girl, I'm so sorry I let you down," Roxie whispered. "I know it's been hard for you to carry all that responsibility on your own." Roxie stroked her dog's ears. "Things are going to be different from now on. I'll be a good leader. I promise."

They sat in silence together for a long while, Roxie softly stroking her dog's fur. Every once in a while, Lilith would look at Roxie, her sparkling brown eyes filled with gratitude. Eventually, a few more dogs wandered by. Some stayed for a bit. Some stayed longer. Eli came to join them, taking a seat on the other side of

Lilith. The dogs licked him and wagged their tails in greeting.

"You're ready to get to work now," he told Roxie, his voice rich and soft.

Roxie looked over Lilith's head and smiled at his handsome face. "I know," she said.

Their next morning hike was a quick one, followed by a breakfast of eggs and bacon and toast.

Eli put the other dogs in the kennel and brought Lilith and Roxanne to the open yard in front of the house.

"Remember, Roxie. This is not an obedience class. Obedience tricks will not change how Lilith sees her relationship to you. What we're doing today is establishing a new world order within our little pack."

She didn't miss his use of the word "our." With Eli, everything had been "our" from the start. Roxanne suddenly smiled.

"Yes?" Eli asked, one brow raised.

"I just realized that you've been serving as pack leader for me *and* my dog, haven't you?"

Eli cocked his head and waited for her to go on.

"You had to show *me* what it felt like to be calm and safe before I could even begin to pass that along to Lilith. Am I right?"

Eli chuckled a little. "Of course. I never tried to hide that from you, Ms. Bloom."

"Yeah, but I only just now figured it out!" She began laughing.

"And?" Eli asked.

"And I should be really pissed off at you," she said, letting her arms fall to her sides as she stared at him in awe. "I didn't give you permission to be my pack leader. I didn't want some man to be in charge of me. In fact, I should be calling you names right about now.

I should feel, I don't know, offended, victimized . . . *manipulated*!"

"So do you?"

Roxanne put her hands on her hips and shook her head. "Not really."

"What do you feel?"

"I feel happy. I feel strong. I feel more powerful now than I ever have in my life." Roxanne stood on her tip-toes and gave him a kiss. "I feel like the warrior priest-ess in the photograph over my fireplace."

"But without the spear, right?" Eli looked a little worried.

Roxie laughed. "No spear."

"Hey, Rox. C'mere." Eli pulled her to his chest and hugged her tight. After a moment he held her away so he could look in her face. "I don't want there to be a misunderstanding."

She frowned, not following him. "About what?"

Eli shrugged. "I've never had this kind of connec-tion with a client before—with anyone at all, really." He lowered his eyes for an instant before he finished his thought. "What I feel for you is just for you. What I'm doing for you and Lilith is separate. It was abso-lutely essential that I show you how to lead by example, but I'm not your pack leader, Roxie."

She smiled at him. "What are you, then?"

"I'm your lover. I'm your friend." Eli took her hands in his. "I'm your man, if you'll have me."

Raymond shuffled down the hall in his pajamas, avoid-ing the mirror that dominated the exposed brick wall of his dining room. He didn't want visual confirmation of what he already knew. He hadn't shaved in two days. He hadn't showered, either, not since the cast was set on his left arm. He hadn't worked out in nearly two weeks. He hadn't had any decent pussy since . . . oh, fuck it. Pussy was the last thing he wanted. Pussy was what got him into this quagmire in the first place.

He staggered into the kitchen, trying to summon the energy to make himself a pot of coffee. It hardly seemed worth the effort. Instead, he stood in front of the refrigerator and gulped down some unfiltered organic pomegranate juice directly from the bottle. It tasted like shit, but at least he could take comfort in the fact that he was drinking nature's elixir of youth. He ratted through the pantry with his good arm and found a half-full box of bran flakes, then scooped a handful into his mouth. Then he scuffled his way out of the kitchen.

"What the hell!"

Raymond grabbed onto the dining room wall, horrified. He'd forgotten all about the mirror, and now he was face-to-face with himself—a bald, crippled old man with a broken limb and a broken libido, alone and unkempt, a deep purple juice stain dribbling down his pajama top.

Raymond rubbed his good hand all over his face. He stumbled closer to the mirror, bringing his red-splotched eyeballs right up to the glass.

The vicious dog hearing was in five days. In five days he would need to waltz into the Animal Control complex well prepared and perfectly groomed, cool and distinguished, at peace in the knowledge that he was the voice of justice and truth. In other words, he had five days to transform from Grandpa Joe into Atticus Finch.

Then it occurred to him—none of his suit coats would ever fit over a cast! What the fuck was he going to *do*? What the fuck did he have to *wear*?

Suddenly, Raymond felt overwhelmed by it all. He

limped back down the hall to his bedroom, thinking that there wasn't a soul on earth he could call on for sympathy and wardrobe advice. He had no platonic female friends. His man crowd had never seen him in anything less than stellar condition, and that's the way he wanted to keep it. He could ask Yvonne to come over and tend to him, he supposed, but his secretary would surely want time-and-a-half.

He collapsed onto his bed and pulled the covers over his head.

As soon as Roxie's fingers hit the keyboard of Eli's computer, a tingle of anticipation raced through her. She felt anxious to discover what she'd missed at www. i-vomit-on-all-men.com after her long absence. Her palms were slick with perspiration as she typed in the password that would grant her access to the inner workings of the Web site. It felt so good to be back in her reality, a world she'd created with her own imagination, passion, and vision.

She found 197 new e-mail messages, at least a dozen from Raymond. She also found sixteen entries for the Jerk-of-the-Week contest, and thirty-four orders for merchandise.

Roxie stared at the screen, waiting for the delight to hit her. This was where she'd always gotten a little thrill. Right about now she should be feeling giddy. Instead, there was nothing.

In fact, she couldn't think of anything less interesting than reading Raymond Sandberg's rages. She felt queasy at the thought of slogging through hundreds of e-mails from hundreds of women agonizing over how badly they'd been treated by hundreds of men. And did she really want to read about the sixteen assholes who'd compete for the weekly crown? No. And the merchandise orders? They could wait until she got home.

Roxie blinked, falling back into Eli's computer chair and crossing her arms over her chest. "Hmph," she said, clicking off Eli's computer. Then she turned off the desk lamp, got up, and moved to the bank of windows on the lower level of his house, staring outside at the earth as it sloped away into the distance. She observed a group of Eli's Angus cattle grazing down in the valley. She saw a hawk sweep down from the mountain and hitch a ride on a gust of air. She heard the happy barking of dogs, knowing Eli was out at the kennel getting everyone their evening meal.

Roxie pressed her cheek against the cool glass, confusion churning in her belly. It was strange that the idea of reading her e-mails made her nauseous. She usually couldn't wait to see what a new day at her Web site would bring. Seeing how women had flocked to the site always provided validation, and occasionally a good belly laugh. And seeing thirty-five new merchandise orders would usually send her dancing through the living room—further proof that she'd tapped into the ultimate consumer market: women with disposable cash *and* a self-replenishing ocean of bitterness to fuel their purchasing decisions.

So why didn't any of that work for her today? What the hell had happened to the way she saw her career—and herself?

The question was enough to jolt her to attention. Roxanne flipped her hair over her shoulder and began to pace through Eli's office, her mind racing in a way that now felt foreign to her.

Oh, *God.* What was she *doing* to herself? If she'd already gotten to the point where she preferred bliss over pissed, then what would become of the Roxie

Bloom everyone knew? What would happen to her business? What would her crew think when their captain abandoned the SS *Man Basher* in favor of true love?

Roxie cracked her neck as she paced, trying to pinpoint the exact moment the change had occurred. It might have been the first time she and Eli made love, at the moment when everything else fell away except for the intense pleasure and connection. Or it could've happened at some point while working with Lilith, maybe the morning Lilith began walking at her side without a leash, as if it were the most natural thing in the world for her to do. Or the evening Lilith began responding to her hand signals without the backup verbal cues. No. It was likely that sunny morning that Roxie floated in the hot spring with Eli, and let her secrets go.

She crumbled to the floor, right there in front of the huge windows. She sat cross-legged and let her hands dangle from her knees. For a few long moments, she sat perfectly still, hearing the rhythm of her own breath, noting the seamless transition from day to night in the Utah desert. She saw how the light slipped away just as the shadows moved in, and she wondered if maybe that's how it had happened with her.

As her anger slipped away, a new phase of her life moved in—a phase of happiness, peace, and love.

"Roxie."

She turned toward the deep, mellow voice. Eli was paused halfway down the spiral stairs that led from the first floor. There was a slight tension between his brows, and his green eyes were filled with concern. "I've been looking all over for you. Is everything okay?"

She nodded, but her chin began to quiver and she pulled her mouth tight to keep from blubbering.

Eli leaned his body against the railing, scanning across the room to the computer desk and back to

Roxie. He gave her a patient smile. "All's well with your Web site?"

She shrugged. "I wouldn't know, Eli. I logged on, but I didn't want to . . . I couldn't . . ."

Eli eased down the remaining steps and headed toward her. He plopped down on the floor at her side.

"Change can be confusing."

"Yeah?"

"Sure," he said. "Knowing you has changed me so much I don't know which end is up anymore."

She laughed. "Are you talking about the edits I made to your aspiring-pack-leader manual?"

Eli grinned. "You did go a little overboard in killing some of my more creative flourishes."

"Spelling isn't supposed to be creative."

He kissed her quickly. "There's something I need to tell you, Roxie. Something about me you should know."

Anxiety rushed through her.

"Nothing too awful," he said, giving her a shy smile. "I mean, let's face it. If you're still here—if you haven't packed your bags and caught the first thing smokin' out of Utah—then you must already be okay with it."

Roxie shook her head. "What on earth are you talking about, Eli?"

He chuckled, raking a hand through his short curls. "Man, this is hard." He sighed, dropping his shoulders. "Do you remember when you told me you were afraid I'd be boring in bed? That I'd be too restrained?"

Roxie laughed at herself. "Pretty silly of me, huh?"

His eyes turned serious. "I'm going to tell you something I've never shared with anyone before. You'll be the only one who knows."

She swallowed hard. She'd never seen Eli like this, and it scared her. *Please, please don't fess up to some boneheaded man moment worthy of my Web site,* she thought.

"I've made a good living by keeping my cool, you know? People ask me to teach them to handle their pets and their lives with balance and stability. I love what I do."

"And you're good at it," Roxie offered.

Eli nodded, letting his attention stray out into the twilight. "The thing is, it's not as simple as that." He stopped for a moment before he continued, his eyes still focused in the distance. "When I was in college I got myself wrapped up in a girl named Bethany. I thought I was in love. I became very possessive of her—the feelings just swamped me, wiped out my self-control. The first night we had sex—" Eli glanced at Roxie and immediately burst out laughing.

She shut her gaping mouth and tried to quell the worst-case-scenario medley now playing in her head. Obviously, Eli was aware of her internal battle.

He turned and placed his hands on her shoulders and peered closer, touching his forehead to hers. "There are no dead bodies in this story, sweet thing. No rape. No theft. No stalking. No felony of any kind. No cruelty to animals. Just let me explain."

Roxie squeaked and nodded.

He pulled away and released her shoulders. "I got pretty wild with her one night. I put my hands all over her when we were having sex, grabbing her everywhere, saying some things that scared the shit out of her. I felt possessed, like a crazy man. The whole thing was way too intense for her and she freaked. She ran from me, in tears, and refused to speak to me after that."

Roxie felt her mouth fall open once more, but didn't bother to try to close it.

"I decided I'd never go there again," Eli said matter-of-factly. "Now that I knew there was this feral, out-of-control part of me, I decided I'd better keep it hidden, and in every relationship since I've been determined to be as stable in bed as I am at work. I've had about six relationships, and every one of those women told me that they loved my cool and collected nature but wanted more than that in bed. I couldn't give it to them."

Roxie gasped. "Are you serious?"

He nodded. "I'd convinced myself that a happy medium wasn't possible for me, that I'd never be able to stop once I got started, so I shut down. I chose boring over the alternative. That went on for about twelve years."

Roxie's jaw dropped again. Eli used the tip of his index finger to put it back into place.

"But—"

"Then last year, with Tamara, it happened again." Eli paused and studied Roxie's eyes. "We were having yet another talk about our future: *'Are we ever going to get married? When? If not, why not?'* Tamara was a pretty even-tempered person herself, but that night she'd reached the end of her patience, I guess, and was throwing things and yelling.

"She said, 'You and your goddamn stability!'" Eli winced, then checked for how Roxanne was taking it. She straightened her shoulders and kept her eyes wide. "You up for the rest of this?"

Roxie nodded. "I'm listening."

Eli sighed. "She told me she couldn't stand it anymore, that living with me was like living with a mannequin. She said, 'Why can't you just let go with me, Eli? Why haven't you ever told me you love me more than life itself, more than the air you breathe?'"

"Go on," Roxie told him.

"She said, 'Why does it always feel like you're holding back? Why can't you just throw me down and fuck the hell out of me? Why can't you—just once—tell me you'd die without me? Why haven't you ever just wanted me so bad that you lost control of yourself?' "

Roxie cracked her neck, which made Eli laugh. They looked at each other for a moment without saying anything.

"So you gave her what she asked for?" Roxie asked.

"Yep."

"And she freaked out?"

"Oh, yes. She left me that night. Moved to Seattle and got engaged to someone else about six months later, someone she described to me as 'passionate yet gentle.' "

Roxie nodded slowly. "So when you met me—"

Eli jumped up from the floor. He walked to the bank of windows and looked out into the night, his back to her. Roxie saw his shoulders vibrate with tension.

"I knew the second I saw you," Eli whispered, not turning around. "You were throwing off this tidal wave of angry energy but I sensed something rare and wonderful underneath it. You fascinated me. You thrilled me. I wanted you more than I've ever wanted a woman in my life. I couldn't look away."

"So you turned me down for lunch," Roxie whispered.

Eli spun around. "Damn, Roxanne! Don't you hear what I'm saying? The pull I felt toward you was so intense I knew I couldn't hide myself from you. I knew I wanted to own you, take you, devour you! And here you were, a woman literally marinating in her hatred of men, suspicious and ready for a fight. I turned you down because I thought it was the best thing I could do . . . for *you*!"

Roxie rose from her perch on the floor. She went to Eli, slipping her hands around his waist and resting her cheek on his chest. She felt him tremble. "Thank you for telling me," she said. "It explains a lot."

Eli laughed bitterly into her hair. "God. You have no idea how often I've worried that I was a hypocrite, a fake, pretending to be something I'm not."

"You're a human being, Eli. You're a passionate, wildly sexual man who happens to be a gifted dog whisperer. They don't cancel each other out."

He gripped her harder.

"You just never found a place where you can be yourself, Eli. Until now. With me."

She felt his body shake. He held on to her while he cried softly, but only for a moment.

"Roxie." He peeled her away from him. "Are you sure about this?"

She nodded.

"Because I don't think I will ever be able to push it down with you, and I don't know everything that's inside me."

She smiled. "We'll find out together."

"You're not threatened?"

She smiled up at him. She went on her tiptoes and kissed the warm piece of exposed flesh above his shirt collar, then leaned back a little so she could look in his eyes. "You've surprised me a couple times, but you've never scared me, Eli. Whatever goes on with us—here in your office or tangled up in your red flannel sheets—it feels just right. I love how we can talk about anything. I love how we fit together." She giggled. "I especially enjoy how you get all worked up and growl *you're mine*."

Eli's eyes widened. "Tell me more."

She slid her fingers up into his curls and massaged the back of his head. He closed his eyes and groaned with pleasure. "You are the most amazing lover I've ever had," she continued. "Sex with you is on a whole new level. Sometimes when you move your mouth all over mine it feels like you're claiming me, marking your territory."

He opened one eye. "Is that a good thing?"

"Yep," she said. "And when you put your hands on my throat or bite my neck, I fall into a trance. It's the strangest thing, but I get this sense that my heart is touching yours while you're taking me over physically. It's pretty fuckin' hot."

Eli's nostrils began to flare. "This is our last evening alone here, did you realize that?"

She might have been completely turned on by this conversation, but a lump of sadness lodged in her chest. "I don't want to go back," she managed to say. "I don't want to leave here."

"My sweet Roxie Bloom," Eli said, kissing her on her cheeks and ears and chin. "That's the beauty of it— you can come back whenever you wish. Believe it. *We* can come back, together."

She nodded. "I believe it," she said, smiling again. "And you can let yourself go with me, Eli. Bring it on. I'm not scared."

Eli chuckled. Then he grabbed her around the waist, lifted her off the ground, and crushed his mouth against hers.

Chapter 17

"Beatrice, be a dear and stay for just a moment longer, would you?"

Bea froze where she stood, looking from Gloria to Rachel, who'd already opened the hospital room door and stepped into the hall.

"It's okay," Rachel assured her. "I'll get the car out of the garage and meet you out front. Good night, again, Mother." With a tender smile, Rachel closed the door behind her and was gone.

"What is it, Gloria?" Bea asked, pulling up the straight-backed chair and scooting close to the side of the bed. Gloria looked particularly gray that evening, and much of the glint had faded from her eyes. She'd had two additional ministrokes, and the doctors had explained that Gloria would require live-in care when—and if—she was discharged from the hospital. It took only minutes for Rachel and Bea to decide they'd move in with Gloria, an arrangement she'd dismissed outright.

"That's the most ridiculous thing I've ever heard," she'd said. "You two just got started! What fun would that be?"

So as Bea leaned close to her now, she expected more of the same fight, and decided to stop it before it started. "No more arguing today, Gloria. You need to rest."

"I don't want to argue. I want to explain something to you."

Bea sighed. "Rachel and I already told you that we want to—"

"I'm dying, Beatrice," Gloria whispered. "I feel it."

Bea patted her hand and tried to silence her with a soft, "Shush now."

"*You* shush," Gloria snapped back. "I need to tell you about the nature of your gift, right now, because soon I may not be able to talk at all!"

Bea opened her mouth to protest but Gloria silenced her with a glare.

"You are blessed with certain abilities, Beatrice. You are sensitive and loving and compassionate. You truly want the best for others."

Bea smiled, but was suddenly feeling uneasy. "That's nice to say, but—"

"I'm doing the talking. You're doing the listening."

Bea's eyes went wide. "All right, Gloria."

"Now." The old woman took a breath. Bea watched her chest tremble with the effort. "You knew Eli was right for Roxie, didn't you?"

Bea stiffened in her chair, realizing that Gloria must have heard what she'd said to Eli at the baby shower. But how could she have? It had been noisy and Gloria was seated on the other side of the room.

Gloria waved her unspoken questions away. "I saw you talking to him. I knew you were telling him to go after her. My question is this: do you know why, exactly, you did that?"

Bea laced her fingers together and let her hands fal

to her lap. Bea had known for a while now that Gloria had a special affection for her, that she'd taken her under her wing. To what end, Bea hadn't understood until quite recently.

But she didn't want Gloria wasting her precious energy on anything that wasn't urgent. And this topic, though fascinating, wasn't urgent.

Unless Gloria really was dying. Bea tried hard not to cry.

"Go on," Gloria said. "Tell me how you knew. There's no time to waste."

Bea offered her a brave smile and took her cool and dry hand in her own. "It felt right, somehow. It's hard to describe."

Gloria smiled back. "Find a way."

Bea inhaled deeply and let her eyes sweep across the hospital room, noting how the evening shadows made even the flowers and balloons look sad and gray. "I don't know, Gloria. I'm not sure there are words for it."

"Oy! You used to know sixty different ways to tell newspaper readers that a man hit a home run. Give it a shot."

Bea chuckled, but stopped when Gloria closed her eyes and seemed to go limp. "I'm resting, not dead. Try to find the words."

Bea rolled her eyes. One of the things she loved about Rachel was that she'd inherited not only her mother's caring heart but also her preference for pointed conversation.

"I sensed some kind of complementary energy, I guess," Bea said. "I know this is going to sound very strange to you, but it was almost as if their *flavors* were what made them go together."

"Go on."

"Well, it was like Eli's qualities had a certain flavor

to them. Every time I met him, his energy tasted pleasing and pure but incredibly strong at the same time. It was a wonderful combination. And Roxie, well, she can be tart on the surface and sweet-spicy inside, like Chinese food."

Gloria blew out a puff of air, her eyes still shut. "So Eli is fine wine and Roxie is sweet-and-sour pork?"

Bea laughed. "I know. It's ridiculous."

Gloria opened her eyes. They were sparkling again. Her grin was wide. "It isn't the words you use to describe the hunch that matter, Bea. It's the hunch itself. Always go with the hunch, no matter how it comes to you. Me? I relied on a spectrum of humming sensations that would course through me, but I've also had that sense of flavor you talk about."

"Seriously?"

"Absolutely."

"Do Rachel and I hum?" Bea asked.

"So loud it's deafening."

Gloria was obviously exhausted from the talking. Bea patted her forearm and told her she'd see her first thing in the morning.

"No," Gloria said, grasping at Bea unsteadily. "Bea, I'm counting on you to carry on the work. Use your gift. Follow your hunches. They are never wrong."

"I will, Gloria." She bent down to kiss her forehead.

"Swear to me," she whispered. *"Swear it."*

Bea stood by the bedside and studied Gloria—frail and ashen, yet, for that instant, her eyes burned with a fierceness that belonged to someone at the peak of health.

"You want me to hook people up? You want me to help people find their beloved? As my *job*?"

Gloria nodded, her eyes welling with tears.

"Well, okay. Why not?" Bea said, not wanting to

agitate her more than she already had. She tucked in the blankets around her bony frame and kissed her forehead once more. "Now you rest."

Roxanne had never pretended to be a gourmand. In fact, she'd never pretended to be a decent cook. But in honor of Sondra and Carole's visit that evening, she'd whipped together one of her staples—fettuccine Alfredo with grilled chicken, a nice salad, and garlic bread. Eli had been put in charge of dessert and made brownies from scratch, which he planned to top with vanilla ice cream.

Roxanne had to admit that cooking in the middle of Utah didn't pose any additional challenge. Eli had a huge walk-in freezer downstairs stocked with enough meat, fish, and staples to last through Armageddon. And a quick trip to the Panguitch Grocery Coop scored some salad makings and a loaf of fresh Italian bread, and they were set.

Sondra and Carole arrived early, because Carole wanted to give the couple a chance to pack up and get plenty of rest before their drive the next morning. That was thoughtful of her, but Roxie suspected it was all part of Carole's plan to ensure she wouldn't have to spend much time in Roxie's company.

Dinner was pleasant. Roxie accepted compliments all around for the meal. Sondra's starstruck enthusiasm over Roxie's Web site had dimmed a bit, but she still managed to ask Roxie a dozen questions about its day-to-day operation.

"Not that I'd ever want to compete with you or anything, but I was thinking how cool it would be to set up my own site—maybe one just for the former partners of serial cheaters."

"*Sondra,*" was all Carole had to say about that.

After a quick cleanup of the kitchen, Eli asked Sondra to help him with evening rounds down at the kennels. Awkwardly enough, that left Carole and Roxie alone in the living room, with nothing to do but sip wine and alternate their gazes from the sunset to the fire in the fireplace. After a few moments of tense silence, Roxie realized it would be up to her.

"Carole."

"Roxanne."

They spoke almost at the same time, which provided a good laugh.

"You go first," Roxanne said.

"No, you," Carole said.

Roxie put down her wine glass and tucked her legs beneath her in the big leather armchair. She hadn't anticipated having a one-on-one conversation with Eli's mother, but figured she'd take advantage of it. "I just want to reassure you that I don't intend to hurt Eli. I don't have my claws out."

Carole blinked, sipping her wine.

"He's been incredibly good to me. We haven't known each other long, but there's been this *potent* attraction from the start. We both feel it, we enjoy it, and we want to see where it goes."

Carole nodded slowly.

"I know you don't approve of what I do for a living, but I assure you it won't influence my relationship with Eli."

"Hmm, interesting," Carole said. "Of course, I have nothing against you personally, Roxanne. You are a lovely and intelligent woman." Her words were carefully meted out and Roxanne wondered whether she'd rehearsed them in advance. "But no mother wants to see her son walk into something with 'heartbreak' written all over it."

"Ah." Roxie crossed her arms over her chest. "You think I'm going to break his heart?"

"Oh, I know so."

Roxie nearly choked. She might not have her claws out, but this mama bear sure did—even though her cub was thirty-two years old and could clearly take care of himself and nearly everyone else in his orbit. "What makes you so certain?"

Carole sighed deeply. She placed her wineglass on a side table and leaned in toward Roxanne. "You're a bitter girl. Someone hurt you very badly and one day Eli will do something really stupid—because all men do. Who knows? The issue may even be something completely beyond his control, something he has nothing to do with!" Carole nodded with certainty. "But you will turn that bitterness on full blast and you'll rip him to shreds. It may not happen right away, but it'll happen."

Roxanne was dumbstruck. And it occurred to her that if they'd had this conversation a week ago, Carole would have been dead right about it all. But not now. Not after what Roxie had learned about herself, Eli, life. Not after what Eli had so lovingly shown her.

"Look, Carole," she said, lowering her voice and speaking as calmly as possible. "I am not perfect, but I'm working on being the best person I can be. How about you? Have you never made a mistake? Have you never gone off course and had to steer yourself back? Have you never had to ask someone to give you a second chance?"

Carole pulled her mouth into a tight line.

Roxanne went on. "So, yeah, I had some bad experiences and I let them get to me, but I'm learning to let it go, a little bit every day, because I don't want to live like that anymore. Eli's been helping me find a different approach. Now, if that's not good enough for you—if my desire to do better and my sincere affection for your son aren't enough—then I guess you're shit out of luck, and *you're* the one who's going to be bitter."

They sat in silence. Roxie's heart was pounding. She could hear her breath sawing in and out of her nostrils. Carole's face had gone as red as the sunset. Just then, Sondra and Eli clomped up the porch steps.

"Point taken," Carole said, reaching for her wineglass and raising it, a wry smile on her face. "To second chances."

Roxanne clinked her glass to Carole's. "I love him, you know. I love him so much my heart hurts," she said. The words spilled from Roxie's mouth and then they were out there. She couldn't take them back.

"I love him, too," Carole said.

Just then, the front door flew open. Sondra came rushing in with a gust of evening air, her eyes alive with excitement. Eli followed behind, looking slightly sheepish.

"Guess what, Mom?" she announced. "You and I are going to fly to San Francisco to lend our moral support at the vicious dog hearing! Doesn't that sound like the best idea *ever*?"

After twelve-plus hours in the truck, they longed to stretch their legs. Besides, Roxie needed to practice her newfound pack leader skills in an environment in which Lilith had only experienced fear and instability.

Eli walked at Roxie's right side, and Lilith was on the leash to the left. As Eli had shown her, Roxie's eyes were to the front or slowly scanning the horizon. She did not talk to Lilith or look at her. She walked with the short leash loosely draped over her fingers, her arm limp at her side, not a twinge of tension anywhere. They'd been walking like this for about twenty minutes, and it had been the best twenty minutes Roxie had spent in the company of her dog within the San Francisco city limits.

"How does it feel?" Eli asked nonchalantly.

Roxie smiled at him. "Surreal. Fabulous. Wonderful."

"Don't get too worked up," he reminded her.

Roxie chuckled. "Whatever you say." She stretched up and kissed him on the cheek.

They rounded the corner of Sanchez Street and, of course, they encountered Mrs. Delano. Roxie whispered to Eli, "This is the Sweeping Lady I was telling you about."

Eli nodded. No one else would have known, but Roxanne could see Eli plugging into the woman, her movements, her energy. *"Yikes,"* he said under his breath.

"Good evening, Mrs. Delano," Roxie said. She and Eli stopped as she continued sweeping her driveway. Lilith sat down calmly at Roxie's side without being asked.

Suddenly, Mrs. Delano stopped her *swshh*ing in mid-stroke. She glared at Lilith and then at Roxie and Eli, her brow furrowed.

"This is Eli Gallagher," Roxie said. "Eli, this is Mrs. Delano."

Though Eli offered his hand, she gripped the broom with a vengeance.

"We don't get many cowboys in this neighborhood," she said, checking him out from boots to the brim of his hat. "Are you one of those Chippendale fellows?"

"No, ma'am," he replied, biting the inside of his cheek.

It took concentrated effort and a couple of deep breaths for Roxie not to bust out in a guffaw.

Mrs. Delano nodded toward Lilith next, and her

frown intensified. "Good thing you finally put her on drugs," she said. "Safer for everyone."

Roxanne smiled at her. "Well, have a nice evening." Their little pack began to move off down the sidewalk.

"Your old flame was here the other day, asking a bunch of questions." Mrs. Delano paused, then chuckled. "He looked like somebody threw him under a bus."

Roxie felt her entire body seize in anxiety. Her back and arm went rigid. Immediately, Lilith began to pull at the leash and whine. Roxie didn't even look at Eli. She knew what she had to do. She took three seconds to breathe, remember her place as pack leader, and feel the stability move back into her flesh and bone. Lilith quieted.

Roxie turned slowly. "Thanks for letting me know," she said to Mrs. Delano.

"He was asking about some young blond woman he thinks you're carrying on with. He kept asking about her. He wouldn't let it drop. It was like he had some kind of obsession problem. Ha! I told him I'd never seen her."

"Well, thank you. Have a nice evening." With that, Roxie turned again and they headed toward the house. "What the hell was that about?" she wondered aloud.

"Who knows? The only thing that matters is that you did real good, Ms. Bloom." Eli slipped his hand around her waist. "Damn good."

"I did, didn't I? And it felt great!" She smiled up at Eli. "Now all I have to do is keep it together when he's standing right in front of me, breathing fire, evil seeping from every pore of his body."

Eli shrugged. "No problem."

"It'll be a snap," she said, opening her front door. She and Eli stepped across the threshold first, then she motioned for Lilith to join them. She toddled in, tail wagging, head held high.

"Roxie." Eli reached for her, pulling her up against the front of his body. She felt the heat coming off his skin, the ease coming into her from him, the way it always did.

"You're going to do great."

"I am," she said, nodding gently.

"I will be right there the whole time."

"I know."

"Raymond Sandberg is just a sad, angry, lost guy, running around chasing phantoms and making threats. He can't touch you. And he can't touch Lilith."

"I know," she said, locking eyes with Eli. She breathed in his absolute confidence, transferred his calm control into her own being. And then he kissed her and his hands were all over her like a man possessed.

Chapter 18

The greeting committee was assembled on the front porch of Rick and Josie's ranch, but Teeny came jogging down the stairs at the first glimpse of Eli's truck. He was followed by a waddling Ginger supported by Lucio, followed by Bea and another woman Roxie didn't recognize, plus four raucous dogs. Josie waved frantically from a wicker lounge chair on the porch, Rick at her side.

Roxie giggled at the sight. She'd missed her friends. She couldn't *wait* for them to see what she'd been up to.

Eli pulled the truck to a stop and nodded for Roxie to hop out. Roxie kissed him quickly, gestured for Lilith to stay, then jumped from the truck directly into Teeny's outstretched arms. He swung her around a couple times.

"My God! You look fabulous!" Ginger shouted. "What have you done to yourself?"

"We have missed you!" Lucio kissed her cheek. "It as been far too quiet here!"

Inexplicably, Bea was crying. She pressed Roxie so ght against her breast that she couldn't breathe, then pulled away gently. "Rox, this is Rachel Needleman, Gloria's oldest."

"Oh!" Roxie shook Rachel's hand, not quite understanding why she was here. "Nice to meet you! How's your mother? Is she feeling better? I have a few things I'd like to talk to her about."

"She's not doing so great right now," Rachel said, slipping an arm through Bea's and pressing up against her in a very nonplatonic fashion. Roxie tried her best not to let her jaw unhinge but didn't succeed. Her eyes flashed to Bea.

"Yeah," Bea said. "We have a lot of catching up to do."

It was then that Eli made his way around the front end of the truck to join the crowd. Lucio and Teeny slapped his back gregariously and Ginger and Bea kissed his cheek. Bea introduced the latest addition to the group.

"Eli, this is my partner, Rachel Needleman. Rachel, this is the dog whisperer I was telling you about." With that, Rachel and Eli shook hands and Bea wiggled her eyebrows at Roxanne.

"You can close your mouth now, Bloom," Bea said. "Come on up to the house. Josie's dying to see you."

"Of course!" Roxie grabbed Teeny's hand and had taken two steps when she stopped. "No! Wait! Hold up!" With that she spun around and returned to the open passenger side door of the truck, where she motioned for Lilith to come out.

The dog hit the dirt and sat quietly. Chen, Tara, Genghis, and HeatherLynn ran up to greet her but slowed as they approached, confused. Lilith's tail was wagging. Her tongue fell out of the side of her mouth in relaxed happiness, and she looked to Roxanne for permission to do her brand-new, favorite thing—run free with her friends. Roxie made a gentle swish of her index finger and Lilith was off, her ears flying back in the wind, the other dogs playing catch-up.

Everyone stood frozen in the dirt lane. Only Ginger moved, and she rubbed her huge belly in concentric circles as she tried to control her breathing.

"What the fuck?" Bea asked, her face slack with disbelief.

With that, Roxie held out her hand to Eli and he moved to her side. They laced their fingers together.

"You can close your mouth now, Latimer," she said. "We've got some catching up to do."

"I'm going tomorrow and that's final," Josie said, once she was settled into bed for the evening. "I don't care what anyone says. I could never let you go through that without my support, Roxanne."

"I'll be fine."

"I want to be there to witness the moment you show everyone how good Lilith is and what an asshole Raymond is. I wouldn't miss it for anything!"

"It might be kind of stressful," Bea offered.

"Teeny's going to freak if you go," Ginger said.

"He's already freaking," Roxie pointed out to the women sprawled on love seats and chairs in Josie's bedroom. "I thought he was going to hack up his salmon croquette when you told him your plans."

"I've done *everything* the doctor's wanted," Josie said, attempting to cross her arms over her belly but giving up when she couldn't quite reach. "I've been a perfect patient. I'm almost to term at this point—only days away from my due date. I feel great!"

Bea shrugged. "Well, the good part is you'll already be in town if something happens. The Med Center is ten minutes away."

"Exactly," Josie said with a nod.

That's when the focus in the room changed. Everyone turned to Roxanne.

"What happened up there in Utah, Roxie?" Ginger asked, adjusting her position for the fifth time in as many minutes. She looked horribly uncomfortable.

Roxie let her head fall back into the mound of pillows on Josie's bed. She turned slightly to see her best friend's freckle-faced smile up close.

Josie grabbed her hand. "First off, you're in love," she said. "We can all see it."

Roxie grinned. "Yeah. I am."

"Yes!" Bea whispered, yanking her fist back in victory.

Rachel laughed. "She's been pulling for you."

"Does Eli know?" Ginger asked. "Have you said it? Has he said it back?"

Roxanne cocked her head, considering that. "Not technically. We've hinted at it. We've even talked about living together. I did tell his *mother* that I loved him, does that count?"

"No. That's just plain *strange,*" Bea said, causing the laughter to escalate.

"Wait! I had a reason," Roxanne said, interrupting the merriment. "She came right up to me and told me I would eventually turn bitter on Eli and break his heart. I told her she was wrong, that I loved him."

Josie's eyes went wide. "That's it? You didn't tell the woman to go screw herself?"

"Yeah, I know. Will the miracles never cease?" Roxie sighed, collecting her thoughts. "All this must strike you as amusing. I mean, I leave here a man-hating demon succubus and I come back a week later floating on a fluffy cloud of love."

"It's not funny," Josie said, squeezing her hand harder. "It's wonderful."

"Love looks really good on you," Ginger said, kicking off her slippers. "If I didn't know better, I'd think you'd gone and got yourself some Botox and a peel."

"She doesn't need a peel," Bea said, exasperated. "She's still in her twenties, for God's sake!"

"All I'm saying is you look stunning," Ginger said.

"And relaxed," Josie added. "Honestly, you look happier than I've ever seen you, and I'm including the pre-Sandberg era." Josie smiled at her. "So? Tell us everything!"

Roxanne laughed. "Everything" might be overkill, but she didn't mind giving them something to chew on. "Josie, do you remember that day at Starbucks when you got steaming mad at me and refused to speak to me for a week?"

Josie frowned. "I did that?"

"You sure did," Ginger offered helpfully. "It was the same day I told everyone about what was going on with Lucio and me."

"And how could we forget *that*?" Bea asked, rolling her eyes. She leaned toward Rachel to explain. "It was scandalous. I had to hose myself off when I got home."

"Anyway," Roxie said, chuckling with everyone else. "Does anyone remember my fateful words that day?"

Everyone shook their heads.

Roxie smiled. "Well, *I* sure do, because I'm eating them now. I said it was a universal law that you can't have great sex and a great relationship with the same man, that you're going to have to settle for one or the other."

Ginger chimed in. "That was right after I said I couldn't get pregnant because I was going through menopause!"

Roxanne had to hold her sides, she was laughing so hard. She fell on top of Josie, and she hadn't intended to, but her cheek pressed against her friend's belly. Almost immediately, Roxanne got kicked.

She gasped, raising her head quickly. "He just said hi to me!"

"It's a she," Bea said.

"We don't know that for sure," Josie corrected her.

"Whoever is in there just kicked me!" Roxie was awestruck. "Josie, that baby is big!"

She sighed and rubbed her belly again. "Yeah. Right about now I wish I'd gone to more of my yoga classes."

"At least you're still in your thirties," Ginger said, massaging her bulge. "I'm the one who's going to snap like a dried-out Thanksgiving wishbone."

Bea shuddered.

"You two will deliver like champs," Roxie assured them.

"And you'll do fine at the hearing tomorrow," Josie said.

"And Bea will ace her agility certification," Ginger added.

That gave Roxie an idea, but she clearly hadn't been the only one whose thoughts had wandered in that direction. Ginger attempted to get up off the love seat. Josie hoisted herself straighter in bed.

"I think we're about to do one of our all-girl pile-ons," Bea explained to a confused Rachel. "Feel like joining us?"

Rachel lowered her chin and stared at Bea in shock.

"Oh. Did I forget to tell you about our little ritual?"

"Your mom joined us the last time we did it," Ginger said, still trying to stand.

"Excuse me?" Rachel whispered.

"Yeah, and now it's your turn!" Bea popped up from her chair and grabbed Rachel's hand. Then she went over to the love seat and gave Ginger the boost she needed. They all approached Josie's big bed.

"Who's going first?" Josie asked.

"I will," Ginger said. "The sooner I do this the sooner I can go sit down again." She wrinkled her nose in thought, then put her manicured hand out in the middle of their circle, palm down. "I, Ginger Renee Montevez, officially promise to pretend I'm younger than I really am and deliver a beautiful, healthy baby in under one hour of labor." She looked quite pleased with her contribution, but then added hurriedly, "With the right to demand an epidural at any time, of course."

"I'll go next," Roxie said. She placed her hand on Ginger's. "I, Roxanne Bloom, solemnly swear to face Raymond Sandberg tomorrow in that hearing room with nothing but inner calm and a deep faith in my dog and myself."

"Whoa. That was good," Josie said, putting her hand on top of Roxie's. "I, Josephine Agnes Sheehan Rousseau—"

"Wait! Are you hyphenated?" Roxie asked, perplexed. "I don't think I ever knew that!"

"Heck no." Josie said, shaking her head. "I stacked everything together only because it sounded more formal. This is an important occasion."

"My feet are swelling, FYI," Ginger said.

"Okay. Where was I?" Josie cleared her throat. "I, Josie yadda yadda Rousseau, shall face my baby's imminent arrival with courage and the trust that everything will be all right."

"Are you scared?" Roxie whispered.

"No," Josie answered, her eyes clear and steady as she looked at Roxie. "I don't have the luxury of being scared."

All the women were quiet for a moment. Then Bea cleared her throat. "You want to go, Rachel?"

"You first."

"Okay." Bea took a breath. "I, Beatrice Latimer, promise to use my gifts to help others, and to offer my services to all those in need. Rachel?"

Roxanne watched Rachel nod her head and smile. She was struck by what a pretty woman she was, with her chin-length silvery-blond hair and funky earrings. She was elegant and feminine. "I, Rachel Diane Needleman, will face my mother's illness and death with grace, and will remain strong for my family."

Roxie's heart dropped. She hadn't realized Mrs. Needleman was gravely ill. She looked to Bea for an answer, but she was occupied with Rachel, who'd begun to cry softly, tucked under her arm.

Out on the porch, the four men sat in rockers and looked at the stars. Teeny and Lucio smoked cigars and drank port wine. Eli had a beer. Rick sipped mineral water.

"We'll already be in the city, Teeny," Rick said, trying to talk his friend down from his worried frenzy. "If Josie goes into labor at the hearing then we're only minutes from the Med Center. It'll be all right."

Teeny shook his head, taking a puff of his cigar, not looking at anyone.

"Here is the good news," Lucio said brightly. "She might go into the labor while you are stuck in traffic—and she will need the services of your mobile birthing unit after all!"

Teeny rolled his eyes. "I think you're making fun of me."

"That is one lucky group of women up there," Eli chimed in, hooking his thumb up toward the second story. His buddies stared at him in surprise, probably because Eli hadn't said much since they'd done the man/woman split after dinner.

"Think about it," Eli continued. "Each one of them is loved. Each one of them is cared for. The pregnant ones are spoiled rotten."

"It is impossible to spoil a pregnant woman," Lucio said. "It is an honor to take care of her when she is carrying your baby."

Teeny sighed. "I think I'm going to cry, man," he squeaked. "I just don't want anything to happen to my Josie Girl."

Rick patted his friend's shoulder, then turned to Eli. "How long will the hearing take?"

Eli shook his head. "Not sure, but I would guess fifteen minutes. They'll read the case notes, review the evidence, then take statements. The complainant goes first—that would be Raymond."

"Okay." Rick said.

"Then Roxie will have her chance to show the hearing officer that Lilith is rehabilitated and poses no threat to the public."

"Is she going to be able to pull that off?" Teeny asked, wiping his eyes dry.

"Absolutely," Eli said. "No doubt about it."

"The puppy is much nicer now," Lucio said, taking a puff of his cigar. "There is no more of the foam, yes?"

Eli smiled. "Lilith is doing great, because Roxie is doing great."

Rick shook his head. "I don't know what you did, man, but I hardly recognize that girl. I've only seen her walking around hunched over with the weight of the world on her back, but now she looks . . . I don't know . . . lighter, happier." Rick cocked his head in curiosity. "How'd you manage that?"

Teeny giggled. "And how about the riot gear? Did that come in handy?"

Eli laughed, then let his laughter fade into a sigh. "Turns out no special equipment was required, just a quiet place and some patience."

Nobody said anything for a moment. Then Lucio cleared his throat. "She holds herself like a woman who is well loved. You can always tell, you know. She is on fire inside yet she is tranquil on the surface, as tranquil as a queen."

Teeny spoke first. "That was damn near poetry, man."

"I have been doing the crosswords," Lucio explained.

"So is that what's happening here?" Rick asked, his voice low and serious. He propped his elbows on his knees and leaned closer to Eli. "Are you in love with her?"

"Most definitely," he said.

"Have you told her?" Teeny wanted to know.

"I have shown her, which was the only way Roxie would believe it," Eli said. "She's had the words before but without the follow-through." He found himself smiling. "I guess you could say I gave her the follow-through first, so that when she hears the words from me, she'll have no doubts."

"But a woman needs the words, too," Lucio said.

"She'll get them," Eli said. "I plan to tell her tomorrow. In fact, I plan to ask her to marry me tomorrow."

Every one of the rockers stopped moving. No one said anything for a long moment.

"There must be something in the damn water around here, y'all running around asking women to marry you like you're under some kind of spell or something." Teeny shook his head, then turned to his best friend. "What was it for you, Rick? Three weeks after you met Josie? Less?"

Rick scrunched his lips together, thinking. "Less."

Teeny glanced at Eli next.

"Yeah, it was fast. A couple weeks. But that's only if you don't count all the times I've run into Roxie in the past."

"They don't count." Teeny leaned toward Lucio. "And you?"

Lucio scowled in concentration. "I do not remember when I asked Genevieve to be my wife, because in my mind I was asking her the moment I laid eyes on her."

Teeny raised an eyebrow.

"All right. It took me exactly eight weeks," Lucio replied.

"You were dragging your feet compared to these two," Teeny said, puffing on his cigar.

"Do you have a ring and everything?" Rick asked. "What is your plan?"

Eli smiled, looking down at his boots in embarrassment. His plan might sound a bit risky, but in his gut he knew it was the right thing to do. "Well," he said with a sigh, meeting the gazes of his friends. "My sister brought my grandmother's ring to my house the other night, so I'd have it with me here in San Francisco. I hope to ask Roxie at the hearing, right after the ruling in her favor, in front of everyone."

Lucio choked on his port. "That is a ballsy thing to do, my friend."

"In front of Raymond Sandberg?" Teeny laughed. "That'll be worth the drive, right there."

Rick tapped his fist on Eli's knee. "You sure about this?" he asked. "You know, we're talking about Roxie Bloom, right? She's not the world's most stable, predictable woman."

Eli grinned. "I'll take my chances."

Chapter 19

They pulled into the parking lot of the nondescript cinder-block building at Fifteenth and Harrison. Eli took a quick survey of the cars, but he didn't see any sign of his mom and Sondra, Rick's SUV, or cars belonging to Ginger and Lucio or Bea.

"Nobody's here," Roxanne said, her voice thin and shaky as she swiveled her head around, scanning the lot. "My God, what if something's happened to Josie? Or the baby? Or Ginger? Or *her* baby?"

"Your dog is as stable as you are," Eli said, repeating his mantra.

Roxanne looked at him and blinked a few times. Then smiled. "I know. I will stay balanced at my core. I will remember to breathe. I will visualize the optimum outcome."

"Sweet thing." Eli ran his hand down her shiny, dark hair. "You're going to do fine. Listen, your entourage may not make it on time. Things like that happen. The traffic is terrible. Just keep your balance, no matter what. Are you following me?"

She nodded.

"Remember why you're here."

"I'm here to save my dog."

"That's right. And remember who you are."

"I'm Roxanne Bloom, warrior priestess."

Eli grinned. "Now you're talking."

They both looked down at Lilith, sleeping peacefully on the seat between them. "We can leave her here for a while and bring her in just before the hearing starts. Would you like to do that?" Eli asked.

Roxie shook her head. "No. I don't want her to freak out alone. She could open her eyes and see this place, and remember what happened to her here, and she could go completely—"

Thankfully, Roxanne stopped herself. She sniffed and tossed her hair behind her shoulder. "Yes, well, she wouldn't do that because dogs don't carry around past trauma the way humans do. They live in the present. And the only thing that would make her nervous today is if I were nervous today. Which I'm not."

"Exactly."

"How about we leave her in here for a few minutes?"

"That's an excellent suggestion." Eli cupped Roxie's pretty chin in his palm and kissed her lips softly. He gazed into her eyes. "Nothing swirling around in this place can affect your core stability. No one can take that away."

She nodded, her chin in his hand.

"You and Lilith are surrounded by an invisible shield of love and calm. Everything bounces off it. The only thing that can penetrate it is more love. More calm. Which I'll be sending you."

"Right."

They entered the hearing room together. The first thing Eli noticed was that the Sweeping Lady was seated in the complainant's witness section. He immediately sensed Roxanne's energy spike.

"She's here to tell the hearing officer what she saw the day of the dog bite."

Roxanne nodded her head and took a deep breath.

"Let's sit over here." Eli guided Roxie to a seat in the front row on the right side of the courtroom, then sat next to her. He leaned in so he could whisper in her ear. "See the little box there?"

Roxanne's eyes shot over to a single chair perched on a raised platform. The platform was surrounded by a solid panel of wood with a hinged doorway built into one side.

"That's where you'll sit with Lilith while you're waiting for the hearing officer to call you."

"Okay."

"Here she is." Eli nodded gently toward the front of the room as a uniformed female police officer walked in. She was probably in her mid-forties, short and stocky, with her black hair pulled back in a no-nonsense bun. But she had a big smile on her face as she greeted the bailiff.

"I've had one other case with her," Eli said. "Her name is Sergeant Donna Liu. She's real levelheaded." He smiled down at Roxie. "This is great news for us, Rox."

She nodded. "Thank God."

"Let me go say hi to her real quick."

Roxie clasped her hands on her lap to keep them from trembling. This was it. The moment had come. No matter what comforting words Eli had, she knew that there was nothing outside of herself that would make a difference at this point. Everything had to come from inside her today—the strength, the calm, and the confidence and bearing of a pack leader.

Roxie actually smiled to herself. Just then, she

realized that everything she'd been through in her life—the abandonment and the rejection and the tough breaks—it had all been worth it because it had made her who she was, *right at that moment*. She was a tough and stable woman who was going to spend the next half hour of her life on the highest possible plane of being, no matter what shit was thrown at her.

"Psst. Bloom."

Roxanne turned around, her body sagging in relief at the sight of Bea, two rows behind. "Where's Rachel?" she asked.

Bea shrugged. "At the hospital. She needed to be with Gloria."

"Of course," Roxanne said. "Is Mrs. Needleman okay?"

"For now," Bea said, smiling sadly.

"Where's everybody else?"

"On their way," Bea said, taking a quick glance around the room. "You ready, Rox?"

Roxanne smiled at her. "Absolutely."

"I know you'll do great," Bea said.

Just then, Roxie saw Carole and Sondra enter through the double doors at the back of the hearing room. Roxie waved them forward, introduced them to Bea, and then turned back around to continue her mental pep talk to herself. Knowing Bea was here had given her a second wind.

Eli came back, gesturing to his mom and sister in greeting and draping an arm around Roxie as he returned to his seat. Just as they'd decided it was time to fetch Lilith, the energy of the hearing room changed, and Roxanne's eyes focused over Eli's left shoulder. It was Raymond. Or was it? He looked like . . . Roxie suddenly remembered how Mrs. Delano had described him: looking like he'd been thrown under a bus. She hadn't exaggerated.

He was wearing a neck brace, the edge of the white bandage visible at the top. His left arm was in a cast and hung limp inside a sling. It looked like he was in pain as he swung a briefcase onto the table. He fell into the chair, then exchanged a few words with Mrs. Delano and . . . *the pizza guy*? When had he shown up?

"I take it Raymond's here," Eli said, not turning around. "You look kind of perplexed."

Roxie's eyes shot to Eli's face. "He brought the pizza delivery kid in as a witness!"

"That doesn't change anything, Rox."

"And Raymond is wearing a neck brace and his arm is in a cast! And I can't tell . . ." She peered over Eli's shoulder again for another look. "I honestly can't tell if he's faking all this for sympathy or whether something else has happened to him, because he sure as hell didn't look this bad leaving the ER. What's he up to?"

Eli frowned. "I'll take a look and tell you what I think."

Eli turned. Instantly, a sharp pang went through him. This was Roxie's former lover? This was the man she had hoped to marry? This old guy pushing himself to a stand had brought the spirited Roxie Bloom to her knees?

He kept looking, inexplicably fascinated by Raymond Sandberg. And confused. The man's energy was frayed. He carried himself as if he were embarrassed. This was not the powerful, cocky man Roxanne had described.

Eli stared, mesmerized, as the older man in a wool sweater vest, button-down shirt, and no tie tried to unhinge his briefcase with one hand, cursing under his breath as he struggled to accomplish the simple task. Then he reached in for a stack of papers and spread them out on the table in front of him.

He must have sensed he was being watched. He turned, looking Eli right in the eye.

And that's when Eli knew.

Raymond Sandberg didn't even acknowledge Eli. He certainly didn't recognize him. Then he limped toward the hearing officer's bench. Eli tried to listen to their conversation, but the words seemed to ebb and flow along with the pulse now pounding in his ears.

Eli heard enough to recognize the deep, soothing tone of Sandberg's voice. Then he noticed how Sandberg tapped the tip of his shoe onto the floor while talking. When the sergeant said something he found amusing, Sandberg lowered his head and bit the inside of his mouth. And there! Eli stared at Sandberg's mostly bald head, and saw that the blond hair that remained carried a bit of curl in it.

Eli stood. He was numb.

"Are you going to get Lilith?" Roxie asked.

He didn't look at her. "Yes. I'll be right back. Don't let them start without me."

Roxie chuckled.

Very, very slowly, Eli raised his eyes to his mother. What he saw on her face answered all his questions. He continued walking to the double doors. Their talk would have to wait. Everything would have to wait. He had a phone call to make.

"Hurry! Faster!" Ginger screeched.

Lucio kept his voice calm when he responded to his overexcited wife. "You have spent our entire married life telling me how good it is that I'm slowing down and staying put, and you want me to go faster?"

"Yes!"

"Josie is not the only woman who is pregnant," Lucio reminded her. "You also are pregnant, *guapa,* and I do not wish to crash the car into a light pole trying to get one pregnant woman to the bedside of another pregnant woman."

"But—"

"You heard Rick. I put him on the speakerphone for this precise reason—I wanted you to know what is going on so that you would not worry."

"But, oh my God. If—"

"Josie had the breaking of the water. They are on their way to the hospital. Everything is under control. This is not an emergency."

"And Roxie!" she wailed, not listening to a thing he said. "Oh, my God! Roxie's going to have to deal with the dog hearing and Raymond Sandberg all by herself!"

"She is not by herself. Eli is there. Bea is there."

"I'm texting Bea to tell her what's going on."

Lucio took the longest, most lung-busting breath he could manage. "Put the phone down, yes? We can text her from the hospital, when we have information to pass on."

Ginger said nothing.

"The most important thing is for you to calm yourself," Lucio continued, taking the corner cautiously. "I do not want you to have the breaking water, too."

More nothing.

"Right, *pelliroja*?"

Lucio glanced to his wife. Her eyes were huge and her mouth was slack.

"What is wrong?" he asked, terror seizing him.

Genevieve nodded down toward her shoes. In a soft, scared voice she said, "My water just broke."

"*¡Hostia! ¡No me jodas!*" Lucio hit the gas so hard he nearly gave them both a case of whiplash.

"I don't care what he's doing. This is an emergency." Eli waited, cell phone to his ear, shoving his way through the glass entrance doors and out into the parking lot.

"Milton Horvath, here," the deep voice said.

"This is Eli Gallagher."

Silence.

"I need you to answer one question for me— immediately."

"All right." The man's voice sounded strained. "But I think it might be better if we met for a drink somewhere. I'm free now. I can meet you wherever you are."

"No!" Eli caught himself, dragging a hand through his hair, spinning on the heels of his boots. This was no time to lose his balance, not when Roxie would be stepping into the ring in just minutes, not when he'd be handling Lilith's leash in seconds. He steadied himself. "I need you to be completely honest with me."

"Look, Eli—"

"Do you know Raymond Sandberg?"

"Uh . . ."

"What happened with my mother and Sandberg? Tell me what you know." Eli fell against his truck with a thud.

"Look, I can't jump to any conclusions for you, Eli. I wish I could, but—"

"What did you mean by 'out of hand'? You told me things got a little out of hand with my mother. Was Raymond Sandberg ever involved? Did he have sex with her, too?"

"Why are you asking me this? Why now?"

Eli gasped, the weight of the truth pressing down on his lungs with such force he could hardly breathe. He pushed up from the truck and did another half spin on his heels. He felt lost. Simply lost. He hissed into the phone. "Because I'm standing outside the animal control hearing room where the very same Raymond Sandberg is trying to get my girlfriend's dog euthanized. I was staring at a man who looks like me, talks like me, stands like me. And my mother is in there—she came for moral support—and one glance at this Sandberg dude and she's about ready to keel over."

"Oh, shit."

"I got ten seconds, Horvath. Then I have to walk back in there and deal with what is sizing up to be a huge fucking mess. Tell me everything. *Now.*"

Milton sighed. He paused for a beat. "Oh, Eli. I don't know how to put this."

"Now."

"Sandberg took a crack at her one night when I was done doing my thing."

Eli's brain froze. *"What did you just say?"*

"Look, I know it's awful. But she didn't even realize it at the time. She was pretty wasted."

At that moment the glass doors opened and his mother stuck her head outside, looking for him, tears streaming down her face. Eli slammed the cell phone closed and shoved it into his pocket.

Eli reached her in seconds. He put an arm around her shoulders and guided her back inside to a bench in the hallway outside the hearing room. "You sit here. Don't go back in there. Can you do that for me?"

She nodded, hanging her head. "I'm . . . Oh, Jesus, Eli. I'm so sorry for everything I've put you through. I didn't even include him because . . . I didn't think we ever . . ." Her head snapped up. "But I do remember him, son! Of course I do! I had a huge crush on him. But I swear . . ." She stared off into nothing and shook all over as she tried to catch her breath. "I don't understand how this could be!"

"I've got to get back in there," Eli said. "We'll have plenty of time to talk after." He put his hand on her trembling shoulder. "I love you, Mom. I always will. Nothing will ever change that."

Just then, Sondra appeared in the hallway. "What in God's name—"

"Sit here with her. Don't let her back in there."

Eli ran out to the parking lot again. He motioned for Lilith to come out. She jumped from the seat and sat obediently on the asphalt. He slipped the leash around her neck and began to walk. She stayed at his side. He went through the doors, past his sobbing mother and bewildered sister, and through the double doors of the hearing room.

At just that moment, Sergeant Liu called the vicious dog hearing to order. Eli headed toward the defendant box. Roxie's head swiveled, her eyes boring into him as he walked. When Eli finally looked at her he saw that fear and panic had deformed her pretty face.

She'd figured it out, too.

No. No. No. This can't be. I won't believe it. It can't be. This can't be real. Oh, God. No. Please, no.

"Miss Bloom, would you enter the defendant box with your animal, please?" The sergeant barely glanced up from the file opened in front of her. She riffled through pages. "Have a seat and I'll ask you to come forward in just a bit. Bailiff?"

Everything was a blur. The bailiff guided her toward

the box where Eli stood, leash draped over his hand. She couldn't look at him because he looked so much like his father. She couldn't look at Lilith because it would make the dog anxious. She couldn't look at Sondra or Carole because they'd already run from the room as if fleeing from Satan himself. And she sure as hell couldn't look at Bea, or she'd lose whatever tentative grip she had on her sanity.

Roxanne sat. She let her arm go limp at her side so that she transferred no tension to the dog. She kept her eyes forward, staring at the Seal of the City of San Francisco, which hung on the paneling behind the judge's head.

The hearing started. Raymond had walked toward the bench and begun speaking. He handed some papers over. Roxanne didn't hear anything. She could hardly see because her eyes were swimming with tears. Her only hope—Lilith's only hope—was that a person in shock didn't transmit negative energy. How could they? She didn't even feel alive inside, and there was no energy without life, right?

What had just happened? Had Eli lied to her? Or was he in as much shock as she was? And if Raymond Sandberg was Eli Gallagher's father, whether he lied or not didn't even matter, because she could never—*never*—find a way to deal with that.

When this hearing was over, Roxanne was going to . . .

"Miss Bloom?"

Roxie blinked, suddenly realizing someone had said her name.

"Yes?"

"Did you hear my question?"

"No, Your Honor, I'm sorry. Could you repeat it?"

And there it was—Raymond's smarmy, self-righteous laughter, floating through the hearing room. Right on cue.

"That's enough, Mr. Sandberg," the judge said. "I would think of all people here today you would be capable of behaving with decorum."

"Yes, of course," he said, clearing his throat and sitting down.

"Miss Bloom, I asked if you had any witnesses?"

"No, Your Honor."

"Are you prepared to respond to Mr. Sandberg's claim that he"—she picked up a piece of paper and read it aloud—"'suffered grave physical and mental injury by the unprovoked attack of a vicious dog'?"

Roxie couldn't help herself. She chuckled. She felt so hollowed out and dead inside that she couldn't think of much else to do.

"Sure, I would like to make a statement about that," she said. "Do I need to stand?"

"No, Miss Bloom, not until I ask you to come forward with your animal. You can speak from your seat."

She nodded. "As you can see from the evidence I submitted to the court, the attack was not unprovoked—quite the opposite."

The judge smiled kindly, clasping her fingers together on the raised table in front of her. "It's not a court of law, Miss Bloom. I am not a judge, so you can call me 'Sergeant' or 'Officer.'"

"I'm sorry Your—*Sergeant*," Roxie said.

"And as far as your evidence goes, I have read the documents you filed with animal control but I'd like to hear it in your own words." The sergeant smiled at her patiently.

"Sure," Roxie said, nodding. She took a deep breath. Miraculously, she felt some life returning to her. He face felt hot. She felt her hands begin to tremble. The only problem was, she didn't want to feel alive. She didn't want to feel anything.

"Uh, Mr. Sandberg and I were in a relationship for about a year. It ended when I overheard him talking about me to a group of his friends, and what he said about me was . . . it was very hurtful."

The sergeant tipped her head, looking puzzled. "This took place in public?"

"Yes. At the Havana Club downtown."

"All right. Who were these friends of his?"

"Other lawyers. I covered courts for the *Herald* at the time, so I had working relationships with many of them." Roxie didn't intend to, but she looked at Raymond. Yes, he was smirking. Yes, his eyes were burning with smug hatred. But suddenly, he looked pitiful to her. What had Eli called him just last night? "A sad, angry, lost guy, running around chasing phantoms . . ."

"You know, Sergeant, it really doesn't matter to me anymore." Roxie shrugged, realizing it was true. "What happened with Mr. Sandberg isn't important. The only thing that is pertinent here is that our relationship ended badly, Mr. Sandberg was very angry with me, and he came to my home uninvited the night of the incident. I went to answer the door. It struck my head when Mr. Sandberg busted it off its hinges. I fell back. Mr. Sandberg called me names and threatened to kill me. My dog attacked him before he could get his hands on me."

"Pardon me, Sergeant Liu," Raymond said from his seat. "I would be remiss if I did not inform you that I am pursuing a tort claim against this woman for defamation of character."

"Really?" The officer frowned. "But *you* were the one who defamed *her.*"

"Of course," Raymond said. "No! I mean, no. I did

no such thing! I am referring to my future civil claim in which I shall seek damages from Ms. Bloom."

"For what?"

"For publishing on her commercial Web site a series of malicious, false, and defamatory statements about me that have harmed my reputation."

"She mentioned you by name on this Web site?" The sergeant looked back and forth between Raymond and Roxie, fascinated.

Raymond pushed himself to a stand, looking somewhat unsteady. "No, but that is not—"

"Then how can you claim she injured your reputation?"

Raymond smiled and shook his head, as if amused by a child's mistake. "How about we leave that point to a real judge?" he said, his voice dripping with disdain. "Someone who understands the many nuances of the law, such as the fact that vilification can occur even without the use of the injured party's name."

"Interesting," Sergeant Liu said, nodding. "Of course, since I'm not a real judge, you'll have to explain to me how she managed to defame you without naming you. This is all way over my head."

Raymond looked up to the ceiling and rolled his eyes, then suddenly winced in pain. He cupped the back of his neck with his good hand. "Look, Officer, Roxanne Bloom provided a detailed description of my person, my position in the community, and various personality characteristics that left little doubt as to whom she was referring. Can we get back to—"

"How did you describe him exactly?" The sergeant was looking at Roxanne. "I'm real curious."

"Well," Roxie said. "I called him 'San Francisco's most successful criminal defense attorney and all around champion pig-faced, misogynistic asshole.'"

Bea's snort of laughter could be heard reverberating through the hearing room. The pizza boy slapped his knee and howled with appreciative laughter.

"What's the name of this Web site?" The sergeant had her pen poised at the ready.

Roxie sighed. "It's www.i-vomit-on-all-men.com. It's hyphenated."

The sergeant's mouth fell open. "Lord have mercy," she said, taking notes as she shook her head slowly. "You two must have made a lovely couple."

Raymond sighed loudly. "I would really appreciate it if we could simply—"

"You know what I'd appreciate?" the officer asked, looking at Raymond as if he were a bug she was about to squash. "I'd appreciate it if you kept your piehole closed until I ask you a direct question. You think you can handle that, Mr. Sandberg, *Esquire*?"

He blinked at her, offended. "Certainly."

"Super." She turned to Roxie. "Now, I've read the police reports about the state of your front door. He must have been pretty ticked off to bust it down like that."

"He appeared to be, yes."

"What type of physical condition was he in at the time? I ask because the man I see right now sure doesn't look like someone who could bust down a door."

"He seemed to be healthy and strong that day." Roxie refused to look at him.

"Out of curiosity, did Mr. Sandberg ever physically abuse you?"

"No," she said.

"Verbally?"

"*Objection*, Your Honor!" Raymond shouted.

"Objection to what, Mr. Sandberg?" The sergeant was clearly furious. Her skin was splotchy across her cheeks and all the way down into the neck of her patrol uniform. "You just objected to a question I asked a defendant in my own hearing room, which would be bad enough, but objections aren't even permitted here. This is not a court of law. There are no juries here. This is *my* hearing room. *I* make the decisions here. Got it?"

Raymond's mouth fell open and no sound came out.

"Miss Bloom." She turned her attention to Roxanne once more. "Did he verbally abuse you on a regular basis?"

She shrugged. "He often insulted and threatened me. But it's all in the past. Raymond Sandberg was a huge mistake, but I'm not living that mistake anymore."

"Uh-huh." Sergeant Liu pulled her lips tight for a moment. She looked at Raymond. "Mr. Sandberg, I see no reference to a cervical collar or broken bone in your medical records. Are those injuries related to the dog attack?"

Raymond paused thoughtfully, nodding. "I would have to say yes, due to the fact that my underlying physical strength was compromised in the vicious dog attack, leaving me susceptible to—"

"He's lying."

Everyone's heads whipped around.

"And who might you be?" Sergeant Liu asked, craning her neck to the back of the hearing room.

A petite blond woman in her early twenties took a step into the center aisle. "My name is Dustan D'Urberville, ma'am. I was Mr. Sandberg's personal assistant at the time he received the injuries in question."

Roxanne felt her eyes grow big. *Raymond's phantom woman was real!*

Chapter 20

Sergeant Liu groaned. She wiggled her fingers impatiently to direct the girl toward the bench. "Come on up here and tell us what you know about the complainant's injuries. Let's get this over with."

She walked slowly and deliberately, giving Raymond enough time to lodge a protest. "This is preposterous! She has no place at this hearing! I must object in the strongest possible—"

"Would you put a *sock* in it, Sandberg?" Sergeant Liu's eyes looked like they were about to pop from their sockets she was so angry.

Bea snorted again.

"All right, let's have it, miss. Were you present at the time he received these injuries?"

"Yes, ma'am."

"And how did they happen?"

The young woman stood erect, clasping her hands in front of her skirt. "Mr. Sandberg and I were in his office. He shoved his hand in my underwear and I pushed him. He fell on his back on the floor." She paused to take a breath. "I left him there, stretched out and not able to move. His secretary later told me he had to be carted away in an ambulance."

Roxie clapped a hand to her mouth. Gasps echoed through the hearing room. Bea snorted.

Sergeant Liu closed her eyes for a moment, collecting herself. "And the arm? Did he injure his arm at that time as well?"

"Oh," the young woman said. "My brother broke Mr. Sandberg's arm trying to protect me from him in a parking garage late one night."

"This is utter fiction! Insanity!" Raymond cried. "I refuse to allow my reputation to be dragged—"

"Bailiff!" Sergeant Liu pointed to Raymond and the bailiff raced across the hearing room to stand in front of him. He collapsed in his chair.

"Thanks, miss. That'll be all." The sergeant shooed her away.

The girl turned and walked up the aisle and out the double doors.

"All right, people." The sergeant shook her head wearily. "I'm an animal control officer, not a talk show host, so how about we just move on to the dog? I can handle dogs. Miss Bloom?" She waved Roxie forward. "Bring the dog on up here and let's have a look."

This was it. Roxie opened the gate and stepped down. She kept her eyes to the front. She kept her arm loose. She kept her breathing steady. She walked calmly to the center of the room and stopped. Lilith sat at her side without being asked.

"Okay, Miss Bloom. There's no doubt this dog attacked Mr. Sandberg. You do not dispute this fact, correct?"

"No, ma'am."

"And you are here today to prove to the City of San

Francisco that the animal is not a threat to the public safety, correct?"

"Correct."

"But this isn't even the same dog! It can't be!" Raymond stood suddenly from his chair but lost his balance and knocked his briefcase off the edge of the table. It slammed to the floor inches from Lilith and sent papers scattering, which spooked her.

"Sit down, Mr. Sandberg!"

The ruckus was all too much for Lilith. She jumped and began tugging at the leash, hairs prickling along her spine, a low growl starting deep in her throat.

Roxie couldn't allow this to happen. Very calmly she turned, leash in hand, and made a wide half circle. Lilith fell into place at her owner's side, and when Roxie stopped again, a few feet away, the dog seemed soothed.

Roxie wanted to look to Eli. She wanted to see his face. She wanted to look into his eyes and know everything was going to be all right. But she couldn't risk it. She was almost there. This was almost over. She had to keep it together.

"Is this the same dog named in the complaint, Miss Bloom?"

"Yes, ma'am. This is Lilith, the same dog that was impounded here at this facility after the incident."

The officer nodded. "Has she ever bitten anyone else?"

"No." Roxanne caught herself. "Wait. Yes. She did bite Eli the first time he came to the house."

"That dog's not right in the head!"

Sergeant Liu glared at Mrs. Delano, who had just popped up from her seat next to the pizza guy. The officer's jaw tightened. "Are you Mrs. Louise Delano?"

"I am."

"I believe you've already given us a written statement about the dog's mental state, but, since you're up, is this the same dog that bit Mr. Sandberg?"

"Ob-*jection*!" Raymond roared.

Sergeant Liu didn't even look his way.

"Oh, sure. It's the same dog, all right," Mrs. Delano said. "You can see the wildness in its eyes."

"Thank you. Please have a seat." The sergeant glanced at Lilith. Out of the corner of Roxie's eye, she could see that her dog was relaxed and still, thank God. The officer clasped her hands on the raised desk. "Mr. Gallagher, would you step forward, please?"

Roxanne felt him move up behind her. She felt his heat and his love for her, and it was too much. She had to keep it together for a few more minutes. But the sorrow had started to build. Fate had asked too much of her. There was no way she could ever link her life to Raymond Sandberg's son!

It wasn't fair! Tears began to well in her eyes, and they were coming on with such intensity that Roxanne didn't think she could stem the tide.

"What have you discovered while working with Miss Bloom's animal?"

"Lilith was a frightened and anxious dog at first," Eli answered. "But Ms. Bloom and I worked on the elements of stable pack leadership, and once that was in place, everything changed. The dog is now calm and confident."

The sergeant nodded at Lilith approvingly.

"Her fear and anxiety level have almost disappeared," Eli said. "She does seem like a different dog."

"That's because it *is* a different dog, you nutjob!" Raymond came eyeball-to-eyeball with Eli, sneering at him. "The dog who attacked me was evil looking, frothing at the mouth. It had its fangs bared and it growled as if it were possessed."

"If I were a dog, I would have attacked you, too," Eli said, his voice soft. "Did you think you could simply go through life terrorizing women and animals and get by without a scratch? It doesn't work that way."

Somebody began clapping. Roxanne didn't have to turn around to know it was Bea.

"That's enough, Mr. Gallagher," the officer said.

"Who do you think you are, for fuck's sake?" Raymond got right up in Eli's face, his voice a vicious whisper. It was then that Roxie noticed the two men were exactly the same height.

"Mr. Sandberg!" Sergeant Liu was on her feet.

"You think you got some little hottie here?" Raymond jabbed his good finger in Roxie's direction. "What you've got is a hot *mess*! She's mean and nasty and she'll turn on you if you give her half a reason. She'll cut off your balls if you even look at her funny."

Eli grabbed him by the shirt collar, pulling him closer. "You should have been castrated years ago, you pathetic excuse for a man."

"What in the world is going on here?" Sergeant Liu stood over her desk with her arms stretched out from her sides in disbelief. "This is an animal control hearing, not some kind of encounter group! I don't care what kind of twisted thing you all have going on here. My only concern is the public safety, and as far as I can tell this little dog here poses no threat whatsoever. You *people* are another story, however!"

"I can explain," a female voice said from the back of the hearing room.

"And who are you? Another of Mr. Sandberg's former assistants?"

"No." Carole moved forward down the center aisle

between Sondra and a gray-haired man Roxie didn't recognize. "I am Eli's mother. My name is Carole Tisdale Gallagher."

"What the *hell*?" Raymond hissed. One of his eyes began twitching frantically.

"Unfortunately, we're all in shock today, Sergeant, and I apologize that it had to happen in your hearing room. We certainly didn't plan it this way."

"Mother—"

"No, Eli. I'm fine."

Roxanne watched as Carole came closer. She could see her body tremble with each step, but her shoulders were back and her chin was held high. In that instant, it was easy to see where Eli got his character. It sure wasn't from dear ole dad!

"I'm afraid that it has only just now been revealed to us that Raymond Sandberg is Eli's biological father."

"Jesus Fucking Christ!" Raymond staggered back until he bumped into the table. "This is complete lunacy! Madness!"

"Nope," the gray-haired man said as he placed a hand protectively on Carole's shoulder. "Madness was what I did all those years ago, the night I stood by while you had your way with this lovely woman. Lunacy was keeping that horrible secret to myself and then living with the sickening guilt all my life."

Sergeant Liu collapsed into her chair.

"Milton Horvath?" Raymond pushed himself away from the table and stumbled a few steps. "Is that you? Damn, you look old, man!"

Bea snorted.

"Do you want him to take a paternity test?" Carole looked to Eli with extreme sadness. "We can get a court order if we have to."

"Now hold on a goddamn minute." Raymond glared

at Carole. "I have no idea who you are, lady, but I can tell you with absolute certainty that I am not this man's father."

"December 1977," Milt Horvath said quietly. "The back office at the Sensation Club, where I was the DJ. Carole was with that group of girls that always sat at the corner table near the window. Ring any bells?"

Raymond clutched at his neck as if he were in severe pain. His eyes shot toward Eli. He shook his head. "No. You're nuts."

Milt Horvath laughed bitterly. "Oh, come on now, Ray. You know exactly what I'm talking about."

"I've had enough of this," Raymond said, turning toward his briefcase and throwing papers inside.

Eli very calmly followed him, slammed the briefcase shut and then leaned on it. He got right in Raymond's face. "I came to Northern California on a quest to find my biological father. I wanted closure. But you know what? I now know who my father was. He was Robert Gallagher, the man who adopted me when he married my mother and loved me until the day he died. I was a lucky, lucky kid. And right now—" Eli swallowed hard as he tried to continue.

Roxie wished she could go to him. But she couldn't move.

"Right now I realize just how lucky I really was," Eli managed. "I never had to know you, Sandberg. I never had to grow up with the knowledge that a lowlife like you brought me into this world."

Raymond stood with his lips parted. His knees shook under the pleat of his expensive slacks.

Bea's phone rang. She immediately ran out into the hallway with it.

"No damn cell phones in the hearing room!" the sergeant yelled, annoyed that the call had interrupted the proceedings. She leaned forward on her elbows. "But now that you mention it, I do notice a strong resemblance."

"Roxie!" It was Bea, poking her head through the doors. "They're both in labor. I've got to get over there."

"What!?" Roxie's stomach felt as if it had dropped to the floor. "Both of them?"

Bea nodded. "They're at the hospital. I'm sorry, but I've got to go."

"No! Wait! I'm going with you!" Roxanne whirled around. "Your Honor. Your Sergeant. I apologize but I have to leave. It's an emergency. My best friends are having their babies. Am I excused? Is there anything else I need to do? Can I come back at some other time?"

Sergeant Liu shook her head and began signing some papers. At first, Roxie thought she'd failed to show that Lilith was rehabilitated. Instinctively, her eyes shot to Eli. He was staring at her, his expression filled with so much hurt and uncertainty that it stabbed her.

"You're good to go," Officer Liu said. "You and Mr. Gallagher have done a fine job. Keep at it." She motioned for Roxanne to approach the bench and she handed her some papers. "That dog sat there like an angel in the middle of flying briefcases and hollering and cussing and stomping and the kind of DNA drama I've only seen on Maury Povich. That little dog deserves a medal."

"Impossible!" Raymond slammed his good fist on the tabletop.

Sergeant Liu stood up and gathered her paperwork. "I find the animal in question poses no danger to the health, safety, or welfare of the community. This hearing is concluded."

"Thank you! Thank you!" Roxie clutched the forms to her chest and began to run for the doors when she realized she couldn't exactly take Lilith along to the hospital. *Shit.* "I'm sorry," she said, placing the leash in Eli's hands and not looking at him. "I've got to go."

"Roxie."

She didn't dare look at him. "I can't, Eli," she said, running.

He stood there, Lilith's leash draped across his palm, the worried eyes of his mom and sister boring into the back of his head, his diabolical father at his side.

What a fucking mess.

"Pardon me," Raymond said, pushing past Eli, heading for the aisle.

"Where do you think you're going?" Milt Horvath blocked his way.

Raymond laughed. "Oh, please, Milton. You've done your superhero duty for the day, don't you think? I'm a busy man."

"Just let him go," Eli said. "I won't be pursuing anything further."

Raymond turned to him and shook his head. "Best of luck with Bitch Bloom. You're going to need it, pal."

Fuck stability. Fuck serenity. Eli handed the leash to Sondra. "Would you mind taking her out to the truck?" he asked calmly.

"My pleasure," she said.

Eli tossed the truck keys to his sister. He turned around slowly, cocked his elbow, pulled it down and back, then slammed his fist up into Raymond Sandberg's gut.

A loud *thump!* filled the air when the man hit the floor. The bailiff shook his head and strolled out the side door, as if he hadn't seen a thing. Then the moaning started. Eli left Sandberg there, in a pile. "Better call an ambulance, Milt," he said.

Eli stormed down the aisle. Bea was waiting for him in the hallway. She got right in his face. "Don't you dare give up on her, Gallagher," she said.

"Let it rest, Bea. Where is she?"

"Outside in the car."

"Shouldn't you two be on your way?"

Bea gripped him by the upper arms. "She loves you. She's in shock right now. So are you. This situation sucks."

Eli laughed bitterly and turned away from her.

"Do you love Roxie?"

Eli turned to face her again. "I love her with everything in me. I wish it were that simple."

"Oh, but it truly is, my friend." Bea smiled at him. She patted his shoulder. "We're going to be on the labor and delivery floor at California Pacific Medical Center. Do you know how to get there?"

"Sure."

"Then be there in a half hour. Don't you dare give up on that woman, Gallagher. You know she needs you. You know you need her."

Eli closed his eyes. "But every time she looks at me, she'll see Sandberg. I can't put her through that. I can't put myself through that."

"What the fuck are you talking about?" Bea asked, laughing.

Eli's eyes flew open.

"Get over yourself, Gallagher," she said with a wave of her hand. "None of us get to choose our parents— are you *kidding*? Do you think I would have gone out and picked Imogene Latimer to be my mother? As if! Do you think Roxie would have picked the spineless loser who was her father?"

Eli blinked. "Uh . . ."

"News flash here, Gallagher—we don't get to choose

our beloved, either. Someone is or is not the right person for us. It's that simple and that mysterious, and you and Roxanne were chosen for each other." She leaned closer and gave him a wicked smile. "Don't you dare tell me you don't *know* what I'm talking about, because I think you do." Bea winked at him. "See you at baby central."

They raced through the parking garage, took the stairs to the street level, and ran through the hospital's main lobby to the bank of elevators, arguing the whole time, the way they'd been arguing since they burned rubber out of the Animal Control parking lot.

"Roxie, give the guy a chance."

"To what end?" She smacked her palm on the up button a dozen times. "I don't blame him for anything. It's not his fault. But I'm just not strong enough for this shit. Leave me alone."

"You mean to tell me you're going to turn away from the best thing that's ever happened to you?"

"I said drop it, Bea."

"This morning you wanted to be with him because he was a loving, patient, amazing man. But this afternoon you don't want him anymore. And why? What about him has changed? Nothing! Only your perception has changed. It's all because you found out where the sperm came from that created him!"

The elevator door *dinged* open.

"I can't believe you, Bloom!" Bea continued. "You're going to let one little measly sperm determine the course of your whole fucking life?"

"Excuse us," a woman said, slapping her hands over her kid's ears as she pushed Bea out of the way and exited the elevator. Roxie hadn't even noticed they'd had company.

"Nice going, Latimer," Roxie said. The doors closed and the elevator headed up to labor and delivery.

Bea snorted, then crossed her arms over her chest. "So you believe the character of a father determines the character of his child?"

"Not necessarily. But I don't want to find out."

"Hmm," she said. "That's real interesting coming from you, because from what you've told me about your dad, he gave up and ran away like a scared rabbit when things got tough."

Roxanne pulled her lips tight and glared at Bea. "That is enough. Seriously. I'd prefer to keep you as a friend, so you'd better stop right there."

Bea laughed loudly. "That's awful kind of you, Rox, but as your friend it's my *duty* to point out that you're acting an awful lot like your dad at the moment. Lucky for Eli, you're cutting him loose now and not six years from now, after he's linked his life to yours and maybe had a kid or two with you."

Roxie swung her arm around and waited for her palm to connect with the side of Bea's face. Instead, Bea grabbed her by the wrist and squeezed tight.

"You've saved your dog, Bloom. Good for you. Now it's time to save yourself."

The elevator stopped. The door opened, revealing the tear-streaked face of Rachel Needleman.

What mattered to Eli most in this life? His integrity, of course, and his family, his friends, his dogs, and his land. Everything else was just busywork.

Then there was Roxie Bloom. He'd wanted her the instant he spotted her, all long and slender with dark eyes and hair, a vision in that soft green bridesmaid dress. He told himself to walk away. It would be better for both of them.

Then he'd fallen hopelessly in love with her that day at the Starbucks, when she'd raised that pretty face and told him she wanted to get rid of the garbage in her life so there'd be room for happiness.

Then he'd watched as her courage and sweetness revealed itself. He'd observed how hard she worked to help a beaten-down mutt. And did she ever make him laugh!

Then there was everything else. How his heart came to life when she was near. How her playful sensuality opened the floodgates of his own. She was his complement. He could be himself with her.

Bea was right of course. This was no fluke. Eli and Roxie were supposed to do this. They were supposed to make a go of it. He would be a fool to pass up this opportunity for his soul's happiness.

Eli pulled into the parking garage and took his automatic ticket, smiling to himself. If it didn't hurt so much, it would be damn hilarious that Raymond-fucking-Sandberg—*of all the male human beings on the planet*—turned out to be his father!

He swung the truck into a parking spot, hopped out, and started to run.

Rachel fell into Bea's embrace.

"Why are you up here on labor and delivery?" Bea asked Rachel. "What's going on? Why aren't you down on the second floor with your mom?"

"You haven't heard?" she asked, pulling away from Bea. Then Rachel glanced at Roxie. "Nobody's called to tell you?"

Roxie's body clenched in fear. "Just tell us what's wrong."

"Oh, God." Rachel took a shaky breath. "Ginger's almost ready to deliver. She's doing great. But, um,

Josie . . ." Rachel blew out a breath of air. "Josie was just rushed into surgery. They said they couldn't find the baby's heartbeat."

Roxie ran. She heard Rachel begin to tell Bea something about her mother's condition but didn't stop to listen. She hit the waiting room at full stride. It was packed with people Roxie usually only saw at baby showers or weddings. Ginger's twin teenage sons were sprawled out on a couple of chairs, accompanied by Larry, Ginger's physician ex-husband, Ginger's mother, and Lucio's father.

Across the room, gathered in a quiet cluster, was Josie's family. Teeny hovered over them, both of Josie's sister's kids asleep in his arms. All the Sheehans looked pale and terrified. Roxie decided not to intrude.

"Larry," she said. "Can I talk to you a minute?"

Larry got up and walked with Roxie to a corner, where they'd have privacy.

"I hear Ginger's doing great."

Larry nodded, his grin widening. "Yeah. She's fully dilated. Looks like the old girl's still got it in her."

Roxie had no time or energy to comment on that vintage Larry Garrison remark.

"I know you're worried about Josie," Larry said, patting her arm. "I don't know for sure what's going on. I'm a urologist, so this isn't exactly my forte, but I know that fetal distress was indicated and they took her in for an emergency C-section."

Roxie nodded, but she felt sick.

"This is not uncommon, Roxanne. The good news is that they got her in there at the first sign of trouble."

"How long's she been in surgery?"

"They just took her in. We should know something very soon—it doesn't take long."

"It is a girl!" Lucio burst through the hydraulic

double doors separating the patient areas from the waiting room, a paper mask dangling from his ecstatic face. "It is a girl! We have a girl! We have a beautiful, healthy baby girl!"

Lucio opened his arms to Ginger's older boys and they jumped together with joy. Ginger's mother joined them along with Lucio's father and they all began to hop and cry and laugh.

"I'll be damned," Larry said, his smile spreading across his face. He took long strides to get to Lucio, and embraced him hard. "Congratulations," he told him.

"Roxanne! You are here!" Lucio ran to her and swooped her into his arms. "I am so happy! I am the happiest man alive today in the city of San Francisco!"

Roxie hugged him back as the tears poured down her face. Some of them were tears of elation for Ginger and Lucio, some were caused by sheer terror for Josie, some were for poor Mrs. Needleman, and yes, some were for Eli.

Why? Why had this happened to them? She'd almost had the fairy tale. But here she was—in the middle of another nightmare.

"What is all this?" Lucio grabbed her by the shoulders. "Roxanne? What is it?"

Roxie refused to spoil this moment for Lucio. "I'm so happy for you both!" She kissed his cheek.

At that moment, Bea and Rachel joined everyone in the waiting room. Lucio took one look at their solemn faces and went into full-blown Spaniard mode. "What has happened?" he shouted, waving his arms around inside his surgical scrubs. He spun around on his paper booties, taking note of Josie's huddled family and Teeny's sad face.

"*¡Hostia!*" Lucio clutched his heart, his eyes searching Roxie's face. "Oh, please do not tell me there is something wrong with Josie or the baby. Somebody! Please!"

"She's in surgery," Larry told him. "We're all waiting."

Roxanne felt him immediately, so it wasn't a shock when she looked up to see Eli rounding the corner from the elevator lobby, walking toward her.

The shocking part was her reaction.

Suddenly, it was so simple. She had to accept the new order of things. *What choice is there?* She was standing in the middle of a combined earthquake, volcano, and direct asteroid hit, and when it was all over, the pieces of her world would never fit together the same way again.

Unearthed secrets. New life. Old age. Pain. Joy. Death. Love.

The facts were the facts. How she reacted to them was the only thing in her control.

She watched Eli strolling through the waiting room as if there were no one else present but the two of them. It was so obvious now. The way he moved. The curl in his blond hair. That smile. Those intense eyes. How could she not have seen Raymond in him from the start?

Maybe she had. Maybe the best parts of Raymond had made their way into Eli, and what she'd once found so appealing in the father she now loved in the son.

Mrs. Needleman had been right! The whole damn thing had been out of anyone's hands from the start!

"You're mine."

Those were the only words out of Eli's mouth. He now stood toe to toe with Roxie, and looked down at her with smoky green eyes alive with confidence, and something else.

"I love you, Roxie Bloom. As God is my witness, I will never rush you. We will take as much time as we both need to figure this out. But here's the way it's going to be. Are you listening?"

She gasped.

"You and I belong together. Do you know why?"

She shook her head, too stunned to say anything.

"Because we make each other feel safe. We make each other feel happy."

Roxanne felt a tentative smile come to her lips.

"So I will be your man. You will be my woman. It's the way it's supposed to be." Eli began digging into the front left pocket of his jeans. He pulled out a ring.

"Yes!" Bea shouted.

"Shhh!" Rachel told her.

Roxie popped out of her daze long enough to notice how everyone in the waiting area had begun circling in slow motion around her and Eli, like a pack of curious dogs.

Eli lowered himself on one knee.

"I know what's in your heart because you've revealed it to me," he continued. "I know you love me, Roxanne. But I also know that what happened today was a painful shock. For both of us."

She nodded, tears stinging her eyes.

"We will wait. Because I'm yours and you're mine, we'll wait until we've come to peace with everything. Wear this in the meantime."

Eli slipped a pretty, old-fashioned diamond ring onto her finger.

"But what does it mean?" she whispered, glancing from the ring to the man.

"It can mean whatever you want it to mean."

She stared at the dainty band of gold and diamonds and had trouble breathing. "But—"

"Someday, when it's time, I plan to be your husband." Eli stood, still cradling her left hand. "Remember what we talked about, Rox—we'll always do things our own way. All I ask today is that you keep your heart open to the possibilities and let me love you."

Roxanne suddenly had the strangest sensation. It was as if something—or *someone*—just moved right through her. It was a force. A rush of power. Then it surrounded her, swirling, building . . . and then there was a distinct humming noise, which turned into words . . . *this man will be different . . . strong enough . . . brave enough . . .*

She stared at Eli, astounded. The sensation was back, that feeling she'd tried to hang on to when they'd stood together on top of the ridge.

She was ready to answer him.

Rachel's cell phone rang. "Hello?" she asked, stepping out of the circle.

Eli pulled her tight. "Do you love me, Roxanne? Yes or no."

"God, yes, I love you."

A newborn's cry pierced the air.

"Do you trust me?"

"With my life."

"Then say yes."

"Yes, Eli. I will wear this ring. I will let you love me. And I will love you back."

Eli grabbed her face and kissed her with the dominance and tenderness that infused everything he did. By now, she knew it was his signature in all things, including the way he dealt with unstable dogs and even more unstable women.

Roxie kissed him back, knowing that her head might be swirling with questions, but her heart was fuller than it had ever been in her life, and wide, wide open.

"It's a healthy boy! Josie's fine!" Rick came stumbling

through the double doors, his mask dangling from his hand.

Everyone erupted in cheers and screams of happiness and relief. Josie's mother fainted. Rick stood in the middle of the waiting room, his eyes wide with awe.

"My God, he's big! Over nine pounds! Perfect, loud, and really, really big! And Josie is . . . she was . . ." Rick suddenly couldn't speak the words. Tears began streaming down his face. "Josie was absolutely amazing." Teeny reached Rick in time to catch him in his arms.

In the midst of all the celebrating, Roxie looked for Bea. She and Rachel stood off together, their heads bent and touching at their foreheads.

Roxie took Eli by the hand and they walked over to them. Roxie knew. And she knew exactly when. Because she had felt it.

The last thing Mrs. Needleman did on this earth was give Roxie another nudge.

"She just now passed in her sleep," Bea said. "The family is downstairs. We're heading there now."

Roxie hugged Rachel and Bea and was about to express her condolences when Lucio came up behind them.

He balanced a tiny bundle in his arms. From inside a tightly wound pink blanket peeked a tiny little pink face, surrounded by a shock of thick black hair. "I would like to introduce you to my daughter, Gloria Beatriz Montevez," he said.

Epilogue

Bea smiled as little Gloria kicked off the wedding procession, scattering petals along the dirt path with wild abandon, her chubby arm sweeping high and wide with each toss. Her parents beamed from their position with the rest of the bridal party, as bewitched by their dark-haired little girl today as the day she came into the world, five years before.

Ring bearer Rocco Rousseau went next. The kid looked about as bored as humanly possible, and kept tugging at his bow tie. Halfway down the path he noticed one of his shoes was untied. He tossed the silk ring pillow into a prickly pile of brush so that he could redo his laces the best he could, which made the crowd gasp. Rocco retrieved the pillow, dusted it off, and announced, "We're good!"

The rowdy ring bearer's parents were next. Bea watched Josie and Rick make their way gingerly along the path, Rick escorting the pregnant matron of honor. This would make kid number four for the couple. Uncle Teeny sat in the front row with two squirming toddlers on his lap. Thank God they lived in a big house, was all Bea could think.

Lucio and Ginger stepped onto the dirt path next, somewhat out of place in this wild setting. They were so glamorous in their formal attire that they seemed destined for a Hollywood red carpet instead of the red dirt of Utah. Lucio delivered Ginger to her position as bridesmaid with a soft kiss on her cheek. That man sure knew how to do it, Bea thought with a sigh.

Next, the groom slid into his place to Bea's left. Eli and Bea exchanged an affectionate glance, and suddenly, Bea felt as though she would cry from the sharp beauty of the moment.

The truth was, everyone she loved most in the world was gathered here that day, in this breathtaking spot in the Utah desert. She'd been to the Dog-Eared Ranch many times over the years, and knew the venue Roxie and Eli had chosen for their ceremony was a bit on the dramatic side. But nothing could have prepared Bea for the magic of it all as it began to unfold in front of her.

The sunset now bathed everything and everyone in a warm blush. A gentle wind ruffled the women's dresses. Enormous cliffs and mountains shot up from an ocean of rolling pastureland, while Bea stood under a natural arch of rock that would serve as the couple's altar. And there, at the opposite end of the path, stood the Goddess Bride, waiting for Bea to give the signal that the time had come.

She grinned at her friend, relieved that Roxie had opted for the real deal of a wedding dress and not some boring get-up. She'd had to sit Roxanne down a few months ago and spell it out for her—*you've made everyone wait too damn long for this day to show up in some off-white pantsuit.*

Bea stood a bit taller, thinking that these days she was not only a canine agility trainer and licensed minister, but a fashion consultant, to boot! *Who'd've thunk?*

Bea gave the nod to Roxanne. With great happiness, Bea watched her friend stroll up the path toward the groom. Eli gasped as she came closer, and Bea couldn't blame him—Roxie looked regal in her creamy strapless gown, her long dark hair loosely pulled off her neck and away from her face, fresh flowers laced through the strands. Roxanne's dark-eyed prettiness had softened over the years. She was now in the fullness of her beauty, composed and sure of herself and radiating contentment everywhere she went. Bea wiped a tear from her eye and patted her pants pocket, double-checking that she'd brought tissues. She was sure as hell going to need them.

Eli beamed at his lovely bride and offered his arm as she joined him at the altar. Together, the couple took a step forward to stand directly beneath the towering stone arch. Eli whispered something to Roxie and she nodded and smiled.

Suddenly, the bride raised two fingers to her lips and a sharp, high-pitched whistle erupted, surprising everyone. Applause began a moment later, when every dog in the vicinity came running up the path, plopping down in a row behind the bride and groom, tails swooshing in the dirt. Each dog bore the indignity of a black bow tie or a white lace kerchief at their necks, depending on their gender. Even Martina.

Bea laughed with delight and opened her arms, the power and beauty coursing through her. Silently, before she said a single thing aloud, she thanked Gloria for showing the way, and for being right here at her side on this day. Of course she was there. If it weren't for her, none of this would have come to pass.

"Welcome, everyone," Bea said. "We are gathered this evening for the marriage ceremony of Roxanne Bloom and Eli Gallagher—*finally*."

A wave of laughter and applause moved through the crowd, only to be gathered up in the breeze and carried across the landscape.

"This is a fortuitous occasion, as many of you are aware, but you may not know all the details. That's where I come in." Bea scanned the gathering of smiling faces. "Did you know that these two people met almost six years ago to the day, at a wedding ceremony held eight hundred miles from here? Did you know they were instantly drawn to each other but spent another year trying to deny the attraction? Did you know that once they acknowledged their feelings it took only days before Roxie had a ring on her finger, but another five years came and went before this day arrived?"

A few chuckles erupted in the crowd.

"We are here to celebrate Roxie and Eli's journey. They could have turned their back on love—God knows they had their reasons. But they didn't. They persevered. They chose each other. They chose to live in the light of their beloved."

Bea's eyes found Rachel's smiling face among the guests, and she was filled with gratitude for how her own life had changed.

"Who would have thought that the four women who stood in the middle of a San Francisco dog park all those years ago and officially gave up on love would be standing here, now, on this windswept ridge, literally surrounded by it? Who could have predicted that the women who'd once vowed to settle for life with their dogs now have a life filled with children, spouses, family, true friends, *and* their dogs?"

With a barely noticeable hand gesture from Eli, the line of sitting canines began to howl in unison. It took a long while for the noise and laughter to die down so Bea could continue.

"To go back to the very beginning, you'd have to say that Roxie and Eli's love story began seven years ago, when a man named Ira Needleman passed away. As fate would have it, our Josie, who was an obituary feature writer at the *Herald* at the time, interviewed his widow, Gloria, for an article. With that single act, a series of events were set into motion, lives were changed forever, and a whole world was brought into being.

"The elderly widow told Josie to be brave enough to ask for what she wanted in life. The very next morning, Josie met Rick and did something completely out of character—she asked him to join her for a cup of coffee. He said yes."

"I have to go to the bathroom," Rocco announced. His father leaned down and whispered in his ear. As the words "hold it" floated in the breeze, Bea knew she needed to wrap this up.

"As fate would have it, Rick and Josie's wedding was where Ginger met Lucio and Roxie met Eli. As most of us know, Ginger and Lucio's grand romance began almost immediately, when she fainted into his arms because her bridesmaid's dress was too tight."

"The best night of my life!" Lucio called out, to applause.

Bea smiled. "However, Eli and Roxie weren't looking for love. They didn't want it. But one day, Roxie needed Eli, and when she asked for his help, he came running." Bea paused for effect. "And he's been chasing her ever since."

Laughter coursed through the crowd, the loudest coming from the groom himself. The second loudest came from his sister, Sondra, the proud (and now very wealthy) head of the i-vomit-on-all-men empire. A movie loosely based on the Web site, starring Jennifer Aniston, was now in production.

"I'm just kidding about the chasing, of course," Bea added, winking at Eli. "We knew they'd get around to making it official at some point—Eli and Roxie have always done things their own way, on their own time-table, enjoying every minute of the journey. Maybe that's what makes them such a resilient couple. Every challenge has only brought them closer."

It wasn't Bea's imagination. Most everyone assembled there on the ridge took that as their cue to steal a glance at Eli's biological father, a bald old man with a cane who stood alone near the edge of the gathering, a cautious smile on his face. These days, Raymond Sandberg's relationship with Eli was polite and distant, which seemed to work for all involved. It said a lot about the old bastard that he showed up here today, Bea thought. He'd lost his license to practice law—along with his looks—but somewhere along the way he'd gained some humility. Bea nodded to him in acknowledgment.

She took a deep breath. "Without further delay, it is my honor to serve as a witness to the love Eli and Roxie share, the love they've built with each other with patience, trust, and faith. The bride and groom will now say their vows."

Bea moved back and to the side, as Eli and Roxie took center stage. They turned to each other in the warmth of the sunset and Bea was overwhelmed by the affection and certainty she saw in their faces.

"My beautiful Roxie Bloom, my lovely warrior priestess," Eli said. "I will forever remember the day you and Lilith entered my life. I knew the second I walked through your door that I was taking on the challenge of a lifetime. Plus, I had to deal with Lilith."

Roxie shook her head at him in mock annoyance, smiling the whole time.

"You have changed me forever, Roxanne. With you b

my side, I know there is no obstacle that can't be conquered, no joy that can't be experienced. I thank you for choosing trust over fear, love over discord. Of all the men in this great big world, I thank you for choosing me."

Roxie blinked rapidly, then shot Bea a look of panic. Bea tapped her pants pocket to reassure her she had the tissues.

"Roxanne, would you be my wife?"

"I will," she said. Rocco handed Eli the ring. Eli reached for Roxanne's left hand and slipped the gold band along the length of her slim finger. Bea made a grab for the tissues—for herself, not the bride.

Next, Roxanne took both of Eli's hands in hers and focused on his eyes. Bea watched her friend's panic simply melt away, to be replaced by a smile.

"Elias Jedidiah Gallagher, you came into my life as a patient and wise mentor. You became a lover and a friend and my partner in all things. You are a unique human being, created by chance, nurtured by love, and blessed with the gift of helping the creatures of this world."

Roxanne nodded to collect herself, her chin trembling so slightly that Bea and Eli might have been the only ones to notice.

"Your love gave me courage, Eli," Roxie went on. "Your love healed me. Your love settled my spirit. When I decided to give you another chance all those years ago, I gave myself another chance, as well."

Roxie took the ring Rocco held out to her. She grasped Eli's left hand and asked, "Eli, would you be my husband?"

"I will," he said softly.

Bea blew her nose, too wrapped up in the moment to realize a lull had settled over the gathering.

"Psst." The ring bearer jerked his thumb toward the couple.

"Oh!" Bea stepped forward again. She crammed the tissues into her pocket and cleared her voice.

"Clearly, Eli and Roxanne were blessed from the start, their union part of a plan too vast for any of us to understand. But it is my pleasure now to add my humble blessings, in front of friends and family and this never-ending sky. Eli and Roxanne, may you keep your feet on the ground and your hearts open to the mystery. By the power vested in me by the state of Utah, I pronounce you husband and wife."

The couple turned toward the cheering crowd and basked in the celebration, their forms in relief against the flaming sunset. After a moment, Eli placed his hand on the small of Roxanne's back, bent her away, and kissed her with such conviction that, but for a few audible sighs, the crowd went silent. They popped to a stand together, laughing.

The bride and groom motioned for the dogs to lead the way home. With hands intertwined, they took their first step forward.

Bea jolted in surprise when someone grabbed her left hand. It was Josie, who gazed at her with wet eyes and a huge smile. Ginger then snatched Bea's right hand and pressed close to her friend's side, grinning in delight. Together, the women watched in awe as their beautiful friend began her newest adventure.

Suddenly, Roxie turned, her face beaming, the breeze ruffling loose strands of her dark hair. She held out her hand to them, motioning for her friends to come along.